Forbidden: Part One

Emilia Emerson

Forbidden: Part One

A Luna & Sol Omegaverse

To anyone who has had to claw their way out of patriarchy and purity culture back to the home of their body.

I hope your days are filled with unashamed pleasure.

Introduction to Omegaverse

This is a Why Choose/Reverse Harem Omegaverse.

Why Choose means that our female main character doesn't have to choose between her guys for her happily ever after.

While each omegaverse is different, in general, it's an alternative world where society is composed of three designations: alphas, omegas, and betas. People are born with a designation, which influences their biology, personality, and social status.

In this omegaverse, the Designation Government came into power five years ago. Ever since, alphas (who are almost always male) have been the ruling class. Alphas are physically the most powerful and dominant of all the designations. The Designation Government believes this means they are superior leaders. Male alphas have a knot at the base of their penis that swells during sex, allowing them to lock inside of an omega, increasing the likelihood that she'll get pregnant. They are highly attracted to omegas' scents.

Omegas (almost all female) are the rarest designation. They are physically small and weaker than alphas. They have a high need for physical touch, and their health will deteriorate without it. Starting in young adulthood, omegas go into heat. During this time, they are highly fertile and emotionally vulnerable. They have a strong urge to nest, gathering soft and cozy items into a bed for comfort. Omegas need to be knotted by alphas to avoid extreme pain and physical harm during heat. Omegas are physically compatible with alphas and can take their knots, although some betas can train themselves to take an alpha knot. Omegas can tell what alphas they're most compatible with through scent, as each alpha smells different to each omega. Omegas are often the center of pack life, the glue that holds the pack together.

Alphas and omegas can bond with each other through a bite, which forms a connection that allows them to sense the others' emotions. Alphas and omegas can be fated mates to each other. Fated mates feel a strong connection to each other, have compatible scents, and are biologically predisposed to be the perfect match for each other.

Betas are essentially what we would consider "normal" humans. They don't have strong scents and do not have fated mates. They form the backbone of society and work most jobs, with the exception of government or other leadership positions. Alphas or omegas can bite betas and form a bond with them.

Author's Note

While a lot of this book feels very cozy, it's set in a world that's very dark. Please take care while reading!

This book is for people 18+. It has explicit sex scenes, including group sex, and elements of BDSM, like spanking.

Trigger warnings include mentions of past sexual abuse, emotional neglect, brief thoughts of suicide, abuse by parents, brief discussion of past forced starvation, and anti-fat bias. Additional triggers include mental health concerns including depression, low self-esteem, PTSD, and disordered eating. None of this abuse happens within our main pack.

This book ends on a cliffhanger that is resolved with a happily ever at the end of *Forbidden: Part Two*.

If you note any typos or errors in this book, feel free to contact me directly at emiliaemersonauthor@gmail.com.

Chapter One

Josie

Absolutely nothing was going my way today. It wasn't as if that was anything new, but hiding between a dirty brick wall and a dumpster was a special level of hell. The garbage stench burned my nose and made my eyes water, but at least it masked the scents of the four alphas currently blocking my exit from the alley.

My heartbeat pulsed in my ears so loudly I was worried one of them would somehow hear me and track me down, trapping me here and... I clenched my fists tightly, allowing the biting pain from my fingernails to keep me from descending into a full-blown panic attack. A few years ago, doing something illegal and rebellious would have filled me with the kind of heart-pumping adrenaline that made me feel alive. Now I just wanted to hide away.

One of the alphas started yelling, and I suppressed a whimper.

"How fucking dare that bitch choose another pack?" he snarled.

"She was a total prude. Bet she would be frigid in bed," another responded.

"Why the fuck do we even let omegas choose packs? They should be grateful alphas like us want to bond with them. They're all whores," a third alpha growled.

Despite my fear, I rolled my eyes at their lack of logic. Which was it—were we omegas all whores or prudes? My guess was this pack had just been turned down by an omega who was doing her pre-heat interviews. My stomach clenched with anxiety. I needed to call Sam, needed to make sure that wouldn't be my fate soon.

The alphas continued to yell drunkenly, spewing unoriginal anti-omega insults at higher and higher decibel levels. The bar, whose dumpster I was currently pressed against, was typically quiet early on a Tuesday night, but these alphas had clearly gotten a head start on their drinking. My inner omega cringed at their rage, and I wedged myself more deeply into the crevice I'd contorted my body into.

My watch told me it was 9:56 p.m., just a few minutes until the nightly omega curfew took effect. Even though the police might not stop and harass me for the next four minutes, the same couldn't be said for these alphas.

The breeze wafted the stench of mold and stale cigarettes over me, and I froze as my skin burned with phantom touches. I gripped my upper arm, feeling pinpricks of pain that lingered almost a full year later.

My breathing evened out as the alphas moved further away, their voices fading into the distance, but I didn't feel safe enough to emerge yet. I couldn't see my destination from my hiding spot, but I knew the gym was there, waiting to embrace me. Even though my nightly journey to the gym was filled with the terror of being caught, the gym itself had become a safe space for me over the past year. Usually, I didn't arrive until well after midnight to start my cleaning job. The streets were deserted in the early morning hours, most of the government patrollers having cleared the area. But on self-defense class nights, I had to be extra cautious.

A yellow taxi van finally pulled up to the curb, and the asshole alphas piled in. I shivered as I waited to make sure they were really gone. The night air was still warm, summer not yet giving way to fall, but I hadn't been able to regulate my temperature all day. I finally squeezed myself out of my hiding spot, my bones and muscles protesting the movement. I burrowed more deeply into my oversized sweatshirt as I watched a silver SUV pull out of the alley beside the gym. I was pretty sure that car belonged to Poppy's alphas. They must have just dropped her off.

My footsteps fell quietly as I made my way across the street, the *Alpha Gainz* sign drawing me like a beacon to safety. Months after I started working for Luc, when I finally stopped flinching every time he spoke or walked near me, I got up the courage to tease him about his gym name. *Why would you put a z at the end?* He mumbled something about it being cool and omegas just not getting it. With enough pestering, I finally got him to admit that his bonded omega also thought the name was stupid. I'd never met Charlie, but I loved imagining her rolling her eyes at her alpha's ridiculous name choice. Or rather, rolling her *eyez*.

I kept my face downcast as I entered the alley by the gym. I was almost to the stairs that led down to the basement entrance when three enormous alphas turned into the alley from the other end. Fear shot through me, freezing me for a second before I realized they hadn't seen me yet. They were talking furtively to each other, giving me enough time to execute the least graceful stop, drop, and roll I could imagine, leaping over the crates blocking the entrance and practically falling into the concrete stairwell. *Fuck, that hurt.* I would be covered in bruises by tomorrow.

I didn't dare open the basement door while they were so close. I held my breath, curling up behind the crates and praying my de-scenter held. The alphas took painfully slow steps down the alley as they continued their conversation. *Don't mind me, take your sweet, sweet time.* Alphas had free rein to move around wherever they wanted, do whatever they wanted, abuse whoever they wanted. I couldn't let myself think about what would happen if they caught me here.

"He said to come in the main entrance and start using the free weights. A guy wearing a green shirt will come over and do the handoff," one of the alphas said quietly in a British accent.

"I don't want to work out again," another one responded, sounding disgruntled.

"Ben, we're not here to fucking work out," a gruff voice bit out.

"How do we even know this hacker is any good? I bet I'm better," the disgruntled one—Ben—said.

"Shh, do you hear something?" the British one hissed.

The three of them stopped right at the top of the fucking stairs. I held my breath, wishing I could freeze my heart for a moment. A breeze stirred and wafted a warm cinnamon roll scent my way. My inner omega automatically relaxed at the yummy-smelling alphas and I clenched my jaw in irritation. Biology was a bitch—these alphas were not safe, no matter how tempting they smelled. But I had to admit, they did smell unusually good.

"Let's go," the gruff one muttered, sounding like he was further away. I caught a glimpse of two other sets of feet turning to follow him.

Once I was sure they weren't doubling back, I eased open

the gym door behind me and slipped in, finally allowing myself a deep exhale.

"Josie!" Poppy squealed as she launched herself towards me, pulling me in for a hug. I stiffened automatically. "You're usually here early. We were worried about you."

Poppy pulled away, and I could see genuine concern in her bright blue eyes, her blonde hair haloing her face in angelic curls. Everyone in our small self-defense class was already gathered—Luc, Anna, and Westin were setting mats up on the other side of the room.

"I had to hide from some alphas for a bit, but I'm okay," I managed to say, proud of how steady my voice sounded. Poppy's concern made me want to simultaneously burst into tears and run away. I wasn't used to anyone besides my childhood best friend, Sam, caring about me.

"Glad you made it safely," Luc grunted as he walked over to us.

Effusive was not a word I would use to describe the grumpy gym owner, but he cared in his own way. He was dressed in his typical all-black uniform (Poppy told him repeatedly that it was boring and he should wear something with more *pizazz* to attract customers), and his dark brown eyes looked me over to make sure I was okay. The only times I had seen Luc show emotion were on the rare occasions he talked about Charlie. The slightest blush would make its way onto his dark olive skin, and a small smile would tug at his lips as if he couldn't help but melt when thinking about his omega. It made my heart hurt and reminded me of the fantasies I'd had as a child, wishing that one day a pack of alphas would whisk me away to a better life.

"I wish you and Westin didn't have to walk here," Anna said. She was a soft-spoken omega who joined our group a few months ago after Westin invited her. I hadn't gotten to know her much beyond the fact that she was bonded to five alphas, which seemed like an exhausting number of personalities to juggle.

"Well, it's not like we're allowed to drive," Westin said, her jaw clenching. We all agreed early on that it might draw more attention to our gatherings if Anna or Poppy's packs picked us up. I was pretty sure Westin's aunt's pack drove her most of the time, as she didn't live within walking distance. "Glad you're okay, Josie."

Westin and I were the two unbonded omegas in the group, and I felt a level of solidarity with her. She was twenty-three, just like me, and though we had never talked about using suppressants, I was sure she was on them. She was petite and striking—her long hair almost silver as she put it in a ponytail. It was hard for me to imagine that someone that looked like her could still be unbonded.

Luc paired me with Poppy and started walking through the objectives for today's class while I stripped off my sweatshirt and set my things down in the corner. I took a sip of water, trying to steady myself as I came down from the adrenaline and fear that had pumped its way through my body.

I walked back over to Poppy and gave her a strained smile, feeling hideous beside her petite frame and luxury workout clothes. Poppy was too sweet to judge me, but I still tugged on my thrifted black tank top, wishing it could magically make my fat rolls disappear. Not for the first time, I wished I had a different body, a different life.

Poppy volunteered to go first, practicing swift, well-executed jabs to the bag I was holding steady. I clenched my jaw as each hit rattled through my too-sensitive body, every twinge a reminder of what was to come if I didn't get suppressants. I needed to call Sam, but I had run out of minutes on my burner phone. He had probably been trying to get through to me all day, and guilt burned in my stomach like acid at the thought that he was worried about me. I would be able to reload the minutes after I got paid tonight, and I needed him to have good news about my suppressants.

A small voice in the back of my head said I could ask to borrow Poppy's or Luc's phone and call him now. But I just couldn't do it, especially when I thought of how much I already owed them. Poppy had paid for my groceries when I was on the verge of starving, and her alphas connected me to the owner of the gym where they were members, who had just so happened to be looking for a new cleaning person. Luc had immediately given me the job, transforming my life. Later, he let me talk him into hosting this class for omegas.

The punching bag smacked me in the face, bringing me back to the room.

"Ahh, I'm sorry," Poppy said, stopping the bag from swinging. "You okay?"

"Yup, totally fine," I said, rubbing my stinging cheek.

"You seem a little out of it today," Poppy said carefully.

"Sorry, just a bit distracted."

"Okay," she said, not sounding fully convinced. "Want to trade spots?"

No, what I want is to curl up in bed with piles of the softest blankets in the world.

"Yep, sure."

I huffed, adjusting my bra straps and tank top for the hundredth time. Even if I had the money to buy workout clothes that fit properly, it wouldn't make a difference with how tight my skin felt. The headache I had woken up with lingered, and my muscles were weak as I threw a punch. I knew what my symptoms meant, but I hoped if I ignored them, the problem would magically go away. *You know, that classic technique that always works.*

"Remember, punch with your body, not just your arm. Josie, try that again and shift your weight into the movement," Luc called from across the room.

I threw the punch again. The bag barely shifted.

"That was better!" Poppy said.

"You're a shit liar," I grumbled.

I threw another unbalanced punch that almost had me landing on my ass. Poppy reached out to steady me, but as her hand wrapped around my arm, I flinched back. Shame flooded me as I took in Poppy's stricken expression.

"I'm just tired," I mumbled, averting my eyes.

I was so fucking exhausted of being scared and jumpy all the time. Omegas needed touch to survive, but I could hardly tolerate even the slightest physical contact anymore.

Part of me wanted to confide in Poppy. We had been talking more since she joined our underground class. She was always kind and encouraging, and her presence at the Designation Academy, where we'd met, had been a bright spot during my time there. But I wasn't the same person I had been back then. Dark memories of betrayal and punishment tried to encroach on my mind, and my whole body tensed. I had placed my trust in the wrong person before. I shouldn't allow myself to get close to others, but I couldn't force myself away. I was a little island floating in the middle of the ocean, and my friends had somehow traversed the waves to find me. Floating away was no longer an option.

I took a strained breath and pushed the memories aside, imagining myself stuffing them all into a box and dumping it into the bottom of the ocean. *You can't let yourself go there, can't let yourself remember.*

"Why don't we take a break? I'm tired today, too," Poppy suggested sweetly.

I wanted to refuse, to insist I could do the exercises when

another wave of dizziness and exhaustion washed over me. I threw her a tight smile, and the two of us sat down on one of the mats by the corner. Westin and Anna were still practicing their punching and blocking. The rhythmic sound of punches landing on the bag almost lulled me to sleep. I shifted my position to keep myself awake.

"You know I'm here if you want to talk about it," Poppy said after a few minutes had gone by.

"Yeah, thanks," I managed to get out, my throat tight. In another world, I would have loved to let myself really be friends with her. It was yet another thing the Designation Academy had stolen from me.

I jolted as Luc called for the end of class. I had no idea how much time had passed.

"I'm not sure when the next class will be, but I'll send out an encrypted message," he added.

I struggled to get to my feet to gather my things and prepare to start working. I was so absorbed in my worries that I almost missed Anna clearing her throat to speak.

"I have an announcement," she said, bouncing up and down. "I'm pregnant!"

The room was silent for a moment before Poppy squealed in excitement and ran over to hug her. Westin and I met each other's gaze across the room with a smile—we had both suspected this was coming soon. Anna had been with her alphas for about a year, and most packs didn't delay pregnancy for long. One of the few things I knew about Anna was her desire to be a mother. She told us she wanted to learn self-defense so she could better protect herself and any omega daughters she might have one day.

I held myself back from giving Anna a hug but joined the others in gathering around her to offer congratulations. The excitement was infectious, and a smile tugged at my lips, the expression almost foreign on my face.

"Why didn't you say something before class? You shouldn't be doing anything strenuous," Luc growled. The four of us jolted, responding instinctually to an alpha's displeasure.

Luc pulled a stool out from a dusty corner of the room. "Sit down, sit down," he exclaimed, guiding Anna onto the stool, to all of our amusement.

"Well, that's something I didn't expect," Westin said dryly, taking in Luc's harried appearance.

"I *am* surprised your alphas even let you come to class," Poppy said, holding in a giggle as Luc ran his hand through his hair with an air of panic. "You know how alphas get around pregnant omegas."

"They're making me stop class while I'm pregnant," Anna said with a pout. "But I convinced them to let me come today so I could tell you all. I wasn't *necessarily* supposed to participate, but what are they going to do?"

Luc groaned. "They're going to fucking kill me."

"No, they're not," Anna said primly. "They're being ridiculously overprotective, but the perk is that they also don't want to do anything to upset me."

I resisted rolling my eyes. I knew Anna was in love with her alphas, but it annoyed me how even the "good" alphas treated omegas as if we were fragile and couldn't possibly make our own choices.

"I did fight with them to keep coming to class, but they wouldn't budge. They said there have been more government crackdowns on mixed designation gatherings, and they don't want to risk me getting arrested. You'll all be extra careful, right?" she asked, her concern for us shining through.

Dread filled me as the others reassured her we would take extra precautions. Poppy started chattering away about planning a baby shower while the voice in my head chanted *all your fault*. I had no idea what bravery or idiocy had led me to ask Luc to start a self-defense class, but to my eternal shock, he had agreed. I suspected it was because a group of alphas had attacked Charlie before she met Luc and the rest of Pack Jang. I didn't know the details of what happened except that she was in a wheelchair. Our classes were the only time I felt alive anymore, the only time I felt even remotely strong or in control of my own life. But if we were found out, I would be the one to blame.

Westin, Anna, and Poppy left in a whirlwind of goodbyes, staggering their exits out the back.

"You seem off today, Josie," Luc said after the other omegas had cleared out. "If you're not feeling up to working today, you don't have to stay."

"I'm fine," I said, even though my legs felt like jelly and my head was swimming.

Luc looked unconvinced. He hesitated before saying, "Your scent has changed."

I froze. *No, no, no, it couldn't be happening so quickly.*

"How obvious is it?" I asked quietly.

"Not obvious yet. If I hadn't spent so much time around you this past year, I wouldn't have noticed. But I'm guessing it will become pretty obvious soon. How long have you been off suppressants?"

"I've only missed two doses." I hadn't known how quickly things would move after missing the medication. "I'll be able to get my normal supply tomorrow, and it will be fine," I added with a confidence I didn't feel. I was sure Luc saw through me, but he didn't push it.

"You come to me if you need help, okay? Maybe my pack can figure out a way to help."

"Thanks," I said, touched by his offer, knowing I would

never take him up on it. Luc had his own omega to protect, and I was already asking too much of him.

I started cleaning the mats and other equipment Luc brought to the basement for me. I would wait until the gym's midnight closure before heading upstairs to the main gym. Luc left after locking up and paying me for the night. He slipped some extra money in the envelope, and shame washed over me as I realized I was too desperate to argue with him about it.

Dizziness continued to break over me in waves, forcing me to sit down and hold my head between my legs in between wiping down equipment. The withdrawal from suppressants was so much worse than I could have imagined, and I held in a groan each time I stood back up and the room spun.

I finally finished around 2 a.m. and carefully headed out the back alley door, locking it behind me. It was only a seven-minute walk back to my apartment, but it was my least favorite part of the day, especially since tonight I had to stop at the 24/7 corner shop and add minutes to my phone.

My skin burned under the thick layer of the de-scenter I sprayed on my baggy clothes. I hated spraying the toxin on me so frequently and knew it would eventually affect my health, but it was worth risking it to avoid attention from alphas. My too-fat body, the source of so much of my shame and suffering, also helped disguise me. No one expected a fat omega. But if anyone gave me more than a brief glance, it would become obvious what I was.

My lip trembled. I wasn't even sure if it was from fear or exhaustion, or both. I just wanted to live a normal life where no one noticed me.

I walked as quickly as I could without looking suspicious. I slipped into the shop and sighed in relief when I saw a female beta working the counter. Some nights it was the owner, a sleazy older alpha who I'm sure suspected my designation. I added the minutes onto my phone, paying in cash and cursing my lack of a bank account before slipping back onto the deserted street.

When my apartment entrance came into view, I forced myself to keep walking instead of breaking out in a sprint. Once I was in the main entrance, I bent over, trying to catch my breath. My muscles screamed in agony after the short walk, my head still pounding. My legs felt like concrete as I dragged myself up the steps to my third-floor apartment. I almost cried in relief as I got to my door. I made my way inside and locked the three deadbolts behind me, each click of the lock telling me I was safe.

Chapter Two

Josie

I collapsed on the couch in a tangled mess, my body shaking. A metal spring from the cushion dug into my back, but I couldn't find the energy to move. I clenched my phone in trembling hands, fumbling as I tried to dial Sam's number.

I was supposed to meet the black market supplier two days ago for my suppressants, but they didn't show. Sam arranged for me to meet a different supplier last night, but they didn't show either. This was the first time I was without suppressants since turning eighteen... with the exception of the two years I spent at the Designation Academy. I had been too starved and stressed to go into heat then. But now, every second without my suppressants felt like I was hurtling towards a dangerous edge, facing a fall I wasn't sure I'd survive.

The phone rang and I bit my lip, wondering if Sam would pick up this late. I exhaled the breath I didn't realize I was holding when I heard his groggy voice on the line. A pang of longing shot through me—being without my best friend for the past year was agony.

"Josie, where the fuck have you been? I've been calling and texting you all day," Sam hissed in a low voice.

"I'm sorry it's so late," I blurted out, my throat tight. "I ran out of money to put minutes on my phone, and I was just able to reload it."

"I don't like you being out on your own so late." I heard rustling through the phone and Gerald's sleepy voice asking Sam what was happening.

"I don't like it either," I responded, trying not to sound defensive. Suddenly, all the terror of the day caught up with me, and I choked out a sob.

"Fuck, Josie, please don't cry," Sam said.

"Sorry," I responded, trying to contain my tears. "Just a lot of alphas around today."

My phone beeped, and I saw Sam was inviting me to a video call.

"Answer it. I need to see that you're okay."

I snorted, unsure how my blotchy, tear-streaked face would be convincing, but I did as he asked.

Sam's face came into focus, illuminated by his phone's light in the dark room. Just seeing his face eased the lump in my throat. Sam was all warmth from his dark brown afro, brown skin, and deep, caring eyes. No one made me feel as seen or cared for as he did.

"No one hurt you, right?" Sam asked, a hint of panic in his voice.

"No, I'm fine," I said, but the words felt false on my tongue. "Except... I'm in withdrawal. If I don't get suppressants, I'll go into heat soon."

"Fuck, fuck, fuck. I'm so sorry, but I don't have good news," Sam said, keeping his voice low. "I spent all day trying to find another supplier, anyone who might be able to get you pills or injections. We got news this morning that they arrested the guy you were supposed to meet yesterday. The black market communication channels over here must have been infiltrated because the cops knew exactly where to find them."

A shiver worked its way down my spine as I realized how easily I could have been caught if the cops had waited a bit longer to arrest the dealer.

"Josie, I don't know what to do." Sam ran his hand over his face, and I heard the exhaustion and desperation in his voice. He always did everything he could to protect me.

Helplessness covered me like a suffocating blanket, and a panic attack clawed at my chest. I needed to get up and move. My muscles ached as I forced myself up and started pacing the dark living room.

"I'm so sorry. Please believe I'm trying everything I can."

"You don't get to feel guilty about this," I choked out, my throat painfully tight. "I wouldn't have survived this long without you. None of this is your fault."

"Fuck, please promise me you won't do anything desperate. Maybe we can get you out, get you into Sol."

Omegas had the same rights as betas in Sol province, one of the many reasons the Designation Government prohibited us from traveling there. In rare circumstances, bonded omegas could move there with their packs, but I'd never heard of an unbonded omega successfully leaving Luna province.

"Luc said my scent is already changing," I whispered. "I have mandatory blood work scheduled in two weeks. I think time's run out on me."

Sam was silent, his face unreadable, but I thought I heard his breath hitch as if he was crying.

"I hate this. I hate them all," he said suddenly, eyes wild.

I started at his raised voice, tripping on the corner of my rug and slamming my shin against my side table. *Fuck, that hurt.* I collapsed back on the couch, rubbing the aching spot on my leg. The pain was grounding, cutting through a bit of my panic.

Gerald murmured in the background, and his hand appeared in the frame, soothingly running up and down Sam's arm. Gratitude overwhelmed me that my best friend wasn't alone. Sam might have more freedom as an alpha, but he had his own secret—his alpha roommate, Gerald, was his romantic partner.

The Designation Laws not only curtailed every freedom omegas formerly held, they also made clear what sorts of relationships alphas could have, and same-sex ones were firmly forbidden. Gerald had lived on the opposite side of the province, and the two met on a secret online network and fell in love without ever seeing what the other looked like. They had planned to form a pack and move in with each other after college, but then Sam's father found their text messages. He threatened to report his own son to the authorities unless Sam left Luna province, all to protect the family from the supposed shame of having a gay son. Fortunately, both Gerald and Sam were offered jobs in Sol after they finished their engineering degrees. It meant an opportunity for them to finally be together.

"I'm going to keep asking around. I'm sure there's someone in the city who can get suppressants. Please don't give up," Sam pleaded. "It would kill me if you did anything to hurt yourself. I need you to promise you will not do anything desperate."

Last year, after two torturous years at the Designation Academy, I had been forced to return to my parents' house. I'd terrified Sam when he'd visited and found me curled up in my dark bedroom, wanting to die. He had been prepared to give up his job, risk being arrested, and lose his chance to be with Gerald just to make sure I was safe. I had flat-out refused, unwilling to let him ruin his chance at happiness for me. We'd finally agreed on a compromise—he worked a loophole in the law that allowed me to move into his vacant apartment as long as his name stayed on the lease and he continued to pay rent. The Designation Laws didn't forbid omegas from living on our own; we just weren't allowed to sign a rental agreement, hold a bank account, or have a job.

I missed him so much it hurt. He was the only one in my life I could trust, and I hated that he was so far away. I hated that I would have to navigate this next bit alone.

"I promise. I won't give up," I said, trying to sound braver than I felt.

There was a long pause. "Maybe you can find a good pack."

I scrunched my nose at him.

"I mean, it's a long shot. But you still get the final say in what pack you choose. You never know; you could find a great fit. There are... good alphas out there." Sam's voice sounded almost strangled.

"How hard was that to say out loud?" I asked with a laugh.

Sam and I grew up surrounded by the worst examples of alphas. My childhood fantasies of joining a pack of strong, handsome, loving alphas had been effectively stomped on and set on fire by my upbringing.

Sam laughed. "Yeah, okay, it felt like shit. No alphas are good enough to deserve you because you deserve the fucking world. I just want you to be safe and happy."

"Thanks," I said, rubbing my aching chest. "I love you."

"I love you, too, so much. I'm going to keep looking for options. We're going to talk every single day. No retreating from me, Josie."

I promised Sam I would stay in constant communication before hanging up the phone, the silent darkness enveloping me.

I sunk down into the couch cushions. I'd been putting off the inevitable for the past five years. While part of me had always known this day would come, I had hoped the world would change before it did—the Designation Laws would be repealed, omegas would be allowed access to suppressants legally, and we wouldn't be forced to join with alphas when blood tests revealed our first heats were imminent.

The unfairness of everything threatened to overwhelm me as I thought of the horrible community I grew up in, my childhood friends whose alphas had forbidden them from spending time with anyone outside the pack, and the news stories of bonded omegas being found dead in the bay and their packs never investigated. I wanted to do something with all my fear and anger, but instead, I curled up on the couch and lay there frozen until the first rays of sunlight crept through the window hours later.

Chapter Three

Theo

A middle-aged beta in a BMW honked at me, throwing up his hands as I slipped into one of the few free parking spots. *You snooze, you lose,* I thought as I shifted the car into park. I hated going to Trader Joe's. The fucking car park was always a mess. *Why don't they plan this shit out ahead of time so it's not such a disaster?*

Cam was being insufferable about getting his candy, claiming I owed him after he'd snagged a signed copy of one of my favorite books last month.

I sat numbly, staring out of the windshield, my eyes unfocused. I couldn't seem to get my shit together lately.

My phone vibrated, forcing me back to the present.

CAM

You coming back soon? Have some things we need to discuss with this new job.

THEO

Just stopped at Trader Joe's to get you Scandinavian Swimmers. What makes them any different from other candy?

I shot off the text, irritated that I had to go across town instead of the perfectly fine supermarket just down the street.

CAM

They are the far superior gummy candy. You owe me.

I sighed, tapping my fingers on the steering wheel. I loved Cam, but he was being even more of a prick than usual. In the early years of being a pack, Cam, Ben, and I leaned on each other for support and comfort. We met as teens after my parents had moved our family to North Woods. I still felt sick when thinking about our old community. The suffering my packmates and I experienced there had brought us even closer, until Cam and Ben were more brothers to me than my own siblings. After we left our community, the trauma of what we went through cemented our bond. But now I felt like I was losing them.

We had all been on edge for the past year. Cam was surlier than usual, Ben was moping around the house, and I felt myself withdrawing from them and hiding out in my office. Lately, all we talked about was work. I missed my best friends and felt useless as fuck that I didn't know what to do to fix us.

CAM

Make sure to get the sour ones.

I forced myself out of the car. As I headed towards the entrance, I saw a woman in black leggings and a baggy sweatshirt walk in ahead of me. I glanced over at her as I maneuvered into the store. I had planned to track down the candy as quickly as possible, but instead, I found myself following the woman down the produce aisle as if pulled by a magnet. She was short for a beta, and her wavy brown hair cascaded down her back as she wove her way through the narrow aisles, leaning heavily on her cart. I hadn't seen her face yet, and I longed to close the distance between us, spin her around, and grip her chin with my hand. I would tilt her face until our eyes met—I was sure she would have the prettiest eyes I'd ever seen—and then I would memorize every inch of her before gripping her round, plump ass and pulling her in even closer, pressing her body into mine.

I stopped abruptly as I realized what a fucking creep I was being. A beta woman behind me swore as she accidentally bumped into me with her cart. I turned to apologize for blocking the aisle and saw her expression transform from one of irritation to apprehension.

"Sorry!" she squeaked. "Didn't mean to hit you."

"It was my fault. No worries," I mumbled, moving out of the way. I would never get used to the anxious and sometimes even terrified glances people gave me just because I was an alpha.

I had lost sight of *her*. I ran my hand through my hair, trying to get a grip. I couldn't remember the last time I had checked someone out or felt even the slightest hint of attraction, yet here I was, practically stalking a woman through the store. My heart pounded, and my inner alpha urged me to go after her. *Am I having a stroke? What's wrong with me?*

I tried to shake myself out of my weird mood and headed in the other direction. I was having trouble focusing as I wandered aimlessly up and down the aisles, trying to ignore the gnawing feeling in my chest as I searched for the candy. Turning the corner to the freezer aisle, I saw her again. I was about to force myself to walk in the other direction when I noticed her eyes were closed, and she was barely remaining upright. I walked towards her with measured steps, inhaling sharply as I got my first glimpse of her face. She was fucking beautiful. Her hair perfectly framed her round face, and I saw she had the cutest smattering of freckles. I wished I could see her eyes, but they were closed as she slumped over the cart. I frowned at how pale she was.

"Are you okay?" I asked hesitantly, a jolt of panic shooting through me at the thought that something was wrong.

Her eyes fluttered open. They were bright green, and I was instantly mesmerized. An explosion couldn't convince me to look away from her.

"Dizzy," she whispered, not lifting her head.

"What do you need? Can I ring someone for you, a friend or partner?" I realized I was clenching my jaw as a burst of inexplicable jealousy ran through me at the thought of her dating someone. I noticed with satisfaction that she wasn't wearing a ring.

"No," she said, her voice carrying a hint of a whine that my inner alpha instinctually responded to.

I froze. *Was she an omega?*

"I'm fine," she mumbled, taking a few steps forward until her knees gave out.

I stepped in without thinking, catching her before she fell. I cradled her in my arms until we were both seated on the floor. I tried to ignore how perfect her soft curves felt against my body.

"What's wrong, love?" I asked, concerned at how warm her skin was under mine. *Love? Where the fuck did that come from?*

I leaned in to see if I could scent her. The chemical smell of de-scenter stung my nose. This little angel was, in fact, an omega trying to cover up her scent.

Her eyes fluttered open, glassy and unfocused. "What's happening?" she asked, her voice so vulnerable it broke my heart.

Before I could answer, an employee interrupted us—a

teenage beta from the look of him. I swallowed an instinctual growl as he crouched down near her. I had no idea why I was feeling so possessive.

"Everything alright here?" he asked. His sniveling little voice grated on me. He was too bloody close to her.

"This woman passed out, and it feels like she has a fever," I said, trying to subtly shift her so my body was between her and the beta.

"Umm, do you know her? Should I call an ambulance or something?" he responded, rubbing the back of his neck. Clearly, the Trader Joe's employees didn't have crisis management training.

I wanted to tuck her close and bring her home so I could care for her or at least drive her to the hospital to ensure she was safe. But there were strict laws against alphas being around unbonded omegas. It would be seen as kidnapping... or, more likely, she would be blamed for seducing me or some shit. Fucking ridiculous.

"Better call for an ambulance," I said, my voice resigned. "Make sure they know she's an omega," I added softly.

"Really? Her?" the beta asked incredulously.

This time I couldn't hold in my growl. Was this pimply-ass pathetic beta daring to insult the angel in my arms?

His eyes widened in terror, and he scampered away to make the call.

"Can you stay awake, love?" I asked gently, brushing the omega's damp curls away from her face. She let out a little whimper but didn't open her eyes. Her cheeks were flushed, and I could feel her warmth seeping through my clothes. Fuck, was she going into heat? Where were her alphas? *Because if she doesn't have any, I will volunteer as tribute.*

"What's your name?" I asked softly. "I'm Theo."

The other shoppers, almost all betas, gave us a wide berth.

It was rare for alphas to do their own shopping and even more so for unbonded omegas... if that's what she was. I couldn't see any bond marks, but she was mostly covered up.

She curled towards me, resting her face on my chest and breathing deeply. My heart jumped in pleasure that she was seeking comfort from me. She was too out of it to respond to my questions, so I contented myself with holding her close and murmuring what I hoped were comforting words.

"Um, they're almost here," the beta worker said, now joined by a manager. I heard the faint noise of sirens in the distance. I gave them a curt nod without looking away from her. I didn't understand the attraction I was feeling. All I knew was I didn't want to let her go.

Too quickly, the medics stormed into the store and pulled her out of my grasp. My arms hung like useless weights by my side, useless because they were no longer holding her. The other shoppers gawked, and I wanted to roar at them to turn away and give her some privacy.

I followed the medics to the parking lot and stood by as they loaded her into the ambulance. I was tempted to lie when they asked me if I was the omega's bonded alpha, but I gritted my teeth and told the truth. Alarm filled their faces, and they started placing frantic calls to the Designation Center and the hospital to let them know they had an unbonded omega who had collapsed.

A medic bumped the stretcher she was on, causing the omega to whimper.

"Be fucking careful with her!" I growled, shoving myself into the medics' faces. I was being unreasonable—my reactions far out of the norm from my usually reserved demeanor. But the thought of anything happening to the unnamed omega enraged me.

"Sir, you have to step back," the medic said weakly.

I clenched my fists and didn't take my eyes off the omega as they took her vitals. I was still standing, frozen in my spot in the parking lot, when they closed the ambulance doors and rushed her away.

Away from me.

Chapter Four

Josie

"Congratulations, hun! We just got your blood work back, and you are officially in pre-heat. The doctor will be in shortly to discuss the next steps so we can get you set up with your pack. It's not every day we have a twenty-three-year-old who hasn't gone into heat yet. This must be such a relief for you."

The young beta nurse was overly chipper as she bustled around the clinical exam room in the Designation Center Clinic. I had spent the night in the hospital and been moved to the clinic this morning.

Yesterday's trip to the store was lost in a hazy mist. I vaguely remembered walking into the store, but my next memory was waking up alone in a hospital room. The nurses told me I passed out while shopping. Despair clung to me. My time was up. My mandatory blood work appointment wasn't for another week, but my body had sped up the process. *Traitor.*

Usually, the bright hospital lights and antiseptic smells were torturous, but I stayed calmer than usual thanks to the delicious scent surrounding me. It took me a while to determine that the scent was coming from my sweatshirt. It was rich coffee and long afternoons spent in the bookstore. I refused to let anyone take the sweatshirt away and slept better than I had in a long time with my face buried in it. Even after showering this morning, I felt like it was still on my skin, imprinted on me and comforting.

The nurse continued to prattle on about my upcoming heat. The lab result wasn't a surprise, but I still felt like a weight was crushing my lungs. Did this woman really think I was happy about my lab results? Could she really be that naïve? I always wondered what betas thought about omegas. We were kept somewhat segregated from the rest of society. *Do they all believe what the news says about us?*

"Don't worry, I'm sure you'll find a pack that won't hold your age against you," she said before handing me a small crinkly gown to change into and finally leaving the room. *Oh wow, what a relief that not all alphas will hold my ancient age of twenty-three against me. Bitch.*

My stomach turned as I hopped up on the exam table, feeling vulnerable and exposed. My mind started blanking out, my heart racing at the thought of having to endure another invasive exam. The scar on my arm burned in phantom pain, and I squeezed it, trying my best to hold on to reality. *It's not in me anymore. They're not here. This is a different doctor.* My body was not convinced by my pathetic attempts to reassure myself. Sweat trickled down from my armpits. I wanted to escape from the room, but my body sat frozen as if held captive by the bright overhead lights.

The door slammed open and a middle-aged doctor—alpha, of course—entered the room with the overeager nurse on his heels. *Not him, it's not him.* This doctor was tall and muscular, with broad shoulders, slicked-back brown hair, and a smile so white it belonged in a dental commercial. I bet all the beta nurses threw themselves at him, dying for a scrap of attention. He smelled like moldy dill and cilantro, almost making me gag.

"Ahh, I see we have a late bloomer omega," the doctor said, consulting his paperwork. "Age twenty-three, the mother is an omega. Regular lab work hasn't returned positive for pre-heat before now. Nurse, what do you notice about this omega?"

I clenched my hands into fists, hating how he wouldn't look at me or address me like I was an actual person.

"Well, besides her obvious late heat, the omega has been consistently overweight since puberty," the nurse answered sweetly, batting her eyes at the doctor.

I resisted rolling my eyes.

"You can see here in the records that she was put on a diet regimen during her time at the DA, which resulted in moderate weight loss, but since graduation, she has clearly gained it back," the doctor said with a sneer, his eyes lingering over my body while he sniffed deeply, breathing in my scent.

I blinked rapidly, refusing to let this asshole alpha make me cry. The diet regimen he was talking about consisted of the DA cutting my meal plan in half, so I was starving. If not for the kindness of my few friends sneaking me food, I probably would have ended up in the hospital. Not that the doctors would have minded as long as I lost the weight.

"Well, the good news is that the omega will be joining a pack. Nurse, I want you to draft a meal plan guideline to give to the omega's alphas so they'll know how to best care for her."

Fucking what? I was not about to let a pack control what I ate. My breath quickened, and I recognized the sign of an impending panic attack. I clenched my fingers into tight fists, my fingernails leaving deep crescents in my hands.

"Lie back, omega, so we can do the pelvic exam. I'll explain what we're doing, nurse, since you're new." The nurse giggled her thanks.

I wanted to punch them both.

The alpha guided my legs into the stirrups and roughly pushed up the paper gown, leaving me exposed. *Just think about the beach, standing in the water as the waves wash over you.* The beach visualization was not fucking cutting it as the doctor shoved his dry fingers up my vagina. I heard him explain to the nurse that he was measuring how tight I was, something that would be included in the report given to prospective packs. Omegas were forbidden to have sex or masturbate—we had to stay pure for our alphas so they could have the pleasure of ripping us open with their massive cocks.

The doctor's words became muffled as my panic intensified. I started running through the latest moves we learned in self-defense class. I imagined shoving my knee into the doctor's groin, knocking him to the ground. He would be too stunned to do anything before I stomped on his balls repeatedly, crushing them. My breathing evened out ever so slightly. *Well, what do you know, that was more effective than the beach visualization.* My awareness of the clinic room faded as I ran through my violent fantasy.

The doctor finally finished up after making some notations in my chart, and they both left me to get dressed. My hands wouldn't stop shaking as I tried to pull on my clothes. I wanted to get out of this cold room with its bright lights and bury myself under a pile of soft, warm pillows. I was pulling on my jacket when the nurse returned. I still felt like I was in a haze and barely took in what she was saying as she led me out of the clinic to the main lobby.

"Alright, omega, just take a seat here, and someone will be with you shortly," the nurse said, gesturing to a chair in the small waiting room off of the main hall before she spun around to head back to the clinic.

I sat down, facing the large posters on the wall staring at me with bold, black letters.

Complete your pack! Sign up for pack interviews today!

There was a large photograph of four alphas standing around a petite omega. Maybe I was projecting, but she looked miserable. Underneath the photo, there was more text.

Research shows that alphas are incomplete without an omega. Omegas are the domestic glue that bring alphas together, providing a warm, nurturing energy in the home.

98% of alphas express complete satisfaction with their omega at six-month follow-up interviews.

The Designation Center ensures all omegas have completed proper Academy training so they can best serve their alphas.

Don't wait! Sign up today.

Sam and I used to roll our eyes at propaganda like this. The Designation Government might only have taken power five years ago, but we'd grown up with these messages in our traditionalist community. The poster didn't seem laughable now that I was days away from being forced to join a pack who would view me as an object for their satisfaction. My hand itched to pull out my phone and text Sam, but if anyone saw it would invite too many questions about how I paid for it.

My leg bounced as I tried to force air into my constricted

lungs. My promise to Sam to not do anything drastic flitted through my mind, but how could I keep living with nothing but years of abuse ahead of me?

I leaned over to see if I could glimpse the front door across the main lobby. What would happen if I made a run for it? Would I make it to the door? I imagined myself walking out calmly, evading security before hot-wiring a car and driving all the way to Sam's in Sol. I sat back up in my chair, forcing myself to cut off the fantasy before I started crying. I needed to prepare for what was coming, not lose myself in what-ifs.

I knew from other omegas who had gone into pre-heat that I would meet with a Designation Center employee and complete a questionnaire covering what I was looking for in a pack. They would use my answers to find compatible packs to interview. Somehow, I didn't think the questionnaire would cover my preferences: In your ideal pack, how many alphas would you bond with? *Zero.* What are your favorite hobbies? *My illegal self-defense class, where I learn how to take down alphas.* How many children would you like to have? *None.*

I could only imagine the horror on the DC employee's face before they had me carted away. Even before the Designation Laws passed, I knew that finding a compatible pack would be challenging. I enjoyed my independence and the hustle and bustle of the city, whereas many omegas preferred quiet pack homes in the country. Most alphas and omegas were biologically wired to want to have as many children as possible, but I had never wanted kids. And then, of course, there was my weight, which, as my mother said, was "disgusting and unnatural." Even if I could find a compatible pack, they would likely never want someone who looked like me.

I was so sucked into my childhood memories of my mother berating my body, forcing me to exercise and withholding food, that I almost thought I heard her voice.

"Josephine!"

Wait... that *was* her voice. She couldn't be here, could she? *Well, why wouldn't she be?* I caught sight of her striding towards me, her heels clicking on the marble floors. *I've obviously gone to hell, and today is my orientation day planned by Satan.*

My throat tightened and a wave of nausea washed over me as I caught sight of my pack fathers, Jericho and Richard, following close behind her. *No, no, no, I can't do this, can't handle seeing them.* Cold sweat prickled on my skin as the room spun slightly. My body screamed at me to get up, to run and hide, but it was as if all my muscles had locked into place.

"Josephine, are you ignoring me?" my mother asked.

She was standing in front of me, perfectly put together in a baby blue pencil skirt and matching blouse that showed off her tiny waist. Jericho and Richard stood next to her, looking impatient. I averted my eyes, hating how visceral my fear was, hating that they could scent it on me.

I forced myself to stand, unwilling to let the three of them loom over me. This was the first I had seen my pack fathers since I moved out of their house a year ago. I had hoped time would make me stronger, would help me get over the icy cold fear that kept me frozen and weak in their presence. Now that they were standing before me, I realized how wrong I'd been.

"What are you doing here?" I asked stiffly.

My mother sniffed. "That's the greeting we get? We're here for you, of course. Director Whiteburn notified Jericho of your lab results. Why didn't you tell us? This is such good news."

There was clear relief in her eyes and even the hint of a smile on her lips. Of course, she was thrilled. The fact that I remained unbonded was an endless source of shame for her.

My mother's face returned to her usual scowl when I didn't respond.

"You better change that attitude if you want to attract a good pack. We just met with the director to ensure you get interviews with the most prestigious packs, at least those who would deign to accept an omega like *you*."

"Lucky me," I said, hoping my sarcastic tone covered the fact that I was on the verge of tears.

My mother grabbed my arm, my skin stinging under her hold. "It's about time you proved to the world you're not completely defective. Twenty-three and no pack—it's an embarrassment," she hissed.

And there it was. All she cared about was how my actions reflected on *her*. I'd spent my whole life hearing all the ways I was a disappointment. Getting out of my parents' pack house saved my life, but it was a massive scandal and my mother still wasn't over it. Most days, her phone calls to me ended in her shrieking at me and crying about what a difficult daughter I was. I had tried blocking her number, but that led to her showing up outside my apartment and shouting loudly enough for all my neighbors to hear. Mrs. Hughes, an elderly beta next door, had thought we were under attack and came out into the hallway with a metal baseball bat to defend herself. She'd looked ridiculous, being close to seventy and wearing a fluffy bathrobe, but even with all that, she'd been a badass and scolded my mother for her behavior. After that day, I decided to just suck it up and answer her calls.

My mother was waiting for a response, but I was worried I would start crying if I spoke. I just shrugged, averting my gaze.

She huffed, eyes burning with anger. "Your late heat has put scrutiny on all of us. I don't know what I did to deserve such an ungrateful daughter," she hissed. "Catherine's daughter found her pack at nineteen and she's already pregnant. Christine's daughter has six alphas and is already on her second baby. I don't know why my daughter wants to punish me like this!"

"Angeline, calm down," Richard said tersely.

My mother's husbands were so cold it *almost* made me feel sorry for her. She stopped speaking, meekly deferring to her alphas in a way that made me want to defend her even after the way she had spoken to me.

"Josephine, we need to talk to you in private," Jericho said, gesturing between him and Richard. "Angeline, stay here."

"They told me to wait here for my interview," I said, trembling.

My omega cowered at the thought of being alone with them, the memories of what happened *that day* flooding my mind—the smell of antiseptic, the cruel laughter, their stares. I dug my fingernails into my palms so hard I thought they might draw blood, the pain the only thing keeping me tethered to reality. I couldn't let my mind go back to that place. I refused to show weakness in front of them.

"Today is not the day to disobey us, Josephine," Richard snarled.

My hatred for the two of them grew as they placed their hands on me and marched me towards a closed door in the small hallway. They opened the door and practically shoved me into the small meeting room. There was a table in the center with metal chairs around it, a TV mounted on the wall, and no windows. I forced myself to keep breathing.

"Let's not waste any time, Josephine. You have been a disgrace to this family long enough, and we cannot allow it to continue. We know you've been taking black-market suppressants. The only reason you're not in jail right now is because we didn't want to subject your mother to such humiliation," Jericho said.

"You have no proof," I said quietly. I knew I was pushing it and should just shut my mouth, but I also knew this was a scare tactic. No medical tests could detect suppressant usage.

"You fucking ungrateful bitch," Richard shouted in my face.

I tried my best not to cower under his aggression. Richard had always had the shorter fuse. Jericho, ever the politician, was more subtle in his manipulation. He placed his hand on Richard's chest to hold him back. As first alpha, everyone in the pack deferred to him.

"We want to be clear, Josephine. You are going to bond with a pack immediately. You will stop rebelling. You will obey your new alphas. You will be the picture of a perfect omega. We have had to put up with you for years. If you continue to cause problems for us, we will escalate things," Jericho said in his dangerously calm voice.

Their hatred towards me was a weight on my chest. A desperate longing filled me, and I wished I'd gotten the chance to know my biological father, the alpha my mother ran away with at seventeen. I couldn't imagine my critical, image-obsessed mother rebelling, but I used to fantasize as a child about what my life would be like if my dad hadn't died. Anything would have been better than being raised by my hateful pack fathers actively fighting to strip omegas of our rights. They had never treated me with any affection, even as a young child, and their anger towards me seemed to only grow throughout the years as my mother failed to get pregnant again, a shockingly rare occurrence for an omega. They saw me as a nuisance, a reminder of my mother's failure. And then, at the DA... my stomach roiled and I breathed through my mouth, trying to block their scents from reaching me and keep myself from vomiting. *Don't think about it. Never think about that day.*

Jericho reached out and grabbed my chin harshly. "Do you understand?"

I ripped my face out of his hand and backed up, holding back a whine. I forced myself to meet his glare with a nod, knowing there was nothing else I could do. I needed to get out of here, to be far away from them.

Richard's phone went off, and he jerked his head at Jericho, who cast me one last look of scorn before sweeping out of the room. I kept as much distance from them as possible, and we returned to the sitting area just in time for a woman to call my name.

Chapter Five

Josie

I hadn't expected the person doing my interview to be so friendly or, for lack of better words, *cool*. She introduced herself as Clementine, and I almost smiled when I got a whiff of her faint, sweet citrus scent. I wondered if her parents chose her name because of it. I liked her already, mainly because she saved me from my mother, who was still sniffling and throwing me dirty looks, and my fathers, who seemed to be on the verge of deciding if it'd be easier to just kill me.

Clementine led me down the hallway without filling the silence with small talk, allowing me to sneak some glances at her. She was a beta, probably around my age or a few years older, with wild, curly red hair that framed her face and set off her freckled skin and brown eyes. Her dark green jumpsuit made her look chic and put together as her heels clicked down the hallway.

Jealousy surged through me—as a beta, she had so much more freedom than I would ever have—but I tried to squash it down. It wasn't Clementine's fault.

I followed her into a large office with dark wood furniture

and a large window on the left side, showing off a view of the bay. I took in the room, still reeling from my conversation with Jericho and Richard when I realized Clementine was speaking.

"I'm looking forward to talking with you privately, Josephine. I work with the assistant director, Amirah Raven, to match omegas with their packs. We wanted to take some time to meet with you before scheduling your interviews."

"I go by Josie," I said. Only my parents called me Josephine, making me hate the name on principle. They adamantly refused to use my nickname.

"Josie! I love that," Clementine said, guiding me into a deep leather armchair while she took a seat opposite me. "Amirah is going to be in shortly. She's finishing another meeting. Can I get you anything? Coffee? Dessert?"

I would have killed to drown my feelings in an enormous slice of chocolate cake, but after my run-in with the doctor and my parents, I couldn't silence the critical voice in my head. *Why did you stop your diet? How are you going to attract anyone looking like that?*

"No, thank you." I looked around the office just to have something to do to fill the awkward silence. "Does the assistant director usually meet with omegas before they do their pack interviews?" I finally asked. I'd never heard of that happening.

"Not always," Clementine said carefully, "But we wanted to make sure we met with you with this being a unique situation."

"You mean because I'm twenty-three?"

"That's definitely part of it. Here comes Amirah. She'll explain better," Clementine said with relief as the office door opened, revealing the assistant director, a petite omega with shoulder-length curly black hair and brown skin.

Even though I'd known the assistant director was an omega,

I still felt my chest fill with shock and... pride? Amirah Raven had been the first-ever omega director of what was then called the Omega Center, a place created to support omegas in all aspects of life. When the Designation Government took over, they swiftly made it illegal for omegas to hold jobs. I had no idea how Amirah managed to hold on to a leadership position. Designation Government politicians were constantly shouting about her on the news, criticizing everything about her, from her appearance to her designation. Glen-*spawn-of-Satan*-Jacoby, the governor and leader of the Designation Government, was one of her loudest opponents. I shuddered as I quickly shut down that train of thought and forced myself to focus.

"Thanks so much for agreeing to meet with us," Amirah said, her tone brusque but not unkind.

As she sat down next to Clementine, her cream-colored blouse shifted, revealing a bond mark at the juncture of her neck and shoulder. The news called her four alphas weak because they allowed her to work—as if that somehow took away from their alpha-ness. I wondered what their relationship was like. Did they support her? Did they love each other? All the packs in the romance books I read were deeply in love, the alphas willing to do anything for their omega. I had long abandoned any dream of that being a reality.

"She goes by Josie," Clementine said with a smile.

"Ahh, thank you," Amirah said to Clementine before turning to me. "Josie, I want to start this meeting by saying that this office is soundproof, and there are no cameras or recording devices in this space. Anything that is said here stays here."

I didn't know what I expected her to say, but that was definitely not it. She must have picked up on my confusion because she continued, "Your mother and pack fathers have just met with the director. Richard Porter has influence as a board member, as does Jericho being senate leader. They seem to be highly invested in you interviewing with Pack Madden—are you familiar with them?"

I shook my head, almost positive I'd never heard that name before.

"One of the alphas works with Jericho, so that's likely the connection," Amirah said, lip curling briefly in disdain before she schooled her expression. "Clementine and I felt it was important to meet you and see what you envisioned for your life."

Her question startled me. What I envisioned for my life? I hadn't been asked that in... well, possibly ever, but certainly not by anyone at the Designation Center. "I'm not sure what you're asking."

Amirah and Clementine glanced at each other, and then Amirah turned her piercing gaze back to me.

"Josie, I have no expectation that you'll trust us. Omegas hold a very precarious position in society. I know that better than most. We wanted to meet with you because it's rare to not come into pre-heat before the age of twenty-three without using suppressants. I'm not asking you to confirm anything, but if you have been using suppressants, it leads me to believe you may not want to join a pack. Unfortunately, I don't have the power to prevent that from happening, but I've made it my life's mission to advocate for omegas. I'm offering our help if you want it."

My heart beat rapidly, but I tried to look as calm as possible. If I confirmed I had been using suppressants, I could be arrested, lose the minuscule rights I had, and be forced to join a pack of my parents' choosing. But there was something in me that desperately wanted to trust the two women sitting in front of me.

"What sort of help could you offer me?" I asked carefully.

The assistant director looked me over carefully. "Trust goes both ways, Josie. I need your agreement that you won't share anything I say with anyone outside of this room. Lives depend on it, do you understand?"

I nodded. "I understand. I promise I won't say anything. You're not, um, wrong about me," I offered, heart pounding at the risk I was taking.

Amirah nodded, a small smile forming on her face for the first time since she walked into the room. "For the past few years, we have been developing an underground network of all designations who oppose the recent legislature. It's called the Omega, Beta, Alpha Alliance. Some of our members include unbonded alphas who want to bond with an omega but disagree with the current laws. While we can't stop mandatory pack selection for omegas, we can try to include some of these packs in the interview process. The one thing you still have power over is deciding which pack you bond with. If you want other options besides who your parents have chosen, we can help you."

My mind was spinning. I knew there was an anti-Designation Government group, but I didn't know Amirah was a part of it. Their underground network was how Sam had gotten me suppressants. He had urged me to volunteer with them, to "use my skills" to help the Alliance. Each time, I made some excuse. He had such faith in me, but I knew the truth—I was nothing, could do nothing. And I knew the cost of challenging alphas. My hand brushed automatically against my scar, touching the forever reminder of what it cost to rebel.

What Amirah offered wasn't a complete escape, but it was more than I had dreamed of. I wasn't sure what sorts of packs the assistant director was talking about, but anything would be better than a pack like those from my family's community—

alphas who believed that omegas were weak, subservient, and needed to be controlled.

Amirah and Clementine looked at me expectantly, waiting for my answer. I looked them over and felt a lump forming in my throat. These two women wanted to help me. For the first time in a long time, I didn't feel alone.

"That's... that's a lot to take in. But yes, I want your help, please. I can't bond with a pack my parents choose. I can't live my life like that."

Amirah nodded as she started scrolling through her phone. "We're going to do our best to have an alternative pack for you to interview. I had two packs in mind, but one of them is out of the country until the end of the week," she said, a slight frown on her face. "The director has insisted we expedite your interview process to take place tomorrow, here at the DC."

"Tomorrow?" I squeaked. Clementine looked at me with sympathy.

Amirah grimaced. "Unfortunately, your labs show your heat is starting within the next week, so we have to act fast, or you'll be stuck with an assigned heat pack."

I shuddered. In the rare circumstance an omega didn't have a pack for her heat, the government would select a group of alphas to stand in. I would rather die than allow that to happen.

Amirah continued, "I'll reach out to the pack we have in mind. Typically, omegas are encouraged to have interviews at pack homes so they can see the house and the nest. It also allows the pack to court the omega and show her they can provide for her. That's not an option for you, unfortunately. We think another reason they've decided to have you do your interviews here is so the director, your mother, and your pack fathers can listen in."

"They're going to be listening?" I asked. "How am I supposed to have a real conversation with any of the packs?"

"You'll have to be very careful with what you say," Clementine said. "Nothing about this is ideal, especially with how soon your heat is coming."

"Is there..." I paused, afraid to ask my question. I took a deep breath and continued. "Is there any way to get me out of Luna to Sol?"

Amirah and Clementine exchanged a sad look.

"Unfortunately, no," Amirah answered. "We have, at times, been able to do that. But our current connection in Sol was just arrested. Even if that hadn't happened, your parents are too influential for us to risk it. There's a high likelihood they would find you, which would jeopardize the entire movement."

I had known that leaving wasn't a real option, but hearing it confirmed sent a dagger through my chest. A few tears escaped down my face.

"I really am sorry. For what it's worth, I've been bonded with my pack for almost twenty years. They are incredibly supportive, and I love them deeply. I know it doesn't change the complete injustice of your current situation, but I am hopeful that the pack I have in mind will be a good fit. I can tell you they are kind and respectful. Also, we will not be abandoning you after your interviews tomorrow. You're part of the Alliance now, and we'll support you however we can going forward."

Amirah reached across the coffee table to grasp my hand, giving it a gentle squeeze before drawing back. I appreciated her straightforward attitude. Having grown up in a pack where manipulation and political games were the norm, the transparency she offered me was a relief.

"Alright, Josie, do I have your agreement? If everything goes to plan, you'll have two interviews tomorrow. The first with the pack your parents have selected, and the second with the pack we've chosen for you. You'll make your choice at the end of the two interviews."

I didn't know what to say. I wasn't okay with any of this, but I also knew Amirah had presented me with the best option I could hope for. So I nodded in agreement and thanked her.

I stood to follow Amirah when Clementine said, "Wait, will you stay here and fill out this questionnaire? We give prospective packs these questionnaires from the omega to get to know them before the courting process. Since you don't have a courting process, they'll get this questionnaire tomorrow before the interviews."

I groaned internally, wanting nothing more than to return to my bed and call Sam. Clementine must have gathered my reluctance.

"I'm sorry. I know it sucks, but it's part of my job." She bit her lip, looking vulnerable, before striding over to a corner cabinet and pulling out a bottle of rosé. She held it out to me with a hopeful glimmer in her eye. "Maybe alcohol will make it better?"

I raised an eyebrow. The stress of the past few days broke down my normal defenses. I was tired of keeping everyone at arm's length. I needed an ally... and maybe even a friend. I *definitely* needed alcohol. At my nod, Clementine beamed and uncorked the bottle, pouring us each a generous glass.

I was drunk. Like suuuuuper drunk. I reached for the box of cookies on the coffee table and accidentally knocked it over. I lunged to catch it and ended up falling off the couch, hitting the floor with a graceless thump. I giggled as I crawled towards the box and fished out a chocolate chip cookie.

"Oh my god, you are suuuuch a lightweight," Clementine said, pouring herself another glass of wine.

"Don't pretend you're not drunk, too," I said in what I thought was a normal volume but came out as more of a shout.

"I am not brunk!" Clementine slurred.

I laughed harder, curling up and clutching my stomach as tears streamed down my face. "You are sooo brunk!"

Clementine joined in and for a few moments, the only sound I could hear was our laughter. This moment felt like the long summer days I spent with Sam when we were kids, escaping our homes and getting into trouble.

"Okay, okay, we have to finish this questionnaire," she said, wiping her eyes.

"Why do these alphas even deserve to know anything about me? I know nothing about them," I whined.

"Well," Clementine said slowly, a mischievous gleam entering her eyes, "No one said you had to give them the correct information."

"You mean lie?" I gasped.

Clementine raised her eyebrows at me suggestively. "If they want to know these things about you, they should have to figure it out."

"You are a genius."

Clementine wiggled happily in her seat while I pulled another cookie out of the box.

"Alright, here's the next question—how do you take your coffee?"

"With seven sugars, seven creams, and a shot of caramel syrup," I deadpanned.

"How do you actually take it?"

"Sweet, but not like that," I said, sending myself into another fit of giggles. I rubbed my cheek back and forth on the carpet I was lying on. I wanted all the soft things right now.

"What about this one—favorite flower?"

"Oh wait! I have a real answer. I love peonies."

"Me too!" Clementine said. "So, hopefully, you'll get peonies and coffee so sweet it kills you. Next question: favorite book genre?"

"Mechanical engineering manuals," I said with a smirk.

"Excellent. Who doesn't love a bit of light reading?"

"Is this seriously what alphas want to know?" I whined, trying to crawl my way back onto the couch, but my limbs were not cooperating. "There's nothing on there about actual compatibility, like where we want to live, if we want to have children, or our values and beliefs. Because I don't get to have a say in any of that—the alphas do."

"Do you need help?" Clementine asked, interrupting my tirade with an amused expression as I tried again to pull myself onto the couch.

"This couch is my Everest."

"We could add mountain climbing as a hobby," she suggested.

"Then they might actually try to make me climb a mountain," I said, finally pulling myself onto the couch. "Although look, I did it! Maybe I would be an excellent mountain climber."

Clementine giggled. "I'll skip the mountain climbing for now. We're almost done. Favorite movie?"

"Hmm... my actual favorite movie is *Pride and Prejudice.* But put down *Silence of the Lambs.* Maybe if the alphas think I'm too creepy, they won't want to bond me."

Clementine shot me a skeptical look. "Unfortunately, I highly doubt that. I hope you know you're a real catch. You're funny and beautiful and deserve a great pack. I've met the alphas Amirah mentioned, and they seem really nice."

I sat up abruptly. "Wait, you know them, and you're just

now telling me?" I screeched, suddenly feeling completely sober.

"Sorry! I just got a message from Amirah saying they've confirmed they'll be there tomorrow. I didn't want to say anything until I knew for sure."

"Well, what are they like?" I asked, my heart racing so fast it almost made me lightheaded.

"I don't know them really well. I met them at a function last year. Their names are Cam, Theo, and Ben. Cam and Theo were more reserved, while Ben was more outgoing. I didn't talk to them beyond basic introductions, but they're, like, really hot. And rich. Not that it matters, but if you have to be stuck with a pack, it might as well be one that can buy you copious amounts of terrible coffee."

"Is there anything else you can tell me?" I pleaded, hating how desperate I sounded.

"I don't know any more right now, but I'm going to try to get more information to you before you meet them, I promise," Clementine said apologetically.

I nodded, sipping more of my wine. The reality of the process was sinking in again.

"I know this sucks," Clementine added softly. "Everything about the Designation Laws suck." The depth of the sadness in her eyes took me off guard. I wondered how Clementine had been affected by the laws. I wanted to ask her more, but I understood not wanting to share painful memories.

"Oh wait, there's one more question on here," Clementine said, breaking the silence. "Boxers or briefs?"

"What, will they switch out their underwear to match my preference?" I sorted.

"Who knows," Clementine said, laughing. "What will it be?"

"Definitely commando."

I looked around, realizing we'd been at this for two hours and had finished two bottles of wine.

"Alright, I just sent those answers off to the match board to give to the packs before the interview. I think we should ask Dave to drive us home."

Omegas were banned from driving four years ago. I remembered watching Glen Jacoby's press conference when he announced the new law, and could still hear him saying omega hormones were too erratic for us to drive safely, as if alphas weren't the real erratic ones. Sam taught me how to drive in secret when we were teens. I loved borrowing his car to cruise around the countryside. It was one of the rare occasions I felt free.

Now I mostly walked or rode the bus since I couldn't drive and didn't have money to hire a car. Omegas were strongly discouraged from riding public transit since our scents could cause the entire bus to erupt into chaos (Glen's words, not mine), but it was technically still legal. But right now, I had no desire to ride the bus in my vulnerable, tipsy state.

"Who's Dave?"

"Dave is an alpha who works here in the center. But he's part of the Alliance," Clementine said without meeting my gaze, a blush forming on her cheeks.

A smile tugged at my lips, and I wondered if there was anything between them. I was tempted to ask but wasn't sure if it was too personal. It had been so long since I really opened up to anyone besides Sam. My self-protective defenses prevented me from getting too close to anyone.

There was a sharp knock on the door before it opened, revealing Dave. He was huge—I was guessing at least 6' 5" with broad shoulders and massive arms. His brown hair was cropped in a military-style cut, and he was wearing an all-black DC security uniform with a gun holstered at his side. My heart rate picked up at his intimidating presence.

Clementine, however, didn't seem remotely concerned. Her face lit up when he walked in, and she started giggling. Dave quirked his eyebrow at her, taking in our mess of wine bottles and opened treats.

"You tipsy, Clem?" There was a warmth in his eyes, fueling my suspicion that there was something between them.

"No, why would you say that?" she responded, laughing so hard she slid out of the chair she was sitting in.

Dave shook his head with a smile before looking at me and introducing himself. The room spun a bit as we picked up Amirah's office, Dave doing most of the work. I kept a wide berth, not wanting to get too close to him. But as Dave moved around the space, I caught his pleasant lemon scent.

Clementine and I gathered our things and made sure we both looked serious and presentable before leaving. Being locked away in Amirah's secure office had almost made me forget we were in the middle of the horrible, oppressive place that was the DC. It would look suspicious if we appeared drunk or too lighthearted, so we quietly followed Dave out of the office. I breathed a sigh of relief once we got to the parking lot. Just being on DC property made my skin crawl.

As we neared the town car, I couldn't help it. I leaned close to Clementine and asked, "Do you like him?"

I meant for it to be a whisper, but it must have come out louder than expected because Dave choked out a cough, and Clementine's freckle-laden face flushed red as we got into the back of the car. I shot her an apologetic look. *Damn alcohol.*

When Dave closed the door behind us, she turned to me and gave a little nod. Before the DC laws, alphas could bring betas into their packs and even bond them. But since the new laws, betas could no longer be with alphas. Tears pricked at my eyes, the alcohol making me more emotional than usual at the reminder that betas didn't have it easy, either.

As the car pulled out of the parking lot, I curled up in the back seat, having far surpassed my limit for the day. I couldn't believe I had gotten my blood work results just this morning. I felt I had lived several eternities since then. The car was warm and dark, a relief after being under bright lights all day, and Dave and Clementine's fresh citrus scents swirled around me as I dozed off.

"We're here," Dave said quietly, startling me out of my sleep. I sat up and saw we were parked in front of my apartment building.

"We'll be here to pick you up in the morning," Clementine said. "It was really nice to meet you. I hope you can get some rest tonight."

"Thanks, Clementine."

Dave opened the door for me, but I hesitated before getting out.

"Some nights, I go to a self-defense class down the street. An alpha there holds a class for omegas, but it's really empowering and you'd be welcome to come with me sometime if you wanted to." Maybe it was the alcohol that made me trust Clementine enough to invite her, or maybe I was just so fucking exhausted doing everything on my own.

Clementine beamed. "Oh my gosh, I would love to. Let me know the time and date and I'll be there."

"I'm going to escort you to the door," Dave said solemnly. "Clementine, don't get out of the car for any reason." He growled that last part protectively. I looked over at Clementine and gave her a wink as she rolled her eyes.

Dave waited until I fished out my keys and unlocked my door before saying goodbye. I headed into my apartment, locked the deadbolts behind me, and stripped off my clothes.

After wrapping myself in my fluffiest blanket, I walked to the kitchen to make hot chocolate, needing something warm and sweet. My hand hesitated over the tin. Even though I didn't want to join a pack, the idea of being around alphas tomorrow and having them judge me and my body made me want to vomit. I blinked back tears as I tightened the blanket around my soft curves and rolls.

See, this is why no one could ever love you or find you desirable. A nasty voice that sounded suspiciously like my mother rang out in my head. I took a deep breath and repeated my mantras to myself. *My body is a good body. My body doesn't exist for the sole purpose of being thin.* The tightness in my chest eased a little, and I forced myself to make the hot chocolate. I shuffled to my bedroom, the blanket still wrapped around me, and set up a fort of blankets and pillows, nestled my way into the middle, and then grabbed my latest romance book. I needed some fictional men to carry away the fears of meeting with the alphas tomorrow. Fictional men would never hurt me or think I'm too fat. *Who needs real men?*

Chapter Six

Theo

I hung up the phone and put my head in my hands with a groan just as Cam walked into the office with a couple bowls of pasta.

"What's wrong?" he asked gruffly as he sat down in the leather office chair across the desk from me.

"You make that?" I asked, eyeing the bowl he'd sat in front of me. It smelled like vodka sauce—my favorite.

Cam snorted. "I don't hate you that much. Ben got back from the store a few minutes ago and took pity on us."

Cam and I couldn't cook for shit and depended on our pack brother for meals. We had subsisted on takeout when we first left our community since none of us had learned to do anything around the house growing up. Ben had discovered a love of cooking and domestic shit. It was another one of the many reasons I was glad we got out of that hellhole. Seeing him bounce around the kitchen in a frilly apron was the biggest fuck you to our pack fathers I could imagine. I didn't know how he managed to be so fucking cheerful all the time, but it made me feel like I had at least succeeded in protecting him from the damage Cam and I sustained growing up.

"Glad he's home already. I just got a call from Amirah at the Designation Center," I said, shooting off a text to Ben. I glanced up from the phone and saw Cam still, a shocked expression briefly crossing his face before he composed himself.

"Is this what I think it is?" he asked.

"Yeah, it is," I said. "Ben will be here in a minute. I'll let you know more then."

Cam and I stared out the window, looking out onto the courtyard and wooded area beyond the house, the food forgotten until Ben bounded into the room.

"What's up?" he asked. "Do you not like the pasta? I'm trying a new recipe."

I cleared my throat. "Oh, no, I'm sure it's amazing, like everything you make."

Ben practically glowed with happiness.

I ran my hand through my hair. "Amirah called," I said, jaw clenched.

Ben furrowed his brow. "Does she have a job for me?" Ben's experience with computer programming and hacking made him invaluable to the Alliance.

"No," I said, steeling myself before I continued. "She wants us to interview with an omega tomorrow."

Since the Designation Laws passed, we hadn't done any omega interviews, refusing to participate in an oppressive system. We'd already experienced far too much of that in the traditionalist community we grew up in.

We met Amirah before the Designation Government took power, back when she was the newly appointed director of the now-defunct Omega Center. We stayed in touch and were one of the first packs to join the Alliance. We provided funding and technical support to the movement—technical support being a nice way to say hacking, encryption, and security. We were currently backing certain politicians who were preparing to propose new legislation to push back against the Designation Laws. The last time we saw her, Amirah asked if we would be open to omega interviews if an omega needed a progressive pack option, and we'd agreed. It seemed like a good idea at the time. Now I wasn't so sure.

The three of us longed for an omega to complete our pack. We had been together since my family moved us to North Woods from England when I was fourteen. We'd been inseparable for the past fifteen years, leaving our community together and starting our company. I could feel through our bonds that my brothers were lonely. As alphas, we were meant to have an omega to cherish, love, and care for. I hadn't let myself believe it could be possible for us unless we moved to a more progressive province, but our Alliance work kept us here.

"This is good, right?" Ben asked, looking between Cam and me. "Amirah knows us. She knows what we're like as a pack and what sort of omega we could bond with. This could be what we've been waiting for. Why don't either of you look happy?"

I glanced over at Cam, who I knew shared my skepticism.

"Amirah kept it pretty cryptic over the phone since we never know who might be listening in. All she said is there's a twenty-three-year-old omega in pre-heat who's doing pack interviews tomorrow and asked if we could come in at two o'clock."

"Twenty-three?" Cam asked, leaning back in the leather chair, his brow furrowing. "Unusual for an omega that age to not have had a heat yet. You think she might have been using suppressants?"

"That would be my guess," I responded. "If that's the case, she probably doesn't even want a pack. They've increased arrests lately for people supplying black market suppressants. I'm not going to force someone to be our omega."

Growing up, it was drilled into our heads that omegas were essential to alphas but never equal to us. We were told that when we bonded with an omega, we would be highly possessive and protective, so much so that we wouldn't be able to control our behavior. We had seen some terrible things—omegas being isolated from family and friends, forced into having sex and babies. And then, of course, there was Cam's sister. My throat felt tight as I thought about her. Even though we all wanted our pack to be complete, we refused to change our values, to change ourselves. It seemed safer to stay unbonded. We didn't want to control an omega; we wanted an equal partner.

"But she'll be forced to choose a pack," Ben exclaimed. "And if we don't interview, she might be stuck with a terrible pack that will take advantage of her."

"We can't be sure that she's been on suppressants. Some omegas are just older when they have their first heat," Cam said. "I think we owe it to Amirah to at least do the interview. We should go in without any expectations, and we need to be prepared for it not to work out." He directed that last part at Ben.

"So, we'll court her?" Ben asked, bouncing up and down on the balls of his feet. "If it all works out," he added when he saw my scowl.

I sighed. "Not exactly." This was the part I was most nervous about. "Apparently, she's going into heat in the next few days. If she selects us, we'll bring her home the next day."

"Shit, that's quick," Cam said, leaning forward. "They want us to bring her home and help her through her heat? Is that what she wants?" His tone was fierce, and I knew he was thinking of his sister.

"We're not going to force her into anything," Ben said as he paced around the room. "What happens after her heat?"

"I guess we'll see if we're a good fit for each other? If we're not, at least this would be a safe place for her to live. We could put her in the pool house if it became an issue," I said, trying to keep my tone matter-of-fact.

Ben growled, and Cam and I looked up, startled. I couldn't remember the last time I heard Ben growl.

"We're not going to put an omega alone in the pool house. That's cruel," he said.

"What? It's a nice space," I responded, unsure why he was defending this nameless omega who likely wouldn't even fit in with our pack. A pair of big, green eyes came to mind, and I shoved the image aside.

"But omegas need touch and connection," Ben said, biting his lip.

"Ben, she might not want those things. She certainly might not want those things from us," I said.

My mind returned yet again to the breathtaking omega from the grocery store. I dreamed of her last night. I desperately wanted to know if she was okay and wished more than anything that I had been able to scent her. Something told me that she would have been all sugary sweetness.

Cam leaned back in his leather chair. "I think we're obligated to do this for the Alliance, to give her a safe place and help through her heat, if that's what she wants."

I shifted uncomfortably in my chair. "You two are fine having sex with a stranger? During heat?"

"I don't know," Ben said. He stopped pacing and sank down in a chair.

"It's not fair for her to suffer," Cam said.

My chest clenched. I didn't want an omega to suffer just because of her biology, but it was rare for me to experience sexual attraction. The idea of having sex for the first time with a heat-crazed omega I'd met the day before set my teeth on edge. Fuck, this was the least romantic scenario I could imagine—sex as a medical procedure instead of something borne out of love. Omegas could sustain significant physical damage during heat without sex and knotting from an alpha.

"I won't be participating," I said finally. "But you two can make your own decision, of course." As I said the words, fear wormed its way into my chest. What if Cam and Ben became close to this omega and I was left out? What if they ultimately chose her over me? I ran my hand through my hair and tried to shield my anxiety from the bond.

"So, we're doing this?" Ben asked, a broad smile on his face.

"Yes," Cam said. His expression was reserved, but I could feel his excitement pulsing through the bond.

"We can meet her. But we all have to agree to accept her into the pack, if she's even interested in us," I said firmly.

"Of course!" Ben said, bouncing up and down. "What should we do to prepare? Do we bring anything?"

"Amirah just said for us to meet her at the DC. She'll give us a file on the omega to review ahead of time, and then we'll meet her." I sighed, having totally lost my appetite. "I'm going for a run. I can't work anymore."

I abandoned my lunch and quickly changed my clothes, heading out for the trails that ran behind our home—one of the reasons I had wanted to buy this house in the first place. As I ran, I repeated to myself, "Don't get your hopes up. This won't work out." The words drummed in my brain to the time of my furious steps as I sprinted through the woods. After a while, the words somehow changed. "Maybe she could be the one," pounded through my head as I pushed myself to run faster. So much for not getting my hopes up.

I am so fucked.

Chapter Seven

Josie

I was curled up on the small window seat in my living room, my head leaning against the windowpane, my hands gripping my e-reader. I was trying to escape my reality by diving into a new romance book, but I kept getting distracted by every movement outside. I hadn't slept at all last night, and now I was nauseous, my entire body on edge. The moment I had run from for years was here.

I dug my fingernails into my palms. My thoughts had turned especially dark in the early hours of the morning, returning once again to the temptation of just... not being here anymore.

My phone vibrated, startling me. I dug it out from where it had slid between the cushion and wall.

SAM

Have they picked you up yet?

JOSIE

Not yet

SAM

Tell me how it went the second you get home

JOSIE

I already said I would

SAM

Don't let them bulldoze over you

But don't be too assertive

JOSIE

Thanks for this super clear advice. Really helping with the stress.

SAM

Sorry, Josie-girl. I wish I was there with you.

Gerald just yelled at me to chill the fuck out.

JOSIE

I wish you were here, too.

Actually, I wish I was there with you. Anywhere but here.

SAM

I know. I love you.

JOSIE

Love you

A black SUV pulled up to the curb, and my heart started pounding. I eyed the fire escape at the back of my apartment, itching to escape. I tried to run once before, back when I was stronger. But they had broken me. I wouldn't survive being caught again. I clutched my stomach as memories assaulted me, sweat trickling down my spine. I stumbled to the bathroom, barely reaching the toilet before I threw up. *Look at you, so pathetic. Pull yourself together.*

I sat on the bathroom floor as the room swam around me. I tried to breathe, reminding myself that Amirah and Clementine promised to help me. Maybe the pack they selected didn't want an omega, either. Best-case scenario, I would move in and we could live as distant roommates who occasionally made small talk about the unseasonably warm fall and our favorite TV shows.

A nagging voice in the back of my mind reminded me of my heat.

In just a few days, I would be writhing in agony, desperate for a knot to soothe the pain and fever. If I was left alone through my heat, the fever could cause an infection and kill me. I let out a scream so piercing and primal I almost scared myself, but I needed some way to express the injustice of it all.

I was holding out hope that I could have a suppressant-assisted heat, which was survivable without any alpha involvement. Sam thought he'd found someone to get me suppressants. And if that didn't pan out? I would just have to find a way through it alone.

I struggled to my feet and rinsed my mouth before looking at myself. The girl in the mirror stared back at me with dead eyes. I hated that I cared what I looked like for these alphas, that I felt the need to put on makeup, which was now smeared, and blow dry my hair for the first time in ages. Hated that I wished my face wasn't so round... that all of me was less round.

This morning, my mother had her assistant drop off a girlish blue dress with a flouncy skirt and embroidered flowers, along with matching velvet blue high heels. Of course, the dress was too tight—she always bought me things that were too small, as if that would somehow force me to lose weight. Instead, I put on a black jumpsuit I knew my mother hated. The jumpsuit didn't do much to hide my stomach and hips, with their rolls and curves that were too much for a typical omega, but it was one of the few outfits I felt confident in. My mother would be furious when she saw I wasn't wearing her outfit, but I needed to exercise any control I had in this terrifying situation.

A whimper escaped me as I heard a knock on the door. I eyed my bedroom with longing, my bed calling me, tempting me to return. My nesting instincts kicked in last night, but I hadn't given in to them. It would have felt like giving up, like accepting my heat was inevitable.

I had never had a real nest—my parents always said it would be something my alphas would give me as long as I was a good omega. At the DA, they showed us pictures of beautiful nests—dark, cozy rooms with twinkling lights, soft music, and every plush pillow and blanket you could imagine. They dangled these images in front of us as incentives: if we stayed in line and behaved, one day, we could earn a nest like that. They told us they intentionally created our dorm rooms without those comforts so that we would be motivated to find our packs.

Our DA rooms had been sparse. There were no decorations, and we were allowed one pillow and blanket. If we did what they wanted, we could earn more items as a reward. Of course, it also worked the other way. They had systematically stripped my room of every item until I had a thin mattress on the floor and nothing else.

Sam encouraged me to make my room in his apartment into a nest, but I'd never been able to. Even if I'd had the money to buy more than the occasional thrift store blanket, a part of me didn't want to give in to my inner omega's desires. She was to blame for the position I was in right now. I'd held on to the hope that if I didn't give in to my instincts of finding alphas, making a nest, or having a heat, I could destroy the omega part of myself. Obviously, I hadn't succeeded.

Dread pooled in my stomach as I heard another sharp knock. I slowly gathered my things and opened the door. Dave was standing in the hallway, a serious expression on his face. He lifted an eyebrow at me.

"For a minute, I thought you might try to run away."

"I thought about it," I mumbled, locking the door behind me. "Is Clementine here?"

"In the car," he replied, his gaze continuously sweeping the stairwell as if someone was going to jump out and attack at any minute.

When we got to the car, I cried out in surprise as Clementine threw her arms around me. Her fiery red curls were pulled up in a messy bun on top of her head, and she was dressed in a loungewear set.

"Sorry! Didn't mean to startle you. Get in here quick. We've got to be focused," she said, a whirlwind of energy.

I forced myself to buckle in and stared longingly back at my apartment building as we pulled away from the curb.

"We only have a few minutes for me to give a rundown of the two packs you're interviewing. Usually, you would only do one interview a day, so you aren't overwhelmed. Especially with your heat coming up, you're probably going to be more overwhelmed by alpha pheromones. But your parents are pushing for you to match with someone immediately, so they've set up two interviews today. The first will be Pack Madden."

Clementine handed me a folder. Inside was a photo of four alphas in suits. It was no surprise that they were all tall and muscular, but what was surprising was that they all had the exact same haircut and unsmiling facial expressions.

"They look like clones," I said, giving Clementine an unimpressed look.

"Oh, just wait; it gets worse once you hear about them," she responded with a smirk. "Personality? None. Favorite activity? Lording their power over everyone and kissing Glen Jacoby's ass. Likelihood they can bring a woman to orgasm? Absolutely zero."

I laughed as I flipped through the rest of the pages in the folder. "I don't think those are their questionnaire answers."

"Don't worry, I'm just saving you time reading their fake-ass answers. This is not going to be your pack. There are a lot of rumors floating around of them assaulting betas, and they support even stricter Designation Laws. They need an omega to cement their status and legitimacy as a pack so they can run for office, and I'm guessing they'll just keep her locked up in their mansion."

My palms grew sweaty, and my chest tightened as I clenched the Pack Madden folder. The partition separating us from Dave lowered.

"Clem, that is not helpful," he said. Clementine looked up from where she was pulling another folder out of her bag.

"Oh my god. Josie, are you okay? I didn't mean to freak you out. They're not going to be your pack. Forget about them."

I was too far gone to process what she was saying, my panic dragging me deep underwater. No matter what, I still had to be in an enclosed room alone with those alphas.

"Omega," Dave said gruffly. "I need you to breathe nice and slow for me."

I wanted to hate him for calling me omega, but I could feel myself instinctually responding to his deep alpha voice. My breathing evened out.

"I can't do this," I whimpered. I blinked quickly to keep my tears from falling. Clementine pulled me in for a hug and rubbed her hand up and down my back. I stiffened at first before allowing myself to relax into her embrace.

"You can do this," she said. "I know it sucks to have to do the interview with them, but they can't touch you or do anything to you. You just have to get through the interview and then you never have to see them again. Omegas always have the final say on the pack, no matter what your parents want. And you have a much better pack option. I might even call them dreamy."

I pulled away from her and shot her a skeptical look.

"I know, I know," she said. "It's hard to believe. But this is Pack Ashwood." She handed me the folder with an exaggerated flourish.

I opened to the first page, where it listed the alphas' names: Cameron, Benjamin, and Theodore Ashwood.

"I told you they were hot," Clementine said, giving me a pointed look.

Dave made a growling coughing sound.

She wasn't wrong. I bit my lip as I looked at the photo of the three of them. They were standing next to each other in some sort of garden, arms around each other. Cam, on the left, was pure muscle. His tan arms were tattooed, and his black t-shirt clung to his massive chest. His dark brown hair was tied up in a bun and his beard was neatly trimmed. He looked like a combination of a secret service agent/hipster and exuded authority. He was the type of alpha I would usually write off, but there was something about his relaxed stance, the way his arm was slung around his pack mates' shoulders. His smile seemed genuine, crinkling the skin around his eyes.

I shifted my eyes to Ben, standing in the middle. He was almost as tall as Cam, wearing a fitted gray button-down, rolled up at the sleeves, and black square-frame glasses that looked adorably nerdy. His bright blue eyes were lit with laughter, and his messy brown hair was faded on the sides with beautiful curls at the top of his head. His presence felt lighthearted and playful even through the photo.

The alpha on the right, Theo, was the smallest of the three, although I guessed he was probably still six feet tall and all lean muscle. His dark brown hair stuck up in an endearing way, and his brown eyes felt warm. Theo looked over at the two other alphas with a reserved smile on his clean-shaven face. His formal black button-down and tie felt out of place in the photo, but the three of them somehow worked together.

My eyes skimmed the bios. *Fuck, Theo is British? I love a good accent.*

"How long have they been a pack?" I asked, frustrated as I read through the sparse bios.

Clementine shuffled through her notes. "They formed their pack fifteen years ago."

I raised my brows in surprise. "Why haven't they bonded an omega yet?"

Fifteen years was an almost unheard-of amount of time to be without an omega, especially for a pack this powerful and wealthy.

"They travel quite a bit for their work. Most omegas don't want a pack where the alphas will be gone a lot."

I barely kept from rolling my eyes. God forbid omegas have their own lives or jobs or want to travel themselves. Once we found our pack of possessive, overprotective alphas, we were expected to stay at home, pining for the alphas to return while always being sexually available. For the millionth time, I wished I were a beta.

"Once the Designation Laws were passed," Clementine continued, "they didn't want to be a part of the corrupt system. Amirah convinced them to be a possible pack option for omegas who are part of the Alliance. They have some non-traditional traits as well. For one, they don't want children."

I perked up. I'd never heard of alphas that didn't want children. Usually, they were obsessed with impregnating their omega. *Just another way to keep us trapped at home and dependent on them.*

"All three have been involved in lobbying efforts to get the government to remove the Designation Laws. They've given us a ton of money under the table so we can keep fighting for equality." Clementine raised her eyebrows suggestively when she said the last part. Damn her for knowing that would pique my interest.

I kept being pulled back to the photo, something warm sparking inside me, but I quickly shut it down. *I have to stay on my guard.*

"So, after the interviews, I just... go home with them?" I asked, hearing the edge of panic in my voice.

"After the interviews, you'll let us know which pack you choose. Technically, you could say you want more interviews, but any other packs would likely be ones chosen by your parents. Amirah had to fight to get Pack Ashwood approved as an option. Assuming you choose them, you'll move into their house tomorrow. Your parents will accompany you for the traditional hand-off meeting."

"We're just moving on down through the levels of hell," I muttered.

Clementine shot me a sympathetic look. "There's someone monitoring the interview room to ensure you're safe. The alphas aren't allowed to touch you or force you to decide on the spot. If they do anything like that, the monitor is supposed to intervene. I'm guessing your parents and the director will also listen in. Don't talk about anything you wouldn't want them to know."

Way too quickly, we pulled into the DC parking lot. I clenched my jaw, steeling myself to enter this terrible place to meet with terrible people. I forced myself to take a deep breath. *You are capable. You can do this.* I didn't believe my own words, but I kept repeating them, hoping they would become true.

Chapter Eight

Josie

"It must be *so* hard having to take care of yourself all alone in your apartment," Hale said, his dark eyes intent on my face.

Kill me now. I wasn't sure how much longer I could tolerate these condescending asshole alphas. Hale, Duke, Pierce, and Henderson Madden. *What fucking annoying names.* We were only a few minutes into the interview, and my fight or flight warred within me. I didn't know if I wanted to punch them all in the face or flee from the room.

The alphas looked like models with their perfect hair and clothes and were styled so similarly it was hard to tell them apart. They started the interview by going on about how much money and political influence they had. My guess was that one of their suits cost more than all of my possessions combined. It was a good thing I didn't want to impress them because I felt painfully underdressed in my jumpsuit. I wished they would stop raking their eyes up and down my body.

Hale had explained that he and Pierce worked with Jericho, helping him pass new Designation Legislation. This pack was at least partially responsible for my choices being taken away, but by their tone of voice, you would think I should be down on my knees thanking them. I had been prepared to hate this pack on principle, but they did a great job of providing me with actual reasons to despise them.

The alphas had chosen separate chairs around the room, making me feel surrounded. I quickly glanced at the door, hating that Duke's massive frame was between me and the exit. I struggled to breathe, not just because of my anxiety but also from their pungent scents burning my nose.

"I've enjoyed living alone," I said, meeting Hale's gaze. "I like being independent and can take care of myself."

I heard what sounded like a scoff coming from Henderson, who was sitting in a lounge chair with his legs spread wide. He ran his hand through his bleach-blond hair, and a waft of his dill scent washed over me. *Fucking disgusting.*

"I'm sure you've done the absolute best you could to take care of yourself," he said in a voice more suited to talking to a young child. Or a dog. "But with us, you won't have to worry about anything. We will make sure that all your needs are met with *complete satisfaction.*" His eyes darkened as he leaned forward.

There was no missing the innuendo there. My chest tightened uncomfortably.

"Omegas thrive under care, and that's what we would give you," Pierce said from his position on the couch across from me. His damp cardboard scent matched his dour expression. "You wouldn't have to worry about anything. All of your meals would be prepared for you. We have a state-of-the-art nest and, of course, the gym in the lower levels. You can find anything you need in the house."

My skin crawled at the thought of being stuck in their house day in and day out.

"A personal chef, a nest, and a gym... what more could a girl want?" I asked, trying to keep the sarcasm out of my voice.

"Don't worry, between the strict meal plan and the gym, you'll be in perfect shape in no time," Duke said with a flawless smile that didn't reach his cold eyes. He looked down at his watch as if *I* was taking up too much of *his* time. His acidic vinegar smell left me wondering how these alphas ever had women interested in them. They probably only slept with betas who couldn't scent them. I clenched my jaw, tamping down any thoughts of them touching me to prevent myself from bursting into tears.

It took me a minute for my brain to catch up with what he had said. "Wait... what do you mean?" I asked, my heart pounding faster.

"We're sure you've tried so hard on your own," Henderson said, "But obviously, the state of your body is evidence enough that you need to be under the supervision of strong, capable alphas. We would handle everything, so you wouldn't need to worry about anything except being a good, obedient omega for us."

What. The. Fuck. I had reached my limit. Everything in me was on edge, having to sit here with these alphas who talked to me like I was stupid, treated me like garbage, and who not only hated my body but felt comfortable enough critiquing it our *first time meeting*.

We had more time left in the interview, but I needed to end this now. There was no way I could choose this pack. The alphas Amirah had selected could be aliens or monsters or shifters that turned into houseplants, and at this point, I would not care. I would rather die than go home with Pack Madden. They didn't seem all that interested in having an omega join their pack, and they certainly weren't interested in me. They needed me to elevate their status as a "completed" pack.

Many traditionalists believed alpha packs weren't complete or legitimate until they found an omega—a critique occasionally levied against Glen Jacoby, who was unbonded. I imagined with Pack Madden's interest in politics, bonding with an omega would increase their legitimacy with politicians and voters—none of whom, conveniently, were omegas anymore.

Duke smirked as he looked around at his pack mates. "At least one thing's for sure, no matter how fucking ugly an omega is, you can always count on her having a sweet cunt."

The other alphas smirked. I froze in total disbelief as the room spun around me. I couldn't believe he had just said that.

"Look, Josephine," Pierce said in his bored tone. "You're twenty-three years old. Your records show you caused significant trouble while at the Academy. You can't hope to get offers from any decent packs. Here's how this will work—you will move in with us and we'll bond. We will provide you with everything you need in the house. We can be generous. In return, you fulfill all of our needs and follow our rules. If you break our rules, there will be consequences. You obviously need a firm hand to keep you in line. You'll get to enjoy being with a wealthy, highly respected pack. You can choose your own dresses for the parties and functions you attend with us. This is the best offer you're going to get."

"This has been a mistake," I said, trying to keep my voice from shaking with anger as I stood. "This interview is over."

"We have not dismissed you," Duke snarled, moving to block the exit. "Sit back down."

My inner omega instinctually wanted to obey alphas, but even she wasn't impressed by this asshole.

"No, I would like to leave," I said again, walking quickly to the door, trying to keep as much distance between Duke and me as possible.

"You're making a mistake," Hale growled as he lunged towards me, grabbing hold of my wrist.

My heart raced, adrenaline pumping through my veins. Last week during self-defense, we learned how to get out of wrist holds. My body moved seemingly without my awareness as I took a step towards Hale, placed my hand over his wrist, and yanked my arm down hard towards his thumb. He let go, shock flashing across his face, and I backed away from his reach. The door opened and Dave stormed in, quickly moving his body between me and the alphas.

"Are you alright?" he asked, looking down at my wrist.

I nodded my head, unable to talk. My wrist throbbed and was going to bruise, but I didn't think it was seriously injured. Terror pumped through my body, but I was also proud that I had used my self-defense skills instead of freezing.

"Can I leave?" I whispered, my voice cracking a bit. The urge to wrap myself up in a pile of blankets in a dark, warm room was overwhelming.

"I thought we made clear that you were not to touch the omega or do anything to make her uncomfortable," Dave growled at them. The alphas looked furious, and I was scared they would fight Dave or try to hurt me again.

"We have authority over the omega," Henderson said snidely. I almost gagged as his putrid scent filled the room.

"She is not your omega," Dave responded. "You have no authority over her, and you violated the interview policies. This interview is over."

Dave gently ushered me out of the room and down a hallway. He was muttering under his breath. I couldn't catch everything he said, but I thought I heard "little pieces of shit alphas" and "should be castrated."

I asked Dave to point me to the nearest restroom. I leaned on the bathroom counter, feeling too dizzy to stand. The thought of doing another interview made me want to cry, even though a part of me—a *very* small part—was curious about Pack Ashwood. But mostly, I just wanted to go home, get in my pajamas, and pretend I had a different life.

There was a knock on the bathroom door.

"Josie, are you okay?" Dave asked. "It's been a while."

"I'm fine," I squeaked out, sounding completely unconvincing.

"Can I come in?"

I didn't want to be in an enclosed space with an alpha, but Clementine trusted Dave and he had just come to my rescue. I hesitantly unlocked the door, backing away as he entered.

"Can I see your arm?" he asked more gently than I would have expected, keeping as much distance between us as he could.

My tears finally started falling. I couldn't handle tenderness right now. I was feeling too vulnerable.

Dave took a deep breath and slowly moved closer, leaning down so our eyes were level and he was no longer looming over me. He gently took hold of my wrist. There was just the slightest redness, but I knew the bruises would form by tonight. Omegas bruised and injured easily—another excuse for alphas to control us *for our own protection.*

Dave seemed satisfied that my wrist didn't need medical care and released it.

He sighed, staying crouched down. "Sweet omega, you are a gift. Those alphas don't deserve you. You deserve a pack that will worship the ground you walk on and gives you whatever you want and need. Do you understand?"

I realized Dave actually wanted me to answer, so I gave him a little nod, even though what he said didn't make sense. Even before the Designation Laws, I had been taught that omegas existed to serve their alphas, not the other way around. I had never heard an alpha outside of Sam and Luc say anything to the contrary.

"Very good," he said. "Now, dry your tears. We need to eat lunch, and then you'll meet Pack Ashwood."

He led me to a small outside courtyard and pulled two sandwiches out of his coat pocket.

"I'm not hungry," I said, taking the sandwich from him.

Dave gave me a stern look. "You need to keep your energy up."

I wrinkled my nose but unwrapped the sandwich and took a small bite.

"Do you know Pack Ashwood?" I asked quietly.

"A bit," he hedged. I knew he couldn't talk freely here—we never knew who was listening. "They seem like reliable, trustworthy alphas."

I nodded, feeling slightly less panicked. I didn't know Dave, but he was unlike so many of the alphas I grew up with—his calm presence made me feel like I could trust what he said. We sat in companionable silence while we ate until Dave's phone vibrated, alerting him it was time to take me into the second interview. I followed him inside, feeling like I was on autopilot until we reached the interview room door.

"You remember what I said?" Dave asked me.

"Yes," I whispered.

"Good," he said with a brief nod. He then opened the door, revealing the three alphas waiting for me. I took a deep breath and walked into the room.

Chapter Nine

Josie

Three alphas stood in the center of the room, their eyes snapping to mine as I walked in.

Fuck, they were hot.

The alpha closest to me was dressed casually in a light blue button-down shirt and black jeans, his messy curls and glasses making him feel approachable even though he towered over me.

"You must be Josephine. I'm Ben. We're so excited to meet you. Please come in!"

Ben said all of this so rapidly I could hardly understand what he was saying, but there was something so genuine about him I felt my lips curl into an involuntary smile. He had a huge grin on his face, and his body brimmed with energy. His gaze didn't feel predatory like Pack Madden, and his enthusiasm put me a little more at ease. The alphas I was used to were stoic and aggressive—Ben seemed to be the complete opposite. I moved further into the room, and my knees almost buckled when his spiced apple scent hit me like a crisp autumn day. It was energizing and comforting at the same time.

"Ben, you've got to calm the fuck down," a low voice said from behind him. Ben stepped to the side, and my eyes fell on an alpha with massive, broad shoulders and thick, tattooed arms.

"I'm Cam. Like Ben said, we're glad to get the chance to meet you."

I didn't know what scent to expect from this intimidating alpha, but it definitely wasn't the cinnamon roll scent that hit me. It was so perfectly sweet my inner omega urged me to lick him. *What the fuck is happening to me?* I felt dazed as the third alpha of the pack stepped towards me.

"Hi Josephine, I'm Theo. It's nice..." his voice trailed off as he froze, eyes wide.

I wasn't sure what to make of his reaction until his warm coffee scent surrounded me. I almost whimpered. It was the same scent I had been inhaling off my sweatshirt for the past two days. How did his scent get on my clothes? Did he work at the hospital? As I inhaled another lungful, I got the briefest flash of memory of strong arms holding me in Trader Joe's. Had Theo been there when I fainted?

My mind reeled with questions, but I was also acutely aware we were being watched. Ben cleared his throat as Theo and I continued staring at each other. Theo looked as shocked as I felt. It didn't seem like he expected to see me here, either.

"Is everything okay?" Ben said, shooting Theo a pointed look.

Theo nodded almost imperceptibly towards the camera in the corner while still holding my gaze. I gave him the tiniest nod in return. Best not to talk about what happened in the store, just in case they would hold it against us.

"Everything's great," Theo said with an easy smile. "Like I was saying, it's really nice to meet you, Josephine."

Fuck, his accent was sexy. His dark hair was neatly combed

back, but some stray pieces fell on his face. My fingers itched with the urge to run my hands through his hair, and I was starting to get lightheaded from all my deep breaths. They all smelled *so fucking good,* and I had no idea why—no alphas ever smelled like this to me. I knew I should be intimidated being alone with them, but I felt strangely safe. Part of me longed to move even closer, which scared me—I didn't know these alphas and couldn't let my guard down around them, no matter what my biology said.

I took some deep breaths through my mouth to calm myself down. I realized I was just standing in front of them like a complete idiot without introducing myself.

"Hi. Um, I go by Josie," I squeaked out. *Wow, your conversation skills are incredible.*

"Josie, that suits you," Ben said with a smile.

"Thanks," I said quietly. We fell into silence—the four of us standing in the room, staring at each other. The air was electric, and instead of feeling self-conscious under their gaze, my inner omega wanted to preen and impress them.

Theo cleared his throat. "Why don't we all sit down? Josie, can I get you a drink?"

"Water, please," I said.

I moved towards the same chair I'd sat in for the last interview. As I walked past Cam, he lifted his hand to touch me but stopped abruptly, forming fists at his side. A pang of disappointment washed through me as he lowered his arm, even though I didn't want him to touch me. *Or maybe I did?*

I lowered myself into the seat, feeling shaky. Theo held out a glass of water, and as I reached out to take it, our fingers brushed against each other. A little jolt of electricity ran through me at his touch, and it seemed that he felt it, too, by the way his eyes widened. He blinked and shook his head before sitting next to Ben and Cam. It was almost comical how tightly they were squeezed together, the couch straining to hold the three massive alphas.

The silence stretched on uncomfortably. Their eyes remained fixed on me as if they couldn't look away, their bodies almost vibrating with intensity. Were they disappointed by how I looked? I shifted in my seat, tugging at my jumpsuit, hyperaware of how it highlighted my stomach area while sitting. They were probably thinking I didn't look like a real omega and trying to figure out how to end the interview early. They were only here as a favor to Amirah. What if they rejected me after this interview? I would be stuck with Pack Madden.

The vise-like grip on my chest returned and made me feel like I was slowly suffocating. I clenched my hands into tight fists, desperate to stop my panic attack so I didn't reveal any vulnerability to these alphas. It would probably be on their long list of reasons they wouldn't bond me. I felt myself growing almost hysterical with the idea that they wouldn't want me, which didn't make sense since *I didn't want them.* But the thought of their rejection made me feel so sick I was worried I would throw up.

Slowly, I realized that the three alphas were saying my name, their voices distorted as if I were underwater. I felt like I was drowning again—terrified of having to bond with these alphas and in complete despair of their rejection.

A warm hand pressed into my thigh, giving a gentle squeeze. The stressed scent of burnt cinnamon hit me, jolting me out of my haze. My omega wanted to know why an alpha was upset and for me to fix it. I blinked. Cam was kneeling on the floor in front of me, his brow furrowed in concern.

"Are you okay, sweetheart?"

I didn't know how to answer. I was not okay, but I also knew I had no choice but to get through this. I gave him a nod and glanced over his shoulder to where Theo and Ben were looking at me anxiously. I could scent their distress and wondered why they stayed back. Maybe they were trying not to crowd me, a stark contrast to most alphas who felt entitled to touch any unbonded omega they came across. I realized I didn't mind Cam's touch on my leg. In fact, it felt comforting and warm in a way I couldn't remember touch ever feeling.

Cam slowly moved in closer, his head level with mine, even though he was kneeling on the floor. He pressed his lips against my ear and whispered, "You can get through this, sweetheart. We've got you. Just get through this next hour." He pulled away. He then said a little louder, "Are you alright, Josie? Has your dizziness passed?"

He was helping me play this off as a physical illness, so I said in a shaky voice, "Yes, I'm better now. I've been feeling dizzy and tired lately, with my heat coming on soon."

All three alphas nodded their heads, and Cam slowly stood to return to the couch. I let out the tiniest whimper as he moved away, not wanting him to leave. He froze, and for a second, I thought he might turn back around to touch me again. Theo cleared his throat and looked meaningfully at Cam, who stiffly took a few steps forward before sinking back onto the couch. I knew this was a precarious situation, but I suddenly felt alone and abandoned in my chair. Cam shot me an apologetic look, his hand clenching the couch's armrest so tightly I was worried it would splinter.

Alphas had the instinctual urge to comfort omegas, and I was sure Pack Ashwood's care had nothing to do with me and everything to do with biology. A wave of sadness washed over me. I wished there was someone who wanted to hold me without expectations. I had never been hugged or comforted as a child, at least that I remembered. Sometimes I had flashes of a man with bright green eyes just like mine, twirling me and laughing. As a child, I believed these were memories of my dad, but now I thought they were probably just wishful fantasies.

Omegas, more than any designation, needed touch. If deprived of physical affection, our health slowly deteriorated. Growing up, Sam and I cuddled together in secret. That ended when I went to the DA.

Silence blanketed the room, and I searched for something to say to appease whoever was watching. I took a deep breath, clenching my hands tightly, and asked, "Will you tell me about yourselves?"

This seemed to startle them out of their stupor, and Ben jumped in. "Ahh, of course! Sorry, it's been a while since we've done an interview and you've surprised us. In the best way," he added, probably when he saw my face fall.

Surprised them? Probably shocked them. They're just too polite to kick you out.

The three of them seemed on edge, and Theo kept looking at my fists where my fingernails pressed crescent-shaped marks into my palm.

"We've been together for fifteen years," Ben continued. "Cam and Theo are like brothers to me. We met as teenagers and quickly became close friends. About ten years ago, we started our own company, Ashwood Consulting Firm. Other companies hire us to review their security systems. Cam has the most experience in security, I work with computer programming, and Theo is the company director and keeps us all in line. We have about twenty employees working for us, so a lot of what we do now is managing and directing, but we still travel quite a bit to meet with companies and set up their security evaluations."

I was envious that they got to run their own company and travel while I couldn't even legally get a job.

"I think that's cool that you... umm... decided you wanted

to work together. What else do you do besides work?" I asked lamely.

"We have a small home about an hour north in the mountains. It's quite beautiful and secluded," Theo said. "Have you ever been to the mountains?"

I shook my head. Growing up, we never took vacations. I hadn't even been allowed to leave our community, which was situated in Forestside, a suburb of New River. Moving into Sam's apartment last year was the first time I'd even been downtown. I tried to imagine what it would be like to be alone in the mountains with these alphas. My heart rate increased, and I felt anxious... but also excited?

"You don't have to be nervous, sweetheart," Cam said gently, or as gently as he could in that deep voice of his.

That was the third time he had called me *sweetheart.* I should hate it, but the traitorous omega part of my brain loved it and wanted to hear what other pet names he would call me. My eyes caught on his thick forearms, and my fingers itched to pull his hair down from his bun.

"So, Josie," Theo said in a soft, soothing voice, "What do you enjoy doing?"

"I like reading and baking," I said, sticking with the omega-acceptable hobbies.

"What do you like to bake?" Ben asked excitedly.

"Oh, uh... I like to bake all sorts of things. Lately, I'm really into bread making."

"Ben loves baking and cooking," Theo said. "He keeps us from starving. Cam and I are rubbish at preparing meals."

We kept the small talk going for a while. Ben told me about his favorite recipes, and they told me about their home in the historic district. I had only been to that area of the city once with Sam, but it was charming. I had even thought about how amazing it would be to live in one of the gorgeous old brick homes.

Finally, the clock in the room showed that we had been talking for an hour. The longer I was surrounded by the swirl of alpha pheromones, the stronger the urge was to curl up with Cam, Theo, and Ben and make sure I was drenched in their scents. I was already out of control with this entire situation, and now it felt like my body was betraying me, urging me to trust these alphas just because they smelled good.

Ben's voice broke through my spiraling thoughts. "Josie, I hope you know how special we think you are, and we hope you choose us."

"We know you don't really know us yet," Theo added, "But we would love to get to know you more and would be honored if you chose us as your pack."

"We promise to protect and care for you," Cam added.

Their words sounded sincere, but I knew they were just putting on a good show. I should have been grateful that they were willing to take me on as a favor to Amirah, but my heart ached with the reality that this was just another situation where I wasn't really wanted. They had been a pack for fifteen years without bonding an omega, and there was no reason for them to change their minds now. I was defective—too fat, too outspoken, too much *everything*. There was no question that I would choose them, and I hoped they wouldn't grow to resent me for becoming their burden. Maybe over time, we could become friends? Or perhaps I could at least be useful and clean their house? I tried not to think about other ways they might find me *useful*, holding onto hope that these alphas were as kind as they appeared.

I didn't know how to respond to their sweet words, so I gave a little nod.

My legs were unsteady as I stood to move towards the door.

I swayed, reaching out to grab hold of a chair to steady myself, but before I could, Cam's arm wrapped around me. I leaned into him automatically, my face brushing his chest. His touch sent shivers through me, and I had to stop myself from pressing my body flush with his.

My slick had never come in after years of being on suppressants, but I felt it now for the first time, dampness in my underwear and a warm burning sensation rippling from my core into my stomach. The alphas jerked to a stop, and I knew they could scent my arousal. My inner omega was thrilled—she wanted the alphas to know how they were affecting us, but the fact that they could scent my arousal felt invasive.

"Sorry," I muttered, looking down. Cam reached out and gently grasped my chin, lifting my head until I was gazing into his dark brown eyes.

"You have nothing to apologize for."

Theo peered down at me with concern. He tentatively ran his hand through my hair as if he was scared to touch me but knew I needed comfort. The gesture made me want to purr. Ben, by far the most relaxed and exuberant of all of us, pulled me into a quick hug, causing Cam to growl. I blushed at their affection that left me craving more, secretly pleased that their scents were now on my clothes. When I got into bed tonight, it would be like I was surrounded by them.

Theo sighed, his eyes lingering on my face before he moved to open the door, his lips down-turned as if he didn't want to end our time together.

As the four of us exited the room, I saw Dave standing outside the door, his expression hard and protective.

"You're needed in the meeting room to debrief from the interviews," he said.

Dread shot through me. I did not want to face my parents, the director, or anyone associated with the DC. I felt myself wilting—I desperately needed to be somewhere enclosed and safe. A soft whine escaped my lips, and I curled into myself.

Ben, Cam, and Theo moved towards me simultaneously, drawn in by my distress. I had trained myself not to whine to avoid attracting unwanted attention, but my omega wanted these alphas' concern and protection. As they closed in, my chest tightened. I cowered away from them without realizing what I was doing, and they all stopped.

"Josie." Ben's voice was an agonized whisper that almost brought tears to my eyes.

How could I be scared for them to be near me and also hurt that they stepped away?

I gathered myself enough to lift my head. They looked deeply concerned, and I could scent their distress and anger. Were they upset at my reaction? I opened my mouth to offer them an explanation for my behavior, to thank them for being here for me, *something*. But no words would come out. Instead, I turned towards Dave.

"Let's get this over with, I guess," I said quietly.

I followed Dave across the atrium, my boots clicking against the marble floor. I looked over my shoulder to where Theo, Ben, and Cam stood, their eyes locked on me. They looked devastatingly sad. My lip trembled, and I turned away, overwhelmed with the distinct *wrongness* of leaving them behind.

Dave stopped in the middle of the hallway in front of two large wooden doors. My muscles tensed as I prepared myself to face whoever was waiting for me inside. He gave me a little nod and opened the door, gesturing for me to enter.

My stomach lurched when I saw Designation Center director, Marshall Whiteburn, seated at the table with my parents and Amirah. I didn't know him well, having only met him in passing at various functions my parents put on, but he and Glen Jacoby worked closely together. I had often seen them walking down the halls together at the DA. He met my gaze with a sneer, and my stomach churned. He looked at me in the same predatory way Glen always had.

Amirah smiled softly at me, the only person in the room expressing any warmth. My parents were all wearing disgruntled expressions, radiating a distinctly pissed-off energy.

"Sit down, Josephine," Jericho snarled, infusing his command with an alpha bark.

Visceral hatred born out of years of abuse filled me. How dare he use his bark on me here, forcing my omega to respond to his command?

My vision darkened as the past tried to encroach on the present—the smell of antiseptic and rotting fruit, the cold feel of metal. The scar on my arm burned, and I bit my lip to stop from whining.

For a moment, I fought Jericho's bark, locking my knees against the urge to sit down. He stared me down until I couldn't hold out any longer. My legs propelled me forward, and I crumpled into the chair next to Amirah. Silence blanketed the room as I tried to control my breathing, my heart still racing with the effort of fighting his bark.

My mother was the first to speak up. "What was that?" she asked in a shrill voice.

"What do you mean?" I responded, keeping my voice as monotone as possible. I was sure she was not referencing Jericho using his bark on me. She had never stepped in to protect me before.

"You had no right cutting that first interview short," Richard snarled. "Pack Madden is highly respected. You should be flattered they even wanted to interview with you. You're a disgrace."

"My behavior? They insulted me and grabbed me." I pinned my hands under my thighs to keep myself from launching across the table.

Jericho cut me off. "They were absolutely right that you need a firm hand. You've always been headstrong and unruly. You should never have been allowed to live on your own."

"The law doesn't prohibit me from moving out of your house," I said.

"Not yet," Richard responded menacingly.

The director cut in. "Josephine, you've met two packs. You disappointed us with your insult of Pack Madden, an upstanding group of alphas. While you're technically free to choose between either pack, Pack Ashwood did not follow interview procedure when they touched you. We are unsure if they are an acceptable pack option."

Time stood still. I glanced over at Amirah, whose face was a blank mask, but I could scent her burnt caramel anger. It came as no surprise they were trying to pull something like this. I knew from years of experience with my parents that if I showed any emotion right now, they would use it against me. I used all my inner strength to stay calm as I turned towards the director.

"Both packs breached that policy. Pack Madden actually injured me." I held up my wrist. "Pack Ashwood was trying to help me. You shouldn't disqualify them for that."

Director Whiteburn's lip curled and he looked like he'd eaten something sour. He knew I was right. I fought the urge to smirk and instead met his gaze, refusing to lower my eyes in submission.

Richard burst out, "You can't possibly be thinking of choosing them. This is unacceptable."

Amirah spoke up for the first time. "You would do well to remember that Josie has the ultimate say here. The DC has vetted both packs, and she is free to choose either. Or she could choose to do additional interviews. This is all well within her rights."

The director opened the folder in front of him. "Actually, Mrs. Raven, we don't have time for more interviews. Josephine's updated bloodwork came in and she's due to go into heat in the next two days. She can choose one of today's packs or we can assign her a heat pack and resume interviews after her heat."

"No, that won't be necessary. I'm choosing Pack Ashwood," I blurted out. A slight, glowy warmth grew in my stomach at how right it felt to say it out loud.

The room exploded in an uproar, my pack fathers arguing with Amirah about my right to choose a pack. Director Whiteburn's eyes nervously flicked to Jericho while Amirah reiterated the omega protections listed in the Designation Laws.

I had spent more time with my parents the past couple of days than I had the past few years. Besides *the incident* at the DA, they had never visited me and I had never been allowed to leave. Outside trips were a privilege reserved for *good* omegas. Instead, I was mostly kept in solitary as punishment for various manufactured infractions. A tiny part of me had hoped the past few years had softened my parents—or at least my mother—that maybe she would decide to love me. Absence makes the heart grow fonder, right? But my parents' hatred for me seemed to only grow.

I stared at my mother, her voice cold as she argued with Amirah, trying to find any hint of love or affection in her features. Her head snapped to meet my gaze and I shuddered at the blankness, the complete lack of... *anything* I found there. At that moment, it was as if a hand reached down and snipped the final fragile strings that tied me to her, hitting my heart sharply with the recoil. The finality of it all, the realization that she would never be able to love or accept me, settled like a heavy stone in my stomach.

I turned away from her and sought refuge inside of myself, tuning out the chaos and thinking instead about moving in with Pack Ashwood. It still hadn't sunk in that tomorrow I would be forced to leave my apartment, my first safe refuge, and move in with strangers. My inner omega danced at the thought of getting to spend more time with the sexy, yummy-smelling pack. *Just think, now you'll be able to have their scents on you all the time. Maybe you can even steal some of their clothes.*

I felt... comfortable around them. And aroused. Two things I didn't think possible. I also needed to know what happened with Theo at Trader Joe's.

"Excellent. I'm glad we're all in agreement that the Designation Laws give Josie the right to choose her own pack. I'll contact Pack Ashwood and tell them to expect you all tomorrow morning."

I snapped back to reality at Amirah's terse tone. Dizzying relief washed over me as I processed what she said. For once, the Designation Laws were on my side. Gratitude for Amirah filled me, and I shot her a tremulous smile.

I mumbled an excuse about needing the restroom and slipped away before my parents could vent more of their wrath on me. Alone, the numbness that had settled over my body faded, leaving me with the excruciating pain of my emotions. I stared at myself in the mirror and didn't recognize the person looking back at me. She was wearing my clothes, but I couldn't quite place myself in her body. I was floating, unable to come back to earth.

My breaths came faster and I knew another panic attack was imminent. I hunched over the bathroom sink, trying to force deep breaths when it hit me—the faint scents of the alphas still clinging to my clothes. In my life, there were few alphas whose scents I found tolerable or, even more rare, likable. Sam's floral scent was playful and comforting, the smell of the best days of my childhood spent with him. Luc's earthy leather scent had come to mean safety. But no scent had ever called to me like these alphas. No scent calmed me this easily.

The shaking in my limbs settled, and my breaths came more easily with each slow inhale of their scents. Another wave of slick burst from my core. I crinkled my nose and shifted with discomfort. This was so messy. How did other omegas deal with it? My body was urging me to have sex when I was nowhere near ready for that, nowhere near the point of trusting these alphas. But my omega didn't know that. All she knew was these three alphas were delicious and sexy and... safe? I wanted it to be true, but my hand gripped the scar on my upper arm, forever the reminder of the consequences of betrayal.

I pushed the memories aside, gripping the bathroom counter with my hands. *Don't go there.* I indulged myself in another inhale, pressing my nose against the soft fabric of the jumpsuit. Cam's cinnamon roll scent, Theo's warm coffee, and Ben's spiced apple wafted around me, surrounding me like a hug. *Fuck, that was like omega Xanax.* I allowed myself a few more moments in the bathroom's quiet before moving to the door.

I was about to open it when I heard raised voices. They were muffled, but I could pick out Jericho's deep alpha tones. I pressed my ear against the door to hear more clearly.

"Remember what you owe us, director. You want to keep us happy, or you know what the consequences will be."

To an outsider, Jericho's tone may have sounded calm, but I had spent a lifetime trying to decipher his moods. Right now, he was as dangerous as I'd ever heard him. A shiver ran down my spine.

"Of course, Senator Porter. You have my word. I'll do everything in my power to fix this situation," said Director Whiteburn, his voice simpering. I was correct in my read of him in the meeting—he was desperate to appease my pack fathers.

"In your power or not, it better be done. We had a deal with Pack Madden..."

Jericho's voice faded as their footsteps receded down the hall. My hand gripped the door handle until my knuckles turned white. I let go, running my shaky hand through my hair, tears pricking my eyes. I knew something more was going on with Pack Madden and this was confirmation, although I didn't know what that meant for me. Were Jericho and the director going to try and separate me from my alphas?

I jolted internally—*my* alphas? *They're not your anything*, I firmly told my inner omega, who was all but purring, imagining the alphas wrapped around us. *They're not safe. They're not ours. You better get used to it.*

I could almost feel her smugness when I took another surreptitious hit of their scents before exiting the bathroom.

Chapter Ten

Cam

My chest ached as I watched her walk away with that damn alpha guard. I hated him on principle. My hands clenched into fists as if urging me to punch him for being in her vicinity, for leading her away from us.

Josie. The perfect omega. My mate.

The second she walked into the room surrounded by a cloud of sweet cupcake scent, I knew she was our fated mate. It was as if the universe aligned, reorienting with her at the center. I had almost lost control, so swept up in my need for her, I forgot where we were. Ben took over, his enthusiasm like a ping-pong ball of energy through the bond. Theo had placed a restraining hand on my arm, and I had forced myself to take a deep breath. Not that it had done much good. All I succeeded in was inhaling more of her potent scent, causing me to get rock-hard.

Alphas and omegas could bond with anyone, but a mate was a perfect match, one who called to our designation and biology. In the past years, the designation-obsessed traditionalists produced propaganda to convince us that fated mates were practically myths. The published studies showed that alpha packs had a one in two hundred thousand chance of finding their mate. Most of us knew those studies were utter shit. I knew a dozen packs who had found their mate. This was a government ploy to convince us to give up the idea of a fated omega and bond with whoever they deemed appropriate.

Even though I knew finding my mate was possible, I gave up on the idea years ago—had given up the idea of bonding with an omega altogether. I refused to coerce an omega, and my pack and I had never found someone compatible with our specific desires. None of that mattered anymore. Everything changed when that sweet little omega with bright green eyes and the most luscious curves I had ever seen walked into the room. I ached to claim her, protect her, do anything I could to make her happy. Even though I didn't know her yet, I would sacrifice everything for her.

As she walked away from us, she looked back with a sweet, concerned expression. I hated how stressed she was. Nothing should ever make my mate feel that way. She should be fucking happy all the time. It was taking everything in me to let Josie walk away from us when all I wanted to do was wrap her around me and carry her home.

When she disappeared down the hallway, I finally tore my eyes away and looked at my brothers. Ben and Theo had equally desperate looks in their eyes. My emotions were too chaotic to even sense their feelings through the bond.

"Let's get to the car," I said quietly, knowing that we couldn't talk openly here. The DC gave me the creeps, and I knew we were under surveillance.

Ben looked like he was going to say something, so I growled, "To the car."

As we walked out of the building, my alpha urged me to turn back, to not leave my mate here with these bastards. When she first walked into the interview, I was so overwhelmed, so focused on maintaining my control, that I didn't notice that she was clearly not okay. She was pale and shaky, her eyes red-rimmed. Had something happened to her before the interview? Or was she upset to be meeting us?

Theo bumped my shoulder as we crossed the lot, and I realized I was growling. I couldn't get the image of Josie having a panic attack out of my head. What happened to make her anxiety that bad? I needed to know so I could stop it from ever happening again. All I wanted to do was pick her up and cradle her. A small warmth bloomed in my chest at the reminder that I had been able to calm her. I rubbed my fingers together, wishing I could feel her soft skin against mine again.

The car doors slammed as we piled into the car.

Ben exploded, "She's our mate!"

"I fucking know," I said, turning to look at Ben from where he was sitting in the back, his eyes wide.

"Wait, what was that weird moment when you first introduced yourself, Theo?" Ben asked. "I could feel your shock through the bond."

"I... I already met her two days ago," Theo mumbled, not making eye contact.

Ben and I stared at him in silence.

"You met our mate two days ago and didn't tell us?" I growled. Anger and betrayal washed over me.

"I didn't know she was our mate. She was the omega who collapsed at Trader Joe's. She was covered in scent blocker. I didn't know she would be here today."

Being away from Josie was putting me on edge. The pull towards a fated mate was painful to ignore. My inner alpha roared at the fact that she wasn't safely tucked away in my arms.

"So you didn't feel anything towards her the other day?" Ben asked.

"I did feel pulled towards her. It was agony letting her leave in the ambulance. I just didn't know why I felt that way, so I didn't mention it. I didn't mean to keep anything from you." Theo's hands tapped a rhythm on the steering wheel, the only sign he was on the verge of losing control.

"Important thing is we've all met her now," I said after a long pause. Talking things out was not my strong suit, but if we were going to bring an omega into our pack, we needed to step it up. I could tell Theo still felt bad, so I clasped him on the shoulder.

"She has to choose us," Theo said, running his hand through his hair, desperation creeping into his voice.

"She's our mate. Of course, she's going to choose us," Ben said, looking between Theo and me for confirmation.

I took a deep breath, trying to slow my pounding heart, catching a hit of Josie's vanilla scent off my shirt. I worried the DC would coerce her into choosing another pack. I knew too well how the system manipulated omegas and forced them into packs they didn't choose. Then another horrifying thought gripped me.

"Do you think she knows she's our mate? Can omegas sense it the same way we can?" I asked.

"She should be able to," Theo responded. Then he hesitated. "Unless... I remember reading some pre-Designation Government research that suggested omegas on suppressants can't fully sense the mate connection."

I growled at the thought that our mate didn't know we were meant for each other.

"How soon until we find out if she's chosen us?" Ben asked, his legs bouncing up and down.

"Amirah said she'd be quick to inform us either way. Josie will move in tomorrow if she chooses us. She also said Josie could opt to do additional interviews, although she doubts she'll go that route since the other packs are all ones her parents want to set her up with."

"Who are her parents?" I asked.

Now I was kicking myself for not paying attention to her file. I hadn't wanted to get my hopes up, telling myself I was doing it as a favor for Amirah and the Alliance. But now I wished I had spent the time to learn every single thing I could about my mate. I needed to know everything so I could keep her happy and give her whatever she wanted.

"One of her pack fathers is Jericho Porter," Theo said.

Ben and I both growled.

"That monster is her pack father?" Ben exclaimed. "No wonder she's twenty-three and without a pack. I wouldn't want a pack either if I had grown up with that fucking asshole." Ben rarely swore. I could feel his emotions unraveling in the bond.

"Shit," I said. Jericho Porter was a fucking snake. We suspected he had even more influence over the Designation Government agenda than Glen Jacoby. I couldn't believe our omega had grown up with him.

"I assume she lives with them?" I asked, my jaw tight.

"No, she actually moved out on her own. She lives in an apartment owned by Sam Larsson, an alpha currently working in Sol province," Theo said, reading off a document on his phone.

"Who is this alpha?" I shouted. "Why is she living in his apartment?" An unhealthy amount of possessiveness surged through me. Was Josie involved with this alpha? Images of hunting him down and tearing his head from his body danced through my brain.

"I'm not sure," Theo muttered. I could sense his frustration through the bond. Theo prided himself on always being prepared and doing extensive research, but this situation caught us all off guard.

"We'll wait here to hear from Amirah and then drive to her apartment to watch over her. We can't leave her alone. We have to make sure she's protected," I grunted. An omega living alone was almost unheard of since the Designation Laws, and my inner alpha was growling at how unsafe it was.

Theo and Ben nodded their agreement. I might be the most stereotypically alpha of the three of us, but I knew they would do anything to ensure our mate was safe.

"Did you see how she moved away from us at the end?" Ben asked quietly.

Of course, I had. The image of her flinching, as if she needed to protect herself from us, kept playing back in my mind.

"We'll need to be careful and take things slow if she's scared of alphas," Theo said, a deep sadness permeating his voice.

I would find out who had hurt her and end them. My alpha was feeling bloodthirsty and wanted revenge for our mate.

We lapsed into silence as the next hour stretched on. I stared out of the window into the Designation Center as if staring hard enough would allow me to develop x-ray vision and see Josie wherever she was. I just wanted her to be safe. I had a sense that Josie was stronger than she appeared. She had to be strong to survive as an omega, especially in the pack she grew up in. At the same time, I was concerned about how fragile she was.

Theo's shrill ringtone cut through the silence, startling me from my thoughts. He shot us a quick look before answering the call.

"Hi Theo, this is Amirah. Are Cam and Ben there?"

"Yes, you're on speaker," he responded.

"We're on an encrypted line so we can speak freely, but it has to be quick. I just came out of the meeting with Josie, Director Marshall, her mother, and two pack fathers. Josie has decided that she wants to join your pack."

The three of us sighed with relief. Now we had the opportunity to get to know her, court her, and prove to her we were worthy mates. Although I wasn't sure I could ever be *fully* worthy of her. She was pure fucking sweetness.

"Josie chose to join your pack, but her parents and the director strongly opposed the decision. They spent the full meeting shouting, trying to convince her that this was a terrible mistake." Amirah's voice sounded strained.

I growled. The idea of anyone raising their voice at my mate made me murderous. How dare they try to influence her omega instincts?

Amirah continued, "The updated lab work showed Josie's heat will start the next day or two. She needs to move in immediately. Her parents insisted on doing the traditional parent meeting and will be at your house tomorrow morning at ten. You need to be prepared and stay very calm. If you give them any sign that you are volatile or in any way unfit to bond with an omega, they will try to remove her. You must do nothing to jeopardize her position in your pack until you're fully DC approved and bonded."

"How was she after the meeting?" I asked, angry I hadn't been there to protect her.

"She's had a hard couple of days. Being around so many alphas can be overwhelming for any omega, but it's particularly hard on an unbonded one right before heat. I didn't have time to talk with her after the meeting, but she will be leaving shortly with Dave to head back to her apartment so she can pack her things."

"Do you know what she likes? How can we best prepare her room and make her feel at home?" Ben asked.

"Honestly, I don't know. I've barely gotten to talk with her. She seems smart, brave, and pretty skittish. She has a lot of anxiety, and no wonder with the way her parents treat her." Amirah's voice sounded as bitter as I'd ever heard it. I didn't know how she worked alongside alphas who belittled her on a daily basis, but I had never been more grateful for her leadership in the Alliance.

Amirah continued, "She's probably going to need to take things slow and to feel like she is in control as much as possible. She needs to have a nest available immediately, and you must remember that you cannot enter the nest without her explicit invitation."

Theo eyed the phone with hesitation before asking, "Can you tell us if Josie has been on suppressants?"

Amirah was silent for several long moments. "I don't typically share confidential information, but it might help you prepare better. Yes, she's been on suppressants. I don't know the details of her usage, but prolonged suppressant use can cause irregular heats once the omega goes off them. Her heats in the future might be closer together or vary in length."

I was worried about how the suppressant use would affect Josie's health long-term, but I glowed with pride that she had managed to be on them for this long without getting caught. Our little omega was smart and resourceful.

"I have to go now, but I'll pass along to Josie and her parents that you'll be expecting them at ten tomorrow. I'll also tell the rest of your Alliance contacts that you'll be out of communication for the next ten days or so."

"Let Josie's parents know we'll have breakfast for them," Ben called out.

I shot him a look.

"What? We need to be good hosts. And we need to feed our mate."

At that, I softened. I didn't want to host her parents, but Ben was right. We needed to make the meeting as relaxed and seamless as possible for Josie's sake.

After hanging up the phone, we all sat and stared at each other. Theo, ever the planner and organizer, said, "We need to get the house ready, need to make sure we have plenty of food and stuff for her nest. If she's going into heat, we won't be able to leave, so we have to stock up."

When we bought our house, we hadn't paid much attention to the nest, assuming we would never have an omega to fill it. Now I thought of the empty room and it made me furious. Why hadn't we prepared better for her? We should have known that she was out there, waiting for us. Now we didn't even have a proper nest to offer her.

Theo continued, "One of us needs to make sure that we're at her apartment tonight. We can take it in shifts."

I jolted as the front door to the DC opened and Josie walked out with Dave. Our car was partially hidden in a secluded corner of the parking lot, so she likely couldn't see us. Her shoulders shook, and my heart clenched as I realized she was crying. I opened the car door, ready to run out to her and comfort her. Theo grabbed my arm.

"Cam, we can't do anything to jeopardize things now. She's already chosen us, but they could take her away if we do anything outside the rules. She'll be with us in less than twenty-four hours."

I snarled, needing to be with her. Josie and Dave neared a large black SUV and he opened the back door for her. *That should have been me.* A woman was waiting in the back seat and pulled Josie in for a hug. My distress eased slightly that Josie wasn't totally alone right now. As they pulled away, Theo started the car. I was already counting the minutes until we could bring our mate home.

Chapter Eleven

Theo

I downed my fourth cup of espresso, the caffeine hitting my system with a jolt. My hands trembled slightly as I set the cup down. I needed to get my anxiety under control before Josie arrived, but I felt like my heart was going to explode out of my chest.

I groaned, involuntarily running my hand through my hair. *Fuck, now I have to fix it again.* I stopped at the hallway mirror, trying to force my hair to look effortlessly styled as if that would somehow mask the chaos inside me.

I tried to block my anxiety from the bond I shared with my brothers, not wanting them to know how unmoored I felt. I couldn't stop my racing thoughts, couldn't stop obsessing about Josie. *How had her night been? Did she resent having to move in with us? Would she be happy here?* I wouldn't feel settled until she was with us, preferably in my arms.

I sat down on one of the sofas in the sitting room and stared at the clock, willing time to go faster. The minute hand mocked me with its slowness. Sunlight streamed in through the large windows, illuminating the sparse room. We bought this house several years ago, falling in love with the historic charm and quiet of the neighborhood. None of us had cared much about the interior, filling it with furniture that was practical and not much else. It lacked the coziness and charm an omega deserved. At least everything was spotless. The welcoming smell of Ben's baked goods wafted out of the kitchen, and the nesting supplies I'd purchased were waiting for our mate upstairs.

Yesterday I had gone to our friend Jewel's high-end boutique while Cam took the first shift watching over Josie's apartment. Jewel was a rare female alpha—one of only twenty in the entire province. We had known her for years and trusted her with our lives. She had greater cause to hate the Designation Government than most after what she had endured under their female alpha experimentation program.

Jewel had gifted me a rare smile when I told her we had found our mate.

"You finally going to have sex, then?" she had asked with a smirk.

A few years ago, I had confessed to her, late one night after copious drinking, that I was a virgin. She had cackled and teased me, but I knew she didn't judge me. Jewel was all about breaking out of the strict designation expectations and living as freely as possible.

Under Jewel's guidance, I purchased half the store, buying a huge variety of bedding and pillows for the nest, along with toiletries and clothes. She had also convinced me to buy a selection of sex toys, which had made me blush, much to her amusement.

I wished I'd had more time to research omega heats. What if the things I'd chosen weren't right for her? I felt terribly unprepared to invite our mate into our home. I was still reeling from seeing her walk into the interview room. I hadn't let myself hope I would ever get to see the angel omega from the grocery store again, but there she'd been. A clawing discomfort had settled in my chest the moment the medics took her away at the store. Now I could finally take a breath.

She had been gorgeous in her black jumpsuit, her delicious curves on full display... and I knew I was a goner. To my astonishment, I had grown hard when I scented her. I'd never felt instantly attracted to someone like that. After the interview, I refused to change out of my clothes, wanting her vanilla scent to surround me as long as possible.

I couldn't wait to get to know her more. The questionnaire she submitted had been... interesting. So what if our girl had varied interests? I didn't give a fuck. She was perfect.

I checked the clock again, and it was official: it must be broken—the hands weren't moving at all. Irritated, I leapt up and started adjusting and re-adjusting one of the cushions.

Ben walked in, a tray of pastries in his hands.

"You're worse than an omega in their nest with all your primping," he teased.

"Like you're any better," I grumbled, knowing that he had a breakfast spread in the kitchen so elaborate it would put most restaurants to shame. "I just want her to feel at home."

Ben set the tray down on the coffee table and turned to me, taking me in.

"It's going to be okay," he said gently.

"I know," I said, shoving the offensive cushion back on the couch and moving to leave the room. Before I could take a step, Ben launched himself at me, wrapping his arms around me in a tight hug.

"Cam!" he yelled.

"Fuck, what are you doing?" I asked, trying to push out of his hold.

"We need Cam," he said. "Cam!"

"You're going to burst my eardrum," I grumbled.

"What are you shouting about?" Cam asked as he entered the room.

"We need a group hug," Ben announced.

To my surprise, Cam didn't protest. He came over to my other side and wrapped his arms around us.

"I know we're all stressing," Ben said. "But it's going to be okay. We have each other. We'll figure this out together. We've just got to focus on Josie."

I allowed myself to relax into the embrace. I couldn't remember the last time we hugged like this. Ben thought he lacked emotional depth—he sometimes made these self-deprecating comments about himself that killed me. I knew the truth. My brother was kind and thoughtful and often intuitively knew what Cam and I needed.

After a few minutes, we pulled apart. I opened myself up to the bond and could tell we all felt more settled.

Cam snorted. "You really thought you could hide that you're anxious from us?"

"I guess not," I said, chagrinned.

"You know you don't have to do that," Cam said gruffly, crossing his arms.

I nodded. I hadn't been allowed to show any weakness growing up. I hid my anxiety from my family, but Cam and Ben had always known my struggles and supported me. Sometimes, though, I fell into old habits and tried hiding what I felt from them.

"Is the nest set up?" I asked, needing to change the subject.

"I put all the bedding and supplies near the bed and hung up those lights," Cam responded. He surveyed the living room and gave an approving nod.

An article I found about nests suggested omegas enjoyed

softer lighting, so we'd gotten string lights to hang around the room.

"I can't believe we're having to host those two assholes," I said, referring to Josie's pack fathers.

Jericho and Richard Porter were well known in Alliance circles for being power-hungry, designation traditionalists. We'd had the misfortune of running into them at a dinner party last year. We hadn't spoken beyond our frosty introductions, but I remembered thinking how smarmy they were. They kept their personal lives private, which wasn't unusual for politicians who worried public scrutiny could put their families in danger, particularly if omegas were involved. I hadn't even known they had an omega daughter until I read Josie's file right before the interview.

Sympathy rolled through me, thinking about what she must have experienced growing up. Just the other day, Jericho had been on the news talking about how the current Designation Laws were too lax and omegas were destroying the very fabric of society with their sex-obsessed manipulations. Now, rage pumped through my veins, knowing that my mate's family had betrayed her with their political actions. The only thing keeping me grounded was knowing we would protect her from them moving forward.

While my packmates and I kept our political involvement quiet to deflect attention from our role in the Alliance, it was clear we weren't traditionalists. I hoped Richard and Jericho wouldn't make today's meeting difficult for Josie. I hated that she would arrive with her parents, and we would have to wait even longer before we could talk with her freely.

"They're the fucking worst," Cam agreed, clenching his hands tightly. I stared pointedly at his fists.

"I'm not going to do anything," he said with an eye roll. I nudged him in the side with my elbow and he shoved me as we moved towards the foyer. We stood at the large dining room window, keeping an eye on the driveway.

Time was finally on my side as a luxury BMW pulled into our circular driveway. Jericho exited first from the driver's side, with Richard shortly following from the passenger's side and Josie's mother exiting from the back seat. I held my breath as I waited to see Josie. Finally, she emerged from the car.

Josie wore a frilly blue dress with long, lacy sleeves and a full skirt. The top of the dress was tight and pressed up her breasts, which was hot. But the dress didn't seem to suit her, and as I took in her face, I noticed she looked uncomfortable and unhappy. My heart clenched with the fear that maybe it wasn't just the dress... maybe she was unhappy because she didn't want us.

Josie's mother rounded the car with a furious expression on her face. She gripped Josie's arm, jerking her closer. Once her mother had turned away from her, Josie's scowl transformed into a heartbreakingly vulnerable expression, and I thought I saw her blinking back tears. I clenched my jaw as Cam growled next to me.

Josie's pack fathers ignored the altercation between their bonded and daughter, looking distinctly bored. Jericho checked his watch before saying something to his daughter, his lips curling with disdain. Josie's shoulders curved in, and her parents left her to drag her small suitcase out of the boot of the car while they all moved towards the front door.

My blood pressure rose, witnessing how our mate's family treated her.

"Don't give them any reason to take her away from us," I quickly reminded my pack brothers as our combined rage vibrated through the bond.

Everything in me screamed to pull my mate into the house and lock the door behind her, leaving her parents on the front porch. And then it could start pouring down rain. With lightning. *A little electrocution of your enemies never hurt anyone.*

The knock at the door jolted me out of my thoughts. Ben rushed to welcome our guests, pulling Josie into a hug the second she crossed the threshold. My insides melted when I saw her cheeks flush pink at Ben's exuberant greeting. We could get through this meeting. How hard could it be?

Chapter Twelve

Josie

This meeting was a disaster. I entered Pack Ashwood's house in a daze, allowing Cam and Theo to shepherd me along until I was sandwiched between them on their living room couch. Across from us sat my mother, who had already made several snide comments about my weight, and Ben, who looked heartbroken when I refused to eat the incredible pastries arranged on the coffee table in front of me. My pack fathers sat in front of the gorgeous marble fireplace, looking entirely at ease as they presided over us.

I had tossed and turned in bed last night, wondering what sorts of stunts my fathers would pull to separate me from my chosen pack. I had to hand it to them—Richard and Jericho were in rare form this morning. They'd already managed to insult, belittle, and threaten me on the short drive over. My well-honed dissociation skills blocked out the worst of it, but I was trembling by the time we arrived at Pack Ashwood's house.

I sat rigidly, my eyes straight ahead as I did my best to maintain a stoic, disinterested expression. The little glimpses of the room I had allowed myself had sparked a bit of... excitement? The house was sparse but filled with historic touches. And the best part was that it smelled like *them*. I had expected to spend this meeting on the verge of a panic attack, but being surrounded by Cam, Theo, and Ben's cinnamon roll-coffee-apple-pie scents kept me calm. I fought the urge to crawl into their laps and press my face to their necks to breathe them in more deeply. My omega really didn't understand appropriate social behavior.

My fathers attempted to get a rise out of Pack Ashwood with snide critiques aimed at their home and business. The guys hid their reactions well. If I hadn't been watching them so closely, I would have missed Cam's narrowing eyes, Theo's restless fingers tapping on his legs, and the way Ben's smile faltered for a split second. Most alphas I knew wouldn't let any insults stand, but these three kept it under control. When Jericho and Richard realized these tactics weren't proving successful, they guided the conversation towards designation politics and, their favorite topic, insulting me.

"It's astounding how much power we give omegas when the research is clear they don't have the capacity to make logical decisions. It's not their fault, of course," Richard said, his tone patronizing, "but it means that alphas need to protect them from making their own choices."

Jericho jumped in, "I hope you three are fully prepared to bring Josephine into your pack."

"We've prepared a bedroom with all the nest supplies..." Cam started to say before Jericho cut him off.

"I'm not talking about the house. Josie needs a firm hand. She thrived at the Designation Academy. They gave her plenty of structure, monitored her food intake, and ensured she had everything she needed to succeed. Josephine is, unfortunately, a strong-willed omega. We have worked hard to raise her well and keep her in line, and it's imperative that you continue."

My cheeks heated as waves of humiliation washed over me, turning my scent bitter. I was used to my parents talking about me like this, but now my new pack was bearing witness. Would they believe what they were saying about me?

Theo shifted to place his coffee on the table in front of us. When he sat back, his body pressed close to mine. I didn't know if he had done it on purpose, but his closeness was so soothing it made me want to cry.

Richard added with a smirk, "We've found that she needs frequent correction and punishment. You shouldn't give her too much freedom. She likes to test and push boundaries. I hope you three can handle an omega like her, or the center will have to find a more suitable pack."

Cam and Theo stiffened, and I could scent the burnt edge of their anger. Theo shifted even closer to me. This time, I knew his movement was intentional. Cam moved his hand to my thigh and gave it a squeeze. A lump formed in my throat at their silent comfort and support.

"Our plan is to support Josie and provide everything she needs," Theo said coolly.

"The DC will come by to check and make sure that's the case," Richard said. "Terrible things happen when omegas are left to their own devices," he added ominously, looking pointedly at my mother.

She sat demurely, showing no reaction to her bonded's critique. Growing up, I had dreamed she would fight back against them, dreamed of seeing even the tiniest glimpse of the omega who had defied expectations to follow her heart. But she never did, content to be weak and subservient, content to do nothing while her bonded alphas abused her daughter.

"It's a shame the newly proposed bill to give omegas'

fathers the power to select a pack hasn't yet passed," Jericho mused. To my surprise, he looked pointedly at Cam. "Don't you agree, Cam? It's always better when the fathers choose the pack."

Cam tensed and the color drained from his face. Jericho looked delighted, as if he had expected this reaction and wanted to see how it played out.

Without thinking, I reached out and placed my hand on top of Cam's. A spark of energy, like a warm current, ran through me. He turned to me, eyes wide in shock before his face transformed into the most heartbreakingly gorgeous smile I had ever seen. He threaded his fingers with mine and gave my hand a gentle squeeze.

Jericho's face soured briefly before returning to its usual controlled mask. I met his gaze, feeling powerful. For the first time in years, I wasn't alone.

Ben took the opportunity to change the subject. "Josie, you sure you don't want anything to eat?"

My stomach cramped with hunger and my mouth watered. Ben's hopeful expression made me want to do anything I could to please him.

Before I could answer, my mother cut in. "Josephine should not be eating any pastries with her figure."

I curled in on myself, trying to make myself a smaller target, and withdrew my hand from Cam's.

All three of the alphas bristled with anger, a growl slipping from Cam as he firmly threaded his fingers back into mine. Theo gently ran his hand up and down my back. Ben looked like he was going to say something, but I caught his eye and shook my head. I wanted this to be over with, and anything he said would get my parents riled up.

An uncomfortable silence descended over the room. My mother adjusted the collar of her blouse. Richard's foot tapped impatiently against the floor. I stared at the coffee table books in front of me: *Modern Cottages of the English Countryside. A Baker's Encyclopedia of Yeast. A Passionate Knitter's Pattern Guide.*

Huh, I wonder who the knitter is.

Jericho looked at his watch. "We have a lot to do today. Josephine, behave yourself. Let's go, Angeline."

I kept my face blank as a surge of happiness rushed through me as Jericho and Richard stood. The guys glanced between my fathers and me, confused by their abruptness, but I was fighting the urge to smile. Jericho and Richard would never admit it, but they had lost today. Their goal had been to provoke my alphas into reacting and they had failed. I was sure it was a temporary victory—they wouldn't give up that easily—but I would take it.

Ben stood, looking befuddled as he offered to escort my parents out. Jericho and Richard stalked out of the room, saying nothing to me, not that I expected them to. There was a moment when my mother hesitated, and I thought she would say something, but she clenched her jaw and walked out of the room. With her departure, the adrenaline pumping through my system crashed, leaving me cold and shaky.

Cam stood and I jumped, my breath hitching. His body vibrated with tension as he clenched and unclenched his hands, almost as if he were readying for a fight. He abruptly sat back down, his body angled towards me.

"Can I touch you, sweetheart?" he asked in a surprisingly tender voice.

A refusal was on my lips when I paused. I was so damn tired of being on my own. My omega took over and I found myself nodding.

I let out a startled squeak as Cam picked me up and cradled me in his lap. I sat stiffly for a moment and then his scent washed over me, releasing all the tension I was carrying. I pressed my face into his neck where his cinnamon roll scent was strongest and inhaled deeply.

"Is this okay?" Cam asked gruffly.

I nodded again, feeling settled beyond words.

"Good. Because I need to hold you," Cam murmured, tightening his arms around me. It scared me how right it felt.

Theo leaned in beside me, brushing the hair away from my face. I wanted more, wanted them to all press their bodies against me, have their hands on me... but I shouldn't want it, right? I should be strong enough to not need their comfort.

Ben returned to the living room. His irritated expression transformed when he saw us.

"Is it cuddle time?" he asked, throwing himself down on the couch and gathering my legs into his lap, placing his hand on my bare calf. "Josie, beautiful, I hate to say it, but I got this *slight* feeling that your parents might not like us."

I snorted, a smile tugging at my lips.

"Sorry, they're awful," I said, hiding my face in Cam's shoulder and taking another hit of his sweet scent.

"Not your fault," Cam grunted.

"I'm sorry we didn't say more to defend you," Theo said. "We're worried they'll use any excuse to say we're not proper alphas for you."

"Should have said something anyway," Cam grunted. "No one gets to talk to you like that."

My cheeks heated. When was the last time someone cared about me like this?

"Do you really think they could force me to be with another pack?" I whispered. This morning I had been terrified to move in with these three unknown alphas. Now I was terrified of someone taking me away.

Cam growled. "Fuck no. We won't let that happen."

"You're stuck with us, beautiful," Ben said. "Now that they're gone, what do you want to eat?"

"Oh, um, I'll just have coffee. I don't usually eat breakfast." I could still hear my mother's voice in my head. *Alphas don't want a fat omega.*

"We'll need to change that," Cam muttered, to my confusion.

Ben handed me a cup of coffee, and I took it from him with shaking hands. The three of them stared at me intently. I avoided eye contact and took a sip of the coffee. A sickeningly sweet taste hit my tongue, causing me to almost choke in shock. My eyes watered from the piles of sugar I had just consumed.

Ben looked alarmed and took the coffee out of my hands so I didn't spill it.

"Are you alright?" Theo asked, running his hand up and down my back.

I tried to keep my voice judgment-free as I cleared my throat. "What is in this?"

"I prepared it the way you said you took your coffee in the questionnaire. Is it not right?" Ben asked.

Oh. My. God. The questionnaire. With the stress of the interviews, I had completely forgotten the questionnaire answers I gave in my tipsy state. I could practically picture the glee on Clementine's face when I told her about this. The ridiculousness of the situation overtook me, and an unbidden giggle bubbled out of my chest.

"What is so funny?" Theo asked with a smile.

I laughed harder. Now that I'd started, I couldn't seem to stop.

Theo picked up the coffee and took a sip before grimacing. "What the fuck is this?"

"Seven creams, seven sugars, and a shot of caramel sauce," Ben listed defensively.

Theo started laughing, and I thought it might be the best sound I had ever heard. Cam still looked bewildered, but I could feel him growing hard underneath me. I knew it was an involuntary reaction to my scent filling the room, but part of me wanted to pretend it was because he was attracted to me.

"Hmm, I think our girl may have lied to us," Theo said, wrapping my hair around his hand and pulling lightly so my face turned towards him. "Did you lie to us, angel?"

"Maybe," I said, feeling playful. *He called me our girl.* My inner omega jumped with happiness. The feeling evaporated instantly when Ben looked down at the coffee like it had insulted him.

"Are you mad?" I whispered, freezing. Was this the moment they turned on me? Was my prank too much for them?

Ben looked up, shocked. "What? No! But now I am wondering what else is a lie on your questionnaire." He smiled warmly and squeezed my leg.

I relaxed into his touch. Maybe Ben liked me being playful with him? A lifetime of having to second guess all my actions out of concern for others' responses had left me unsure.

"I guess you'll just have to find out," I said softly.

Ben grinned. "How do you actually take your coffee?"

"One cream, two sugars."

Theo and Cam snorted.

Cam shifted me closer to him on his lap, and I could still feel his *rather large* hardness under me. "How're you feeling about being here?" he asked, pressing his face into my hair.

God, being pressed against the three of them made me want to purr. I clenched down on the urge before I let a purr slip out. Growing up, I was taught it was something an omega should only do for a bonded partner. I had tried it once when I was younger, and my mother's eyes had flashed with rage before she slapped me hard across the face. I never heard her purr for Richard or Jericho, but then again, why would she? There was no affection between them.

I realized Cam was waiting for an answer. I took a deep breath. "It's... just a lot to take in. Thanks for being so nice to me."

Cam just grunted in response.

Ben handed me a new cup of coffee. As I reached out to take it, the sleeve of the horrid dress my mother had forced me to wear this morning shifted back, revealing the finger-shaped bruises left by Pack Madden. Before I could pull my sleeve down, a vicious growl erupted from Cam's chest.

"How the fuck did you get those bruises?" he asked, gripping my wrist in a tender hold that didn't match the rage in his voice.

I flinched at his anger, even though I knew it wasn't aimed at me.

"It's nothing," I said, tugging my sleeve back down.

"It's not nothing," Cam said fiercely.

"Did one of your fathers do this?" Theo asked, his voice almost too calm.

"Oh no. Um, it was the other pack I interviewed with yesterday. I cut the interview short, and they tried to stop me from leaving."

"What's the pack's name?" Theo asked, the rage in his scent betraying his tone.

"It's just some bruises. It's okay," I said. My survival instinct was screaming at me—*don't make a big deal of it, downplay your needs, placate the alphas.*

Cam shook beneath me, and Ben couldn't tear his eyes away from my wrist.

"It's our job to protect you. If someone hurts you, we need to know," Cam said through gritted teeth.

The energy in the room crackled, the tension acting as a warning sign to my system. The warmth of their bodies, their touches, turned suffocating. I was too vulnerable here. I pushed myself out of Cam's embrace—ignoring how his grunt of displeasure pulled at my heartstrings—and stood up.

I tugged the dress again, trying to ignore the way the fabric pinched my rolls of skin, and looked down at the three of them. Their scents were bitter with distress, but I couldn't sense any anger. That gave me the confidence to take a deep breath and launch into the speech I had practiced all night.

"I know your alpha instincts are telling you to protect me, but you shouldn't feel obligated. I know you don't really want an omega and this was just a favor for Amirah. I really appreciate you doing the interview. You saved me from a really terrible pack. But I get it if you don't really want me here. If you let me stay, I promise I'll be really quiet and not bother you. I can also clean and do other things around the house." My words came faster, a far cry from the measured, collected way I had delivered them in my mirror.

The three alphas froze. The silence stretched on uncomfortably. Cam broke it with a growl.

"You're our mate," he said, his voice deep and rough. "We'll do anything for you and want you here more than anything. I'm so fucking grateful we were asked to do the interview because I would murder any other pack that got close to you."

My eyes had been fixated on the patterned rug under my feet, but at his words, they shot up, meeting his gaze. My heart pounded a million beats a minute, and a delicious warmth ran through me, hopefulness that what he was saying was true. But then, an icy wave of disbelief covered it. *They're messing with you, getting your hopes up so they can betray you.*

"Mates?" I croaked out. "What are you talking about?"

"You don't feel it?" Ben asked gently. "We knew from the moment you walked in the room that you were ours."

Theo nodded his agreement. Hazy numbness was washing over my body and my legs trembled. I clenched my hands again, pressing my fingernails into my palms just to *feel* something. I had always dreamed of finding my fated mates, always hoped that someday someone would want me, *love* me. This was too good to be true. Life had taught me that good things would always be ripped from me.

Theo reached out and unfurled my fists, soothing the crescent-shaped marks I'd pressed into my hands.

"But I thought that never happened. Aren't fated mates a myth?" I whispered.

"The Designation Government has made it seem that way," Theo said gently, "but we know quite a few packs that bonded with their mate. We think it's more common than the government wants us to believe because they can be more in control of who matches with a pack."

"But how do you know? You could be wrong. You don't even know me," I said, my words coming out high-pitched and strangled.

"None of us have any doubts," Ben said. "Your scent does things to me I've never felt before. I already know you're so kind, strong, and precious. You already feel like the center of our pack."

Ben gently caressed the bruised spot on my wrist before dropping his hand again. He looked so genuine, so hopeful. What if... what if this was real? But then, why didn't I feel it? A heaviness settled in my stomach. Maybe my parents had been right all along. I was defective. I couldn't even tell if these alphas were my mates.

"Then why don't I feel the same thing?" I asked, panicked.

Ben let out a distressed noise.

"We think there's a good chance that being on suppressants might temporarily suppress your omega from recognizing us as mates," Theo said, continuing to rub my hand soothingly.

I stiffened. Fuck. They knew I was on suppressants. *See, now they can blackmail you. Can't trust them.* I shifted back and forth and tried to keep my voice from shaking.

"What makes you think I'm on suppressants?"

The three of them exchanged a look before Ben answered me.

"We were curious because of your age, and then Amirah confirmed it," he said before continuing quickly. "She was just trying to be helpful so we could know how to best support you. We're not upset about it, gorgeous. Not at all. You deserve to make decisions about your own body." He tentatively took my hand. I threaded my fingers through his, and his responding smile looked like I had just given him a gift.

The shaking in my legs became more pronounced as I struggled to keep myself upright.

"Will you sit back down, sweetheart?" Cam asked. As soon as I nodded, he reached out and pulled me back onto his lap. I softened, enveloped in his embrace.

"You might not recognize us as mates yet, but I wonder if you feel more comfortable around us than other alphas you've been around?" Theo asked.

I shifted so I could see his face, unconsciously leaning towards him so I could breathe in more of his coffee scent.

"Yeah, I do," I responded hesitantly.

"Of course you do, baby girl. We would never hurt you," Cam said, pulling me closer.

Ben picked up a cheese Danish and held it up to my mouth. I took a bite without thinking, and the guys' scents intensified with pleasure. That was the best Danish I had ever tasted. I wiggled happily as I took another bite from Ben. Cam grunted, tightening his hold on me, his cock rubbing against my thigh.

"The fact that you feel more comfortable around us is probably your omega recognizing us as mates, at least to some extent," Theo said, running his hand through my hair. "I couldn't scent you at Trader Joe's, but I was drawn to you from the moment I followed you into the store."

I scrunched my nose. "Your scent was on me when I woke up at the hospital, but I don't really remember anything that happened."

"You collapsed in one of the aisles and I held you until the paramedics came. It destroyed me to let you go. If I had known you were our mate, I wouldn't have been able to. I had no idea the omega we were meeting was you."

Was the reason I had found his scent so comforting in the hospital because we were mates? Part of me recognized what they were saying made sense. I traced little patterns on Cam's arm, thinking through everything as the quiet fell soothingly around us.

Suddenly, I jolted. If we were mates, they might expect us to bond right away.

"I'm not ready to be bonded yet," I blurted out.

Cam pressed a tender kiss to my temple. "Of course. There's no rush. We're going to court you. Give you everything you deserve. You'll learn that we'll do anything to make you happy."

I melted back into his embrace. *Fuck*, it was like Cam was an omega whisperer.

"You don't have to get me anything," I said.

My inner omega almost whined. She wanted all the courting gifts she could get her greedy hands on. Traditionally, alphas courted an omega for weeks before she joined their pack, and they would usually live together for a while before bonding. Once they marked me, we would be forever connected, able to sense each other's emotions.

"Amirah said that your heat is coming on in the next day or two, and I know it's fast. We need to know how to make you the most comfortable during this process," Theo said.

Cam continued, "We'll also need to make a list of all the things you want during your heat—your favorite snacks and drinks, anything else you need for your nest, safe words and preferences during sex."

My chest tightened and my cheeks heated. *Of course, they're expecting to have sex with you during your heat, you idiot.* I needed to tell them my plan... but what if it made them angry? Before I chickened out, I forced myself to just say it.

"I don't want to have sex."

Chapter Thirteen

Josie

Well, I meant to deliver that with more tact, but there you go. I hid my face, expecting them to start yelling at me at any moment.

After Dave dropped me off at my apartment yesterday, I ran inside, piled up all the blankets I owned, and buried myself underneath. I'd just gotten settled when Sam called to let me know someone in his network could get me suppressants. Apparently, an Alliance doctor had been traveling but was returning to town and bringing suppressants with them. I'd burst into tears on the phone. I blamed my surging heat hormones, but the reality was I couldn't believe how lucky I was to have someone who cared for me like Sam did.

Suppressants wouldn't stop my heat at this point, but taking them meant I wouldn't be forced to choose between having sex with alphas to satisfy my heat or being in excruciating pain that could leave me with permanent damage. I knew the simplest way to avoid conflict was to go along with what Cam, Theo, and Ben expected and have sex with them during my heat. A part of me loved their hands on me and wondered what it would be like to have them see me through my heat. But the thought of having sex with three practical strangers, three *alpha* strangers, especially while I was most vulnerable... My stomach clenched with nausea. I couldn't do it. But what if they rejected me because I didn't want to have sex? What if they disregarded my wishes and did it anyway?

I jumped when Ben finally broke the silence.

"What do you mean, gorgeous? What about your heat?" He quickly added, "We never want to pressure you, but I'm worried about your safety in your heat if we don't, you know..."

"I've found a way to get suppressants. They'll dull the heat enough so I can get through it," I said carefully.

It wasn't until this moment that I realized I hadn't thought this through. Telling them I wanted suppressants gave them even more ammunition to use against me. Even though they had said they weren't angry that I had been on them, I couldn't quite believe it.

A quiet growl rippled through Cam's chest and I tensed, ready for him to lash out at me. The growl abruptly stopped.

"Sorry, sweetheart," he said. "The idea of you suffering even a little bit puts me on edge. I just want you to be okay."

I wasn't expecting that response. It was enough to make me brave enough to uncurl slightly and make eye contact with them. I inhaled sharply when I saw their expressions of care and concern. I searched their faces for disappointment or anger and couldn't find any. Somehow, this was even more unsettling —I didn't know what to do with their reactions.

"I don't want to make things hard for you or disappoint you," I almost whispered. "But we just met and..." I trailed off, not knowing what to say.

Theo shifted to sit on the coffee table in front of me.

"Angel, just breathe. Everything is okay. None of us are

mad at you. We want to support you." Cam and Ben murmured their agreement.

Theo held his hand out to me, allowing me to decide whether to take it. I waited a minute to see if he would grow frustrated by my hesitation, but he sat patiently. I tentatively reached out until my hand was resting in his. My building panic and tension dissipated at his touch.

"Who is the suppressant supplier?" he asked, giving my hand a squeeze.

"It's a doctor my friend knows through the Alliance. They've been out of town but are supposed to be back tomorrow. They're going to call me to set it up," I whispered.

I didn't want to share too much, especially not Sam's involvement, in case they turned around and reported me. Although the longer I was with them, the less likely it seemed they would betray me.

Cam brushed my hair back from my face. "Okay, sweetheart. We'll help you get the suppressants. No one will push you to do anything you're uncomfortable with. No sex unless you want it," he said firmly.

"We'll do some research and see how we can support you through a suppressant-assisted heat," Theo said.

"I don't think you'll be able to find any information on it," I said. "The government removed all of that stuff from the internet."

"Ahh, but you now have a hacker at your disposal," Ben said with an easy smile. "We'll get the information and do whatever we can to make you safe."

Relief washed through me, and my eyes grew heavy. The intense conversation, all the stress I'd been through, and a string of sleepless nights were finally catching up to me.

"You look done in. Do you want to take a nap?" Cam asked.

I felt like I should say no, but I couldn't keep my eyes open. I couldn't remember the last time my body had been this relaxed. Their scents drugged me and turned me boneless. Cam stood, holding me tight to his body. I tried to force my eyes open, but instead, I pressed my face into his chest. I was vaguely aware we were walking through the house and going upstairs. I wanted to see what the rest of the house looked like, but I was too comfortable, too sleepy, to look around.

A door clicked and Cam set me down on a bed, his hands lingering for a moment before he let me go and took a small step back.

"This is... um... your room. Sorry it's not better. We'll fix it up," Cam said, his voice gruff as he rubbed the back of his neck.

Without his hands on me, I was suddenly wide awake. I opened my eyes and took in the room. Even though it was sparse, it was nicer than anything I'd ever had. I could tell they had made an effort to get what I needed for my heat—the bed was massive and piled high with blankets and pillows and string lights crisscrossed the ceiling.

Cam, Ben, and Theo stood near the bed, shifting from side to side as if nervous about my reaction. Cam scowled at the room as if it had personally offended him. I'd never been in a situation before where alphas wanted to please *me,* and it made me feel powerful.

"The room is great," I said, stroking one of the soft blankets. The three of them puffed up, looking thrilled by my assessment. I had to stifle a grin at how easy they were to please.

A haze of awkwardness settled on the room. None of us knew what to do next.

"Um, could I have a few minutes to myself?" I asked. I desperately wanted to change out of my horrible dress and needed some space to process everything.

"Of course," Theo said. "We'll be downstairs. Just let us know if you need anything."

They filed out of the room slowly, as if they were forcing themselves to leave. When the door shut behind them, I felt empty. I pushed myself off the bed and walked to the suitcase someone had brought up. I quickly stripped off the too-tight dress my mother had gotten me, frowning at the marks left on my skin, and dressed in sweatpants and a sweatshirt. I looked around, at a loss for what I was supposed to do. *I should feel relieved that they're gone, right?* This was what I wanted—time alone to process. But as I took in the room, I felt deeply alone.

I glanced longingly at the bed. My omega pushed me to wrap myself up in the bundle of blankets and start nesting. The urge was stronger than it had ever been now that I was going into heat, but part of me still resisted. If I made a nest, it would make my heat real, and I wasn't ready for that.

Resisting the bed, I walked over to the wall of blackout curtains, curious to see the view. I pushed them aside and saw that the windows were actually French doors leading out to a private balcony. The nasty voice in my head spoke up again: *You don't deserve this room. As soon as the alphas see how defective you are, they'll kick you out.* I closed my eyes, resting my forehead on the cool glass door pane, and wished I could be kinder to myself.

I hesitated before grabbing my phone and slipping onto the balcony, sitting on one of the plush outdoor chairs. The balcony looked out over the back of the house, revealing a magical wonderland of a courtyard. Pale pavers surrounded a serene pool, and roses climbed on a brick wall towards the back. It looked like something out of *Pride and Prejudice.* Trees provided shade around the perimeter, and a large wooden dining table and chairs sat next to a fire pit and outdoor kitchen.

It was an unusually warm day for October. The sun was shining and a slight breeze played with my hair, wafting the scent of wild roses over me. I had been so overwhelmed when we pulled up this morning that it hadn't truly registered how gorgeous this home was. I could picture myself waking up in the mornings and enjoying coffee on the balcony or curling up in one of the lounge chairs by the pool to read.

A burst of anxiety shot through me as I realized I was already envisioning myself in this home, bonded to these alphas. What if I let my guard down and they hurt me? I quickly dialed Sam's number.

"Josie, are you okay? Why the fuck haven't you answered my texts?" Sam asked, sounding pissed.

I bit my lip and saw I had eighteen unopened texts from him. *Oops.*

"Sorry," I said. "I've been a little busy."

Sam took a deep breath. "Didn't mean to snap. Are you at their house? What are they like? How are you doing?"

I opened my mouth to answer him and a choked sob came out instead.

"Have they hurt you?" Sam all but shouted. "That's it. I'm coming to get you out. This whole thing is fucking ridiculous."

"No, wait, it's okay," I managed to get out. "I don't even know why I'm crying."

"Are you hurt?" Sam asked.

"No, it's actually... good? I don't know. I'm so confused."

"Take a deep breath, Josie-girl, and tell me what's going on," Sam said.

I heard Gerald in the background asking who they needed to kill. Gerald was the kindest, gentlest alpha I had ever met. If not for his scent, I would never have guessed his designation. Hearing him make threats in my defense eased the tightness in my chest.

"We got here this morning. My parents were awful, of course, but they weren't here that long. The alphas—Cam, Ben, and Theo—have been really kind. The house is beautiful. It's in the historic district and all brick and covered in roses. They showed me to my room, which has its own balcony because, apparently, these guys are like super rich. So that's where I'm sitting now."

Sam didn't say anything for a minute. "I mean this in the nicest way possible, but I don't give a flying fuck about the architecture of the house. Tell me why you were crying and what the fuck is going on with the alphas."

"I'm scared," I said softly.

"Scared of what?" Sam roared.

I had to be brave and tell Sam everything or he would try to organize a rescue attempt.

"I feel more comfortable with them than I ever have around alphas, except you, of course. They're funny and kind and I'm really attracted to them. I didn't even get freaked out when Cam held me in his lap. I thought I wanted time alone, but now I have it and I just want them to be here with me. Oh, and they said we're fated mates and want me to stay and bond with them."

There was another long pause before Sam finally responded. "That all sounds... good."

I started tearing up again. "But what if it's all a lie and once I trust them, they'll turn around and hurt me?"

Sam let out a deep breath. "You, more than anyone, have the right to be cautious about trusting alphas. I also know you have great instincts. What's your omega telling you?"

"Oh, she's thrilled about everything and trusted them immediately," I said. "But I don't know how sound her judgment is."

"I think pretty sound," Sam said, and I could hear the smile in his voice.

"Do you believe in fated mates?" I almost whispered.

"Yeah, I do. I don't trust anything the Designation Government has put out the past few years, including whatever bullshit research they've published. Fated mates used to be pretty common. I remember you reading quite a few romance stories about them," he said, his voice teasing.

"Yeah, well, those are just stories," I mumbled. But he was right. I had always dreamed of finding my mates, and most romance books featured them heavily. "I'm literally living out one of my fantasies right now. Three super hot, rich alphas who happen to be my mates and have an amazing house and are super nice and supportive. So why am I so terrified?"

"Did you tell them about what Glen..."

"No," I said quickly. "I can't... I don't want to."

"You have nothing to be ashamed of," he said sharply.

When I didn't respond, he sighed. I imagined him sprawled across the couch in the living room I had only seen in our video calls.

"I think you'll need to tell them, but the timing's up to you."

He was probably right, but I couldn't think about it right now. No matter how often Sam told me what happened wasn't my fault, I couldn't shake the feeling that I was dirty because of it.

"So... the house is in the historic district?" Sam prompted, taking pity on me and changing the subject after I still hadn't responded.

I grinned. "You would love it." I paused for a second before dropping my voice, even though I knew no one could hear me out here. "I still want the suppressants. I'm not ready to go through heat with them."

"They on board with that?"

"Yeah."

"Good. Or I'd have to fucking punch them. Mates or not, you're still your own person. My contact confirmed that the doctor will call you tomorrow. They're being cagey and not telling me the doctor's name, but my contact assured me they're reliable."

"Thanks, Sam. I couldn't do this without you."

"You know I'm always here for you. I know how hard it is for you to trust your omega, but just try to follow your instincts, okay? Just because it feels like something bad is going to happen doesn't mean it will."

After I hung up, I was overwhelmed by the sudden urge to be with my alphas. I walked back into the room and stood by the door, my hand on the doorknob. What now? Could I just go downstairs? What if they didn't want me around right now? The thought of them rejecting me froze me to the spot. And there I stood, unable to take a step towards them.

Chapter Fourteen

Cam

I paced the kitchen, each movement laced with agitation at being away from Josie. Her sweet vanilla scent clung to my skin and clothes, making me grow hard. Fuck, having her on my lap, pressed against my cock, had been the sweetest form of torture I'd ever experienced. I wanted to camp out by her door just in case she needed something, but that probably didn't send the right message after she'd asked for space. Leaving her, even to just go downstairs, felt wrong. She'd looked so tired and vulnerable in the room. I hoped she would at least be able to sleep.

I knew I needed to back off and take things slowly, but it went against my instincts. I had no doubts about our mate and couldn't wait until she trusted me to take care of her like she deserved. My alpha was riding me to have a courting gift ready for her when she got up, but I couldn't think of anything to get her that would be special enough.

"Shit," Theo said, leaning over the kitchen island and looking at his tablet with disgust.

"What?" I asked, distracted by an article I found online: *Forty-two failsafe courting gifts for your omega.*

"The DC sent over this *Omega Care Instruction* booklet for us," Ben said, anger seething from him through the bond.

My skin crawled with dread.

"Brace yourself. It's fucking disgusting," Theo said as he handed me the tablet.

I grabbed it and started skimming the multi-page document, white-hot rage pulsing through me the further I read.

> *Josephine Porter, omega, age 23, was assessed via blood work on October 7th to be in pre-heat. Through examination with the Designation Center medical specialist, she is a confirmed virgin with a rated vaginal tightness of 9/10. Ms. Porter is in good health with the exception of her weight, which is significantly higher than the average healthy omega. While at the Designation Academy, Ms. Porter was put on a strict diet leading to significant weight loss. In the intervening year, Ms. Porter has been without alpha supervision and has regained that weight. It is strongly recommended that her food intake be stringently monitored by her alphas for her to maintain optimal weight. A sample diet and eating schedule are attached below.*

I could hear my heartbeat in my ears as other sounds fell away. The "sample diet" wasn't enough food for a small child to subsist on, let alone an adult omega woman. Josie was curvier than most omegas, and she was perfect. I didn't give a fuck about her weight. Reading that they'd practically starved her made me want to feed her right now.

"What the fuck is this about vaginal tightness?" I asked, my voice deathly quiet.

"I don't know," Theo snarled as he paced the kitchen.

"Does that mean someone touched her? What kind of examination is that?" Ben asked, his voice growing louder. Theo shushed him, not wanting Josie to overhear.

"What are they doing with omegas at that fucking academy?" I asked, my horror growing as I flipped through more of the document outlining Josie's "significant behavioral issues."

April 14th: Ms. Porter challenged her teacher and disobeyed a direct order to be silent. Consequence: Two days of punishment carried out by disciplinarian alpha.

April 26th: Ms. Porter argued with the teacher about designation hierarchy. Consequence: blanket and pillow removed from room for thirty days.

There were pages and pages of similar statements documenting near-constant punishment sessions.

"What the fuck is a disciplinarian alpha?" I growled, accidentally snapping the tablet in two.

"I didn't think the Academy was good, but I didn't realize it was..." Ben trailed off, looking stunned.

"I'm going back up to check on her," I said, throwing the tablet in the trash.

"She said she wanted space," Theo said, although I knew through the bond he was longing to be with her.

"Don't give a fuck," I growled. "She's alone and vulnerable and has been treated like shit by everyone, apparently. I need to make sure she's okay."

I stormed off, taking the stairs two at a time, only hesitating once I was outside her room, breathing hard with the anger and adrenaline pumping through my system. *They hurt our mate. We need to end them.*

My alpha and I were in total agreement. I needed to touch

her, scent her, and make sure she was okay, but I couldn't bring myself to barge into her room. It was obvious now why she didn't want to be around us. Shit, she probably didn't want to be here at all.

We could move her to the pool house if she wanted more space. The thought filled my chest with hollow despair and I sank to the floor, resting my back against her door. I already knew I couldn't refuse my mate anything that would make her more comfortable, but the thought of being separated from her, of her not wanting to be near us, was agonizing. Just then, there was a click of a door handle, and I fell onto my back as the bedroom door swung open.

Josie peered down at me, confusion written all over her tear-streaked face. I scrambled to my feet and we stood in silence. I hesitated before opening my arms to her. She immediately launched herself into my embrace.

Relief washed through me. I didn't know what had made her cry, but she wanted *me* to comfort her, trusted me enough to seek my touch. I pushed away my fears that I would let her down, that I would fail to protect her like I had my sister. Right now, she needed me. It was the greatest fucking feeling in the world.

I gently picked her up and her legs curled around me tightly. Her head rested on my shoulder and she let out a long, shuddering breath, her eyes fluttering closed. Nothing would ever feel better than this, than having her safe in my arms. I lay down on the bed, arranging her so she was sprawled out on top of me, one of my hands gripping her upper thigh and the other rubbing her back in a gentle rhythm.

"Rest now, baby girl. I've got you," I murmured.

Chapter Fifteen

Josie

I woke slowly, feeling deliciously warm.

The sweet cinnamon roll scent I'd already started associating with safety surrounded me. A soft blanket was laid over me and underneath me was... I jolted awake fully, remembering that I had fallen asleep *on* Cam.

"Shh, it's okay. You've been asleep for about an hour," he said, his hand resuming its soothing path up and down my back.

"I didn't mean to fall asleep on you. Am I crushing you?" I asked, biting my lip.

Cam snorted. "Baby girl, you could lie on top of me all day, every day, and not crush me."

I blushed, pressing my face against his chest before trying to scoot off of him. No matter what he said, I was sure he'd be more comfortable if I moved.

Cam's arms tightened around me.

"Please don't," he said, his voice almost pleading. "I need a few more minutes."

My body melted with contentment as I settled back on top

of him. I tried not to second guess everything and embrace my instincts like Sam suggested.

"We need to order more things for this room," Cam said as he massaged the tension out of my shoulders. "It's not good enough for you."

"You don't need to get me anything," I murmured as I closed my eyes, holding back a whimper at how good his hands felt. I had only been here a couple of hours, but I already hoped these alphas would keep me. I didn't want to come across as needy or high-maintenance.

"We definitely do, sweetheart. Need to get you everything you could need or want. If you don't like the house, we'll get a new one."

He couldn't possibly mean that, could he? I cracked my eyes open and took in his serene expression.

"You can't just change houses for me."

"Of course, we can," he snorted. "You say the word, we'll move. We have our other home up north that's more secluded. If you want to be in a different part of the city, we'll just buy a new house."

"You're ridiculous," I said with a smile, snuggling back into his chest. "I love this house." Cam gave me a little squeeze, the steady beat of his heart creating a calming rhythm.

"Why were you crying earlier?" he asked.

I tensed, not sure what to say. I was used to hiding my emotions, but I found myself wanting to be honest with Cam.

"I got really overwhelmed," I finally said. It was the truth but didn't reveal too much.

"Tell me how to make it better," he demanded.

I hid my smile in the crook of his neck. That was cute.

"You already did when you came up here," I said, running my nose along his neck and breathing deeply. "I'm confused why I feel so safe with you all when I don't even know you. I needed time to process everything, but when I was alone, I just wanted to be with you all."

"You feel comfortable with us because you're our mate," he said, his voice filled with... satisfaction? "Your omega recognizes me and knows I would never hurt you. Leaving the DC without you felt like I was being ripped in two. I'll try to give you space when you need it, but it will be hard for me. Let me know if it's too much and you need me to back off."

I nodded, my mind wandering as I traced the abstract patterns of his tattoos up and down his arm. I wondered what Ben and Theo were doing and found myself missing them. Maybe Cam and I could go downstairs, or maybe they could come up in bed with us. I was imagining what it would be like to be sandwiched between all three alphas when I noticed Cam's scent turning bitter, like burnt pastry.

"What's wrong?" I asked, my chest constricting with anxiety. Did I do something wrong?

Cam rolled us so we were both on our sides facing each other and tenderly brushed my hair out of my face.

"The DC sent us documents about your care and records from your time at the Academy."

I stiffened. I didn't know what exactly the Center had sent over, but I knew it wouldn't be good.

"Do you not want me anymore after reading it? Or do Ben and Theo not want me here now? Is that why they're not here?" I asked, my voice high-pitched. Tightness built in my chest, forcing me to push myself into a seated position.

"What are you talking about?" Cam asked in a low voice, sitting up with me.

"I'm sure it didn't say good things about me. I promise a lot of it's not true, but I'm still damaged. You deserve a better omega than me," I responded, blinking quickly to keep my tears from spilling over.

Cam growled and pulled me onto his lap, his arms forming tight bands around my waist.

"Listen to me," he said sternly. "You are not damaged, and we will *never* want anyone else. I'm so fucking pissed at how they treated you. I had to see you or I was going to go to the Center and kill them. You deserve to be fucking cherished, not punished or starved or whatever other shit they did to you." He grasped my chin, forcing me to meet his gaze. "I never want to hear you talk badly about yourself again. If anyone else does, you tell me and I will take care of it."

Cam's intensity startled me, his protectiveness filling me with warmth.

"Theo and Ben stayed downstairs so they didn't overwhelm you because they're better alphas than me. But I'm finding it hard to care since now I'm here with you and they're jealous as fuck. I know you have doubts, and I understand why after seeing how other alphas have treated you. But you have to know, sweetheart, that we are all in."

I moved without thinking, straddling Cam's lap. He hadn't told me what had happened at the DA was my fault. He was angry *for* me. A warm, happy feeling suffused me as Cam pulled me in close, one hand on my ass and the other gripping the back of my neck. I wrapped my arms around his neck, wanting to be as close to him as possible. My movement caused his cock to line up with my core, sending a jolt of pleasure through me.

My body froze as doubt rushed through me. What was I doing? I barely knew this alpha and now I was pressed up against him. I waited for panic to take hold, but all I felt was pleasure. The torturous punishments the alphas at the DA delivered if an omega was caught masturbating had ensured I never touched myself. I'd never felt this way before. Now I wanted to stop thinking, stop over-analyzing, and get more of this feeling. My omega took over. I experimented with rolling my hips against Cam, and he groaned.

"Fuck, baby, you're so beautiful."

He pulled me tighter into him and his lips crashed against mine, somehow soft and hard at the same time. *My first kiss!* Or, at least, the first one I'd wanted.

He nipped my lower lip before deepening the kiss, continuing to rock me against him in a steady rhythm, his cock hitting the perfect spot that made me moan. A gush of slick soaked my underwear and I whined, embarrassed by the wetness.

"So fucking sexy, you smell so good," Cam murmured, not allowing me to pull away and peppering kisses down my jaw and neck. "I want your slick to coat me, want to be drenched in your scent."

He moved his hand under my sweatshirt, cupping my breast with his hand before rolling my nipple between his fingers. Even through the fabric of my bra, the slight pinch pushed my arousal higher, and I ground against him until my legs trembled. I sucked on his lush bottom lip before pressing my tongue into his mouth. He growled, sending vibrations through me, and grasped my hip with his hand, urging me against him faster. I whimpered as the pleasure grew, wanting more but feeling scared at the same time. It felt like I was going to fall off a precipice and I wasn't sure I was brave enough to let go. I slowed my movements, overwhelmed with how good everything felt and unsure if I could handle more.

"What's wrong?" Cam asked, concern etched on his face.

"I'm scared," I whimpered. "It's too much."

Cam pulled me closer and pressed tender kisses on my cheeks and eyelid.

"I've got you, baby girl. You can let go. I'll catch you."

I believed him. The familiar warning sensation in my body screaming *not safe* was silent. I rolled my hips against him, the pleasure continuing to build until I shattered with Cam's name on my lips. Electric shocks of pleasure tingled through my body until I felt like I was floating. I took a shuddering breath as I collapsed onto him, my limbs feeling warm and heavy.

"So goddamn perfect, baby girl. So fucking beautiful when you come," he murmured, pressing his face to my hair and breathing deeply.

"I didn't know it would feel that good," I said after my heart rate had finally slowed.

"What do you mean?" Cam asked, his hand stilling on my back.

"Umm, you know, coming. It exceeded the hype. Ten out of ten recommend."

"You've never come with someone before?"

"Yeah. Or... at all," I said, squirming, suddenly feeling embarrassed.

"Sweetheart, are you saying you've never had an orgasm before?" he asked, his voice strangled.

"Omegas aren't allowed until we join a pack," I whispered.

"Who says?" he asked sharply.

"I don't want to talk about it."

My face grew hot. Cam and I were wrapped up in a peaceful bubble, and I didn't want to let memories from the DA intrude.

For a moment, it seemed like Cam would press the issue. Then he let out a long exhale. "Okay, sweetheart, we don't have to talk about it now."

I relaxed into his embrace as he held me in silence for a few moments.

"If I had known it was your first one, I would have made it better for you," he grumbled.

"Better than that? Not sure it could get better," I said, giving him a teasing smile.

Cam quickly flipped us so he was lying on top of me. He kept most of his weight on his forearms, but I loved the feel of his body against mine.

"That sounds like a dare," he said, a wicked smile on his face.

"Maybe it was," I responded, trying to sound flirty. His hair was still in a bun and my fingers itched to take it down. I wondered what it would be like to kiss him with my fingers threaded in his hair.

"I'm going to make you come every way possible, over and over. You're going to be so overwhelmed with pleasure you won't be able to move. But right now, I think my brothers are seconds away from breaking down this door if I keep you to myself a moment longer."

Slick drenched my underwear at his words. My first orgasm had truly lived up to the hype and I wanted to experience it again, but I was also missing Theo and Ben.

"Let's go downstairs," I said, pressing my lips against Cam's for a quick kiss.

Cam looked like he wasn't sure if he would let me up. "We won't talk about it now, but I want you to know I'm fucking pissed with whatever bullshit the DA did to you. And, because I'm a selfish bastard, I'm also fucking thrilled your first orgasm was with me."

I blushed as Cam got up and gently pulled me to standing next to him.

"I need to change," I said, wrinkling my nose at how wet my underwear was. I looked over at Cam and saw a dark wet spot on the front of his pants.

"Is that from me? I'm sorry," I said, my face burning with embarrassment.

"Umm, no, I mean, it's not. It was just really hot, seeing you come..." Cam trailed off, and I saw he was blushing. A grin spread across my face as I realized what had happened.

"Did you come, too?" I asked.

Cam nodded curtly, his blush deepening.

"Why are you embarrassed?" I asked, confused.

"Just don't want you to think I'm a fucking teenager who won't make it good for you," he mumbled.

"Did I not make you feel good?" I asked, worried.

Cam drew me in, a firm hand at the back of my neck.

"That was the hottest fucking experience of my life. You made a grown-ass man come in his fucking pants."

"Oh good," I said, smiling. I felt proud that I had made Cam feel good, too.

Cam laughed. "Fucking cute. Alright, change your clothes and then come downstairs. We need to feed you."

He kissed me on my forehead before heading downstairs, leaving me feeling more relaxed and settled than I could remember.

Chapter Sixteen

Ben

I tossed and turned in bed, my sheets tangling around me as I sighed in frustration. I hated going to bed early and often had trouble falling asleep, but knowing that my mate was on the other side of the hall, probably all curled up under the covers looking luscious, was torture. What if she was cold or uncomfortable or lonely? *She would probably sleep much better if I was wrapped around her body, one arm curled right underneath her amazing breasts, my knee shoved up between her legs in the perfect position for her to grind her sweet pussy on my thigh.*

I groaned, throwing my fisted hand over my face. I had already jacked off three times in the shower earlier and once in bed, but my dick was a fucking rock again.

Josie seemed to enjoy me touching her, but there had been a few times when her mask had slipped and I had seen flashes of fear and uncertainty. It killed me that she felt anything but confident and settled with us. I wasn't upset that she wasn't ready to have sex yet, but I couldn't stand the idea of her being in pain during her heat and being helpless to fix it.

When she and Cam came downstairs earlier, it was obvious something had happened between them. Cam was drenched in her scent and had a proud, satisfied look in his eyes. A burst of jealousy had flared through me—I wanted to be the one who made that soft expression appear on her face. But it also made me hopeful that she was already getting more comfortable around us.

Josie was more settled at dinner, her scent bright and sweet. But she had still been quiet, picking at her food. I'd offered her something different to eat, but she refused and then went to bed early. Alone.

My heart pounded as I heard the soft padding of feet and the opening of a door. I leapt out of bed, straining my ears to listen. There were footsteps down the hall, followed by the slight creak of the stairs. It had to be Josie. Was she okay? Did she need something? I forced myself to take a calming breath, but I got a lungful of her scent through the door, making me grow even harder. I pulled on some sweatpants before slipping out of my door to follow her.

I heard the click of a light switch and saw the faint glow coming from the kitchen. I followed the faint glow of light, drawn towards her as if a beautiful, golden thread connected us both. Josie was leaning over the counter to reach the brownie container. Her tiny sleep shorts were riding up and her tank top showed off a sliver of her waist. She looked soft and adorable and utterly sexy.

I cleared my throat softly, not wanting to startle her. She let out a small shriek and spun around, throwing the brownie she had grabbed straight at me. It hit my face with impressive accuracy. I would have caught it before it hit me, but I was so surprised that I only snagged it after it bounced off my cheek.

"I'm really impressed with your aim, beautiful. Next time

I'll know to be ready and catch it in my mouth," I said with a wink.

"Oh my gosh, I'm so sorry I threw that at you. I didn't hear you come down here. I shouldn't have left my—umm—the guest room. I hope I didn't wake you up. I'll just go back to bed," she squeaked out, her cheeks turning red as she started moving around me. Moving on instinct, I quickly stepped towards her, grasped her around the waist, and set her down on the kitchen island.

"Take a breath, precious," I said, concerned with her quick, shallow breaths and the scent of her rising shame.

"I'm really sorry, Ben," she whispered, tears gathering in her eyes.

"Beautiful, why are you crying?" I asked, panic tightening my chest as one of her tears spilled over and ran down her cheek. I stepped between her legs, pulling her close and running my hand through her hair. "It's my fault for startling you. You did nothing wrong."

"I shouldn't have left the room."

She trembled beneath my hands and I tightened my hold on her. My inner alpha urged me to purr for her, something I'd never wanted to do until this moment, but I wondered if it would freak her out, so I refrained.

"You can leave your room whenever you want," I said with a bit of confusion.

"But I shouldn't be walking around your house or touching your things."

"Of course, you should, precious. You should do anything you want to do, anything that makes you happy."

She shuddered in my arms, her tears turning into soft sobs. My chest tightened and a sick feeling grew in my stomach. I was failing her as an alpha. Cam or Theo would know what to do. I was the inadequate one who could never be serious enough, never good enough. I almost offered to go get one of them, but couldn't stand the thought of leaving her for one second.

"I'm sorry I'm bad. I'm such an inconvenience," Josie said through sobs.

What the fuck was she talking about? Who had told her she was bad?

I squeezed her tighter against me, one hand firmly cradling the back of her head and the other on her lower back. Her skin felt hot even through the fabric of her tank top.

Then it clicked.

Her heat was starting.

Growing up with sisters taught me that heats made omegas feel emotional and vulnerable. I wished we had gotten a chance to spend more time with her before her heat started. Then we would have at least had a better sense of what comforted her. Hoping it was the right thing to do, I leaned into my alpha instincts.

"That's not true, gorgeous. You are such a good girl. Your alphas want you here. We are so thrilled to have you. You are perfect, so sweet and beautiful, such a good omega." I kept murmuring praise until her tears slowed and she took some deep breaths.

"I'm sorry I'm keeping you up," she said softly, running her nose back and forth along my collarbone as she breathed in deeply.

I wished I knew what I smelled like to her—omegas could pick up alphas' scents just like I could pick up every note of her mouthwatering cupcake vanilla scent. I pressed my face into her hair. She needed to stop apologizing to me, but at least she wasn't crying anymore.

"You're not keeping me up, gorgeous. I stay up late most nights."

"Why did you go to bed so early tonight?"

"Everyone else was going to bed," I said, shrugging. "And the guys like to get up early so we can work out in the morning."

She scrunched her nose. "I hate waking up early. And working out."

I laughed. "Same. It's what I've always done, but maybe I should reevaluate now, especially if that means I get to have you to myself in the mornings."

"Morning cuddles sound nice," she mumbled into my chest.

"You can have all the morning cuddles you want. Now, tell me what you need. I'm assuming a brownie unless you only use those in self-defense."

Josie blushed the cutest fucking shade of red. "Umm, no, I don't just use them for self-defense."

"Good answer, precious. Let's get a plate of brownies, then. What else do you need? Water? More food?"

"You don't have to get me anything," she said quickly as she tried to slide off the island. I gripped her hips tightly, keeping her glued to the marble counter.

"I know this is a lot," I said softly, my lips brushing her ear as I pulled her close again. "But I would love to take care of you right now."

Josie pulled back and looked at my face intently like she was trying to figure something out.

"Oh... okay," she responded.

"Thank you, precious," I said, smiling. "Now, you stay there while I gather up our supplies."

I tried to sound stern, but I didn't know how convincing I was. Cam and Theo were the commanding ones, but maybe I had something to offer my mate right now. I wanted to make her smile and feel at ease. I quickly gathered a platter with brownies, chips, popcorn, soda, and water. I turned back to Josie, who was still on the counter.

"Good girl for doing as you're told," I murmured, running my hands up her bare thighs. Josie huffed an exasperated sigh, but I could scent her arousal swirling around me. *Our girl gets off on praise.* I suppressed a smile, tucking that tidbit of information away, hoping it would come in handy soon.

"Let's go to the den and eat our snacks," I said, helping her jump down from the island.

I guided Josie to the massive sectional. As she curled up into the deep cushions, I grabbed a blanket and spread it over her. My alpha was giddy with the simple act of taking care of our omega. I settled beside her, sitting as close as I could without crowding her. I grabbed a brownie and held it out, disappointed when she poked her hand out from the blanket to grab it instead of eating it out of my hand.

Usually, I felt the need to fill any silence with chatter, but sitting with Josie calmed me. We both ate our midnight snacks, and I relaxed into the couch. While I loved meeting new people, I sometimes felt like I couldn't be fully myself in social settings. I was more at ease with Josie after one day of knowing her than with some people I had known for years.

Josie's eyes grew heavier as she put down her snacks and curled up tightly under the blanket. Her vanilla scent was heady, and a smile tugged at my lips as I realized it would saturate the couch for days. I shifted so I was facing her, feeling like I would die if I had to look away, and took in her flushed cheeks, rosy pink lips, and the way her hair framed her face. I had to resist palming my cock, which had grown harder than I had ever felt. *I might be a creepy stalker watching her sleep, but at least I'm not going to sit here and jack off. It's called boundaries.*

I must have dozed off because I started awake some time

later. Josie was shifting around, fluffing one of the couch pillows and rearranging her blanket, letting out a frustrated sigh. I glanced at my watch and saw it was three o'clock in the morning.

"Josie, precious, what's wrong?" I murmured.

"I didn't mean to wake you up," she said with a whimper.

She looked so small and lost sitting next to me. I itched to pull her close to me, but I knew I needed to be careful.

"It's okay. I would rather be awake so I can take care of you. Do you want to go back to bed and make a nest?" Her heat was settling in more strongly and I guessed she wouldn't feel relaxed outside of a nest.

"No," she said. "I'm not in heat. I don't need a nest."

I looked pointedly down at the pillow she was currently fluffing and re-fluffing.

"I'm not ready," she whispered.

I caressed her face, my thumb catching a single tear at the corner of her eye. Feelings of inadequacy resurfaced, causing me to hesitate for a moment. I reminded myself that I had grown up in a house filled with omegas. I could do this. I could help her.

"I have four sisters and they're all omegas," I shared.

Josie's eyes widened. "That's a lot of omegas in one home."

I chuckled. "Yeah, it was. I loved it." A pang of sadness gripped me at being separated from them, especially my youngest sister Lilah, who I'd been closest with. I pushed it aside. "I know from talking with my sisters that first heats are intense. You're in a new environment and don't know us well yet. It's a lot to handle."

She nodded, resting her head on my shoulder. "I wish I wasn't an omega."

Her whispered confession broke my heart. My mate had

never gotten to experience the joys of being an omega, had never been lavished with the care and affection she deserved.

"I guess we'll just have to spoil you enough that you change your mind," I said, gently brushing my fingers through her hair. "Now, what do you need to feel more settled?"

Josie tensed up again. "I don't know," she said. "I'm not ready to nest yet."

"That's okay. Do you want anything else to eat or drink? Do you want to stay here or go back to bed?"

Her stress increased with my questions and I cursed inwardly, remembering that omegas didn't like to make decisions during their heat. She needed alpha dominance right now to make her feel secure.

"Never mind, precious. I'm going to take care of you so you don't have to worry about it."

She looked relieved, her green eyes wide with vulnerability as she gave me a nod.

"Come here," I said before pulling her into my arms, not giving her a chance to overthink it. I held her firmly to my chest, forgoing a blanket when I felt how hot her skin was. She immediately pressed her nose to my neck, where my scent was the strongest, and inhaled. *I hope she likes my scent because I want to fucking drown in hers.*

I arranged her so she was lying on top of me, my arms encircling her waist. Slowly, the tension melted from her limbs. I hoped my dick wasn't bothering her—it was fully hard, pressing against her perfect, soft stomach—but then I saw she'd already fallen asleep.

My cell vibrated and I cursed the timing, trying to pull it out of my pocket without disrupting my mate. I wasn't surprised in the slightest to see who it was.

CAM

Is Josie with you?

BEN

We're in the den. She's sleeping now. Her heat started.

I knew it would be a matter of moments before Cam was down here, and I was sure Theo would join us before the morning. Josie was already pulling us towards her like a magnet. For a moment, I felt frustrated, wanting to have more alone time with her, but the feeling passed as I heard Cam's footsteps on the stairs. I had dreamed of this for years—sharing an omega with my brothers—and I couldn't have imagined anyone more perfect for us than Josie.

Chapter Seventeen

Josie

I was burning from the inside out.

My limbs were hot, I was cramping, and... my underwear was soaked. *Fuck.* I knew I couldn't avoid my heat forever, but knowing it was inevitable and experiencing it were different things.

"Are you awake?" a deep voice murmured.

My eyelids were still too heavy to open, but a restlessness ran through my body like a current. I whimpered, trying to fight my way to consciousness.

"You're okay, love," another voice said. *Theo.* His British accent sent a little shiver through me.

I vaguely remembered falling asleep on the couch with Ben, but his crisp fall scent was absent. My eyes flew open, and I realized I was lying on top of Cam.

"Morning," he said, his arms banded around my waist. "Ben is making you some breakfast. You need lots of fuel for the next few days."

I tried to push myself off him, still feeling confused and

foggy. An intense cramp squeezed my uterus and I let out a strangled whimper.

"You want to sit up?" Cam asked, concerned.

I nodded, breathing through the pain. He helped me sit but arranged me so I was still in his lap. The gesture was possessive and tender at the same time. I didn't know if I wanted to pull away, lean into him, cry, or all of the above. Theo took my hand and rubbed my palm as if he could sense I'd been about to dig my fingernails into my skin.

Suddenly, it hit me what a vulnerable position I was in—surrounded by alphas while in heat. They had been sweet and protective so far, but what if they started getting pushy? My heart rate picked up and I felt exposed. I pushed off Cam, needing space. His arms around me felt too good, too comforting. *What if they're hiding their true personalities so they can lure me in?*

Cam reluctantly released me and I slipped onto the couch, momentarily distracted by the softness of the cushion. My omega was urging, *begging* me to cover myself with a pile of blankets *and a pile of alphas*. Stupid hormones.

"How are you feeling, angel?" Theo asked carefully. "Ben said your heat started in the middle of the night."

I scrunched my nose in confusion when I saw Theo was wearing slacks and a button-down. Then my mind wandered to different places, and I wondered what it would be like to strip him of all his clothes and have another orgasm.

"Josie?" Theo spoke again.

I'd been running my eyes all over his body and hadn't answered his question. *What had he asked me?*

A shy smile spread across his face. He shifted in his seat, adjusting the front of his pants. I quickly averted my eyes, my cheeks burning.

The burning. My skin flushed as the burning spread across my body.

"I feel really warm," I said.

Yeah, stupid. It's called heat for a reason. Tears pricked behind my eyes and there was a lump in my throat.

"Please don't cry, love," Theo pleaded, cupping my cheeks. "I did some research on heats. In the first phase, your temperature will rise, you'll start cramping, and you'll have mood swings."

Well, check, check and check. I hated feeling trapped by my own biology.

"It also says that getting in a cool bath could help you feel calmer," Theo continued.

"Do you want to get in the water, baby girl?" Cam asked.

"I... I don't know," I responded, overwhelmed. "I'm sorry I'm being such an inconvenience."

Yesterday they said they wanted me, that I was their mate. Now, that felt impossible.

"You are not an inconvenience," Theo said, squeezing my hand.

I opened my mouth to argue when another cramp hit, much stronger than the last one. Cam wrapped his arms around me, pressing a hand over my stomach while he murmured sweet words. I stayed slumped against him even after the cramp passed, no longer having the energy to move. Fuck, I needed suppressants immediately. This was just the beginning, and it already felt like my insides were being torn apart.

"I need my phone," I said, my panic rising. "The doctor is supposed to call to get me the suppressants."

"I'll run and get it for you," Theo said, kissing me on the forehead before heading up to my room.

Cam's hand was still on my stomach and I cringed, thinking

about how he could feel every fat roll. But his touch helped with the cramps, so I didn't want to push him away.

"I've got you," he said softly.

"Everything's out of control," I blurted out, sounding pitiful and whiney. "I don't even know you and this is so embarrassing and I don't know what to do."

Cam pressed a gentle kiss to my temple. "I know you're not used to being taken care of, but deep down, you need your alphas to take control."

I wanted to argue with him, to tell him I could take care of myself, but my omega melted at his words. I leaned into him, hiding my face in his chest and closing my eyes.

"Good girl," he murmured.

The couch shifted as Theo returned with my phone. "I'll make sure I keep this on me for when the doctor calls," he said, stroking my hair.

"Here's what we're going to do," Cam said. "We're going to get up and get you in the pool. We turned the water temperature down so it will help your fever come down and the cramps lessen. While you're in the pool, we'll make sure you eat and hydrate. After you're done, we'll come back here and cuddle you and watch a movie or whatever the fuck else you want. You're going to let us take care of you, baby girl, and I don't want to hear you call yourself an inconvenience again."

The intensity and sternness in his voice sent a shiver down my spine, and I felt a burst of slick in my panties. Cam and Theo groaned as they scented my arousal. My cheeks burned and I tried to move off Cam's lap, but he pulled me in even tighter. His hardness pressed against my back. *Fuck, he was massive.*

"Not getting rid of me that easily," he whispered, his lips brushing the shell of my ear. "No being embarrassed. You're going to let us take care of you."

I closed my eyes, blocking out the room. The scared, mistrusting part of me wanted to demand to be left alone. Deep down, I knew Cam would let me go if I really wanted him to.

Ever since I'd revealed as an omega, I'd been fighting my instincts. Now I was here with three attractive, rich alphas who wanted to take care of me. This was supposed to be the dream, so why did it feel so hard to accept?

Neither Cam nor Theo said anything while I quietly processed it all. Finally, I lifted my head.

"There you are," Theo said. "Now I can see your beautiful eyes. What do you say, love? You going to let us take care of you?"

I gave a slight nod.

"Good," Cam said. "Nothing sexual if you don't want it. We would never force you into something you're uncomfortable with, okay?"

"Okay," I whispered. I had learned to never trust alphas, but I believed Cam.

I gasped as he stood, lifting me in his arms and cradling me to his chest.

"I can walk," I said as I wrapped my arms more tightly against his neck. "I know I'm heavy."

Cam snorted. "I'm going to carry you if I want to, baby girl."

I blushed. He didn't seem to strain under my weight, so I bit back my protest.

Cam carried me outside where the sun was shining. It was an unseasonably warm morning for October. I closed my eyes tight and whimpered at the brightness. Omegas needed dark, cozy spaces for their heats. An outdoor pool definitely didn't meet that criteria.

"Too bright," I whined.

"I know, love," Theo said from beside us.

I cracked my eyes open and saw that he'd changed into swim trunks and had taken off his shirt. The brightness suddenly didn't feel so problematic as I took in the smooth planes of his chest.

"We could put you in the bathtub instead, but I read it might be helpful for you to move around, so we thought we would try the pool. If you get in and it doesn't feel good, we can move to the tub."

"I don't have a swimsuit," I said as Cam gently put me down, the front of my body sliding against his until my feet hit the ground. "It's still at my house." I had only packed a small suitcase since I'd only had one night's notice on the move. Also, part of me still hadn't believed it was actually happening.

"We can go to your apartment later today and get your things. For now, you can go in with your clothes or in your underwear. Whatever makes you more comfortable," Theo said.

I looked around, trying to get my bearings.

"Where's Ben?" I asked, suddenly feeling the need to be surrounded by all of them. Ben had made me so comfortable last night. I remembered laughing with him, remembered the feel of his hands on me.

"He's making what's probably going to be an absurdly large amount of food. Fair warning, he's going to make you eat as much as possible. Wouldn't want you fainting on us," Theo said with a wink.

My snort was cut off by another cramp ripping through me. My clothes felt like sandpaper against my skin and I no longer cared that the alphas would see my stomach rolls and thick thighs with stretch marks. I just had to get away from the burning.

I started pulling down my sleep shorts, but my arms and legs were trembling too badly. Cam and Theo's hands were on me instantly, helping me keep my balance. Cam pushed the shorts down the rest of the way, and Theo pulled off my shirt. I was wearing the bralette I had worn to bed.

"Come here, love, let's get you in the water," Theo murmured.

I stepped into the pool, Cam and Theo each holding an arm to keep me steady. The cool water lapped around my legs. I would have hated the temperature on a normal day, but right now, it felt like heaven. The burning subsided as I lowered myself all the way in and let out a contented sigh.

"Does that feel good?" Cam asked.

He had taken off his shirt at some point and was ever so slowly lowering himself into the water. "Shit, that's cold," he gasped.

I giggled at seeing the tough alpha with goosebumps all over his arms—his sexy, tattooed, toned arms that carried me without any problem. I was filled with a different kind of burning as I watched drops of water trail down his bare chest. It was not like me to check out an alpha, but Cam, Theo, and Ben were the exception to every rule. The longer I looked at him, the wilder my thoughts became, so I took a breath and went completely underwater, trying to sink to the bottom.

Theo had been right that the water felt good, and moving my arms and legs seemed to ease the cramping. I knew most people would tell me I was being ridiculous for not taking advantage of the three alpha dicks available to me, but I didn't want my first time having sex to be when I was out of it mentally. Right now, I still felt some clarity, but as my heat continued, things would get hazier. Letting go when I was that vulnerable terrified me.

Suddenly, I felt a warm hand wrap around my upper arm and pull me up to the surface.

"Shit, sweetheart, you can't stay under that long. You're

going to make me lose my mind," Cam said, a flash of panic in his eyes.

I bit my lip to hide my smile. "I was fine. I like being underwater."

He just grunted and pulled me into his chest. "How's the pain?"

I rested my head on his shoulder and breathed in the sweet cinnamon roll scent that made me want to lick his neck. Somehow, I didn't think he would mind, but I held back the urge.

"It's okay," I responded. "Just a little bit of cramping right now. But I don't feel like I'm burning anymore."

Theo pressed himself against my back, moving my wet hair to the side and nuzzling my neck and shoulders. "I hate to see you in pain. When is that doctor supposed to call?"

"Sam just said sometime today." I shoved down my anxious thoughts that something would go wrong again with my suppressant access. I had to trust this unknown doctor to come through.

The patio doors opened and Ben strode out, carrying a massive tray of food. My chest ballooned with happiness at seeing him. Ben felt like pure sunshine.

"I made us some food," he said, beaming.

"*Some* food?" I asked, giggling as he put down an enormous charcuterie board filled with breakfast foods—Danishes, muffins, scrambled eggs, fruit, and cheese.

"I didn't know what you would like best," he said with a sheepish grin.

He stood back up and stripped off his shirt and sweatpants, leaving him in tight black briefs. My eyes wandered down his chest to the v-line of his muscles, taking the quickest peak of his growing bulge before looking away.

"You see something you like?" Ben asked with a wink as he lowered himself into the pool and gathered me in his arms.

"You can look at me anytime you want. I'm always looking at you," he murmured.

I blushed, my insides squirming with happiness. I'd spent my entire life being told my body was ugly, but somehow these alphas wanted *me*.

"What would you like to eat, precious?" Ben asked.

I needed to eat, but my heat made it hard to concentrate on food. Ben pressed his chest to my back and caged his arms around me. As if sensing I was too overwhelmed to choose, Theo held out a pancake rolled up with bacon and maple syrup on the inside. *Culinary genius*. I went to take it from his hand, but he shook his head.

"Let me," he said, bringing it to my mouth.

The omega in me wanted to preen under his care, but I also bristled at the idea that he thought I wasn't capable of feeding myself.

As if he could sense my struggle, Ben pressed his lips to my ear. "Let us take care of you. It's not that we don't think you're capable."

Cam grasped my chin and turned my face so I was looking at him. "What did I say, baby girl?"

I whimpered at his stern tone, my insides feeling like jelly.

"Answer me," he demanded.

"You want to take care of me."

"That's right. So you're going to let us."

"Yes, alpha," I whispered. The words slipped out of my mouth before I could second-guess them.

"Good girl," Cam said with a smile, releasing my face so I could eat the pancake Theo was holding.

We worked our way through the board, the guys always ensuring I got the first bite of everything. After a while, I felt uncomfortably full and pushed away from the wall, wanting to float in the water. Ben pulled me to the center of the pool and guided me onto my back, his hands on me at all times. I couldn't remember ever being touched this much in my life, and I loved it. It was like the alphas knew how to give me all the tenderness I had craved my entire childhood.

I was weightless as the cool water lapped at my skin. Theo, Ben, and Cam stayed close, floating next to me. Their touches didn't feel sexual or demanding; they were pure comfort.

After a while, I heard teeth chattering and opened my eyes. Cam was next to me, and his lips were practically blue. I pushed myself upright and tread water.

"Oh my gosh, you do not have to stay in here with me," I said. I had forgotten they weren't running 106-degree fevers right now.

"S'fine," Cam muttered, barely able to speak as he tried to keep his teeth from chattering.

Seeing this intimidating alpha stay in a freezing cold pool just to make sure I was comfortable melted my heart. I reached out and put my arm on his shoulder to help keep myself afloat.

"I think I'm ready for the next phase of the day, anyway," I said.

"Hmm?" he responded, wrapping his arms around me and pulling me close in a crushing embrace. Part of me still felt I should resist the intimate contact, but I forced myself to relax. His cool skin felt good against mine.

"I heard something about couch snuggles," I said.

"You don't have to get out of the pool yet if you don't want to," Cam said.

"I'm feeling okay," I said.

His eyes narrowed, but his chattering teeth betrayed his sternness, and I couldn't stop myself from giggling. He growled at me playfully, holding me tight as he lifted me out of the pool. Theo was there right away to wrap me in a thick towel. I had another pair of sweatpants and a tank top inside, but I needed to get the rest of my clothes.

"I need to go to my apartment to grab more of my stuff."

"*We* are going to your apartment together," Cam growled.

I hid my smile in the crook of his neck. Cam was being a classic overbearing alpha, but somehow his treatment didn't make me feel like he thought I was weak. It made me feel cherished.

Chapter Eighteen

Ben

Josie's apartment was a small one-bedroom in a busy part of the city, making me irrationally uncomfortable. Her heat had triggered my alpha instincts and I wanted to hide her away, preferably in my bed where I could cuddle and feed her all day.

The apartment itself was... well, *minimalistic* would be a generous descriptor. The living room had a small, scratched-up coffee table and a dingy mustard-yellow sofa. There was a pile of blankets on the small living room window seat and stacks of books lining the walls. All her things seemed worn. I didn't know why it hadn't hit me earlier that my mate had been living alone with no financial support.

"How has she been affording food and basics?" I gritted out, keeping my voice low.

"Maybe her... *friend* helped her out," Theo said. None of us liked the idea of this unknown alpha.

I ran my hand down the chipped laminate countertop in the kitchen. There was barely any counter space. Maybe our kitchen would convince her to stay. We could bake together. I would feed her out of my hand, lick chocolate off every part of her body, bend her over the island and...

Theo cleared his throat pointedly as he felt my arousal through the bond. My face heated. I needed to get myself under control—I would never forgive myself if I did anything to make Josie uncomfortable. The thought was actually painful.

Josie had gone into her bedroom to pack her things. The three of us were awkwardly waiting in the living room, wanting to go to our mate but also needing to respect her desire for space. Cam grew impatient and started pacing, covering the room with just a few long strides.

"What's taking so long?" he muttered.

"It's been five minutes," Theo responded evenly, as if he wasn't feeling just as impatient.

We all waited another minute until Cam couldn't help himself.

"Josie, you alright, sweetheart?" he said through her bedroom door.

"Yeah," a faint voice said from the other side.

The three of us threw the door open before giving it a second thought. Josie was lying on top of a mattress on the floor, shivering so hard her whole body shook. She was trying to pull a blanket over herself.

"What's wrong, gorgeous?" I said, trying not to feel panicked as I pushed the other two out of the way, ignoring Cam's snarl, so I could pull the blanket over her.

"Cold," she said, her teeth chattering. She looked over at Cam. "I guess it's revenge for me laughing at you in the pool."

Cam smiled, but it didn't reach his eyes. I found more blankets in a basket by her bed and started bundling her up, wrapping my arms around her so my body heat could warm her.

"The fever can cause chills," Theo said, a pained expression on his face. "Maybe the pool was too cold."

"It felt good," Josie said. "Maybe I should just stay here." She buried herself further under the blankets.

Cam let out a growl. "Out of the question."

Josie whimpered at his harsh alpha tone.

"Shit, baby girl, that came out wrong. I'm sorry," Cam said, sitting down on the bed and stroking Josie's hair. "Your wet hair probably isn't helping with the chills. Let's see if we can get it dried, and we'll help you pack up the rest of your stuff. Just tell us what to do," he said softly.

Josie peered at Cam from the blanket nest. "Okay," she whispered, her teeth still chattering.

"Do you have a blow dryer, gorgeous?" I asked.

"Yeah, in the bathroom."

"Why don't I bring it in here and dry your hair while Cam and Theo pack?" The bathroom was just across the hall from the bedroom, and I decided to go ahead and gather all her things in a bag.

"You warming up at all, precious?" I asked when I returned, already knowing the answer when I saw her blue lips.

Josie whimpered. "I'm still cold. Why am I cold?"

I gently lifted her up into a seated position, adding some extra blankets to the mountain surrounding her, obscuring all of her except her head. She looked up at me with the most vulnerable expression.

"It must be the fever making you feel cold," I said, cupping my hand against her cheek.

It felt like I had won the biggest prize in the universe when she leaned into me. Her face was hot to the touch and her cheeks were flushed. *Is it okay for her to be covered in blankets? Should we try to cool her down?* My chest clenched with anxiety, echoing what my brothers were already feeling. I took a deep breath and focused on what I could do in the moment, vowing to read everything about omega heats when we got home. Last night I hacked my way into old online archives on suppressants and heats that the government replaced with their propaganda, but I hadn't had a chance to read them yet.

"Let me dry your hair and you'll feel better."

"I can dry my hair," she said as she closed her eyes, still leaning her face into my hand.

"I know you can, but it would make me happy to do it."

I honestly didn't think she could do it right now with how she was shaking, but I also knew that it was important for her to be independent. I was ready to bond her, to make the connection I already felt permanent, but she didn't feel that way yet and I would respect her pace.

I plugged in the blow dryer and started working on her hair in sections. Her hair was soft and brown with golden highlights. Getting to care for her filled me with a sense of purpose.

"How are you so good at this?" she whispered, her eyes still closed.

"My sisters taught me all the important life skills," I said. A lump formed in my throat at the familiar sadness of being separated from them after we left North Woods.

"The omegas?" she asked quietly.

"Yeah," I responded.

"Do they all have packs?"

"They do. The youngest one, Lilah, tried to hold out for a while, but, well, you know. She bonded with her pack after we'd already left North Woods." I hated not knowing if Lilah had found a good pack and it killed me that she would never get to meet my mate.

Josie hummed in response. I finished drying her hair while Cam and Theo packed the rest of her things, including a small stack of books on her nightstand.

"Are these all romance books?" Cam asked as he placed them in a duffel bag.

"Um, yeah," Josie said, sounding shy.

"You and Theo have a lot to talk about," Cam said with a chuckle. Now it was Theo's turn to blush.

"You read romance?" Josie asked, her eyes popping open. Theo threw Cam a dirty look as he grumbled out a yes.

"What's your favorite?" Josie asked, her voice perking up. Theo noticed the change in her tone and smiled, moving closer to where she was sitting on the mattress.

"This is actually one of my favorites," he said, picking one of the books out of the duffel.

"Wait, really? Mine too. I can't stop re-reading it."

Josie and Theo looked like they were about to launch into a long book conversation. *Fuck, she's perfect for us. A book nerd who loves to bake and is sexy as hell.*

I met Cam's eyes over Josie's head. He wore the biggest shit-eating grin, and I knew he was feeling it, too. Just then, Josie shivered, and her teeth started chattering again.

"You done with her hair?" Cam asked me gruffly, his smile falling. I nodded, throwing the hairdryer in the duffel.

"Okay, sweetheart, you and Theo can talk about books when we get home." Cam leaned down and scooped Josie up, taking her blanket pile with her. Theo and I looked around to make sure we'd gotten everything before zipping up the bags.

"I didn't know it would feel like this," he said softly, staring after Cam and Josie. His eyes were filled with longing, and I knew he was taken with this sweet omega.

"I know," I responded. "The idea of her not being with us is painful."

Even now, I felt like I was being pulled to follow her and Cam. Theo looked at me with understanding, and we swiftly followed them out of the apartment and down to the car.

Chapter Nineteen

Cam

Holding Josie in my arms as I headed back to the car felt like heaven, but her suffering felt like hell. I was still kicking myself for growling at her back in her room. I was stressed as fuck that our mate was in pain. I had the overwhelming urge to comfort her, protect her, fuck her. *You are not fucking her. At least not yet.*

I carefully maneuvered us into the backseat of the car, keeping her held tight to my chest.

"How're you feeling, baby girl?"

"It's hurting again," she whimpered.

"You're breaking my heart," I murmured, wishing I could draw her pain into my body.

I barely looked up from her as my brothers joined us in the car.

"Josie, gorgeous, how're you feeling?" Ben asked as Theo peeled out from the curb faster than usual.

Josie was beyond speaking. Her breaths were getting more labored, and her whimpers intensified.

"I knew she shouldn't have left the house. It's too much

exertion," Theo growled, his knuckles turning white on the wheel as he drove faster. "She should be in a nest for her heat. She needs the suppressants now."

The panic and despair running through the bond overwhelmed me as Josie choked out, "It hurts, it hurts," tears streaming down her face. I held her tighter, gently stroking her hair, and shot a panicked look at Ben, who was turned around in the passenger seat, his eyes glued on our omega.

"What do I do?" I mouthed to him. I was failing her. She was in my arms, crying in pain, and there was nothing I could do to help. Ben shook his head, looking helpless.

"You two need to get a grip," Theo hissed out. "Calm down and focus. We're almost home, and then we'll get her more comfortable."

The last five minutes of the drive were unbearable. By the time we pulled into the driveway, Josie was screaming from the pain.

The second he parked the car, Theo opened my door and reached in to grab Josie, but I growled at him, refusing to let her go. Theo clenched his fists but backed off.

"Get a bath started with hot water," he said to Ben, who took off in a sprint towards the front door. Theo grabbed Josie's things out of the car and I carried her in, hoping that a hot bath would work some sort of miracle.

A shrill ring cut through the air as we walked up the stairs.

"Thank fuck. It's her phone," Theo said, pulling it out of his pocket. "Wait, don't hang up," he said quickly to the person on the other line. "This is Josie's phone."

There was silence for a moment. "Josie, love, did Sam give you a code word to identify yourself to the doctor?"

Josie's eyes fluttered open. "Um, yeah, it was..." she moaned and clenched her hand to her stomach. "God, I can't think clearly. The codeword is *cupcake*."

I left Theo to manage the phone conversation and rushed Josie into the bathroom. Ben was lighting candles to line the tub so we could keep the lights off.

"Let's get you in the bath," I said after testing the temperature of the water. Ben and I gently stripped off her clothes, leaving her bra and underwear on. Josie seemed to have left lucidity behind, and I was worried she wouldn't be able to stay safe in the tub. I stripped down to my underwear and got in, sitting behind her to hold her up.

"The doctor's coming now. She's an omega," Theo said, keeping his voice low as he entered the room.

"How is that possible?" Ben asked, moving to the side of the tub so he could stroke Josie's face.

"She's from Sol, apparently, and did her training there. She and her pack live just down the road and should be here in a few minutes."

Chapter Twenty

Josie

I felt like someone had reached into my body and ripped my insides out.

Please, just kill me.

"Can't do that, baby girl."

I started. Had I said that out loud? Where was I? My eyelids felt like they weighed a thousand pounds as I opened them. The room was almost pitch black, the darkness only broken by flickering candles. I realized the warmth surrounding my limbs was water. I was in the world's largest bathtub, my head resting on Cam's naked chest. Sitting next to us outside the tub were Theo and Ben.

"I keep waking up with you holding me," I mumbled.

"Didn't want you to drown, sweetheart. Also, don't want to let you go," Cam responded, his lips right by my ear, making me shiver.

"Josie, love, we just talked to the doctor and she's on the way over to give you suppressants," Theo said. His hand gripped the edge of the bathtub, his knuckles white.

"No, I don't want the doctor. He hurts me," I whined, panic

washing through my body and intensifying the cramps even more.

"What doctor hurt you?" Cam asked angrily.

"At the DA," I whispered. Cam's growl vibrated through my body.

Theo reached out and cupped my face with his hand. "It's not a doctor from the DA. This is the doctor Sam knows, remember? And she's a woman."

I heard Theo speaking, but the words weren't registering. My core clenched, feeling painfully empty. Their scents were so delicious, and my hormones screamed at me to just sit on a dick to make the pain disappear. I didn't feel like myself and was scared of what I would say aloud. Memories of *that* doctor's hands on me flooded my mind. *Can't think his name. That will make it real.* But all I could feel were hands on me and alpha scents surrounding me. *Unsafe, can't let anyone close.*

"Don't touch me," I whimpered, jerking away from Theo's touch and pushing against Cam's body. I moved to the opposite side of the bathtub.

Cam reached out towards me, and in that moment, his arms belonged to someone else. To the alphas I never let myself think about. The ones who had haunted my dreams for years. I cried out and pressed my back against the tub, splashing water onto the floor. Cam's expression was stricken as he got out of the tub.

Being alone in the bathtub didn't ease my panic. Even though I'd wanted to be alone, I felt rejected. Now all I wanted was for my alphas to hold me close. I curled into a ball, the water coming up to my shoulders, confused and overwhelmed.

"The doctor just pulled up, love," Theo said gently, his voice breaking through my panicked fog. "Is it alright if I bring her up? If she gets here and you want her to leave, just say so."

"Wait, the doctor is a woman?" I asked, startled. Only male alphas could be doctors.

"Yes, I spoke to her. She's coming here to help you." He kept his sentences short as if he knew I was floating in and out of lucidity.

I nodded, keeping my eyes closed.

"Josie, this is Dr. Angela Walker. She wants to talk with you for a minute," Theo said a few moments later. "I'm going to turn on a lamp."

Standing in the doorway was a woman who looked to be in her mid-thirties with straight black hair, golden skin, and a matching set of hot pink loungewear.

"Are you sure she's a doctor?" I mumbled, barely able to keep my eyes open.

"Hi, Josie. Yes, I trained in Sol as a doctor before moving here. Please call me Angie. I've been out of town and just got back, which is why I'm dressed like this," she said, gesturing at her outfit. "One of my old colleagues knows your friend Sam, and I've been working with Ms. Raven through the Alliance for quite some time. I believe all omegas deserve to make their own choices about their bodies. I want to talk for a few minutes to see how I can best help you."

Another cramp surged through my body and I did my best to hold in my scream. My alphas moved in closer as if they could do something to protect me from the pain. I finally processed what the doctor had said and sat up a bit with a jolt.

"Did you say... your pack?"

"Yes, I'm an omega and I have a pack of two alphas. We live down the street. One of my alphas is waiting downstairs," Angie said, sitting down next to the tub.

"Your alphas let you be a doctor?" I whispered, filled with awe at this no-nonsense omega sitting in front of me.

Angie smirked. "They know better than to stop me from

doing what I want. They're very supportive. Omegas are just as capable as any other designation and it's time the world caught up. Now, I can see you're in a lot of pain. I haven't had a chance to fully review your chart, but I understand this is your first heat and you've been on suppressants for the past year."

"Yeah. I ran out a few days ago."

"When did your heat start?"

"Last night, just after midnight," Ben responded.

Angie nodded. "I was able to get injectable suppressants, which are stronger than the oral variety. This shot will last three months and will shorten your heat and make it more manageable to get through without being knotted."

"How much will it shorten and what does manageable mean?" Cam gritted out. I vaguely noted that he was standing further away, closer to the door.

"It's hard to tell, but suppressants usually stop a heat within two days. You'll still have cramping, but nothing that will cause permanent damage or require medical care. I also have pain medication that I plan to inject to help with the cramps you're experiencing since I couldn't get here earlier. I can also give you a birth control injection."

I nodded, wondering what the guys thought about babies. Because I was a firm *no*.

"What else can we do to help her the next couple of days?" Theo asked.

"Baths are great if she feels up to it. She probably won't want to eat much, so make sure to give her lots of small snacks and plenty of water. Nesting is still critical. Have you been able to make a nest yet, Josie?"

"No," I whispered. "Don't know how." What if everyone had been right that I was defective? What if I made a nest incorrectly? Then my alphas would know something was wrong with me and kick me out. I whimpered at the thought.

"There's no right or wrong way to make a nest," Angie said gently. "Your omega will let you know what she likes and what makes her feel safe. Trust her to guide you. I also wanted to mention that even without being knotted, physical touch from alphas can be very soothing. It's not a requirement if you don't feel comfortable. Remember, you are in control."

Angie spoke with such authority I almost believed her.

"I like them touching me," I slurred out.

"Why is she talking like that?" Ben said, a hint of panic in his voice.

"Omegas reach a point in our heats where we're not quite lucid. Let's get her the injections now before she's too far gone. These do need to be injected into your buttocks, so I'll need you to get out of the tub."

I dreaded having to move. Angie grasped my forearm to help me keep my balance, my other hand resting on Ben's shoulder. Theo was at my side immediately with a huge towel and helped pull me out of the tub. Cam was still standing near the doorway and I frowned, wondering why he was so far away.

Angie was quick with the injections, but they still burned, and I clung to Theo for support. Once it was over, Theo gently guided me onto a stool and I leaned on Ben.

"I need a moment alone with Josie," Angie said firmly. Ben growled, the vibration rocking through my chest and sending a burst of slick into my cold, wet underwear. "This is non-negotiable—it will just be a few minutes," she continued, not remotely deterred by the three territorial alphas.

"It's okay," I whispered, patting Ben on the arm. "I'll talk with her."

After a long hesitation, Theo spoke. "We will be right outside the door, love." He caressed my face and reluctantly walked out of the room, taking Ben and Cam with him.

Once they were gone, Angie lowered herself to the floor so our faces were level. "Josie, I'm sure this has been completely overwhelming, and I'm so sorry you didn't get the care you needed earlier. You are my patient now, and I will ensure you get through this heat as comfortably as possible."

"I don't want to inconvenience you."

"You are absolutely not. Us omegas have to stick together, right?" she said with a smile. "I know Amirah helped set you up with this pack. Do you feel safe with them? If not, we can send someone to stay here with you if you feel you need protection."

"I... I feel safe. Or safe enough. I just feel like I'm such a burden to them and everyone." I swiped at the tears falling down my cheek.

"You are not burdening anyone. You have people who care about you and want to make sure you're okay. I can say with confidence that you are certainly not a burden to these alphas." Her lips quirked into a smile.

"What do you mean?" I asked, confused.

"Those three overprotective alphas out there are clearly completely taken with you. Being an omega is hard, but we have great instincts. So, Josie, what are your instincts telling you?"

"They feel safe to be around," I whispered, still convinced a reality TV show host was going to burst out of the walls at any moment to tell me I'd been pranked and none of this was real.

"Have you felt unsafe around alphas before?" she asked gently.

"Most alphas are unsafe."

"I'm so sorry that's been your experience. It shouldn't be that way. All you need to focus on right now is getting through the next couple of days comfortably and safely."

I was nervous about revealing too much to Angie, but this might be my only opportunity. "I have a question."

She nodded reassuringly.

"They told me we're mates, but I can't feel it. I mean, I felt comfortable around them pretty much from the start and I'm attracted to them." I felt like my face was on fire. Why was this so hard to talk about? "But I'm not sure what else I'm supposed to be feeling."

"There's no test we can run to see if you're mates. We do know that taking suppressants will suppress some of that instinctual reaction. That blocking effect will wear off after you stop suppressant use. Unfortunately, there's no way for you to know for sure until then."

I appreciated her straightforward answer. The knot in my chest loosened at the confirmation that the guys hadn't lied to me about suppressants blocking my ability to recognize them as mates.

Angie gently placed her hand on mine, holding my gaze for a few long moments. "I know what it's like to be hurt by alphas and how scary it is to let go and trust. Those three out there have to earn your trust. I also know how easy it is to hold yourself back from something good out of fear... or because you don't think you deserve it. You deserve goodness, Josie. I hope you'll let yourself have it."

My throat tightened. I couldn't believe how kind this stranger was being.

"Thank you," I whispered.

"Remember, I live right around the corner. You have my number. Reach out if you need anything. I'll call tomorrow to check in on you and see how you're doing."

"You don't have to do that."

"But I'm going to. You're not alone in this, Josie. I'm part of your team now."

"Okay," I said, smiling. I still wasn't sure this magical take-charge omega wasn't a figment of my imagination, but it was safe to say I was obsessed.

"Alright, I'm sure those alphas are about to break down the door. Let's bring them back in so they can take care of you, and I can return to my grumpy alpha, who is currently very irritated I made him stay downstairs."

I giggled as Angie opened the bathroom door. Ben ran in and gathered me in his arms. I heard Angie say the medication would make me tired and to let me sleep as much as possible. My eyes closed of their own volition, and the last thing I remember was inhaling Ben's apple pie scent before losing consciousness.

Chapter Twenty-One

Theo

"Why hasn't she woken up?" Ben hissed for the one-hundredth time as he paced around Josie's room.

Josie was curled up in a tight ball in the center of the massive bed, her messy hair and flushed cheeks the only part of her visible under the blankets and pillows we'd piled around her.

"You're going to wake her," I hissed, my irritation growing as I sat beside the bed. "Dr. Walker said she should sleep a lot, so please just sit the fuck down."

Ben wasn't the source of my irritation—I was frustrated with myself, with the helplessness I felt. I'd pulled up countless articles about suppressant-assisted heat, and all said the same thing: excessive sleep was normal and to be expected.

But what if she is sleeping too much? It's been twelve hours. Something is probably wrong, and she needs you to get on the bed and wrap your arms around her tightly and...

A growl slipped through my clenched jaw. Ben shot me a dirty look, but I focused on Josie, who had stirred. Her eyes were still closed, but she started to slowly stretch, her arms pressing against the pillows we'd laid around her.

Last night, after I'd carried her to bed, the three of us awkwardly stood around, unsure of what to do with the cozy nesting items we had gathered. None of us knew shit about making a nest, as evidenced by the messy piles surrounding my mate right now.

Josie let out a soft sigh as she blinked her eyes open. She looked around, her little nose scrunching up in confusion. *Fucking adorable.*

"Morning, love. How are you feeling?" I asked softly, holding myself back from crowding her.

"Where am I?"

"In your room, precious," Ben replied. "We brought you here after you fell asleep in the bathroom last night."

Josie had a slightly dazed look. I wondered if she was always this groggy when she woke, and I couldn't wait until I was the one waking up beside her, giving her little kisses while we were both half asleep.

Her sweet voice jolted me out of my daydream.

"Um... why are there piles of blankets and pillows on the bed?" she asked, her cute nose scrunching again. I wanted to kiss it. Fuck, I hardly recognized myself. I'd never felt like this, never had someone I wanted like this.

"Angie said you would feel more comfortable in a nest, so we made you one," Ben said enthusiastically.

Josie looked around again at the bed. "You made this... nest?"

"Is there something wrong with it? Do you not like it?" Ben asked, his face falling.

"Oh no, it's not that. It's... really nice," Josie responded carefully.

She and I made eye contact, and I quickly had to look away

to keep from laughing and crushing my brother's beaming expression.

Clearing my throat, I asked again, "How're you feeling?"

"Much better than yesterday," she said, pushing herself up to a seated position. "Cramps are really light and I don't feel feverish."

"Angie called earlier this morning while you were still asleep. She said for us to call and let her know how you were feeling once you woke up," I said.

"Where's Cam?" Josie asked, eyes searching for him.

Ben and I looked at each other, unsure of how to respond.

"Last night, when you were in the bathtub with him, you got upset and didn't want anyone to touch you. He's worried he upset you," I said carefully, deciding being direct was probably the best course of action.

Cam was off in another part of the house, sulking. After we'd gotten our omega settled, he had pummeled the punching bag in the downstairs gym for hours. Nothing Ben or I said could calm him down.

"I'm really sorry if we made you uncomfortable. None of us will touch you without your permission," I added.

"But I... I don't really remember last night," she said. She was shifting the blankets nearest her on the bed and I could scent her agitation.

"Please don't stress, gorgeous. We can leave you alone if you would prefer that," Ben said, clearly having picked up on her anxiety as well.

Josie's head snapped up from where she was diligently rearranging the blankets. "You want to leave?" she asked, her voice containing the edge of a whine, tears gathering in her eyes.

Fuck! Fix this!

"No!" Ben and I growled, causing Josie to shrink back and burst into loud tears.

"Go get Cam," I quietly growled at Ben so Josie wouldn't hear. For a moment, Ben looked like he was going to argue, but when Josie's sobs got louder, he quickly ran out of the room.

"Josie, love, please don't cry," I said softly. "We're not going to leave if you don't want us to."

Josie didn't respond. She was buried by blankets, whimpering quietly. I had no fucking clue what to do, but I couldn't leave her alone. Desperately hoping I wasn't making things worse, I crawled to the center of the bed and peeled back the blankets until her face was visible. Her eyes were screwed shut and tears leaked down her cheeks.

I took a deep breath to calm myself down before gently wrapping my arms around her. I ran my hands up and down her back, trying to soothe her. Her sobs quieted down and she curled closer to me, rubbing her face against my neck and breathing me in. I didn't know if it was intentional, if she even knew what she was doing, but my mate had just scent-marked me for the first time. Joy and possessiveness welled up inside me, and I pressed my face to her hair. *She's mine and I'm never letting her go.*

"I'm sorry I'm such a mess," she said, trying to pull away.

"You have nothing to apologize for," I said, tucking her head under my chin. Her scent was still intoxicating, even with its bitter edge. "I've got you, and I'm not letting you go."

Josie's breath hitched as she relaxed into my hold. "Is Cam mad at me?"

"Of course not, love."

"But he's not here, and I was rude when he was just trying to help me."

"It's not rude to let us know what you need or to tell us to back off when you need us to. We want you to express yourself. Cam feels bad because he thinks he hurt you, but that's his problem. You did nothing wrong."

I gently gripped her chin and pulled away just enough so I could lift her face and look into those beautiful green eyes.

"But it's my fault," she said, her eyes filling again with tears.

"It's not your fault. You have to be honest with us."

Josie's brows furrowed in confusion, as if she couldn't quite believe what I was saying. I forced myself to wait in the silence, keeping my breathing steady. And then she gave me the tiniest of nods.

A smile teased at the edges of my mouth. "Now that you've agreed to be honest, what do you think of your nest?" I asked.

"Well, it's very sweet that you made it for me," she said diplomatically.

"You being honest with me?" I growled.

She giggled, and it was the sweetest sound I'd ever heard. I felt myself breaking out in a broader smile than I could remember.

"Okay, so it's... not good."

I laughed. "Tell me how to fix it, sweetheart. Dr. Walker said you need to get lots of rest and stay comfortable for the next few days, so we need to fix this..."

"Disaster," Josie supplied, to my delight.

"Don't let Ben hear you say that, love," I said with a wink.

"We better fix it quickly then," she said, pulling away from me. I reluctantly let her go, helping her into a seated position before sliding off the bed. Josie's gaze snapped to mine, and to my horror, she was tearing up again.

"Angel, what's wrong?" I asked, trying and failing to keep the edge of panic out of my voice.

"You said you wouldn't leave," Josie cried, her lower lip trembling.

"I'm not leaving," I almost shouted, frantically looking around the room as if a *How to Stop Fucking Things Up and*

Upsetting Your Omega You Dipshit manual would appear. Josie's tears turned into sobs as she curled up in the bed again, bringing her knees to her chest in a defensive position. Acting on instinct, I threw myself back in the bed and crushed my omega close to my chest. Almost immediately, Josie stopped crying.

"You... didn't want me to leave the bed?" I asked hesitantly, wrapping her hair around my hand so I could keep her head pressed into my neck, her rapid breaths warm on my skin. She shook her head, keeping her eyes squeezed shut.

"I'm so sorry I upset you. Fuck, I keep doing everything wrong. Everything I read said alphas are supposed to wait until their omega finishes building their nest and then only enter with permission. I left the bed not because I wanted to but because I thought you would prefer it. I would never let you out of my arms if it were up to me."

"Never?" Josie whispered.

"Never."

"You'd get bored."

"Nope. Could never be bored around you."

Josie was still, and I held my breath, hoping I hadn't said the wrong thing. "What if I wanted to sit around and watch baking shows for twelve hours?" she asked, her voice *almost* teasing.

"You ask as if that would be torture. I'd hold you tightly just like this for all twelve hours."

"Wait, really?" she asked, pulling back and looking at me suspiciously.

"Yes, really."

"What if I wanted to peruse the romance section of a book-store all day?"

"I'd peruse right along with you, but of course, I would also find all my favorite books and whisper the dirtiest parts in your ear all day long." *Until you were so wet, you begged me to bend you over the nearest book display and fuck you until you screamed.*

Josie's lips parted in surprise before she smiled and relaxed into me.

"I'm sorry I panicked. My emotions are totally out of control," she said quietly.

"So much has happened the past couple of days. Your body is going through a lot. Of course, it's overwhelming. You never have to apologize for that. I'm sorry I keep fucking things up."

"No, you're not. You're all being too sweet. I keep messing up being an omega," she said, pressing her face against my chest again so she didn't have to look me in the eye.

"There's no way for you to mess this up, love," I said.

She didn't realize how serious I was, how she already had us completely wrapped around her finger.

"Now, how do you want to make your nest?"

"Oh," she said, looking around at the disorganized mess around us. She pushed herself up to a seated position. This time I didn't allow any distance between us, pulling her onto my lap, my arms circling her waist.

"I'm supposed to make my nest on my own. So I guess you should move off the bed?" Her voice was laden with uncertainty as she twisted in my lap to face me.

"Do you want me to move off the bed?"

She shook her head and I couldn't stop myself from bringing my hand to her face, gently cupping it and brushing the briefest kiss over her lips. It had been ages since I'd kissed someone, and the feel of her lips against mine sent butterflies in my stomach.

"Then I won't move an inch."

Josie looked a little dazed. "But this isn't the right way to do this."

"The right way is whatever feels best for you. If anyone makes you feel otherwise, you let me know and I'll throttle them."

"You might have to let me go to do that," she said seriously. It took me a minute to recognize that my mate was, in fact, teasing me. I couldn't stop the huge smile that broke across my face, stretching muscles I hadn't used in a long time.

"Are you doubting me? I would keep one arm around you and use my other hand to throttle them. No problem." Josie giggled and my cock hardened to the point of pain. Josie shifted her ass on my lap, making me groan. I was worried I had made her uncomfortable when she shot me a mischievous smile, her eyes twinkling.

"You're trouble," I growled as I winked at her. "You better fix this nest quickly before Ben comes back. He was bragging last night about what a great job he did."

Josie grinned as she instructed me on which blankets and pillows she wanted to keep and where to move them, making small adjustments to their position until somehow everything came together, creating a cozy nest with space in the middle to cuddle and little walls around the sides to give a sense of protection. My perfect omega had made the perfect nest and hopefully, when she felt more comfortable with me, I would fuck her in it for hours on end.

I was lost in my fantasy when I noticed Josie kept adjusting and re-adjusting the same throw blanket, her movements growing more unsettled.

"What's the matter, love?"

"Something's not right and I can't figure it out," she said in a small voice.

"It looks beautiful to me. You did such a good job," I praised.

"No, I didn't. It's wrong!" Josie grabbed a pillow and threw it across the room.

She turned to look at me, eyes wide in shock, like she couldn't believe her outburst. I thought her tantrum was cute and would have smiled, except I was afraid she might cry again. The paperwork Angie left said one of the side effects of suppressed heats was "volatile mood swings."

The door opened and Ben walked in with a sullen, sleep-deprived Cam on his heels. Ben immediately threw himself onto the bed, apparently not giving a fuck about nest rules. He lay down on his side next to us and placed a firm hand on Josie's thigh.

"Looks like you two did some rearranging to my master-piece of a nest," Ben said cheekily, clearly not reading the room. Josie's bottom lip trembled and Cam stood frozen by the door. I felt his anguish through the bond. My brother was always so worried about causing anyone harm, of turning into his asshole alpha father.

"Gorgeous, what's wrong?" Ben asked, finally catching on.

"The nest isn't right," Josie whimpered.

The three of us looked over the nest, and I could tell none of us had a fucking clue what was wrong. In fact, my inner alpha preened that we had such a beautiful, clever mate to build a perfect nest. Ben pulled Josie out of my arms so she was lying half on top of him. I growled my displeasure at him stealing my mate before lying down and sandwiching Josie between us.

"This is better," she mumbled. "Need all your scents in the nest."

"We'll get you some of our clothes if you want them," Ben said.

"Yes, please, but not right now. This is good. Except..." She lifted her head and locked eyes with Cam.

"I should go," he said gruffly, reaching for the door.

Josie whined and the three of us stiffened.

"You don't want me?" she asked.

"What? Of course I want you, but I never want to do anything to hurt you. And I did that last night. I failed you," he said, hanging his head in shame.

Josie shifted out of my and Ben's grasp, crawling to the edge of the bed. I tried and failed to look away from where her oversize t-shirt—one of mine, I thought smugly—had ridden up, revealing the creamy, soft thighs I wanted to bury my face into.

"You didn't do anything wrong. I was overwhelmed. I'm sorry I hurt you," Josie said, tears starting to fall.

Cam growled and quickly covered the ground between the door and the bed, tenderly gripping Josie's face with both hands.

"You never apologize for telling me what you need. Do you understand?"

"Yes, alpha."

Arousal shot through the bond as my brothers and I groaned.

"Will you come into my nest?" she asked sweetly. I could feel Cam's stress and trepidation melt away.

"I would be honored, little omega."

Josie beamed and Cam moved onto the bed, lying between Ben and me. He pulled Josie on top of him, pressing a gentle hand to the back of her head. I cupped her thigh and gave it a squeeze, causing her to let out a whimper.

"You belong here," Cam murmured.

Josie sighed and made a contented noise, snuggling deeper into Cam's chest, her eyes drifting shut.

Chapter Twenty-Two

Josie

Cam's hand trailed up and down my thigh, the movement slow and unhurried. I let out a happy sigh and pressed my nose to his neck, loving the feel of his bare skin against mine. I didn't see any reason for my alphas to wear shirts. Or pants. I hadn't seen them without underwear, but honestly, that could probably go too, right?

I let out a little giggle, noticing how much more settled I was compared to the last time I woke. The nest felt cozy and secure, and I felt calm and cared for with my alphas pressed against me.

Not my alphas.

I tried to remind myself that they weren't mine, but the words felt hollow.

Cam noticed I was awake and tugged me even closer, gripping my thigh firmly in a move that made me feel warm and tingly. Ben grumbled and scooted closer, pressing himself to my side and curling one hand around my waist.

"You have to learn to share," Ben said, his tone adorably sleepy.

"I think fucking not," Cam murmured into my ear. I shivered, suppressing the urge to grind against him as heat pooled in my core.

"Cranky cinnamon roll," I mumbled to Cam.

"Did you just call him a cranky cinnamon roll?" a sleepy Theo asked, amusement in his voice.

"Mmm, yeah," I said, still not opening my eyes.

"What does that mean?" a disgruntled Cam asked.

"You smell like a warm cinnamon roll. So yummy and sweet, just like you."

Ben and Theo burst out laughing, but when I cracked my eyes open, Cam smiled as he tucked me in close against him.

"Only sweet for you," he murmured before flipping off his brothers.

"What do I smell like to you?" Ben asked, nuzzling my neck.

"Not telling. You made fun of Cam's scent."

"Nooo, you wouldn't punish me like that, would you, precious? I want to know," Ben whined.

I smiled into Cam's chest. "You'll just have to be patient."

Ben let out a long-suffering sigh that made me freeze.

How could you say no to an alpha?

Not safe.

Not safe.

My omega cringed, waiting for the punishment to come.

"Wait, no, it's okay. I'll tell you if you want to know, don't be mad," I whispered.

A long silence followed, and my heart beat faster.

"Precious, I was just playing around with you," Ben finally said, his voice soft. "Just teasing. I'm not... I'm not angry or anything."

My scent turned bitter as I lay perfectly still on Cam, waiting to see if Ben would change his mind and lash out.

"Will you tell me my scent if I get you food?" Theo asked.

The subject change was abrupt enough that I looked at him. Theo's eyes were narrowed with concern, but his smile was teasing.

"Then Ben will be the only one who doesn't know." He winked at me.

"Seems a little mean," I said, but the tightness in my chest was fading. I said *no*, and nothing terrible happened.

"Nah," Cam said. "It's what he deserves for laughing at me."

"Theo laughed too," Ben exclaimed indignantly.

"Yeah, but you're the one who needs to learn to be patient," Theo said, his eyes sparkling. He leaned forward and kissed me on the nose.

"Shouldn't you smell like tea?" I asked. "It's more British. But you smell like coffee."

Theo grinned. "Coffee?"

"Mmm, like really good coffee on the best cozy days," I sighed.

Theo leaned in to kiss me, his smile evident against my lips.

"I'll get you some coffee, angel," he murmured as he kissed down my jaw. "What else do you want to eat?"

"I'm not really hungry." I didn't want food. I wanted more of *this*. More of my alphas touching me, kissing me.

"You need to eat to keep your strength up. I'll bring different snacks and you can choose," Theo said, giving me a final kiss on the forehead and leaving the room before I could argue.

Ben's hand caressed the small of my back, and I automatically stiffened before forcing myself to relax. I knew Ben wouldn't hurt me, but the fear of retribution was ingrained in me.

"I didn't mean to scare you," he said, his voice unusually solemn.

I turned my head to face him. He smiled tightly before reaching out and brushing my hair out of my face. The smooth glide of his hand continued as he threaded his fingers through my hair, massaging my scalp. My shoulders softened as the minutes passed in silence.

"We like to tease each other, but I promise it's not serious. I would never lash out at you, never get angry at you for telling me no." Ben's voice was quiet. Soothing. "It's really important to me that you know that," he added.

"It's going to take a little while... for me to believe that. It hasn't been my experience with alphas," I whispered.

Cam growled, but the vibrations somehow settled me.

"Fuckers deserve to die," he grunted.

"You can tease me anytime you want," Ben said as he stilled his hand on my neck, then leaned forward until his face was inches from mine. "Now that we've gotten that settled, you're going to tell me what my scent is, right?"

"Insufferable," Cam muttered, taking me with him as he rolled onto his side so his back was to Ben.

Ben's head popped up over Cam's shoulder, his face so indignant I couldn't help but giggle. His face broke out in a huge smile upon hearing my laugh.

"Prettiest fucking sound in the world," Cam said, a tender expression on his face. He leaned in for a gentle kiss.

I tried to ignore the obvious hardness pressed against my stomach and the way it made my vagina clench as another wave of slick drenched my underwear. *Good grief, this is so obnoxious.* I needed some sort of absorbent underwear if this kept happening. At least Ben and Cam weren't drawing attention to it, even though I knew my scent was filling the room.

Before I could do something embarrassing like grind myself

against Cam, Theo returned with one of those fancy breakfast-in-bed trays. Cam's gaze was heated as if he knew what I'd been thinking, but he didn't push it as he helped me sit up against the headboard.

"Sorry we messed up the nest," he said, referring to the tangle of blankets and pillows after our nap.

"It's okay," I said as Theo placed the tray over my lap. I meant it. The nest was saturated with their scents, which my omega felt was the most important part. I could rearrange the blankets later.

I absentmindedly ate some cheese and crackers. I realized I hadn't seen any bond marks on the guys. Alphas who formed a pack could choose to bond with each other even before they found their omega. Many alphas waited, and some alphas chose to never bond with each other. These guys were so close and had been a pack for so long that I was surprised they hadn't bonded.

"Why aren't you guys bonded?" I asked as Ben stole a piece of chocolate from my tray.

Theo blushed and bit his lip. The whole lip-biting thing almost succeeded in distracting me from his chagrined expression.

"What?" I asked when none of them answered my question.

"Who says we're not bonded?" Cam asked.

I raised my eyebrows. "Where are your bond marks, then?"

Ben groaned, covering his face with his arm. "It's too early for this story."

I glanced over at the clock on the nightstand. "It's three o'clock in the afternoon."

"Well then, I'm way too sober for this story," Ben grumbled, trying to shove Cam to the side so he could get closer to me.

Cam was not having it and pushed him so hard he almost toppled out of bed.

I scowled at Cam's antics, but he just smiled and kissed me on the cheek.

"That was cold, brother. Cold," Ben growled, popping back up in a seated position.

"I don't know why you're acting embarrassed," Theo said. "It was your fucking idea."

"True," Ben said, a mischievous glint in his eye. He pulled my legs onto his lap and started massaging my calves. "But I also distinctly remember being absolutely wasted, and you two went along with it."

Theo rolled his eyes and put his arm around me. "We bonded once we left North Woods. One night, we got really drunk and just went for it. Maybe not the smartest decision in hindsight, but we were sad and alone and, I don't know, guess we wanted the emotional connection." He pressed his face into my hair and my heart twinged at how vulnerable he sounded.

I wanted to ask more questions about why they left their community, but I held back. I could tell it was a tender subject, and they hadn't pushed me to share about my past. I hoped they would tell me when they were ready.

"So, where are your bites?" I asked, studying their bare chests as if the marks would pop out at me. Also, it was an excuse to stare at their bare chests.

"Remember that we were drunk. And Ben thought it was fucking hilarious," Cam grunted.

"What can I say? I wanted to be a pain in their asses for life," Ben said with a wide grin.

It took me a minute to register his words. "You bit each other in... the butt?" I asked. Usually, bond marks were placed on the neck or in a similarly visible location.

"Don't knock it 'til you try it," Ben teased.

"Fine, maybe I will," I flirted back.

I stilled, realizing what I had said. We hadn't had a conversation yet about bonding. I was scared to let myself think about what it would be like to be connected to my alphas' emotions in such an intimate way. I'd never thought I would be good enough for a pack like this.

Ben smoothed over my mini internal freakout with a sweet kiss on my forehead.

"Just putting it out there that I would like my next bond mark to be highly visible where everyone can see it," he said, lips brushing against my ear.

I shivered, eyeing his neck as I imagined myself sinking in my teeth, marking him forever. The thought sparked something low in my belly.

Cam grunted. "The healing process was a bitch."

A sharp laugh burst out of me as I realized what he was alluding to. Bond marks needed to be tended to by licking the bite for several days. Imagining the three alphas, stone-cold sober, having to drop their pants for each other and lick each other's ass cheeks was too fucking much. My laughter increased until tears were streaming down my face. Theo moved the tray out of the way and then tackled me.

"You think that's funny?" he growled, his eyes bright.

I quickly schooled my face into a not-even remotely convincing serious expression. "No, not at all. Nothing funny about this. Nope."

"Brat," Cam said, a smile stretching across his face.

"You need to eat more," Ben said, snagging a bowl of strawberries for me. I tried to eat a few, but my cramps returned and I finally pushed them away.

"You full?" Cam asked, his brows furrowed as he stared at the almost untouched tray of food.

"My stomach hurts," I said. "I just want to lie down."

They didn't look happy but didn't push things further. Cam settled me back on his chest, and I absentmindedly traced the outline of his abstract tattoos. My body felt worn out, but I wasn't sleepy anymore. A little spark of curiosity grew. I hadn't seen any evidence that the guys were... intimate with each other. But if they had bitten each other in the butt, maybe they were?

"I can hear you thinking way too hard about something," Cam said.

I pushed myself up on my forearms. Cam's eyes were closed and he wore a blissed-out, relaxed expression. He gave my leg a little squeeze as if to encourage me to say what was on my mind.

I opened my mouth but then hesitated.

"You can ask us anything, love," Theo said, running his hand down my arm.

My cheeks grew hot.

"Now I fucking have to know," Cam said, taking in my blush.

I cleared my throat. "So have you all ever... you know?"

"Ever what?" Ben asked, his face buried in the blankets.

"Have you ever been *together* together?" I blurted out before hiding my face in the crook of Cam's neck. His chest shook with laughter.

Theo cleared his throat. "Are you still hungry? You need more food." He moved as if to leave again.

"Wait, no, you don't get to change the subject," I squealed, throwing myself across Theo's body to prevent him from getting up. Now that I'd asked, I needed to know.

"There's nothing to tell," Theo said, but his blushing cheeks suggested otherwise.

I turned my gaze to Ben, who was being surprisingly quiet.

"Ben," I purred, "You're going to tell me, right? You wouldn't hide something from me."

Ben burst out laughing. "Are you trying to play me, precious? Because it's totally working. I'll tell you if you give me a kiss."

Suddenly, the heat I'd been keeping at bay flooded me full force. I crawled to Ben and straddled him, shocking even myself with my boldness. His gaze was heated as I lowered my face to his, reveling in the feel of his lips brushing against mine. Ben wrapped a hand around my neck, deepening the kiss. His hold on me was light, always giving me the choice to pull back.

I allowed myself to get lost in the kiss, letting out a whine as he nipped my bottom lip. His hardness rocked against me and I shivered, my thighs warm and wet with slick.

"Fuck, that's hot," Theo groaned out.

Oops. I forgot Cam and Theo were literally on the bed with us. I pulled back, nervous they would be jealous, but all I saw were their lust-filled gazes. My eyes dragged down their bodies to the large bulges in their sweatpants.

Ben gripped my chin and forced my gaze back to him.

"Do you want to come, precious?"

I nodded with a little whimper. The pain wasn't nearly as intense as yesterday, but the desire was still there—the need to have their hands on me, to feel that same pleasure I had with Cam.

Ben's hands traced my hip and side, moving down to squeeze my butt. Suddenly, he flipped us so I was underneath him. I let out a surprised cry that turned into a moan as he moved his hand to my mound, gently pressing through my clothes.

"Can I touch you here?"

I gasped out a yes, craving his touch. He slipped his hand

under my clothes, parting me to run his fingers through my wet slit and circle my clit.

I felt like I was on fire.

Cam pressed against my side, kissing my face and breathing deeply. "You smell fucking edible, baby girl. I bet you're all warm and wet for Ben. Are you going to come on his fingers?"

I gasped and writhed, the dirty talk almost as hot as what Ben was doing. My legs trembled and my skin flushed.

I wanted more, wanted everything.

Ben continued circling my clit, building intense pleasure that had me arching off the bed. Then Theo's hand was on my thigh, pressing me to the bed. I didn't know when he had moved to my other side, but I was glad he did—I wanted all their hands on me.

My orgasm built. I noticed the same feeling as last time—as if I were about to jump off a precipice into the unknown. Then Ben pressed the tip of his finger into my entrance and I flinched, the pleasure inside me turning icy cold.

Ben noticed and paused, gently pulling his finger out. "You don't want that, gorgeous? That's okay, I won't, promise."

Chills ran through me, a cold sweat breaking out over my skin as blurry flashes of memory of Glen and Dr. Bishop standing over me, fingers inside me, flickered before my eyes. Suddenly I felt like I was gagging on the scents of rotten fruit and burnt plastic. I rolled into a protective ball, my eyes closed shut. Logically, I knew I was in a warm bed with three caring alphas, but I could almost feel the cold steel of the exam table underneath me, the smell of antiseptic cutting through Cam, Ben, and Theo's scents. Scents that had turned bitter in the last few moments.

I forced myself to open my eyes. I needed to be prepared for their anger.

You're defective, unlovable.

But all I saw was their caring concern. Ben looked devastated—shoulders shaking with emotion like all he wanted to do was scoop me into his arms.

"I'm so sorry," he said softly. He was sitting up now, and all three of them had pulled back to give me space.

I took a few deep breaths, the panic that had gripped me so instantly loosening its hold. I didn't know what to say, so I settled for holding my hand to Ben. I knew he hadn't meant to trigger me and I wanted to put a smile back on his face, to bring back the playful energy we'd had just minutes ago. I also felt strangely sad at the loss of their touch. They were being thoughtful by giving me space, but my omega whined at their withdrawal, the feeling of rejection rolling through me.

Ben gently placed his hand in mine. "Please don't cry," he said. "I'm so sorry. I didn't mean to hurt you."

Tears rolled down my cheeks and it pissed me off. I was surrounded by the three sweetest, hottest, tastiest alphas I had ever met. I wasn't going to let my abusers take away this experience.

I wiped my tears. "I want to keep going." My voice was a little shaky, but I was confident in a way I hadn't felt in years.

"Sweetheart," Cam said with all the tenderness in the world. I had a feeling he was holding himself back from gathering me in his arms. But I didn't want gentle cuddles right now. I wanted my second-ever orgasm.

"No, I want to keep going," I repeated, meeting Ben's gaze. This time, my voice sounded strong and sure. "I got triggered by having your finger... umm... you know. Just not ready for that yet." My voice petered off.

Why couldn't I be as confident as Poppy when talking about sex? During one of our self-defense classes, she had given us a graphic play-by-play of heat sex with all five of her alphas.

Westin and I blushed so hard I thought we might both spontaneously combust.

"You want to continue?" Ben asked quietly.

"Yes, please," I said. If I was ever going to get close to these alphas, I needed to tell them what I wanted. "Oh, um, only if you want to," I added hastily.

Ben's lips twitched, and a smile slowly broke across his face. "Yes, please, beautiful."

The alphas seemed even more nervous than I was as they slowly lay down beside me, Ben pressed tightly to my side. I tensed, unsure if he would jump right back to where we left off. Instead, he pulled me in for a kiss. It was unhurried, his soft lips coaxing mine open and soothing the ragged edges of my anxiety. Ben moved his kisses down my body, his mouth hot against my skin.

Theo caressed my face, leaning towards me with a question in his eye. I closed the space between us, our lips connecting in the sweetest kiss. Theo had an awed smile on his face as he pulled away. He was the shyest of the three, which bolstered my confidence. I threaded my fingers through his hair and pulled him in for another kiss as Ben slipped his hand under my underwear. A little jolt of anxiety ran through me until Cam stroked his hand down my hip.

"Good girl," he said. "So brave for us, so beautiful. Just relax, sweetheart, and let Ben make you feel good."

My orgasm built slowly, Ben's fingers circling my clit in a steady rhythm. I panted, arching off the bed as my pleasure built. I forgot about cold tables and alpha smells that made my stomach turn as I let myself get lost in their touch, building until my orgasm crested over me in a gentle freefall. Ben's fingers slowed, his hand cupping my mound and pressing steadily as little waves of pleasure continued to roll through me.

Ben removed his hand and gathered me up in his arms.

"Thanks for trusting me, precious," he said, kissing me softly.

I pressed closer, hoping my touch conveyed my gratitude even as words caught in my throat. Cam and Theo curled around me until I was surrounded by their comforting warmth. I didn't know how long we stayed like that, but a heavy blanket of peace fell over me. I had never imagined I could be this comfortable with my alphas. A little jolt of realization shot through me.

They were *mine.*

Chapter Twenty-Three

Josie

For the first time since my heat began, I was alone in my nest.

I hated it.

What is wrong with you? You've been alone for approximately three minutes. Since when did you become so codependent?

"Shut up," I groaned at the critical inner voice, a painful cramp gripping me. I didn't care how unreasonable I was being. I was vulnerable and in pain and I needed my alphas here, dammit.

Cam got an emergency call this morning from one of their employees, resulting in a lot of cursing and grumbling before he reluctantly left to see to the crisis. Ben had cleared the mostly untouched lunch spread he'd prepared and was putting it away in the kitchen. Theo cryptically said he "needed to get something" and left me here. Alone.

My uterus cramped again and I whimpered, curling up in a ball. I knew the suppressants were working, and without them I would likely have ended up in the hospital. But that didn't do anything to comfort me when my insides felt like they were on fire.

My hand brushed against something soft and I lifted my head to see what it was. It was a folded-up knitted blanket. I shifted so I was propped up against the headboard and unfolded it.

What the hell? It was the ugliest blanket I had ever seen. It looked like it had been knit by a color blind two-year-old. But something about it made me want to curl up with it. It smelled just right and was knitted with a super soft yarn. I rubbed it against my cheek before tucking it around me and curling up in the center of the bed.

The door opened and my heart leapt as Theo walked in. He wore black sweatpants and a soft gray t-shirt that clung to his muscular chest. His rich coffee scent washed over me and the tension drained from my body.

When he didn't immediately come into the nest, I forced my eyes away from their perusal of his body. Theo was holding something behind his back and shifting side to side, barely meeting my gaze. Were his cheeks flushed?

"I got something for you," he said, running his hand through his hair.

My omega perked up. "Like a courting gift?"

So far, the guys had given me candles, bath bombs, and the massive, fuzzy blanket I had wrapped around me. Growing up, I had never been given gifts, even when other kids got them on birthdays and holidays. When I was little and asked why I didn't get presents on my birthday, my parents told me I didn't deserve gifts just for being born. If I worked to be a better omega, I might be lucky enough to one day have alphas who would give me gifts.

I hated how much I wanted gifts from the guys. I didn't want to be too needy, too stereotypically omega. Designation traditionalists often talked about how omegas were too easily swayed by gifts, leaving us open to bribery and corruption. That was one of the many reasons we could never serve in leadership positions or hold jobs. There was also the nagging fear in the back of my head that anything my alphas gave me came with strings attached, although more and more, that argument didn't make sense to me.

"Umm... maybe?" he responded.

I raised my eyebrows, feeling impatient. Slowly, Theo brought his hands in front of him, cheeks flushing further to a dark crimson.

I stared at it. He stared at it. Then we stared at each other.

"You got me... a dildo?" I stammered.

"It's not just a dildo, technically. It also vibrates and can... um... move."

Theo looked like he wanted to run from the room, which somehow put me more at ease.

"You want me to use a vibrating dildo?" I stared intently at Theo's face, refusing to look at what he held for fear of bursting into flames.

"I... I just got it for you in case you wanted to use it. You might already have one. But I just thought, just in case..." He paused and ruffled his hair for the third time in thirty seconds, muttering an embarrassed curse to himself before dropping his hands. If it was possible, his cheeks grew redder. "I can take it back. But you can also take it. I mean, not *take it* like that. Well, of course you *can*, that's what it's for." Theo looked hopelessly lost, then his expression morphed into shock as the dildo began to vibrate in his hand.

"Shit!" he flung it away and it landed next to me on the bed, where it kept making a furious buzzing noise. We both watched it for a moment, wearing twin expressions of shock before we burst into laughter.

"Come here," I said, patting a spot next to me in the nest.

Theo picked up the dildo and turned the vibration off before sitting down stiffly next to me with the dildo in his lap. Unfortunately, it was positioned over his crotch, making it look like he had a huge erection. I covered my mouth but couldn't stop a giggle from escaping.

"Fuck, I'm terrible at this," he said, setting the dildo on the nightstand and scooting down into a more relaxed position. He draped his arm over my shoulder and I snuggled into him.

"You're not terrible at this," I responded.

He arched an eyebrow.

"Well, maybe you are," I said with a smile. "But so am I, so that's okay."

"It's not just a random gift," he said. "I did some research on what can help with suppressant-assisted heats. I know you've been in pain all day." He squeezed me closer. "Apparently, using something like *that* can help reduce the cramps."

I pressed my face into his chest as a happy warmth flowed through my body.

"I can't believe you did that for me," I said.

"Of course, love. Anything for you." Theo ran his fingers through my hair, and I wanted to purr. Theo might not be as demonstrative as the other guys, but he was thoughtful and paid attention to the little things.

"Can I see it?" I asked hesitantly.

Theo handed it to me, and I reached out to touch it. Sex toys were strictly forbidden for omegas, and I'd never held one before. I was told from an early age that alphas wanted pure omegas and that sex toys were a fast route to becoming used goods.

"It's really big," I said finally, wrapping my fingers around it. I couldn't imagine it actually fitting inside me. I knew, in theory, that omegas were built to take large penises and knots, but this seemed excessive.

"I wasn't sure what size to get. There were a lot of options," Theo mumbled.

I looked over at him and said in what I hoped was a flirty voice, "Did you get it to match your size?"

Theo blushed, but then his face transformed into the cutest smirk I had ever seen. "No, love, this is a size *small*."

Wait, was he serious? He was bigger than this? My eyes bored into his crotch as if I would develop x-ray vision and magically see through his pants. He cleared his throat, and I jolted.

"Do you need to see a comparison?"

Now he was the one flirting with me. My face grew hot. My omega was screaming at me to take him up on the offer, to ask him to pull his cock out of his pants and let me run my hands over it to see its size and shape. But what I actually said was, "I'll take your word for it."

I put the dildo down on the bed and leaned on his shoulder. I felt more lucid now, but I guessed the cramping would return with a vengeance. Everything inside me ached with need and I felt so empty. The thought of putting it inside me was becoming more appealing. And now I was thinking about what Theo was packing and putting *that* inside me.

He picked up my hand and started playing with it, tracing his fingers over mine. As the shock of Theo's present wore off, tendrils of concern snaked through my chest. The guys didn't have any experience with omegas, so maybe they didn't understand what would happen if I used a sex toy. I fidgeted with the corner of one of the blankets and tried to gather my thoughts enough to verbalize my concern.

"Theo, won't this break the inner barrier?"

Theo looked at me with confusion. "What are you talking about?"

"You know, the inner barrier," lowering my voice. "Would this prevent us from bonding? An alpha needs to break it the first time."

Theo looked bewildered. "Angel, I'm not sure what you're talking about. Can you explain a bit more?"

My hands felt sweaty. "Omegas have an inner barrier inside us when we're virgins. When we have sex for the first time, the alpha breaks the barrier. If the barrier is already broken, your bond won't be as strong when you do have sex with your chosen alphas. If I use the dildo, it will break my barrier, and then if we all decide to bond, it will never be as strong."

Theo squeezed my hand. "Who told you that?" he asked carefully.

"It was drilled into me by my parents since puberty, and then they taught us all about it in our anatomy class at the DA. Why?" I asked, apprehension creeping into my stomach.

Theo started to say something when Ben burst into the bedroom. "Why was I not invited to the party?" He threw himself onto the bed without a care, then made a face.

"What's this?" he asked, pulling the dildo out from underneath him with a huge grin.

I groaned and flipped over onto my stomach, burying my face in the blankets. A meteor was more than welcome to hit me any moment now and take me out.

"It's nothing," Theo said. Ben didn't answer, and I could imagine Theo gesturing furiously to get across what was happening. I tried burying myself further into the bed so I could shut the world out.

A tender hand stroked down my spine and a warm, crisp apple scent surrounded me.

"Didn't mean to make you embarrassed, precious," Ben murmured as he lay beside me.

The bed shifted as Theo lay down on my other side, sandwiching me between them.

"Is this okay?" he asked, brushing my hair away from my face.

I nodded and opened my eyes to meet his gaze. My face still felt hot.

"We don't have to continue our conversation, love," Theo said. His eyes were filled with such tenderness, and it hit me again how caring these alphas were. I could trust them to tell me the truth.

"Was what I said not true?" I whispered, almost afraid to hear the answer.

"What were you two talking about?" Ben asked, his voice gentle as he continued stroking my back in a soothing rhythm.

"Can you tell him?" I asked Theo, knowing I wouldn't be able to say it again.

"Josie told me she's been told all her life, including at the DA, that omegas have a barrier inside of their vagina that has to be broken by an alpha or they won't be able to bond properly."

Ben's hand stilled on my back and I waited for him to say something. When the silence stretched on, I shifted my head to look at him. Ben looked confused, his eyes locked with Theo as if they were having a silent conversation. My omega wanted his eyes on me. On instinct, I reached out my hand and gently cupped his face. He leaned into my touch and let out a long exhale.

"I've never heard that," Ben said carefully, bringing his gaze to mine.

"It's not true, love," Theo said, kissing the back of my neck.

A sick feeling worked its way through my stomach, chest, and throat, squeezing me until I could barely breathe.

"Oh my god, I'm so stupid," I sobbed.

"No, don't say that," Theo soothed.

"I believed them! My whole life. You must think I'm the most idiotic person you've ever met."

Theo and Ben pressed their bodies tightly to mine, making twin sounds of protest. Being sandwiched between them was the only thing preventing me from having a full panic attack.

"Of course you would believe them," Theo said. "It's not your fault. They were the ones in the wrong for lying."

"I'm sure you're not the only one who thought they were telling the truth," Ben said in a hoarse voice.

"If it's not true, why did they do all those exams?" I choked out, and the sick feeling in my stomach redoubled.

Ben looked at me with concern. "What... *exams*?"

"Every month, we had to submit to a pelvic exam to check for virginity."

I tried to block out the memories, but they flooded me and pulled me back to the forced examinations. Those times at the beginning where I had fought them and they had strapped me down to the table. The sadistic doctor who wanted to cause me pain by being rough and inserting multiple fingers inside me without lubrication. Why had I believed what they said? Why had I never questioned it?

Theo let out a strangled sound. "They did *what*?" His voice had a dangerous edge that sent a thrill of fear through me, and I whimpered.

At the sound, Ben and Theo entangled my legs with theirs and stroked my face, hair, arms... any skin they could touch.

"Not mad at you, love," Theo said quickly. "They never should have done that to you. Never."

Their steady breaths and firm hold settled my body, but my mind was racing. What other lies had I believed about myself? About omegas in general? Suddenly, something else dawned on me. Cam had been shocked when I said I'd never masturbated. Did that mean...

"Is... is it..."

Shit. I didn't know how to get this question out. My face was flaming red, and part of me didn't even want to know the truth. My omega snarled. We had been told lies about us, about our needs, about alphas. She was pissed.

"You can ask anything," Theo said. "We'll never judge, never mock you. Promise."

I took a deep breath. I still half expected their ridicule, but my need for answers was at the forefront right now.

"What happens if omegas masturbate?" I finally blurted out.

"I'm guessing the answer you're looking for isn't 'they orgasm?'" Ben said, planting tender kisses down my cheek.

"What have you been told?" Theo asked, his tender touch on my hair a contrast to the anger permeating his scent.

"That omegas aren't allowed to come at all before we bond with alphas and we should never touch ourselves. If we do before we bond with an alpha, we'll never be able to bond as deeply. And then, once you're bonded, your alphas are the only ones who can make you come."

Hearing myself say the words out loud made me realize how absurd it all sounded. Somehow, it seemed so logical and scientific when I was at the DA.

Theo and Ben sat in silence. *Well, I guess that's my answer.*

"Why would they lie about that? Just so they had another excuse to punish us?"

Anger flared in my chest. I had been invaded, punished, and controlled by alphas who got off on my subjugation, and now others knew more about my body than I did.

"What punishment?" Ben choked out.

Flashes of memory assaulted me again. I didn't want to talk

about it, didn't want to remember. But part of me wanted to share. I didn't want to keep the DA's secrets anymore.

"If they found out an omega had, *you know*, they would burn her fingertips. Every morning, we had to line up for inspection to make sure we were following all the rules. They said they could smell it on us, but we also suspected they had cameras everywhere. If they caught someone, they would burn her in front of us."

Ben growled, grasping my hand and flipping it over to examine my fingertips.

"They never because I never..." I mumbled.

I was ashamed of how thoroughly the DA stamped out my rebellious tendencies. Where was the omega who talked Sam into teaching her how to drive and stayed out all night hurtling down back roads? Where was the omega who pulled pranks on teachers growing up? I felt her loss so profoundly. Tears gathered in my eyes.

Ben tenderly kissed each finger and then planted a kiss on my palm.

"I hate them," I said.

"Us, too, precious," Ben murmured.

The two of them kept stroking and kissing me, murmuring sweet, soothing words as I tried to detangle my emotions. My eyelids fluttered closed, heavy with exhaustion as my alphas' scents swirled around me. Before I fell asleep, my anger and sadness gave way to determination—determination that I wanted to reclaim some pieces of myself that the DA took and embrace what Ben and Theo were offering me.

Chapter Twenty-Four

Ben

Josie's scent settled as she slept between Theo and me. Her scent had been all burnt sweetness during our conversation, and I hated it. Hated her suffering, hated what those fuckers at the DA had done.

"This all started because I brought the vibrator to help ease her cramps," Theo whispered.

"Will that work?" I asked. My alpha roared with anger that our mate was in pain, furious we weren't doing anything to stop it.

"I've been going through those research articles you dug up. One suggested that using the vibrator while surrounded by alpha pheromones can ease cramps."

My heart broke as I thought about the exams and punishments Josie had endured. "They assaulted her," I hissed. "Every month. Just because they could."

I knew the two of us were imagining all the punishments we could mete out to the DA staff. I usually hated violence, but my alpha and I agreed: we would find the ones who hurt our mate and destroy them.

Later. Our mate needs us right now.

Theo and I lapsed into silence. At some point, I dozed off, jumping awake when I heard a whimper. Josie squirmed as Theo pressed himself to her back, trying to soothe her. Her cheeks were flushed and her hair tousled. I could imagine waking up with her like this every morning, except she would be trembling with desire. I would pull her close, part her legs, and slide home so tenderly, holding her before we were fully awake.

I shifted so I was flush against Josie's soft body. I hoped I wasn't crowding her too much, but I couldn't stand any distance between us.

"You alright, precious?" I asked, brushing my hand through her tangled waves. Her scent was so potent I had to breathe through my mouth so it didn't throw me into a rut. I couldn't even imagine what her scent would be like without the suppressants.

"I need..." she gasped out in a whine. "I need..." She tangled her hands in my hair, pulling me in for a desperate kiss.

"What do you need? Anything you want, we'll give it to you," I said between kisses.

"Feel empty," she whined.

"Do you want to try the vibrator, love?" Theo asked softly. "It should help with the cramps."

Tears streamed down her face, and helplessness rose in me, almost choking in its intensity.

"Yes," she said, pressing her face to the crook of my neck and breathing in deeply.

"How about you start with your own fingers, beautiful? That way, you can see there's nothing there, no barrier," I suggested. I remembered how scared she had been when I had pressed my finger just the slightest bit into her. I had a feeling she needed to be in control of this experience.

"I don't know if I can," she said, her glassy eyes meeting mine.

"You can, precious. Can I pull these off?" I asked, tugging on the waistband of her sweatpants.

Josie bit her lip. "I guess that's kind of essential."

Her scent had an acidic edge to it, and I bristled at the thought of doing anything that made her uncomfortable. Theo solved the problem for me.

"Do you want a blanket over you?" he asked.

Josie let out a deep breath and smiled. "Yeah, if that's okay."

"You're in charge of this," Theo said firmly, turning Josie's head so she met his gaze.

Her lips parted and her pupils grew as she gave him a nod.

I grabbed a blanket from the side of the bed and placed it over her lower half before tugging again at her waistband. She nodded and I slipped her clothes off, leaving her bare under the blanket.

"You're doing so well, such a good girl," I murmured, kissing her nose.

Theo stroked her back, pressing little kisses to her neck. I gently took her hand in mine, moving slowly so she had time to pull away. When she stayed relaxed, I slipped our hands under the blanket and guided them to her pussy, holding in my groan as our fingers ran through her hot slick. I willed my dick to chill the fuck out. *This is so not the right time to be turned on as hell.*

"You can do it. Just move your finger to your entrance. Feel it there?"

She nodded.

"Now, just ease one of your fingers in."

I felt her finger disappear inside her and I had to swallow a moan.

"I... I don't feel anything there," Josie said softly. "What if my fingers aren't long enough?"

"You could try the vibrator?" I suggested.

Josie paused, tension lining her shoulders. Then she took a deep, shuddering breath, gripping my wrist before whispering, "Will... will you check for me?"

"Of course," I grunted. "But only if that's what you want and you're sure."

"I'm sure. I trust you both," she said, arching back into Theo. He gave her one of his rare smiles, tilting her head back so he could kiss her.

I moved my fingers to her entrance and realized she had tensed up again. I changed tack, cupping her pussy with my hand and gently pressing the heel of my palm against her clit. She squirmed against me and I continued playing, circling her clit with my fingers. She was drenched with slick, the scent of her pussy making me grow harder than I thought possible. She was pure sex and sweetness. I would never get enough of her.

Her body tensed and her breaths came faster. I knew she was close to coming. I kept up a steady rhythm until she came with a small cry. Her legs shook with the aftershocks of her orgasm, and she pressed her face into my chest.

"So good," she breathed out.

I smiled with satisfaction. I had given my mate this pleasure and wanted to give her more. I placed my finger at her entrance, just holding it there. When she stayed relaxed, I finally eased into her channel. My finger slid in until it was seated as far as it could go.

"I don't feel a barrier, beautiful, just your hot, wet pussy gripping my finger," I almost growled.

"You feel so good," she said. "I didn't know it could feel good." There was awe and grief in her voice.

I pressed my forehead against hers, swallowing against the

lump in my throat. I wished she had never experienced a single bad thing. As I pumped my finger slowly in and out of her, I was struck by the fact that I loved her.

My mate, my omega, my girl.

I loved Josie.

The feeling overwhelmed me and filled me with warmth and joy.

"Open your eyes, precious," I whispered.

Her green eyes met mine and didn't break away as she came again, her pussy clenching around my finger.

Nothing would get better than this moment. I wanted to tell her how I felt, but didn't want to overwhelm her.

I removed my finger, bringing it to my mouth and sucking down her sweetness.

Her eyes widened, fixed on my fingers and mouth.

"Pure sweetness, precious. The best taste in the world."

She whimpered, wiggling her hips.

"You need more, beautiful?" I asked, kissing her gently.

"Yes, more," she said.

I smiled at her demanding tone. She could demand anything she wanted from me.

"Are you going to let Theo use the vibrator on you? Let him slide it deep into your pussy, fill that emptiness inside you while he plays with your clit?"

Theo swore, shifting her so she faced him.

"You want that, angel?" he asked.

"Yes, please touch me, Theo. Make me feel good."

Theo groaned, grasping the dildo. He kissed Josie deeply, running his hand down her body. I marveled at how not-weird this felt. There was no jealousy, just joy at their happiness.

Theo tugged at the bottom of Josie's shirt, a question in his eyes. Josie immediately covered her stomach protectively, and he backed off, kissing her softly on the cheek.

"Is it okay if I touch you over your shirt?" he asked gently.

Josie nodded, waiting a few long moments before uncovering her stomach. Her stomach was so soft and luscious, and I wished she was comfortable with her body, but one thing at a time. That she trusted us to be with her in bed, to touch her at all, was a miracle.

Theo moved slowly, cupping her breast. When Josie arched into his touch, he tweaked her nipple. I couldn't hold back, doing the same on her other side. Her nipples poked through her tank top. I squeezed them before lowering my mouth and sucking them through the material.

Theo moved the dildo under the blanket, the wet noises telling me he was running it along her pussy.

Josie whimpered, and I lay down beside her, kissing her face and throat.

"Ready?" Theo asked.

Josie nodded. "Yes, please," she said, arching her hips.

Theo slipped the dildo in and Josie made a strangled sound, throwing her head back on the pillow. A fire could burn through the house, and I wouldn't be able to tear my eyes away from the pleasure on Josie's face. Her slick made obscene wet noises as Theo moved the dildo in and out.

"I need... something," she cried with a whimper.

Theo's brow furrowed. "I think this will help. Can you shift on your hands and knees for me?"

I could almost imagine Theo reading an article that said presenting for alphas was shown to help omegas during suppressed heats.

Josie nodded, and we helped her get into position, keeping the blanket around her. Her arms immediately collapsed under her, and she lowered her head and shoulders to the bed, her ass pointing high in the air. The two of us groaned and palmed our cocks. Our omega was presenting for us.

"What a good girl, our good omega," Theo murmured. He curled around Josie's back, snaking his hand around to continue pumping the dildo.

"Does this thing vibrate?" I asked, almost giddy as I lay down next to Josie and stroked her hair. Her eyes were glazed over, arousal permeating her scent.

"How could I forget?" Theo responded. I locked eyes with him and knew we were perfectly united. I felt closer to him than I had in years.

Josie's scream told me he had turned on the vibration.

"That's right, let us hear all those sweet cries of yours," I said, pumping my cock.

Theo wrapped his arms around Josie's waist and pulled her upright onto her knees. I moved in front of her, giving in to temptation and sucking her other nipple into my mouth, drenching her tank top. One day, she would trust me to undress her. I couldn't wait.

"You have the prettiest breasts I've ever seen, the sweetest nipples," I said, running my tongue over the opposite nipple.

Josie groaned, tangling one hand in my curls and the other around Theo's neck as she came again with an orgasm so intense, she would have collapsed on the bed if not for us holding her. Theo pulled the dildo out of her pussy and set it back on the table. My mouth watered, and I had the urge to suck the slick off the toy.

We ran our hands slowly down Josie's body, trying to help her come down from her orgasm. I tilted her face to see how she was feeling and was alarmed to see tears in her eyes.

"Thank you," she said, lip trembling. "Thank you, thank you."

"You don't have to thank us," I said, my throat tight. "That was the fucking hottest thing I've ever experienced."

Josie gifted me with a blissed-out smile. We settled her back into the nest, Theo grabbing a wet cloth to clean her up.

"How're you feeling, love?" he asked tenderly. Josie laid her head on his chest and took a shuddering breath.

"Overwhelmed. But in a good way," she responded.

A sound downstairs signaled Cam was home. I smirked, imagining his reaction when he came into the room that was absolutely fucking drenched with our mate's well-pleasured scent.

Chapter Twenty-Five

Josie

I stared at myself in the bathroom mirror. I'd just showered, blow-dried my hair, and even applied a touch of makeup. I looked... *happy*. It was hard to even recognize the emotion on my face after the past few years of torture.

My heat had broken last night after my playtime with Ben and Theo, and I blushed thinking about it. I dropped my towel, wondering if my body had changed this past week. I bit my lip, hesitating before reaching my hand down to cup my vulva.

I'd had Ben's fingers inside me, and Theo had brought me to orgasm with a vibrating dildo. I expected to feel different somehow, but I still felt like the same omega. A little smile quirked on my lips. An omega who might be addicted to orgasms.

My hand moved up to my stomach. For a moment, I fought the urge to check my side profile to see how much my stomach was jutting out today, but in the end, I couldn't stop myself. I hadn't eaten much during my heat, but somehow my stomach looked as huge and flabby as always. I sucked in, trying to make my stomach flat, but it refused to yield.

I faced the mirror head-on again, trying to shut down the cruel voices playing their familiar berating script. Why couldn't I have a normal omega body—thin and beautiful and perfect like all my friends? It was completely unfair. But then... I'd gotten to spend the past week with three incredible alphas. Maybe I wasn't so unlucky after all.

Shoving aside the panic I felt about my body, I pulled on the shirt Ben had given me—one of his—and a pair of underwear. The shirt was baggy, making me look even larger than I was. But then I remembered the lust in Ben's eyes when he handed it to me with a whisper that he couldn't wait to see me in his clothes.

Be brave. Go out there with confidence.

I gave myself one more look in the mirror before heading out of the bathroom. Ben was lying in bed—Theo and Cam had left to get us all breakfast from their favorite cafe. I told them I was feeling well enough to go out, but they insisted on me staying in bed.

Ben propped himself up, a wicked smile spreading across his face as he raked his eyes down my body. His eyes were heated, and I couldn't stop my blush. I walked towards the bed, adding what I hoped would be a sexy swing in my hips, before crawling onto the mattress.

Ben held his arms out, pulling me flush with his chest. The moment I was in his arms, my anxiety melted away.

"You are so sexy," he murmured, reaching down to cup my ass. "How did I get so lucky?"

I pressed my face into his neck, scent marking him. I thought being out of heat would make me less possessive, less needy for their touches, but none of that had faded.

"One of your courting gifts is arriving in about an hour," Ben said.

I flushed, thinking of Theo's gift yesterday. Was it wrong that I still wanted more?

"Unless you don't want any presents. I'm sure we could return it," Ben said teasingly at my lack of response.

I popped my head off his chest, my bottom lip automatically jutting into a pout. "You would take my presents away?"

"I don't know, precious. Didn't seem like you were interested."

"No, I am," I blurted out. "What is it?"

"Hmm, I'm not sure if I should ruin the surprise."

"No, I think you should," I said eagerly.

"The guys will be angry at me... but I suppose I could handle their anger if you give me something in exchange."

"What do you want?" I asked suspiciously, taking in Ben's gleeful expression.

"I want you to mark me," he said, a slight blush creeping up his neck.

I raised my brows. Did he mean...?

"Umm... like a hickey," he clarified.

Now it was my turn to grin. "You want me to give you a hickey?"

"Right here," Ben said, pointing at a spot high on his neck.

My heart fluttered, and my omega preened with happiness. It hit me that she was ready to bond these alphas. She wanted to see her mark on them permanently. I knew I wasn't there yet, wasn't ready, but marking Ben in this way? Yes, that's something I wanted.

"You drive a hard bargain," I murmured, grinding myself against his hard cock. "But I guess it's a fair trade."

Ben's eyes sparkled with delight, his grip on my backside tightening as I lowered my lips to his neck and started nipping and sucking. The taste of him was everything. I soaked up his scent as I sucked harder, wanting to make sure everyone would see my mark on him. He groaned, cupping the back of my head, holding me to him as he breathed me in.

"Feel what you do to me, precious? This is all for you." Ben thrust his hips into mine, his cock rubbing deliciously against my clit. I pulled away, examining my handiwork. A deep red mark adorned his neck and I smiled, wiggling happily.

"How does it look?" he asked, eyes hooded.

"Like you're mine," I responded without thinking.

Ben's lips parted and his expression turned tender. His fingers were featherlight against my face, running down across my lips before he captured them with his mouth. I got lost in his kiss, the taste and feel of him like lightning through my body. I tangled my fingers in his curls and tugged on them, needing to keep his face close to mine.

"Feels so good," he gasped before nipping my bottom lip.

I whimpered, needing more.

"I've got you, precious," he said, moving his hand down my body.

I arched into him as he tweaked my nipples, the hint of pain increasing my pleasure. My underwear was drenched and I perfumed, my scent filling the room. Ben licked the column of my throat and groaned. I was beyond reason, beyond coherent thought. All I knew was that I needed him closer to me, needed more of him.

"We need to stop," Ben said between deep kisses.

I nipped his lower lip in protest and shook my head. He gripped my hips firmly, trying to hold me still on top of him, but all he did was increase my arousal.

"We need to stop so you can eat breakfast and then get ready for your present."

The reminder that I was getting a gift helped me break through the fog of lust. I planted one more kiss on his lips before pulling away.

"What's my present?" I asked eagerly, trailing my hand down Ben's smooth chest.

"You're so dangerous," he said, a smile on his lips. "We'll never be able to deny you anything."

I flushed with pleasure.

"Our friend Jewel owns a boutique. She's coming over so you can pick out things for your room and get clothes and other stuff." He trailed his hands down my arms, his touch raising goosebumps on my skin even as a sick feeling settled in my chest.

"Who is Jewel?" I asked, trying to keep my voice even, but my omega felt vicious. Who was this woman and how did *my alphas* know her?

Ben's brow furrowed in confusion, scenting my anger. Then a slow smile broke across his face.

"Jewel is just a friend. She's an alpha. We've known her for years, but there's never been anything between us."

I sniffed. I guessed that was acceptable.

"You feeling jealous, precious?" he asked, pressing little kisses all over my face.

"No," I said.

"Mmm, of course not."

"Wait, Jewel is an alpha?" Female alphas were among the rarest designations, second only to male omegas.

"Yeah. She's also part of the Alliance."

Just then, the bedroom door opened and Cam and Theo walked in.

"What do we have here?" Cam growled, swiftly moving to pluck me from Ben's grasp and settling me in his lap, my back to his chest.

"Missed you, sweetheart," Cam said, kissing my forehead.

I snuggled into him, a smile tugging at my lips. He had missed me after being gone for less than an hour. Cam always wanted to be the one holding me, touching me. But we hadn't done anything sexual since my first morning here. A spark of insecurity formed in my stomach. Did he not want me the same way?

I leaned against him, turning so I could press my nose against his chest. As I shifted, I felt his hardness against me and scented his arousal. I took a deep breath. He wanted me. I could *feel* that he wanted me. Was he holding back to be careful, or was there something else?

"We have a surprise for you today, love," Theo said, kissing me gently before pulling food out of the brown paper takeout bags.

Ben and I exchanged looks. He shook his head as if to stop me from tattling on him.

"You told her?" Theo asked, exasperated.

"What?" Ben gasped in mock innocence. "I would never."

I burst out laughing.

"She coerced me!" Ben said. "I'm not good under duress."

"Duress!" I shot back. "As *if*. You wanted to tell me."

Ben winked, ignoring Cam's growl.

"What the fuck is that?" Theo asked, lifting Ben's chin and taking in the hickey.

"A gift from my omega," Ben said smugly.

Cam tightened his hold on me, twining his fingers in my hair. I glanced up at him, worried he was upset.

"You can mark me anytime," he whispered in my ear. "In fact, I might insist on it."

Theo handed me a container piled high with waffles, home fries, and scrambled eggs.

"What are we going to do with you two?" he asked, affection suffusing his voice.

"Feed us, tell us we're pretty," Ben responded, digging

through the bag until he found his breakfast. "Yes! Pancakes! One of these days, I will figure out this recipe."

"Have you always been this insufferable?" Cam asked Ben before turning his gaze back to me. "We can kick him out of the pack, sweetheart. You just say the word."

I grinned. "Let's keep him for now."

I took a bite of a waffle and did a little happy dance at how good it was.

Cam grunted and grasped my hip to still my movements.

"Oh! Sorry. I'll get up so you can eat breakfast," I said.

"No," he grunted.

"No?"

"No. Want you here." He punctuated his words with a small thrust of his hips into mine, showing me just how much.

I rolled my eyes at his possessiveness, but a warm flush bloomed across my body. The breakfast in bed and courting gifts were amazing, but nothing could compare to just being wanted.

"We're not going to Jewel's shop?" I asked. "Wouldn't that be easier?" I loved being in my nest, but I also felt a little antsy. My omega also loved the idea of being out with my alphas... of showing them off and maybe even them showing *me* off.

"She's going to bring everything here," Theo said, a soft smile on his lips. "That way, you don't have to leave your nest."

"She's going to come in *here*?" I asked, my chest feeling suddenly tight.

"Yeah," Ben said, swallowing a massive bite of food. "Concierge shopping service."

I stiffened, my omega unsettled by the idea of another person, especially another *alpha*, in our room. What if she touched my nest? Even if she didn't touch anything, her scent would be in the room. Right now, it was the perfect combination of all our scents—rich and sweet.

But the guys were looking at me, so pleased with themselves, I didn't want to ruin it.

"That sounds amazing," I said, trying to inject my voice with as much enthusiasm as I could muster.

"Why are you stressed?" Cam asked, pressing his face into my neck.

"I just... don't want you to think you have to spend money on me."

I wasn't lying—money was a concern as well. Somehow, it felt easier to speak that worry out loud. Admitting that my omega was on edge about scents felt high maintenance. I needed to prove to them I wasn't a nuisance, wasn't ruled by my omega instincts.

"Baby girl," Cam admonished, his lips brushing my ear. "We want to provide for you. We need to get you everything you want. It makes us happy."

I sighed, forcing myself to relax again. Everything would be okay. And so what if Jewel's presence made me feel stressed? I could get through it to please my alphas.

I was not okay.

After finishing breakfast, I dressed while the guys cleared the food. I'd tried to go downstairs but Cam stopped me, insisting I relax in my room because "omegas need their nests after heat." A little prickly feeling started building under my skin and only intensified in the intervening hours.

Jewel arrived, her very presence commanding and pure alpha. She must have been over six feet tall with jet-black hair down to her waist and almost black eyes. Her scent was pleasant, like springtime flowers, but there was an unusual hint of metal mixed in, which gave me pause. I breathed through my mouth, trying to calm down and suppress my territoriality.

Jewel, to her credit, didn't touch anything in the room and gave me space. She ordered the guys to bring everything she'd brought from her store up to the room, which was how I had ended up surrounded by pillows, blankets, lighting, and decor. The guys kept pulling more things out, asking what I thought about each item.

I was so fucking overwhelmed.

Theo decided I had to have anything I glanced at for even a moment. Previously, my possessions had fit into a couple of small suitcases. Now they were trying to buy me an entire store. It was too much. The cruel voice in my head kept up a steady monologue. *One day, they'll wake up and realize they don't want you anymore and take all the stuff away. It's not really yours.*

A whimper escaped my lips, and my skin was tight and itchy. At the sound of my distress, all three guys flew to my side, petting me and asking what was wrong. Usually, I loved having my alphas close, but for the first time, it felt stifling.

"Nothing's wrong," I said, my voice cracking.

"Do you not like this bedding?" Theo asked, looking at the piles of soft blankets in front of me as if he were going to burn them for offending me.

"Are you hungry?" Ben asked. "I'll make you something to eat."

"Don't worry about choosing your favorite blanket," Cam said. "We'll just get them all."

My breaths started coming faster. Their scents, usually so soothing, felt thick and oppressive. I curled up tightly in my chair, wishing I could be alone in the dark closet with one of the blankets from my nest. I didn't want any of the new blankets. They didn't smell right. In fact, none of the new things smelled right. The room had been perfect this morning, and now there was a mix of clean, sterile scents that felt all wrong.

"Why are you crying?" Cam's voice was panicked and loud, sending sharp spikes of his scent into the room. My omega whined, needing to fix the upset alpha, but I had hit my breaking point. I felt myself shutting down, disconnecting from the room and my body.

"For the love of god, it's like watching a train wreck," Jewel said dryly, a hint of amusement in her voice. "You three, out," she barked.

Cam, Ben, and Theo were all in an uproar, arguing with Jewel, which made my tears come faster.

"You see what you three overbearing assholes are doing to her?" Jewel asked.

"Josie, love, what do you need? Just tell us how to help." Theo crouched next to me, his hand resting lightly on my thigh. His question made me more anxious—how was I supposed to know what I needed?

"For fuck's sake. If you want her to stop crying, get out of the room now. You can return when you've learned to listen to your omega."

I wanted to say something—to apologize for freaking out, smooth things over, *anything* useful. But I was numb, floating outside my body.

It was a testament to Jewel's alpha-ness that she got the guys to leave the room. They were shouting and swearing as they argued with her, but I was too far gone to understand what they were saying. The door shut and I was alone with Jewel, scared and awed by her authority.

Jewel eyed me critically and I cringed, wondering what she thought of me. She nodded sharply to herself as if satisfied by something.

"You are going to get in your nest," she said.

She hadn't used her bark on me, but I followed her instructions automatically. I sat in the middle of the bed, unsure what to do next.

Jewel sighed. "Put that blanket over you."

She pointed at my favorite dark blue velvet blanket. It was soft and smelled most like my alphas. The second I pulled the blanket over me, the itchy, restless feeling faded away.

"Very good," Jewel said. "You stay there. I'm going to move all these things downstairs. I told those idiots it wasn't a good idea to have me here so close to your heat. Alpha males are more than useless."

Jewel kept up a steady stream of insults—towards my alphas, males in general, and the government. Her angry mutterings lulled me into a sleepy daze. Every time she opened the door to remove another bundle of items, my alphas' scents wafted over me. They were staying as close to me as Jewel would allow, and that filled me with tingly warmth.

"Okay, omega, everything's cleared out. Time for you and I to have a chat."

I poked my head out from under the blanket as Jewel dragged the armchair to the side of the bed, sitting on it like a throne. I'd never seen someone so self-assured. I moved to a seated position, waiting to hear what she had to say.

"Why would you let me into your room?" she asked.

"What?"

"You've just finished your heat. You're brand new to this pack. Why would you let another alpha into your private space?"

I squirmed under the intensity of her scrutiny. How did she know what I was feeling?

"I didn't want to be rude," I said, my voice almost a whisper.

Jewel rolled her eyes. "And why the fuck not?"

I scrunched my nose, confused. "Why didn't I want to be rude?"

"Yes. You're an omega. You have needs. Your alphas are here to meet those needs. Those three overzealous, overbearing alphaholes out there are clueless."

"They're not clueless," I said defensively.

A slow smile spread across Jewel's face. "It's cute seeing you defend them. Why didn't you tell them what you needed? Why didn't you tell them to back the fuck off?"

I paused, my thoughts tangled in my mind. Why hadn't I spoken up?

"I didn't want to be a nuisance," I finally said.

"So you're content to be passive? Let them make all the decisions for you?"

I frowned. "That's not what I said."

"Of course, alphas know what's best for helpless little omegas."

Anger flared through me, and I clenched my fists. "That's not true."

"Ahh, so you *do* have some fight in you," Jewel said with satisfaction. "After how Luc described you, I didn't expect you to be quite so pathetic."

"I'm not pathetic," I said without much confidence. Jewel just arched a single, disbelieving eyebrow.

"You know Luc?" I asked.

"I know everyone," she said smugly, looking down at her perfectly manicured black nails. "He told me about this pain in the ass omega who convinced him to run an illegal self-defense class. And here you are, deferring to your new alphas at every turn. It's weak."

My cheeks heated in embarrassment. "You don't know anything about me. You don't know what I've been through."

"Oh, please. Do you think you're the only one who's had a

hard life? That you're the only one the Designation Government has harmed?"

I inhaled a sharp breath as it clicked. Jewel's odd scent, the almost artificial edge to it... had the government done something to try and change it?

"I'm sorry," I said softly, blinking away the tears threatening to form.

Jewel snorted. "No one in this room is at fault for the shit they did to us. But you're letting them win if you stop fighting."

I wanted to protest what she was saying, but part of me recognized the truth in her words.

"Don't you understand why the Designation Government is so fucking terrified of omegas?" she continued. "It's because you rule alphas without even trying. Our biology pushes us to care for omegas, to do whatever we can to meet their needs and protect them. That doesn't mean we're mind readers. The three alphas plastered to the door are decent men. But that doesn't mean they're going to get everything right. They're still men, after all."

My lips quirked.

"If you want to stay on the sidelines and let your alphas make all the decisions for you, be my guest. But something tells me it's not going to go well for any of you. Those three need to learn to listen. You need to learn to speak up."

Her stern gaze was hypnotizing, and I found myself nodding. I had gotten so used to people seeing me as weak that I had started seeing myself that way, too.

"Now, I've left some things in the living room for you. Anything you don't like, bring it back to the store. I'm going to go so you can get rid of my horrific stench."

Her tone didn't betray her emotions, but my heart clenched at her self-deprecating statement. How many times had I said or thought even worse things about myself?

"Your scent isn't horrible," I said.

Jewel arched her eyebrows. "You don't need to lie to me, omega."

"I'm not," I insisted. "There's a little artificial edge to it... almost metallic? But it's not bad. And mostly, you smell like springtime. I like it... just not in my room."

For the briefest moment, Jewel's impenetrable mask fell. She looked stunned, as if she couldn't quite digest what I'd said.

"You're welcome at my shop anytime, Josie," she said, her voice almost tender. And then she strode out of the room without a second glance.

Chapter Twenty-Six

Josie

I buried my face in the blanket and took a few deep breaths, trying to process everything Jewel had said. There was a gentle knock at the door.

"Josie, can we come in?" Cam asked, his voice as soft and hesitant as I'd ever heard it.

"Yeah," I responded, feeling suddenly shy.

Were they upset with me? With Jewel?

Cam, Ben, and Theo shuffled into the room, eyes downcast. They stood in front of me by the bed but didn't move to get closer or touch me.

"We're sorry," Ben blurted out. "We messed up. We wanted this to be a good surprise and courting gift, but obviously it wasn't. We should have asked you first."

My lips parted in surprise. Had an alpha ever apologized to me?

"Thank you," I responded, unable to meet their eyes. "I'm sorry I ruined the present."

"You don't apologize," Cam growled. "We're the ones who messed up, sweetheart. I'm sorry."

The tightness in my chest eased.

"You were upset when we told you Jewel was coming over and you didn't say anything. Why?" Cam asked, his brow furrowed with concern.

"I didn't want to be an inconvenience. Or make you think I'm crazy and hormonal."

"Baby girl, *I'm* crazy and hormonal. Fuck, my alpha won't shut up about needing to protect you and feed you and give you a shit ton of presents," Cam said.

"You're allowed to need things, you and your omega both," Theo said tenderly.

Finally, I looked up, meeting each of their gazes. They looked so genuine and unsure. Theo kept ruffling his hair, and Cam shifted from side to side.

"Will you sit next to me?" I asked.

The three of them moved to the bed instantly. Cam settled against the headboard so I could lean back on him with Ben and Theo beside me.

"We're going to be better at listening, precious," Ben said, kissing my cheek. "What do you need?"

I hesitated, wringing my hands until Theo gathered them in his, soothing his fingers down my palms.

"I don't need to stay in bed all the time," I said. "I'd like to go outside. Unless..."

"Unless what, love?" Theo asked.

"Unless you don't want to be seen with me?" I whispered.

I heard a sharp intake of breath.

"Baby girl, no. That's not... Fuck." Cam pulled me so I was fully leaning on his chest.

"Of fucking course we want to be seen with you," he said. "Except I'm feeling possessive as fuck right now."

"We're unsettled because you've been in pain the past few days and we couldn't help you," Theo said.

My eyes glanced over at the side table, which currently housed the vibrating dildo. Theo cleared his throat, and I realized he was blushing. He was so cute.

"Well, couldn't help as much as we wanted," he said. "But that's our problem, not yours. You understand, angel?"

I nodded, leaning closer to Theo to breathe in his warm coffee scent.

"We're not going to be angry if you tell us we're being idiots," Ben said with a cheery smile. "I tell these two all the time."

Theo huffed in annoyance before winking at me.

"What do you want to do right now, precious?" Ben asked, wrapping his arm around my waist. "We could go out somewhere?"

I let my body relax into his. I was worn out, and my omega wouldn't rest until the room felt right again.

"It smells wrong in here," I said.

"Well, we can't have that, can we?" Ben asked, nuzzling the top of my head.

I glanced at him, unsure if he was mocking me, but saw only sincerity on his face.

"What do we need to do to fix it, angel?" Theo asked, squeezing my hands.

"Umm, we need to open the windows to air it out. And I need your scents back on the nest." Jewel's words echoed in my head. I still felt uneasy demanding anything from my alphas, but I couldn't be passive.

"That's what we'll do then, sweetheart," Cam said, giving me a squeeze before releasing me.

The guys moved around the room, opening the windows and balcony doors. I adjusted the placement of the bedding and blankets. I didn't feel the same urge to nest anymore, but I still wanted to make sure the bed was layered with soft things and filled with my mates' scents. After arranging everything, I noticed the guys standing close to the bed and staring at me.

"What's next, precious?" Theo asked.

"I need your scents on the bed."

Ben's eyes sparkled with mischief right before he flung himself on the mattress, taking me down in a gentle tackle. I giggled, the stress of the past few hours melting away with each messy kiss he planted on my face. I squealed and pushed him away. Cam and Theo moved onto the bed until all three were pressed against me.

"Do we need to do anything else?" Cam asked, brushing my hair from my face.

"It would probably work better if you took your shirts off," I said, snuggling deeper into the bedding.

"You trying to get us naked, precious?" Ben asked with a laugh.

I sniffed, feigning indifference. "Just saying that's what you would do if you wanted this to work best."

"Naughty girl," Cam asked, rolling until he was on top of me, his arms bracketing me on both sides.

"Skin-to-skin does encourage the releasing of pheromones," Theo said.

"See?" I said with a smirk. "It's science."

"Well, if it's for science, I guess I have to," Cam said, stripping off his shirt. His chest was hard and muscled above me, and I couldn't resist dragging my fingertips down the expanse of smooth skin.

"Fuck, that feels so good," Cam groaned, his hardness pressing against me.

I tugged on Cam's arms until he allowed his weight to press down on me. The pressure was comforting as adrenaline seeped from my body, leaving me exhausted.

After a few minutes, Cam shifted us so I was lying on top of him. "Rest if you need to, baby girl."

I bit my lip, wondering if I could make a *request*. God, Jewel was right. If I was this scared to ask my alphas for something I wanted, how would I do anything useful with my life?

"Do you think we could maybe go out tomorrow? Like, for food?" I hated how timid my voice was, but at least I had asked the question.

"Yes! I have so many restaurants I want to take you to," Ben burst out. "I have a list here on my phone."

My eyes widened as he handed me his phone with an endless list of restaurants.

"I haven't heard of most of these," I said.

Sam and I used to sneak out to eat when we were teens, his alpha status offering me protection when we were out and about, but we had always been working with a shoestring budget. I doubted our favorite hot dog cart made the list.

I scrolled back up to the top of the note and noticed the heading: *Places to take my mate.* I blinked quickly to keep myself from crying.

I handed the phone back to him and realized Cam and Theo hadn't said anything. I eyed them carefully. Pack Ashwood didn't have a strong hierarchy like the packs I'd grown up with, but I knew I needed Theo and Cam's approval for the plan.

Cam's grip on me tightened, and his chest moved with his deep inhale and exhale.

"We'll have to choose someplace safe and private," Theo said, his serious gaze falling on Ben, who nodded.

I held my breath, waiting for Cam's response. "Send a couple restaurant options to our team, Ben, so they can scope things out," he said, his voice hard.

I moved up his body so I could see his face. Was he angry at my request? His brown eyes were filled with warmth and tenderness.

"We would love to take you out, sweetheart. And you did so good, asking for what you needed."

I buried my face in the crook of his neck, my chest filling with a strange mix of emotions that felt a little bit like love.

Chapter Twenty-Seven

Cam

"Cam? Wake up."

The urgent whisper created a crack in my nightmare, but dark images clawed at my consciousness, pulling me back under.

Sinister figures dragged Josie away. Her arms extended towards me as she screamed, a sound so piercing and agonizing I felt my heart might break. I roared in anger and charged at them, ready to kill anyone who dared harm my omega.

"Shit, you need to get back."

"No," the sweet voice whined before a small hand shook my arm. "Cam, wake up."

My chest tightened at the panic in the voice, but I was too disoriented, trapped between waking and dreaming.

"Josie, get back. I don't want him to hit you."

A growl tore through my chest as I finally shook free from the nightmare.

Hurt Josie? Fucking never.

I woke with a gasp, prying my eyes open to find my omega's face inches from mine, eyes wide. It was too dark in the room for me to be sure, but I thought I saw her blinking away tears. I didn't need a light to catch the bitterness of her scent saturated with fear.

I had done that.

"Are you okay?" she whispered, tenderly cupping my face.

My throat was too tight to form words, so I opened my arms to her, and she threw herself into my embrace. My heart pounded and my skin burned as I clutched her to me, desperation seeping into my limbs. I needed to protect her. I couldn't let anything happen to her, couldn't fail *again.*

"Sorry for waking you," I said hoarsely.

A cruel voice in my head taunted me, telling me what I'd always feared: I was a failure. I couldn't even protect my omega. I'd upset her and interrupted the sleep she so desperately needed after her heat.

Theo leaned over, grabbing a bottle of water from the side table and handing it to me. I went to sit, but Josie clung to me with a protesting whimper. I rubbed her back and held her close as I sat up against the headboard. She pressed her face to my neck and I secretly loved that she didn't want to let go.

After downing half the bottle of water, I set it aside. My limbs burned with the need to hit, punch, fight, to do something with my fear and rage.

"I'm going to go to the gym," I said, giving Josie what I thought would be a final rub on the back.

Ben and Theo met my gaze over Josie's shoulder and nodded. They knew how I got after nightmares like this.

"No," Josie said, pulling back and looking at me, eyes wide. "Don't leave."

Her lower lip trembled and I was powerless against it.

Shit, now she was sniffling. How did I stop it?

"I'll stay," I said, my hands running down her body to try to soothe her. "Don't cry." My words came out as a demand, and I saw Ben's lip twitch.

"Lie down," Josie said, issuing a command of her own as she pushed my shoulders.

All I could do was obey.

I slowly lay down on the bed, suppressing a growl when Josie moved off of me. But then she started arranging blankets, taking the one I had knitted for her and placing it over me. She let out the cutest fucking omega growl of her own when Theo or Ben tried to interfere. They looked amused, but I felt their worry for me in the bond.

Josie carefully placed soft things around me, and somehow, with every gentle pat and adjustment of a pillow, the tension in my limbs subsided. Once satisfied, she curled up next to me, tugging Theo and Ben so they were lying down. She ran her fingers through my hair, massaging my scalp. My muscles unclenched, surrendering to the care of my omega.

"Do you want to talk about it?" she whispered.

"I'll tell you one day, sweetheart," I murmured, hoping she would understand. I wasn't ready. Not yet.

She traced her fingers down my jaw, all softness in contrast with the roughness of my beard.

"Okay, alpha." She kissed me on the cheek, and something else relaxed deep in the recesses of my mind at her easy acceptance. Her touch made it okay to let go, just this once, knowing my omega was safe in my arms...and maybe I was safe in hers.

Chapter Twenty-Eight

Josie

I bit my lip, glancing at my phone. Luc had texted this morning, letting us know we had class tonight. His text was shortly followed by one from Clementine, asking if there was any way I could pick her up.

I hadn't told the guys about self-defense class and my stomach clenched, nervous about their reaction. I was especially worried about Cam after his nightmare last night. Did he often have nightmares? I barely knew anything about their pasts… just like there was so much of mine they didn't know.

Theo and Cam sat on either side of me at the kitchen island. Theo was on his laptop, and Cam was reading the morning paper. Every few seconds, one of them reached over and absentmindedly touched my thigh, kissed me on the cheek, or played with my hair. Each time they touched me, my omega preened with joy.

"The recipe has to have buttermilk, but I don't understand how they get them so fluffy." Ben sighed, exasperated as he tried to recreate the pancake recipe from yesterday morning. My eyes kept being drawn to the bright red mark on his throat and down the bare expanse of his chest, covered only by a pink apron with cupcakes on it.

"Your pancakes are better, anyway," Cam said gruffly, without looking up from the crossword he was completing.

Ben's face broke out into the cutest smile before he turned back to the stove. Warmth spread through me at seeing how the guys supported each other, a stark contrast from how I'd seen alphas behave growing up. They loved each other and weren't afraid to show affection.

My phone beeped again and I jolted, reminded of the subject I still needed to broach.

"What's wrong?" Theo asked softly, kissing my forehead. "You feeling okay? Do you want to go back to bed?"

"No," I responded. "I... well, I have to tell you something."

My alphas immediately looked at me with a laser focus. *That's not intimidating.*

"What is it?" Cam asked, his eyes canvassing the room as if someone was about to jump out and attack.

"Umm... you know how I've been living alone?" *Good grief, of course they know that. They were literally just at your apartment.* I told the voice in my head to shut up and continued. "Well, I needed a way to make money so my friend, Poppy, introduced me to this gym owner."

"I'm going to fucking kill him," Cam roared as he jumped to his feet, the counter stool clattering to the floor.

I flinched at the sudden movement and noise, whimpering as I curled into myself.

Silence blanketed the room.

"Fuck," Cam said softly. "I'm sorry, sweetheart. I would never hurt you." He slowly reached his hand out towards me and I took it, holding on tightly.

"Who is this gym owner?" Theo asked, his voice icy cold. "We'll take care of him."

"What?" I was so confused by their reactions. I replayed what I had said in my head.

"Oh my god! Nothing's ever happened with me and Luc. He hired me to clean the gym at night."

"You clean the gym," Theo said slowly, as if it were a hard concept to understand.

Cam grasped my chin and turned my face so I was looking at him. "He didn't hurt you? Touch you?"

"No, never," I said. "Luc is a really good alpha."

"He's an alpha?" Cam growled, his muscles tense as if trying to hold himself back from shouting again.

"Wait, his name is Luc? The owner of *Alpha Gainz*?" Theo asked.

I snorted. "Yeah, that's the one. Do you know him?"

"We were just there the other night," Ben said, sliding a stack of pancakes in front of me. "We did a drop there for the Alliance."

"Wait!" I shouted, the puzzle pieces finally connecting in my mind. "You were there, in the alleyway! I totally forgot after everything that happened later, but I scented you."

"You were in the alleyway?" Cam asked, his jaw clenching as he planted one hand on my thigh.

"What did the scents smell like?" Ben asked quickly.

I snorted. "Nice try." I leaned forward to kiss away Ben's pout.

"Ben, fucking focus," Cam growled. "Why were you in that alleyway, sweetheart?"

"That's why I brought this up. Luc leads a self-defense class for omegas. I was on my way to class when you entered the alleyway, and I hid until you were gone."

Theo's eye twitched and Cam's grip on my leg tightened. Only Ben seemed somewhat relaxed, although he was tapping the spatula rhythmically against the counter.

I forged ahead. "We're having class tonight and I invited Clementine, Amirah's assistant. She wants to know if we can give her a ride."

"You want to go to an illegal self-defense class led by an alpha," Cam said. His voice was measured, but his bitter scent betrayed him.

"Yeah." My skin felt hot. I hated the tension in the room, but I forced myself not to back down.

"It's not safe," Cam bit out. "You realize you could be arrested?"

Flickers of indignation and anger sparked through my body. "I'm aware," I said tartly. "You realize most things are illegal for omegas?"

Cam grimaced but didn't respond. I forced myself to take a deep breath.

"How do we know we can trust Luc?" Theo asked.

"You all seemed to trust him enough to do Alliance work with him," I responded, trying to keep my tone even. "I've been working for him for almost a year. I trust him."

"We're not bonded yet, which makes you vulnerable. You need our protection," Cam said.

"So if we were bonded you would let me go to the class?" I asked.

Cam looked away. I guessed that was my answer. A tendril of panic worked its way through me. *Did they want to keep me locked in the house?*

Ben made his way around the kitchen island, wrapping his arms around me from behind. I leaned my head back on his chest and he nuzzled my neck.

"I think we all need to tone it down a notch," he said, shooting a pointed look at Theo and Cam. "I want to hear about the class, precious." He spun my chair so I was facing him and kissed me on the nose. "And then we need to eat pancakes."

A smile tugged at my lips. Ben knew exactly what was needed to diffuse the tension.

"We never got a chance to ask you about your apartment," Theo said, playing with a strand of my hair. "How were you able to live alone?"

I took a deep breath. "After I was... *released* from the DA, my parents brought me back home. It was a really bad situation." I paused, trying to stop the memories of those weeks from invading my mind.

"I'm guessing that's an understatement," Ben said gently, grasping my fisted hands in his warm ones.

I shrugged, not wanting to go into detail. "Growing up, I had a best friend named Sam. He revealed as an alpha the same time I did as an omega. Our parents tried to keep us apart, but we snuck out of our homes to see each other. I hadn't been able to speak to him the entire time I was at the DA. Once I was back at my parents', he came to tell me he'd been offered a job in Sol. When he saw the state I was in, he insisted on staying with me, worried about leaving me alone. We knew there was no way I could get a visa to leave the province, but he had to move so he could be with..." I stopped myself from saying more. I didn't think my alphas would do anything to put Sam in danger if they found out he was gay, but I couldn't risk it.

"Well, it doesn't matter," I continued. "Leaving was going to be the best thing for him. But he kept his apartment so I could escape my family. His new job paid well, so he could pay double rent, or at least that's what he told me. I still needed money so I could buy food and stuff. One of the omegas I met at the DA, Poppy, mentioned that her alphas went to this gym and that I might be able to get a cleaning job because the owner was sympathetic to omegas. That's how I met Luc. He gave me a job and paid me under the table. I've been working there four nights a week for the past year. It's walking distance from my apartment, and I just have to be careful that no one sees me."

"You walked to the gym alone in the dark?" Ben burst out.

The three of us looked at him, slightly stunned. Ben was usually so easygoing. His cheeks turned pink at his outburst.

"Umm right, not important right now. I just don't like it," he muttered.

"You're not working there anymore," Cam said.

"I already let Luc know," I said with as much patience as I could muster.

"So you worked there, and then one day this alpha just decided he wanted to lead a group for omegas out of the kindness of his heart?" Cam snorted.

"No," I bit back. "I pestered him to start the class until he finally gave in. One night, he was at the gym late and I mentioned that I wished I knew how to defend myself. I convinced him to teach me a few things. After a month of begging, I finally got him to agree to do a secret class for omegas. Poppy joined and so did my friend Westin."

"Is Luc's omega part of the group, too?" Theo asked.

"No, I've never gotten to meet her. She has health issues that prevent her from leaving the house. I'm not sure what happened to her, but I think she might have been attacked or something. I think it's part of why Luc cares about omegas being able to defend ourselves."

Theo nodded thoughtfully. Ben asked, "What's the class like?"

Hope bubbled in my chest. I needed to make a good case that the class was safe.

"We practice different self-defense moves, mostly with each other, but sometimes with Luc. We don't meet on a set schedule and class is in the downstairs basement, accessed through the alleyway. We only invite people we know we can trust and keep things small."

"Are you sure you're feeling well enough?" Theo asked. "You've had a rough week."

"I'm sure," I said with a smile. "I'll take it easy if I need to, promise."

The guys exchanged a look. Cam still looked unhappy and wasn't meeting my gaze, but he gave Theo a curt nod.

"Okay, angel, we'll make sure you can get to class tonight and pick up Clementine," Theo said, kissing me on the cheek.

"Can we go out to eat tomorrow instead?" I asked, looking at Ben. I didn't want them to be upset with me for changing plans.

"Of course," he said, kissing me on the nose. "Just gives me one more day to set up the perfect date. Now that we got that sorted, it's time for pancakes."

Cam removed his arm from around me and abruptly stood up. "I've got to get some work done," he mumbled, heading towards his office.

I held back a whine, feeling sick as I watched him go. A mixture of frustration, guilt, and sadness warred within me. It was my fault that he was upset and I wanted to fix it, but part of me also knew I had the right to make decisions about my life. Jewel had been right—I couldn't let my alphas dictate everything.

"Give him a little time to cool off, love," Theo said, caressing my face. "Cam gets scared when the people he loves are in any sort of danger. It's not that he doesn't support you."

I nodded woodenly and forced myself to eat the pancakes Ben proudly plated up for me.

I knocked lightly on the study door, holding my breath.

"Come in," Cam's gruff voice called out.

I took a deep breath and steeled myself for his anger. What I saw when I opened the door made me scrunch my nose in confusion. Cam was sitting in his big office chair and was... knitting?

His head shot up. "Josie! I thought you were Theo." His cheeks flushed, and his eyes darted to his knitting project before quickly dropping it on his desk.

"I didn't know you knit," I said, still standing by the door.

I had been expecting Cam's fury, or at least for him to be cold towards me. Almost all the alphas I knew lashed out with aggression when they didn't get their way. Seeing the muscular alpha in front of me blushing furiously, his craft project in front of him, sent my brain into a fritz.

"I saw a therapist for a while, and she recommended I find a way to channel my emotions into something non-destructive. So I learned to knit," Cam blurted out. He wasn't looking at me and his scent was... embarrassed?

Without thinking, I closed the distance between us. Cam automatically parted his legs so I could stand between them.

"Can I see?" I asked, nodding towards the abandoned knitting project.

He gave me a curt nod. I picked up the needles, revealing the lumpiest, ugliest piece of knitting I had ever seen. I remembered the blanket I'd fallen in love with in my nest, and my heart melted at the realization that Cam must have knitted it for me.

"I know it's not a very *alpha* thing to do," he said. "It's stupid."

I raised my eyebrows in surprise. "Why would that matter? You should do what makes you happy," I said, my tone sharp.

Cam's lips quirked. "Haven't heard you sound that fierce before. It's hot." His blush deepened, as did his scent. He ran his hand across his neck and avoided my gaze.

I bit my lip, unsure of what to do next. "Are you mad at me?" I asked, my voice soft.

Cam's hands automatically went to my hips, gripping tightly. "No, baby girl, not at all." He took a shuddering breath. "I'm pissed at myself for reacting like that, and I'm scared shitless at the thought of anything happening to you. My alpha keeps telling me I need to keep you locked up so no one can get to you, but I know I can't do that." He grumbled that last part, which made me smile.

"Thanks for saying that," I said, running my hand through his long hair. He was wearing it down this morning, and I loved the feel of it. I needed to convince him to let me braid it sometime.

"Come here," he said, tugging me onto his lap and holding me close. "You're so important to me, sweetheart. I don't think you understand how much. I know I'm an overbearing bastard, but I need you to be safe. Can't stand the idea of anyone hurting you."

I placed little kisses down his clenched jaw, feeling his tension slowly release.

"I know you'll keep me safe, Cam," I said. As I said the words, I realized how true they were. Fear had been my constant companion these past few years. Being around my alphas made me feel safer than I could have ever imagined.

"I'm coming with you to meet Luc and check things out. That's non-negotiable," Cam said, bracing as if he expected an argument.

I just nodded, snuggling closer to his chest. Funny how I didn't hate his protectiveness all the time. *Who are you kidding? You love it.*

Cam kissed my forehead tenderly. "I'm sorry I overreacted," he murmured in my ear. "I know you're capable and independent, and I don't ever want to take that away from you. Forgive me?"

"Of course," I said, tilting my head to kiss him.

Chapter Twenty Nine

Josie

"I'm not leaving her here alone."

I anxiously watched Cam and Luc's standoff. Theo and Ben had begrudgingly stayed home to catch up on work while Cam and I picked Clementine up. She and I held a silent conversation in the car, with lots of suggestive eyebrow raises from her and lots of giggles from me. Cam pretended to be annoyed, but I saw the corner of his lips twitch at our antics. His scowl returned once we pulled into the alleyway, as if remembering that I had been venturing out alone late at night for months.

Westin and Poppy squealed in excitement when we walked in, and all of us were currently watching the two alphas argue back and forth like a ping-pong match.

"So you'll be fine to sit here quietly without interrupting, even if she gets hurt?" Luc asked.

"Why the fuck would she get hurt?" Cam asked, getting louder. I needed to de-escalate the situation.

"Cam, please, it's going to be fine. You can go upstairs and work out, and then if something happens, you'll be close by." I started nudging him towards the door even though I knew I had no chance of moving him without his cooperation.

"Be careful. I expect you to be unharmed and in one piece at the end of class. Your safety is more important than anything," he said fiercely, allowing me to slowly push him to the exit.

"Yes, alpha," I said, giving him a quick kiss. He melted at my endearment, and he finally left the room.

"Wow, I thought my alphas were bad," Poppy said, a look of awe in her eyes.

"They are just as bad," Luc said dryly. "Remember your first class?"

Westin and I burst into laughter.

"What happened during her first class?" Clementine asked.

"All five of her alphas showed up. Things got so heated one of them challenged Luc to a fight," I said between fits of laughter.

Poppy blushed with a dreamy look in her eyes. "Yeah, okay, they were over-the-top ridiculous."

"Who won?" Clementine asked.

"Luc and Poppy's alpha each landed a punch, and then Poppy threatened to withhold sex if her alpha didn't stop," I said.

"I've never seen an alpha freeze that fast," Westin added with a giggle.

"We had the most amazing angry sex when we got home. And the way he spanked me was sooo..."

"Poppy!" Westin and I shouted, doubling over with laughter. I turned to Clementine, whose cheeks were red.

"Poppy has a very active sex life with her alphas and likes to tell us all about it," I said, rolling my eyes. "But she's the best, so we put up with it." I winked at Poppy and she blew me a kiss.

"Okay, now that we got the overprotective alpha nonsense out of the way, let's start class," Luc said.

"Are you saying you're not just as overprotective of your Charlie?" Poppy asked teasingly.

"Not relevant," Luc muttered. "Partner up. We'll start with punching and blocking practice, and then we'll review how to get out of various holds."

I partnered with Clementine and caught her up on everything we'd learned so far. As a beta, she was naturally stronger than omegas, and she caught on quickly. We practiced getting out of holds and she was a great partner—she made me work for every escape. The hour flew by and before I knew it, there was a knock at the basement door.

"I wonder who that could be," Westin said in a sing-song voice.

Luc opened the door and Cam strode in. He had changed into workout gear and his gray tank top was damp with sweat, showing off his muscular, tattooed arms. I hadn't understood what people in romance books meant when they said they wanted to climb their partners like a tree, but it was rapidly becoming clearer to me.

"Damn, Josie, if you don't bond with him, I will," Poppy said in a stage whisper.

I whipped my head around and growled. He was *mine.* Poppy just laughed and sauntered away to grab her things.

"Ignore her," Westin said with a grin. "I'll see you next class. Enjoy your time with Mr. Scary Hottie."

Cam stalked over to me and ran his eyes up and down my body.

"What's this?" he growled, gently grabbing my forearm and inspecting the red marks before turning to glare at Luc.

"I got those practicing holds with Clementine. You going to beat her up now?" I asked, my lips twitching with amusement.

Cam whipped his head to look at Clementine and then back at me. "No, of course not," he said gruffly.

"Good," I said cheerfully, launching myself into his arms. His scent was deep and sweet, making me want to rub against him. He gripped me by my thighs and lifted me up.

"Did you have a good class?" he murmured in my ear.

"It was great," I whispered back, trailing my tongue down his ear and neck.

"Baby girl," he growled out in warning. I felt him growing hard against my core, but I resisted rubbing against him since we had an audience.

"Thank you for letting me come and only being medium ridiculous and overbearing," I said.

"Only medium overbearing, huh? What would push me to the highly overbearing category?"

"You would have to fight Luc to reach that category like Poppy's alpha did. But I'm very pleased with the medium level."

"As long as you're pleased," he said, giving me the sweetest smile.

I signaled him to let me down and I gathered my things.

"Ready, Clementine?" I asked.

"Yep!" she responded with a bright smile as she looked between Cam and me. We both thanked Luc—Cam offered a gracious grunt—before heading out.

Chapter Thirty

Ben

I walked into the kitchen, a little thrill going through me when I spied Josie trying on my glasses. Her warm brown waves framed her face, and she was wearing a loose sweater and leggings, looking deliciously cozy. She must have made her way down here while I was in the shower. Theo and Cam were holed up in the office after they'd been pulled into work—so much for taking time off.

"Are we doing a sexy librarian role-play?" I asked, leaning against the door frame.

Josie jumped, whipping her face towards mine. I cringed internally, hating that I'd startled her. She seemed more at ease the past few days, but moments like this reminded me of everything she had been through.

Relief rushed through me as she snorted out an adorable giggle. "I just wanted to see how bad your eyes are."

"And?" I strode across the kitchen, wrapping my arms around her, reveling in the feel of her soft body against mine.

"Let's just say, if you cuddle up with Theo at night thinking he's me, I won't be surprised."

I laughed, taken off guard by her sassy response. Any glimpse of playfulness from her felt like a gift.

She took off my glasses and placed them gently on my face before returning my embrace, sighing as she pressed her face into my chest. It killed me not knowing what I smelled like to her, but I also secretly loved our game. It made me feel like we had something just between us. I'd spent most of my life overshadowed, unsure of what I had to offer, but Josie made me feel seen.

"You looked adorable in those, precious," I murmured, leaning down to kiss her. She wiggled happily in my embrace. "Just so you know," I continued, "I'm down for sexy librarian role-play anytime the mood strikes."

She shivered in my arms and I was momentarily anxious I'd made her uncomfortable, but then I caught the scent of her arousal—deep and sugary and so completely Josie. My dick was rock hard and I wanted to strip her, to slip my fingers into her wet heat again. We hadn't done anything sexual since the vibrator, *aka the hottest fucking experience of my life,* and I wanted more. I was hesitant to push anything physical, though. I knew Cam and Theo felt the same, unsure of what she needed and what the right timing was.

Josie's stomach growled. I pulled back from her with a chuckle, but she averted her gaze, her cheeks growing pink. My jaw clenched, and I had to force myself to take a breath. I had wanted to rip up the meal plan the Designation Center sent over, but Theo had convinced me we might need it when the DC came to check in on us. I couldn't believe any alphas would agree to deprive their omegas of food. Just the thought of doing that to Josie made me nauseous.

"I'm starving," I said, lifting her chin. "I was going to make cinnamon rolls if that sounds good to you, gorgeous."

I held my breath as she paused and chewed on her bottom lip. But then she smiled. "Can I help?"

"Wouldn't have it any other way."

I leaned down to kiss her, planning on a gentle press of lips, but the moment I tasted her, I groaned and deepened the kiss. Josie brought her arms around my neck, tugging me closer and sucking on my lower lip. Just when I had decided to abandon my breakfast plan and feast on her instead, Josie's stomach made another sound. I broke away, chastising myself for losing focus. My mate needed to eat.

Josie whimpered at the loss of contact, her pupils blown and her skin deliciously flushed. She was a living, breathing dream come true.

"Stop distracting me," I said, squeezing her ass for good measure before reluctantly letting her go and pulling out the baking supplies from the pantry.

"I'm distracting *you*?" she said with indignation.

"Constantly," I replied with a wink.

I took every excuse to touch Josie while we were baking—brushing my hands down her side as I helped her put on an apron, pressing my body against hers anytime I leaned to get an ingredient, guiding her hands while she kneaded dough. I was so distracted I almost forgot to put sugar in the filling. My behavior was absurd, but Josie didn't say a word. She hummed contentedly to the music playing from the kitchen speakers, gently placing the completed buns in the prepared pans.

"You're so good at this, Ben," she said as we placed the last tray in the oven. "You could totally run your own bakery."

I stilled, searching her face to see if she was teasing me. But, of course, all I saw was genuineness.

"Do you really think I could?" I croaked out.

"Of course," she said, scrunching her nose in confusion. "Why wouldn't you be able to? You're amazing."

Warmth bloomed in my chest, and I couldn't stop myself from picking her up and spinning her around. Her giggles filled the air.

"Thanks, precious," I said, sitting her down on the counter and pressing little kisses all over her face. "It's something I've thought about, but I'm not sure I'd actually be good at running a business, you know? Honestly, it's a miracle I can bake at all with how air-headed I am." I forced out a laugh to cover the pain of my self-deprecation as the words I had overheard my father speaking to my mother played in my head. *Can't believe you only birthed a single alpha, giving us that clueless, weak idiot.*

Josie gripped my face with her hands, pinning me with a fierce expression. "You're not allowed to say things like that about yourself. You're brilliant and sweet and funny. If you started a bakery, it'd probably be the most successful in the city. And how could you say you're not smart? Ben, you're a computer-hacking person. That seems, like, really hard."

I couldn't stop a smile from stretching across my face. "A computer hacking person?"

Josie shrugged nonchalantly. "Close enough."

"Not sure Cam and Theo would be thrilled if I stopped my computer hacking activities to start a bakery."

"I'm sure they just want you to be happy," she said softly, stroking her fingers down my cheek.

Part of me knew she was right, but there was another part that was convinced I would disappoint them. Theo and Cam had protected me growing up, believing in me enough to put me in charge of our cyber security team. Leaving the company would betray everything they'd done for me.

"Is there anything you've wanted to do?" I asked, needing to change the subject.

"Oh," she said, looking startled to have been asked. Her

eyes had a faraway look to them. I moved in closer, wedging myself between her lush thighs.

"I used to have plans. Sam and I dreamed about what our lives would be like after we turned eighteen. We were going to find a place together, get jobs, and save money for school. I had thought about studying marketing and graphic design, but really, I just wanted anything that would get me out of my parents' house. Sam turned eighteen a few weeks before me and secured an apartment. I secretly packed all my things so I would be ready to go." She paused as if she was back there. I squeezed her leg, trying to remind her she was still with me.

She took a little breath and continued, "But then, a week before my birthday, the Designation Government took over. Just like that, I wasn't allowed to work or attend college. I was stuck at my parents' house for two years. Honestly, I feel like the past five years are a blur. I can't remember a lot of it."

That last part came out in a hoarse whisper. Her scent turned bitter and she didn't meet my gaze. My heart ached. I wanted to soothe her, but I could feel how precarious this moment was. This was the most Josie had shared with me about her past, and I didn't want to interrupt. I thought she had frozen up on me when she continued.

"Sam ended up going to a college close to home so we could still see each other. He got me suppressants and black-market books. But when they opened the Designation Academy, I was automatically enrolled in the inaugural class. At first, it was like a boarding school. We took classes to help prepare us for a pack. I thought they would force me to do pack interviews, but they didn't... they..." she petered off.

Fine trembles worked through her body and her skin felt cold. I held her tightly against me, trying to lend her my warmth. She shuddered in my grasp, the tiniest whimper escaping her as she melted into me.

"Thanks for sharing that, precious. I'm so sorry for what they did. So, so sorry."

We stayed there, arms around each other until the oven timer went off. I slowly pulled away, my heart clenching all over again when I realized I had a damp spot on my shirt from her tears. She wiped at her face, giving me a tremulous smile. I wanted to destroy everyone who had hurt her, take away every moment of pain she had felt.

I was at a loss for what to say as I pulled out the cinnamon rolls. They looked perfect. I imagined what it would be like to work together in a bakery. Vanilla cupcakes would have to be our specialty.

"Cinnamon rolls were my little sister's favorite," I said.

Josie tilted her head. "You two were close, right?"

"Yeah," I said with a smile, setting the last pan on the stove. "My older three sisters were quite a bit older. They all bonded their packs when I was still young. But Lilah and I were so close. She's less than two years younger than me and was my shadow growing up. God, she's so smart. Like scary smart. She was supposed to go to college... She wanted to be a doctor or researcher and advance omega medicine. She and Cam's sister, Ellie, always kept us on our toes. They were so much trouble. We spent so much time together—me, Ellie, and Lilah causing trouble, and Theo and Cam trying to keep us from getting everyone killed. They definitely would have thought you were too good for us."

"You don't talk with her anymore?"

"I wasn't allowed to after we were kicked out. My parents never really bought into the designation crap, but they were pressured to shun me like the other families. Back then, we didn't have money, so I couldn't hire someone to keep track of Lilah. I know she bonded a pack shortly after I left, but then it's like she disappeared."

Josie furrowed her brow, reaching out to grab my hand. "I'm so sorry, Ben."

"I have to believe she's okay," I said quietly. I missed Lilah so much and was terrified she'd been harmed like Ellie.

Josie nodded. "You'll find her someday."

Somehow, her words eased the tension in my chest. I took a deep breath, wanting to change the subject.

"Maybe I should open a bakery now that I know someone who can handle all the marketing," I said, tucking her hair behind her ear.

Josie's sweet perfume filled the air.

"I probably wouldn't be any good," she said with a shrug.

Now it was my turn to growl at her. "If I'm not allowed to put myself down, you're certainly not," I said, fixing her with as stern a look as I could muster.

She hopped down from the counter with a smile.

"Thanks, Ben," she said with a tender kiss before she started frosting the rolls.

We fell into an easy quiet. Soft music surrounded us and sunlight streamed through the window, catching the golden highlights in Josie's hair. As she plated up the rolls, I got some coffee brewing.

"Mmm," I said. "Cinnamon rolls and coffee. What a great combination. I wonder what could be missing..."

I waited to see if she would catch on to my ulterior motive for choosing cinnamon rolls this morning, and she did not disappoint.

"Oh my gosh, Ben! Cinnamon rolls and coffee. Is this all a ploy to get me to slip up and tell you what your scent is?" she asked, her eyes lighting with laughter.

I arched my eyebrow. "I would never be so diabolical," I said, placing my hand on my chest in mock horror. "Although, if you want a cinnamon roll, you better tell me what I want to know." I snagged the plate of rolls off the counter and held them above my head.

Josie gasped. "You would deprive me of breakfast?" Her lip jutted out in a pout, and she blinked quickly.

"What? No!" I exclaimed, setting down the plate on the counter and placing my hands on either side of her face. "Never."

Suddenly, Josie's sad expression transformed into laughter as she leaned into me with a giggle.

I slumped over in relief. "Fuck, precious, I thought I made you upset."

Josie wrapped her arms around me and squeezed me close. "Sorry for freaking you out. You're just too easy to tease."

I lifted her by the waist and put her back on the kitchen counter, thrilled when she wrapped her arms and legs around me. I gripped the back of her neck, my other hand working my way higher up her thigh. She let out a breathy moan that went straight to my cock.

"You know how you can make it up to me?" I murmured.

"Hmm?"

"Tell me what my scent is."

Her laughter started again, and it was the sweetest sound in the world.

"Pleaasse."

"Don't do it!" Theo yelled from the next room.

"Make him work for it," Cam added as he entered the kitchen. He went straight to Josie, shoving me aside to pull her in for a heated kiss.

"No breakfast for you," I said, glowering at Cam.

Josie sighed happily in Cam's embrace. "You're right, Ben, there *is* something missing. And it would be perfect now that it's getting to be fall."

"Aha! A hint," I said, rubbing my hands together. "I can

work with that." I pulled out my phone and started searching for top fall recipes.

Cam sighed with exasperation, partly at me but mainly at Theo, who had tugged Josie out of his arms.

"This looks amazing, you two," Theo said, kissing Josie's forehead.

"Ben's a creative genius in the kitchen," Josie said easily.

"That he is," Cam said, slinging his arm around my shoulder.

Happiness bubbled through my body. After years of waiting, our family felt complete, and it was better than anything I could have dreamed.

Chapter Thirty-One

Josie

I glanced over at Cam. His jaw was clenched, and his eyes kept sweeping the restaurant as if he were ready to jump into action. I realized he probably was. He hadn't told me much about his past, but I knew he had served in the military for several years. It wasn't hard to imagine Cam commanding people in dangerous situations. And right now, he was acting as if we were at imminent risk of being under attack.

When we arrived at the restaurant, one owned by a friend of Ben's, Cam had demanded they seat us in a booth in a far corner where he could see the exits. He also insisted I slide into the booth first so he could better protect me. His anxiety caused an uncomfortable kernel of guilt to form in my stomach. I had been the one who wanted to go out to eat, and now Cam was upset.

I reached under the table and tentatively took hold of his hand. "Do you want to leave?" I asked in an almost whisper.

Cam tore his gaze from the restaurant entrance and looked at me with a bewildered expression. "Why would I want to leave?"

"You seem stressed," I said, shifting in my seat. "Maybe this was a bad idea."

"Fuck," he said, running his free hand over his face. "Trust me, sweetheart, I want to be here with you."

I thought I caught Theo scowling at Cam from across the table, but his expression transformed into a relaxed smile when he saw me looking.

Cam placed his hand on my thigh and gave it a squeeze. I leaned into him automatically, reveling in his warmth. He was wearing a tight black t-shirt that showed off his tattoos, having taken off the leather jacket he'd worn to the restaurant. I was feeling a little drunk off his scent and lamented that I hadn't had a chance to explore every one of his tattoos yet.

"What looks good to you, love?" Theo asked.

In contrast to Cam's casual outfit, Theo wore a black suit and a green plaid tie. His dark brown hair was neatly combed back and the candlelight danced across his chiseled jaw. God, he was like an even sexier James Bond.

Ben cleared his throat. I had been staring at Theo without saying anything for an inappropriate amount of time. My cheeks heated as I finally tore my eyes away.

"Next time, I'll know to wear a tie," Ben said, his eyes dancing with amusement.

I bit my lip and looked down at the menu. "I like what you're wearing, too," I mumbled.

I meant it—Ben had layered a soft blue sweater that brought out the color of his eyes over a white button-down. It looked perfectly cozy, and my omega wanted to curl up on his lap.

"I don't know what I want," I confessed, feeling overwhelmed by being out to eat for the first time in years. Ben had already taken charge of the appetizer order, getting almost everything on the menu.

"If Ben's in charge, he'll just order every entrée and make you try them all," Cam snorted, squeezing my thigh again. Was I imagining it or had his hand moved closer to my core?

"Not all," Ben responded with a glint in his eye. "Josie doesn't like shrimp, so we'll skip that one."

I opened my mouth to say they shouldn't spend so much money on me—I had planned to just order the smallest, cheapest thing on the menu—when Cam pressed his face to the top of my head.

"Don't even try to argue with him, sweetheart. Ben takes his food ordering very seriously," he said. Then he moved his lips to my ear and murmured, "I'll get better at this, I promise. Can't tell you how much I love being seen with you, to have all these people know you're mine."

My body tingled with warmth at his words and I snuggled close to him, unable to suppress a smile.

"Hate this de-scenter on you, though," Cam said, his voice almost a growl.

My breath caught and I went to shift away from him. De-scenter could have an unpleasant metallic smell, but the idea of going out in public without it had been too much to cope with.

"Didn't say I wanted you to move away, now did I?" he asked.

My lips parted as the authority in his voice sent a shiver through me.

"I'm sorry. I know it doesn't smell good," I said. "I just... don't feel comfortable being out without it."

"I understand, sweetheart. I shouldn't have said anything. I want you to be safe and comfortable."

I let myself relax, listening to Ben animatedly review the menu options and tell me which ones he thought I would like the best.

The waiter came to drop off our drinks—I'd ordered a

cotton candy martini that sounded equal parts disgusting and delicious—when I noticed a group of women being led to a table near ours. I froze when I saw it was my mother and a group of her friends. Sam and I had dubbed the group the Omega Bitch Squad as teens—OBS for short. Sam's mother, Victoria, was part of the group, along with several other omegas whose alphas were all Designation Traditionalists.

My mother and I locked eyes as she found her seat. Her mouth curved into the briefest frown before she turned away from me and sat down. I couldn't be bothered to be hurt by her rejection—I was just relieved that she had decided to ignore me. I looked away, hoping Cam's large body blocked me from the view of the rest of the OBS.

"This looks revolting," Cam said, eyeing my drink. He picked it up and took a sip.

"Hey!" I exclaimed, trying to tug it out of his hands without spilling.

He chuckled and set the drink down. "That's fucking disgusting."

I scrunched my nose at him in irritation, but secretly I was thrilled that he had relaxed enough to joke with me.

I looked up and realized Theo had noticed the new arrivals.

"Josie, isn't that…?" he asked.

"Nope," I snapped, cutting him off. Theo's eyes widened in shock and I bit my lip, ashamed of my rudeness. "Sorry," I said, not meeting his gaze. "I know she's here and she saw me. But I just want to ignore her."

Theo reached across the table for my hand and gave it a gentle squeeze. I closed my eyes, relieved he wouldn't punish me for my outburst.

"Who are we talking about?" Ben asked, looking up from the menu and turning around in his seat.

"Don't look," I whispered urgently. "It's my mom and her friends."

But it was too late. Sharon, the OBS ringleader, had spotted us. Her eyes raked over each of my alphas in a way that made me feel profoundly possessive before her gaze landed on me. A wide smile spread across her face, a sinister gleefulness in her eyes. She nudged my mother, who turned to look at me, her eyes tight. I was sure my mother was ashamed to be associated with me, but now she couldn't reasonably continue ignoring me.

Soon, all five omegas turned to look at us and Sharon got up, gesturing for them to follow her to our table.

"Fuck," I muttered, every muscle in my body clenching with dread.

"Josephine, darling! I never would have expected to see you here. And who are these alphas?" Sharon asked, tossing her blond hair.

I clenched my fists to keep myself from shrinking down in my seat. I hated myself for feeling intimidated, but being around these women for the first time in years brought up all the terrible memories of my childhood.

I cleared my throat. "This is Cam, Theo, and Ben. My alphas."

I swear all my guys sat a little taller at my words. Did they like that I had called them mine?

"This is Sharon," I continued. "Victoria, Linda, Elizabeth, and, of course, my mother, Angeline."

"Angeline told us you finally came into heat and found a pack," Elizabeth said. "We were simply blown away. We had quite the betting pool going on if you would ever find alphas." She laughed, a hollow, fake sound.

Cam tensed next to me.

"Oh?" I asked, feigning indifference. "Who won the bet?"

Sharon giggled, the sound high-pitched and girlish. "It was actually Victoria. Angeline was the most optimistic when she guessed you'd find a pack at twenty."

My mother shifted her weight ever so slightly, the only tell that this conversation made her uncomfortable. She had never hesitated to remind me that my failure to find a pack reflected poorly on her.

My gaze landed on Victoria, who had the decency to look embarrassed.

Sharon leaned forward so much I thought her breasts would pop out of her tight dress.

"It's so kind of you to take on such an unconventional omega," she purred.

Then she *touched Cam's arm.*

A red haze came over my vision as I stared at her hand. All sound fell away. Nothing mattered anymore except getting her off my alpha. I wanted to leap across Cam's lap and tackle her, wanted to rake my nails down her skin for daring to touch him in front of me.

Before I could act, Cam firmly moved Sharon's hand off of him with a scowl and pulled me closer to his side, rubbing little circles on my hip. The red haze eased enough for me to take a breath and focus on the conversation. I felt a foot run down my calf and looked across the table to Ben, who gave me a wink.

Sharon opened her mouth to say something else but was interrupted by two servers carrying large trays with all our appetizers. I shifted with discomfort, already prepared for the food-related comments they were about to make.

"Goodness, you must be starving," Linda said, eyes wide.

I didn't think I'd ever seen her eat at any of the countless dinner parties my parents forced me to attend.

"Of course, alphas such as yourself need to eat to keep up

your physique," she added, practically eye fucking each of them.

Sharon let out a theatrical gasp. "Did you not get the omega-approved diet list?" she asked my alphas. "I barely recognized you at first, Josephine, with all the weight you've put on. I'm so concerned about your health."

Cam vibrated next to me, his scent almost acidic with anger. We gripped each other tightly as if to prevent the other from attacking.

My mother glared at me, the epitome of *if looks could kill*. I tried to find a witty retort, but to my shame, all I did was shrink lower in my seat. It's not like I didn't know I had gained weight, but for her to say it in front of my alphas hurt.

My mother's steely gaze flitted between me and the appetizers. "Don't embarrass yourself, Josephine," she said. It was obvious to everyone that what she meant was *don't embarrass me*.

"Josie is perfect the way she is," Ben said, his usual mirth absent from his tone. "We don't need her to look a certain way."

"Oh, I'm sure you don't," Sharon said with a wink. "I'm sure you're not lacking side options to satisfy you."

The red haze returned and I had to hold back a growl. How dare she suggest my alphas were cheating on me?

"I suppose there are limits on what we can expect from you," Elizabeth said airily. "Nothing can make up for bad breeding."

I crinkled my nose slightly, wondering how my mother would respond to the insult. But she didn't react. Didn't say a single thing.

"It's time you return to your table," Theo said, standing up, his accent deepening with his barely suppressed rage.

"Of course," Sharon said with a girlish laugh. "It was so

nice to meet you all." She trailed one last finger down Cam's arm before flouncing away, leaving us in silence.

I kept my head down, staring at the napkin in my lap. Suddenly, all three guys moved into action at once. Cam and Theo shifted their seats so they were blocking me from view of the OBS table, Cam pulling me in so close I was practically on his lap. Ben signaled for the waiter.

"We need all of this boxed up immediately," he said. "And please box up some entrées and desserts as well—Seb will know which ones. We'll be waiting in the parking lot. You can bring them to us out there."

The waiter's eyes widened, and he stammered in confusion. Ben clasped the waiter's hand as he moved out of the booth. As the waiter pulled his hand away, his confused expression transformed into one of amazement.

"Right away, sir," he said, gathering the appetizers and whisking them away.

"Did you just slip him money?" I asked, momentarily distracted. "I thought that only happened in movies."

Ben winked at me.

"Let's go, sweetheart," Cam said, tugging me out of my seat.

"We don't have to leave," I said weakly. No part of me wanted to stay. Being this close to my mother and her vicious friends made me nauseous, but I didn't want to be a nuisance either.

"If we stay, I'll do something I regret," Cam said, pulling me out of the booth. "Probably best we go unless you want to pick me up from jail."

I wasn't sure what it said about me that his words didn't remotely frighten me. Instead, I pulled him down for a kiss, uncaring that the OBS was watching. For the first time, I left an encounter with them feeling like I came out on top. They could do their best to insult me, but I was the one leaving with three hot alphas who cared about me, while they all had to go back home to cruel alphas who didn't give them the time of day.

The guys ushered me to the car, and Ben slipped into the back seat with me.

"I'm sorry," I said, breaking the silence. I wasn't sure what I was apologizing for, except that I had been the one who wanted to go out, and it had turned into a complete disaster.

"Baby girl, none of that was your fault," Cam said tenderly, turning in the passenger seat and grasping my hand in his. "I'm sorry we didn't do more to defend you."

"I just kept hearing Amirah's voice in my head saying the DC will try to take you away from us," Theo said, a vulnerable look on his face. "We don't believe anything they said. Forgive us?"

It took a minute for my brain to catch up to what he'd said. *He* was asking for *my* forgiveness?

"There's nothing to forgive," I stammered.

Theo reached out and held my other hand, rubbing my palm where my fingernail indentations had been.

"Don't worry, we'll get our revenge," Ben said. "I'm texting Seb." He kissed me on the cheek before continuing to text furiously. "Those women are about to have a terrible dining experience."

"What? Who's Seb?" I asked.

"Seb is my good friend who happens to be the owner and head chef. And he owes me a favor."

"Ben, you shouldn't do anything," I said without much conviction, a smile spreading across my face.

"Oh, but I should," Ben responded before letting out an evil cackle.

"You're such a dork," Cam told Ben with a grin.

"I have to tell Sam his mom won the betting pool," I mused.

"That was Sam's mom?" Theo asked.

"Yeah, Victoria. She's always been super quiet. I wasn't even sure she could speak for a long time. But she came by Sam's apartment right before he moved out to say goodbye, and I heard her tell him she loves him." Of everyone in the OBS, Victoria was the least evil.

"You grew up with all of them?" Ben asked.

I nodded, but before I could say anything else, there was a tap on the car window. A middle-aged alpha wearing a white apron stood outside with several large paper bags. He was all warmth with brown skin, dark brown hair, and a beard streaked with silver. I caught a hint of his cardamom-orange scent as Ben opened the car door, instantly putting me at ease.

"Seb!" Ben exclaimed, taking the bags from the chef and putting them in the trunk. The two of them clasped hands in greeting. "I didn't think you'd be the one running these out here."

"I had to," he said, turning his gaze on me. "Had to apologize to this sweetie for her less than stellar dining experience."

"More like you were feeling nosy," Theo said with a smirk.

Seb's eyes sparkled. "Can you blame me? I've never seen Ben this excited. I just had to meet the lovely lady." He held his hand out to me, and I giggled as he bowed dramatically before kissing it. Cam growled and Seb's smile grew wider.

"It's wonderful to meet you, Josie."

"Nice to meet you, too," I said.

Seb released my hand, and his face grew more serious. "I am truly sorry you had such a poor experience in my restaurant, sweetie. My servers and cooks have received special instructions for how to deal with a certain table, so rest assured we have everything under control," he said with a wink. "Now I have to run, but please come back soon." He clasped Ben on the shoulder before jogging back to the restaurant.

"How about we set up a picnic in the courtyard?" Theo suggested as he pulled out of the parking lot.

"That sounds nice," I responded.

I still felt bad about ruining the evening, but then Ben moved to the middle seat and wrapped his arms around me. I leaned into his embrace, running my nose along his neck to breathe in his scent. He gently massaged my neck and I groaned, not realizing how tight my muscles were. He kept up the massage all the way home until I was slumped against his chest, totally relaxed.

Cam opened the car door for me, taking my hand firmly in his as we walked to the courtyard.

"You need string lights," I mused, looking around the garden.

"It's your house now, too," Cam said, squeezing my hand. "And you're right, *we* do."

Ben set up the food, laughing as he pulled out plastic drink cups. "Looks like our cocktails came with us."

"Gimme," I said, holding out my hand.

We all sat around the outdoor table, and Ben plated the appetizers for me. I stared down at the overflowing plate, mouth watering at the array of food. But I couldn't get Sharon's voice and my mom's disappointed glare out of my head.

Cam moved closer and squeezed my thigh. "You need to eat, baby girl."

I forced myself to take a bite of the fried mac and cheese and hummed in delight. I looked up and saw all three alphas beaming at me.

"Why are you looking at me like that?"

"We like seeing you happy and knowing you're safe and fed," Theo said.

I blushed. "I haven't had much of that in my life."

"No kidding, if that's who you grew up with," Ben said.

"What's the deal with them?" Cam asked. "Didn't seem like your mom's friends are very nice to her."

"Yeah. I'm not sure they're nice to anyone, but they've always treated her like an outcast." I responded, taking another bite of the mac and cheese. "Sam and I call them the Omega Bitch Squad."

Ben choked on his drink, snorting out in laughter. "Perfect name."

"Why would they treat her like an outcast?" Theo asked. "I would have thought being bonded to your pack fathers would give her some clout."

"It probably would have, except she ran away from the community with my father when she was young. No one could ever really forgive her for that crime," I said.

"Wait, your father?" Cam asked.

"Yeah," I said.

All three of them looked at me with confusion.

"Oh, I'm not related to Jericho or Richard. My mom fell in love with my father when she was seventeen."

"Why didn't she stay with him?" Cam asked.

"He died," I said, a lump forming in my throat. "I've never even gotten to see a picture of him."

I took a sip of water and blinked away my tears. Cam's grip on my thigh grew tighter, his touch reassuring me I wasn't alone.

"I'm sorry, angel," Theo said. "Do you know what happened to him?"

I swallowed past the lump in my throat. "My mom never talked about him, except for one night. She came into my room and she was really drunk. She sat on my bed and told me about him. It's the only time I've even heard her say his name. It was Jonas. They knew each other growing up, and she'd had a crush on him for years. He was an alpha but didn't have a pack and wasn't interested in forming one, so he wasn't eligible to mate with an omega. But they loved each other, I guess, so they ran away. She said he wore a leather jacket and drove a motorcycle."

A smile tugged at my lips. I couldn't imagine my mom running away with a bad-boy alpha. It made me wish I could have met her before everything else happened.

"A year after they left, my mom got pregnant with me. She said that the pregnancy added stress to the relationship because they didn't have much money. Growing up in a Designation Traditionalist community, she usually would never have been allowed to get a job, but she worked as a secretary until she had me. Then Jonas started drinking to deal with the pressure of caring for an omega and a child."

"We're not meant to do things alone," Theo said. "They needed more support."

I nodded, but deep down, I knew it was my fault. They were happy until they had me.

"My mom started crying, and she kept saying, 'I love you, Jonas, I miss you, please come back,' over and over. I didn't know what to do. I've never seen her like that."

"How old were you?" Ben asked.

"Nine."

"Shit, that's a lot for a nine-year-old to process," Theo said.

I shrugged. It wasn't the worst I had experienced growing up.

"When she finally got up to leave, she stopped in the doorway and said, 'I wish you and I had died alongside him so we wouldn't have to live this misery.' I think it's the only honest thing she's ever said. She said she hates looking at me because I look like him. He had green eyes."

"Fuck," Cam said, his jaw clenched. He tugged me into his lap, his strong arms wrapping around me and his face pressed to the top of my head.

"It's my fault that things got bad between them," I said, tears streaming down my face.

"How can you possibly figure that?" Theo asked.

"He started working more to make money for me. If he hadn't been so stressed, maybe he wouldn't have started drinking. And then maybe he wouldn't have died."

"No, love, it wasn't your fault," Theo said, his expression devastatingly sad.

"Not at all," Ben said, scooting closer to me so he could hold my hand.

I took a shuddering breath. I'd never told anyone this before except for Sam. It hurt to talk about, but something in me wanted to keep going. I didn't want to be crushed beneath the secrets anymore.

"My mother didn't have anywhere to go. She had a two-year-old and was an omega alone. So she returned to her parents' house. I think they're the ones who set up the match between her and Jericho and Richard. I don't know if they ever loved each other, but they certainly don't now. I knew I wasn't biologically theirs because they told me all the time. My grandparents did, too. They made sure I knew, even as a child, that I didn't really belong with them."

"Fucking bastards," Cam growled, the vibrations in his chest running through my body.

"Yeah, the whole family is horrible. And I..." I wasn't sure if I should share this next part.

"What, sweetheart?" Cam asked, cradling me closer to his body.

"I don't know. It's probably stupid. But one time, my grandmother was talking on the phone when I was at their house. They had locked me in a closet. I think she forgot I was there, so she was standing nearby and said, 'It was good we got rid of him.' I don't know if she was talking about my dad, but what if she was? What if they did something to him?"

"They locked you in a closet?" Cam growled, outraged.

I scrunched my nose. "I feel like the possibility of them murdering my dad deserves more of a reaction than them locking me in the closet."

"Fucking does not," Cam bit out. I looked at Ben and Theo for support, but their faces were both hard with anger.

"Did they do that often?" Theo asked, his voice low and cold.

I squirmed. "Umm, no."

"Josie," Cam said. "Don't lie to us."

"I mean, sometimes they would. But it's actually a good thing because it forced me to learn how to pick locks. Which, you know, is a handy skill," I said, trying to lighten the mood. It didn't work. A heavy blanket of silence fell.

"Don't be mad," I whispered, looking up at Cam.

He took a deep breath and met my gaze. "I'm not mad at you, baby girl."

I wrapped my arms around his neck, squeezing tightly.

"Why would your grandparents treat you like that?" Ben asked.

"They didn't approve of my dad," I said with a shrug. "I think they also blamed me because my mom couldn't have any more kids. She was in and out of doctor's offices most of my childhood, but I don't know if they ever figured out what was wrong. It gave my mom some status when I revealed as an omega. Everyone had been convinced I would be a beta, so it was a relief for her. But I'd always been fat, even as a kid, and that didn't change once I revealed. They took me for testing multiple times to ensure I was an omega and to figure out what was wrong with me. But the doctors could never figure anything out. Everyone just decided that I was the problem."

My alphas protested at once, so fierce in their disagreement that I let out a startled laugh.

"Love hearing you laugh," Cam murmured, his lips brushing my ear.

"Thank you," I said, looking at each of my alphas. I couldn't believe how lucky I was to have them.

"I feel like there has to be something wrong with me, though, because my mom hasn't been a mother to me, but I still feel sad for her. I can't remember seeing her happy—she was definitely never happy with me. And I know Jericho and Richard treat her like crap. She's never stood up for me, never helped me, so why do I feel so sad? Why do I still love her?"

"Because you have a kind heart, beautiful," Ben said, his eyes shimmering. "You're so sweet and incredible. They don't deserve you."

"Maybe her criticizing you is a way to protect you from repeating what she had to go through," Theo mused.

"Yeah, maybe," I said, staring back at my food.

"Doesn't make it okay," Cam grunted.

"Of course not," Theo said easily. "She obviously doesn't have your strength or compassion."

The conversation lulled, and I picked at my food.

"Okay," Ben said, clapping his hands. "Enough sadness." He handed me his phone. "Pick out some music, precious."

I looked at the music app, unsure of what to choose. "What do you all like?"

"Nope," Ben said cheerfully. "Pick something you like. And let's get these cocktails poured."

I finally selected an album by a popular female artist.

There was speculation that she might actually be an omega. I figured if the guys hated it, we could always change it.

The bass pumped as the melody of the first track started playing through speakers I hadn't known were hanging on the courtyard wall.

"Excellent," Ben said. He handed me my martini in a plastic cup and I took a long drink. Cotton candy flavor exploded in my mouth. The energy at the table eased with Ben's enthusiasm for the food and the upbeat music. I found myself humming along to the songs and eating everything Ben put in front of me.

Theo launched into a conversation about his favorite books, and I eagerly joined in. I saw Cam out of the corner of my eye sneaking sips of my martini when he thought I wasn't looking. Finally, I turned around fast enough to catch him in the act. His cheeks blushed furiously.

"Next time, you have to order one for yourself," I laughed. I leaned forward and kissed him on the cheek. "But don't worry, your secret's safe with me."

Cam set down the drink and gripped my chin with his thumb and forefinger. "I guess I just like tasting sweet things." My body heated at his words and I swayed closer to him. His firm hand on my face guided me into a deep kiss. I could taste the cotton candy on his tongue.

I held back a whimper when he pulled away. His hand returned to my thigh, giving it a tight squeeze.

"Finish eating, baby girl."

Theo and Ben's eyes were on me, their deep scents swirling in the breeze. I knew I wasn't ready to have sex with all of them yet, but a gush of slick soaked my underwear at the thought of all their hands on me.

I cleared my throat, grateful for the de-scenter masking most of my perfume, and continued to eat.

The night turned chilly. The moment I started shivering, the guys announced it was time to move inside. I caught Ben's hand as he was tidying up.

"Thanks for a great evening," I said. "I didn't think I could feel relaxed after everything, but you made it happen for me."

Ben beamed and pulled me into a tight hug. "You make everything better." He spun me around, making me laugh, before tugging me inside.

Chapter Thirty-Two

Josie

"Look at his hand! He touched her bare hand, and he's feeling things," I shouted, pointing at Mr. Darcy from my perch on the den sectional.

"I thought he hated her," Ben said, his arms wrapped around me and his chin resting on my head.

"Classic enemies to lovers," Theo said, squeezing my hand.

Cam grunted from his spot next to Ben. "Don't fucking get the appeal. If they like each other, they should just say it. Waste of time."

Theo and I grinned at each other. We had convinced the guys to watch Pride and Prejudice. It was a rainy Saturday and we'd spent most of the day curled up together, watching movies and letting Ben ply us with snacks.

Just then, Cam's phone rang. He fished it out of his pocket and swore.

I tensed. "Who is it?" After our encounter with the OBS, I was feeling more on edge. Would my mother say anything to my fathers? Would the DC or Pack Madden do something to try to separate us?

"Sorry, sweetheart, nothing to do with you, just a fucking annoying client. I'll be right back." Cam kissed my forehead before leaving the room.

Theo paused the movie.

"What's going on with the client?" I asked.

Ben groaned. "They've been obnoxious from start to finish. We did a complete overhaul of their cybersecurity, but they keep coming up with new things for us to check. Their headquarters are about two hours away, and we've sent several teams to address their issues, but they keep complaining."

Cam stormed back into the room. "Fucking obnoxious motherfuckers. I'm going to murder them."

"What did they say?" Theo asked.

"They're being paranoid. They said we missed things with their building security and the cybersecurity of their servers," Cam said with disdain.

"I've hired so many people to try to hack into those servers," Ben said, rubbing his eyes. "They're solid. No one can get in. This is such bullshit."

I curled up against Theo. I knew none of them were mad at me, but the tension in the room set me on edge. My body still wasn't convinced I wouldn't be harmed.

Cam sat on the ottoman in front of me and put his hand on my thigh. "Not frustrated with you, sweetheart."

"But you haven't been working much since I've been here and it's making things harder for you," I said.

"Our team is completely capable of running the day-to-day," Theo said.

"This company, in particular, wants to feel important by having us there. They don't want to settle for any of our staff," Cam said, rolling his eyes.

I felt obnoxious for needing their constant reassurance, but I loved that they were willing to give it to me.

"We have to follow up with them in person," Cam said, capturing one of my hands and rubbing it tenderly.

"What?" Ben whined. "Just tell them to get over themselves."

Cam sighed. "I said we would do one more in-person eval and then we're done. If they want more after this, they can hire someone else. I wouldn't even agree to this, except they're one of the biggest companies in the province, and I don't want to burn bridges if we don't have to."

"So you all have to go?" I asked, trying to hide how anxious I felt about being left on my own.

"I'll stay," Theo said, kissing my temple.

"Why do you get to stay?" Ben asked, snuggling closer to me and trying to pull me out of Theo's grasp.

"Because you need to look at their servers, and I have to evaluate their building security," Cam said unhappily. "We'll leave soon and be back tomorrow by midmorning."

"Okay," I said quietly. *Don't go, I'll miss you.*

"Are you sure you want to go to class tonight?" Cam asked.

Luc had texted our group chat earlier and asked if we wanted a quick class tonight. A guest trainer was coming to lead classes in the gym for the next week and it would be too risky for us to go in, so it would be our last opportunity to meet for a while. I had hesitated to ask the guys if I could go, but they all agreed without argument. I knew Cam still wasn't comfortable with it, though, and a part of me wanted to succumb to his hopeful expression and tell him I would stay home.

I bit my lip and exhaled slowly. "Yeah. Is that okay?"

Cam's jaw clenched almost imperceptibly. "Of course, sweetheart." He kissed me on the forehead before he and Ben went upstairs to pack.

"Want to finish the movie?" Theo asked.

"Sure," I said without enthusiasm.

"They'll be back before you know it, love," Theo said, tucking me into his chest.

"I'm being silly."

"Not at all. Being separated from your mates is always hard, especially at the beginning. If it makes you feel better, those two will be miserable the whole time."

I scowled at him. "I don't want them to be miserable." But my omega preened at the thought of them missing us.

"You're sweet," he said, pulling me in for a kiss. My stomach fluttered when I realized this meant I would get alone time with Theo. The other two often overshadowed his more reserved personality, and I wanted to get to know him better.

I heard Cam and Ben coming down the stairs, and I pushed myself off the cozy spot on the couch to say goodbye.

Ben picked me up and twirled me. "I'll miss you, precious. Don't have too much fun with Theo without me," he said with a wink.

He cupped my face with one hand and pulled me in for a kiss, backing me up until I was pressed against the kitchen wall. I wrapped my hands in his loose curls, trying to hold him tight enough so he would stay. I whimpered as his hips rolled into mine.

"Can't wait to be inside you, to feel that sweet pussy coming on my cock, hear more of those breathy little moans you make when you're close."

I swear I almost came just from his words. The guys had been careful not to pressure me to do anything sexual, but hearing Ben didn't make me anxious. It made me want to strip and have him fuck me right here, against the wall.

Ben was ripped away, Cam standing in his place.

"Fuck, Ben, you can't get her worked up like that before we leave," he grumbled.

"I've got to be sure you don't forget me," Ben said cheekily, giving me a tender kiss before heading out to the garage.

My body felt like it was on fire. I whined, wanting Ben to come back, wanting someone to make me orgasm.

"Come here, sweetheart," Cam said. "Got to help you calm down a little."

He pulled me in close and ran his hands soothingly over my back and arms. His pace was slow and he kept a steady pressure until my muscles felt like jelly. I sighed and relaxed fully against his chest.

"I'll miss you," Cam said.

"I'll miss you, too. Come back quickly."

"Be safe in class tonight. No risks. No injuries." Cam tilted my chin up so I met his gaze.

"Are you upset that I'm going to class again?"

He hesitated, running his thumb across my cheek. "I'm not going to say I'm comfortable with it, especially since I'll be out of town. It's not because I don't want you to do the things you enjoy. It's just because I feel like I should be protecting you, and it makes me uncomfortable to have you away from me."

"Thanks for caring about me and for letting me make my own choices," I said.

Cam rubbed his head against mine, scent marking me. I hid my smile against his chest. My possessive alpha wanted me to smell like him before he left.

"I have a gift for you."

I pulled away, my omega perking up at the promise of presents. "What is it?" I tried to reign in my eagerness, but Cam's grin told me I had failed.

He pulled a pink gift bag out of his duffel bag and handed it to me. I reached into the bag and pulled out the softest, nicest workout set I'd ever held. The leggings were butter smooth and made from special performance fabric. The tank top was made of similar material and there was a fleece-lined black pullover, perfect for the cooler temperatures. At the bottom of the bag was a pair of brand-new sneakers. They were black with glitter.

"I wanted to get you some colorful clothes but thought I should stick with black since it will be less noticeable when you're going in and out of the gym." Cam rubbed his neck and I could swear there was a slight blush on his cheeks. Was he nervous about my reaction?

I threw my arms around him, and he picked me up. There were tears in my eyes.

"Thank you," I said, pressing kisses up and down his neck. That he wanted to support me in going to class because it was important to me, even though he wasn't comfortable with it, filled me with warmth.

"It's nothing," Cam said, looking shy again. He was wrong. It was *everything*.

He gave me a light kiss on the lips and a final squeeze before setting me down and heading out to the garage. Theo pressed behind me, making me shiver as his lips skimmed my neck.

"Let's get you some dinner before heading to class."

Chapter Thirty-Three

Josie

Theo took a circuitous route to the gym. He held my hand, but his other was tense on the wheel, and his eyes kept darting to the rearview mirror.

"Do you really think there's someone following us?" I asked as he took another unnecessary turn.

He shot me a quick smile and squeezed my hand. "No, I don't think so. But I'm not taking any chances with your safety."

Finally, we pulled into the small alleyway leading to the back entrance.

"Remember, don't step outside until you see me pull up. Call me if you need anything or want me to come get you early. I'll be right upstairs in the gym."

I hid my smile at his fussing.

"I know, Theo. I'll be super careful, promise."

He looked like he would start lecturing again, so I leaned over the center console and kissed him. I loved how pillowy soft his lips were, loved the warmth of him as his coffee scent intensified. He wrapped his hand around my neck and deepened the kiss. I moaned at the feel of his tongue against mine, our breaths coming faster. I strained against my seatbelt, trying to press my body against his.

Theo broke away from me with a groan.

"Fuck, angel, I can't go into the gym covered in your scent. The other alphas will lose their shit."

I whined. I wanted him to be covered with my scent, wanted everyone to know that he was mine.

Theo smirked, taking in my scowl. "You're a possessive little thing, aren't you?"

I huffed and unbuckled my seat belt. His statement stung. Was he criticizing me? Maybe he pushed me away because he didn't want me.

Before I could get the door, Theo was there, holding it open and offering me his hand. I refused it and got out of the car on my own, crossing my arms. Theo gently placed his fingers under my chin, lifting it so I was forced to look into his warm brown eyes.

"Have I mentioned how much I love that you're possessive of me, angel? Because I'm possessive as fuck over you." He planted little kisses down the side of my face and I melted into him. I was feeling extra vulnerable with my other two alphas gone. I knew they had to leave for work, but my omega felt rejected.

"You owe me kisses later," I said, still not liking that he had stopped me in the car.

"We could just leave and have kisses now," he suggested, running his hand down my arm.

"Nope," I said. "You pushed me away, so now you have to wait."

Theo growled, pressing me back until I was against the car.

"You like teasing me, little omega?"

My heart pounded, and I wanted more. I wanted to feel his

cock pressed against my core, wanted to know what it would be like to feel him inside me.

His body stilled before he backed away. "Fuck! This is all your fault for being irresistible. Now I've got to use fucking descenter spray. Get inside before I put your cute little ass back in this car and take you home."

My inner omega preened with satisfaction that we had caused our alpha to lose control. I practically skipped the few steps to the back entrance stairwell as Theo kept a firm grip on my hand and scanned the alley again.

"Behave yourself," he said sternly, placing a quick kiss on my forehead and adjusting his pants before heading back to the car.

When I stepped into the dim basement, Clementine, Poppy, and Westin were by the door, staring at me with huge grins.

"Why didn't you bring in your alpha, Josie? We haven't seen this one before. He looks soooo sexy and mysterious," Poppy said, a mischievous expression on her face.

My omega snarled, not liking anyone talking about our alpha.

"Poppy, do you want to get attacked?" Westin asked, a smirk on her face.

"Don't worry, Josie. He's all yours. My alphas keep me plenty busy. Although I don't have one with a sexy British accent," Poppy mused, twirling her curly blonde hair.

Possessiveness seized me. Poppy was my friend and I knew she was teasing, but part of me wanted to tackle her.

Clementine threw her arm around me. "It's not like you would be successful, Poppy," she said. "Theo only has eyes for Josie."

That's right, he only wants me. A thrill went through me as I realized I believed my own words. I still wasn't sure why they wanted me when they could have anyone else. But they had chosen *me*, made clear their attraction to *me*.

"Where's Luc?" I asked, looking around.

"He had to deal with some issue upstairs. He said we should get started on our warm-ups," Clementine said.

"I don't want to," Westin whined, lying down on a mat.

I raised my eyebrows. Westin was usually so focused, never one to complain. As I examined her more closely, I saw she looked paler than usual, her eyes squinting as if the basement lights were bothering her.

"I'm just tired today," she said with a shrug, averting her gaze.

I bit my lip, wanting to press her further, when Poppy interrupted my train of thought.

"I think we should forget about the warm-ups. I need girl time," Poppy said, flopping down next to Westin before turning back to me with a playful smirk. "Josie, I want to hear how things are going with your alphas."

I scowled at her.

"I pinky promise no more teasing. They're your alphas. I would never dare try to get between you and them." She held out her pinky towards me.

"Okay," I said, squeezing her pinky with mine. "I forgive you."

Poppy beamed and patted the spot on the mat beside her, and I lowered myself down.

"Are you happy with them?" Westin asked, her earnest eyes meeting mine.

"Yeah, I am," I said. "I was so scared to join a pack, scared to even be around alphas. But they're the best. They make me feel so safe."

I thought I saw *longing* in Westin's eyes. Did she want a pack?

"Aww!" Poppy said. "Look at that ridiculous smile on your face."

It had been so long since I had other girls to talk to. The vulnerability of opening up clawed at my stomach, but I needed to process everything that was happening.

I took a deep breath. "But I feel so... needy all the time? Is something wrong with me?"

"What do you mean?" Clementine asked, leaning her chin on her knees from her spot across from me.

"Cam and Ben left this afternoon for a work thing, and they won't be back until the morning. I know they're not going to be gone for long, but I already miss them, and I feel all raw inside."

Poppy nodded. "That's totally normal. The first time one of my alphas left the house to go to the store, I sobbed the whole time they were gone. Freaked them all the fuck out," she said with a smirk. "The fact that you're not bawling right now means you're doing leaps and bounds better than I did. Us omegas are needy. It's how we're made. It gets easier, but you shouldn't feel bad about it. And your alphas should definitely help you when you're feeling that way."

The weight on my chest lessened at her words. What I was experiencing was normal. That didn't mean I liked it, especially after a year of almost complete independence, but at least there wasn't something wrong with me.

"Okay, I've been dying to know—have you had sex yet?" Poppy asked, practically bouncing on her spot on the mat.

"Poppy! Not everyone is as comfortable talking about sex as you are," Westin said.

"But I want to know! Did you see how he pressed her against the car? That was so hot."

My face was on fire. "Umm, no. We haven't."

"Why not?" Poppy asked, looking as if I had stolen her favorite toy.

"I want to," I said quietly. I knew no one could hear us, but I still felt like this subject required hushed voices. "With the other two guys gone, I thought Theo and I might..."

"Tonight?" Poppy squealed loudly.

"Shh," I said, lunging at Poppy.

"No one can hear us," she said, laughing.

"Theo is upstairs," I hissed.

"Okay, fine, fine. I'll be quiet," Poppy said.

"So you're thinking tonight?" Clementine asked gently.

"I don't know," I groaned, flopping back on the mat. "I'm scared."

"What are you scared of?" Clementine asked, her eyes wide.

"Mostly that I'll freak out... that it will remind me of what happened at the DA." My voice was a hoarse whisper, my gaze focused on a crack in the cement brick wall.

Clementine's hand gently landed on top of mine. "I don't know exactly what you went through, but I'm sorry it happened."

I nodded, still averting my gaze.

"There's no rush to do it," Westin said gently. "Do you feel like they're pressuring you?"

"No, not at all," I said, biting my lip. "But I think I want to do it? I don't know." I covered my face with my arms. "I want to have sex with Theo. With all of them. I don't want what happened at the DA to control me, to make me scared forever. But what if I lose it on him?"

"So what if you do?" Poppy said. "If he's worthy of you, he'll understand and be kind about it."

I shifted my arms to glance at Poppy.

"Look, I don't know what happened at the DA after I left,

but I'll never forget what you looked like when I saw you after you got out. You scared the shit out of me. It was like you were dead. And the past few weeks, it feels like you've come back to life again," Poppy said. I was shocked to see her brush away a tear. "There's nothing wrong with you for being scared. I had issues trusting my alphas at first. The DA really messed us up."

"You did?" I asked, sitting up to face Poppy. She had such a vibrant sex life and her relationship with her alphas seemed so fun and easy.

"Yeah. I freaked out anytime I was alone. I cried a lot. And they didn't really know what to do, but they were there and kept trying. They earned my trust over time. Remember that I've been with them for almost three years now. We weren't like this at the beginning."

It hadn't dawned on me that someone as confident and carefree as Poppy could have struggled, too. She scooted closer to me and ran her hand through my hair. I leaned into her, something I wouldn't have been able to do a few months ago.

"Okay, so hypothetically, if I decided to have sex with him tonight, what would I do? I don't want to mess it up," I said, glancing at Westin and Clementine.

"You can't mess up sex," Westin said with a small smile. "As long as it feels good and you're comfortable, it's right."

"But what if he doesn't think I'm attractive?"

My friends snorted and rolled their eyes.

"I'm serious!"

"Josie, come on. They already know what you look like. And you're fucking hot," Poppy said with a confidence I didn't have.

"I don't know what to do to make it good for him," I confessed.

"Alphas are so easy," Poppy said with confidence. "Everything feels good to them."

"But I've never even seen a... you know," I said, gesturing at my crotch.

"Do you need me to draw you a diagram of a cock?" Poppy asked with a giggle.

"Ugh, no! I just don't know what to do with it."

Westin giggled. "Well, mainly put it inside you, right? But you can also give a blow job. They're easy—you just grip the base with your hand and move it up and down for a bit. Keep gripping the base and put your mouth on the tip. Use your tongue a lot. And then put as much as you can in your mouth and suck. That's pretty much all there is to it."

Clementine nodded. "You can touch their balls, too. Some guys go crazy with that."

"Am I supposed to, like... swallow it?" I asked, my voice getting high-pitched.

"That's up to you. But you'll probably want to. Alpha jizz tastes really good to omegas," Poppy said, a dreamy look on her face.

The three of us stared at her before bursting into laughter.

"Fuck, I'm missing out being a beta," Clementine said, tears streaming down her face. "I think it tastes so gross."

"Maybe that's an incentive for me to try alphas," Westin said, her face pink. "Because beta males do not give me that dreamy expression."

"I want to know about knotting," Clementine said.

I whipped my head towards her with a squeal. "Wait, Clementine—have you and Dave done it?"

"Who's Dave?" Poppy demanded.

Clementine cleared her throat. "Umm, just an alpha I know. And no. He said it's too dangerous for us to be together. But I think he doesn't want to be with me because he wants an omega."

"Fuck that!" Poppy said. "You're hot and amazing. Any alpha should crawl on his knees to be worthy of you."

Clementine raised her eyebrows at me.

"Poppy has strong opinions," I said with a smile. "But she's right."

"Of course I am. Okay, so obviously, knots are easier for omegas to take. We have an extra pleasure spot internally that the knot rubs against when it's inflated and it feels amazing. It can still feel intense and overwhelming the first few times, but it shouldn't hurt. I know betas that have been able to work up to take a knot. You just have to practice," Poppy said.

"I get being scared, though," Westin said, patting my hand. "I've never been with an alpha, so obviously, I've never experienced it. It kind of scares me, the idea of being stuck together."

"That's why it's important to do it with someone you trust," Poppy said. "But you don't have to be knotted tonight if you're not ready. You just have to communicate your needs."

"I don't like having to do that," I whined. Poppy gave me a little shove.

I covered my face and groaned. "Why am I so nervous?"

"You just have to do it," Poppy said. "Just get home and seduce him."

"Seduce him?" I squealed, quickly covering my mouth at how loud I'd been. "I can't seduce him," I hissed.

"Just walk up to him, grab his cock through his pants, and say, 'Daddy, I want your big, fat cock inside me,'" Poppy said, forming a pout with her lips and blinking her eyes.

"Oh my god, Poppy!" the three of us shrieked.

She fell over with a cackle. "Okay, that might be a little advanced. Why don't you suggest giving each other massages? And then, if things feel right, you just build from there?"

I took a deep breath. Massages. Okay, that might be doable.

Before we could say anything else, the door opened and Luc walked in.

He looked at the four of us, sprawled out on the mats.

"Why did I think I could leave you to your own devices?" he muttered.

"I don't know, Luc," Poppy said. "But thank goodness we have a big, strong alpha here to direct us now."

Luc rolled his eyes, but I swore I saw his lips twitch.

"Alright, let's get going," he said, voice firm.

Poppy pulled me up and gave me a hug. "I'll text you tomorrow morning to see how it was," she said with a wink.

"Hey, Clementine," I said, keeping my voice low as we partnered off. "I was wondering if there's been any word from the DC about my pack. I thought they'd be more, I don't know, meddling? But they haven't gotten in touch with us at all. Do you know what's going on?"

Clementine brought her head close to mine, her voice low and conspiratorial. "Things aren't going well for Glen Jacoby or Marshall Whiteburn," she said in a hushed voice. "We thought they would be more interfering, too, especially with how angry your pack fathers were with your selection. But the Alliance has been doing a ton to dismantle the government, so I think that has them distracted. Typically, the DC does a home check before officially signing off on a pack. I'm guessing Amirah can swing it so I'm the one who does that check."

"Oh my gosh, that would be perfect. And we could hang out at the house after," I said, bouncing up and down with excitement at the idea of actually being able to have friends over.

"I'm so glad we're friends," she said softly.

"Me, too."

Chapter Thirty-Four

Josie

Theo was waiting for me after class, his SUV parked right by the gym's back exit. As soon as he saw me, he rounded the car to open the passenger side door. My stomach filled with little butterflies as I bounded towards him and threw myself into his arms. He automatically picked me up and squeezed me in for a crushingly tight hug. He'd clearly showered after his workout, and his hair was damp and falling across his forehead.

"Hi," I said, my face pressed against his chest and breathing in his scent.

"I missed you," he said quietly, pressing his face against my hair.

"It was only an hour," I responded, pulling away from him as he set me back on the ground. "But I missed you, too."

Theo's lips quirked up in a smile as he kissed me on the forehead and helped me get in my seat. The heat was blasting in the car and my seat warmer was on. I knew it wasn't because Theo needed it—he never seemed to get cold—but because he knew I got chilled easily. I wiggled happily at his attentiveness.

"I thought we might stop and get some ice cream," he said, resting his hand on my leg as he drove through the downtown traffic. Heat pooled in my core as I imagined his hand inching further and further up my thigh.

"I would love that," I responded, resting my hand on his.

"How was class?"

"It was so good," I said. "Luc used his bark on us and we practiced resisting it."

It had been a challenging class and different than usual. We usually practiced physically defending ourselves and fighting off opponents, but today was all about psychological resistance. Omegas were hard-wired to respond to an alpha's bark, making us vulnerable no matter how physically strong or capable we were.

When Luc first suggested it, I had panicked, taken back to all my horrific memories with... the device. The scar on my arm had burned, and I'd almost refused to try. But with my friends encouraging me, I'd given it a shot. Being able to resist him, even just a little, had given me back the confidence *they* had stolen. And it felt fucking amazing.

Theo fell silent, and his grip on my leg grew painfully hard. I whimpered and he immediately snatched his hand away, throwing me a horrified look.

"I'm so sorry, love. Did I hurt you?"

"I'm fine," I said, waving a hand. "Why are you upset?"

"Upset?" he responded, his voice getting louder. "I'm fucking livid! Using an alpha bark on an omega you're not bonded with is illegal. I'm going to kill him." Theo whipped around in a U-turn, causing angry drivers to honk as he cut them off.

I wasn't sure what to feel at his over-protectiveness—grateful? Annoyed? A little nervous? Theo was kind and gentle at his core, and for some reason, I found myself giggling at his over-the-top reaction.

"Love, what could you possibly be finding funny right now?" he asked in a deadly, measured voice that would have made me shrink back a week ago. But I knew this alpha now and couldn't stop more laughter from bursting out. Theo's face, which had been contorted in anger, turned towards me in confusion.

"What's the plan?" I asked in between peals of laughter. "You're going to roll up and kill Luc?"

"You think I won't?" Theo growled. "You don't think I'll do anything to protect you?"

"No, of course, I know you would," I said, my voice softening. I brushed my hand across his cheek and he leaned into my touch. "But then, what will you do with the body?" I asked, my laughter kicking up again.

It had been so long since I caught the giggles like this and it felt so good to laugh with abandon as the streetlights flickered, my pissed-off alpha next to me. *I love this man so much.* The thought caught me off guard, taking my breath away before spreading warmth across my body. Something about this whole situation made me feel safe and secure. I grabbed Theo's wrist, gently pulling his right hand off the wheel so I could hold it in both of mine.

I turned my body to face him, taking in the profile of his strong jaw and the pieces of his dark hair falling down around his face.

"You haven't answered me," I said, keeping my voice serious as I reached one of my hands out to brush his hair from his face. "What will you do with Luc's body after you kill him?"

The corner of Theo's mouth twitched. "I have a tarp and rope in the boot. I'll wrap it around his body to transport it, throw him in the car, and then take him out to our cabin property to burn," he said, his voice still serious but lacking the anger from before.

"We'll have to circle back to why you have a tarp and rope in your car. But it sounds like I'll have to help you? Be in the car with a dead body on the way to the property? Not very thoughtful, making me an accessory to the murder. Also, you promised me ice cream."

"I'll make sure you get extra sprinkles for your help," he said, squeezing my hand before putting his back on the wheel to turn the car around. "Or I suppose we can skip the murder for tonight. Don't want the ice cream shop to close on us."

"Mmm, good thinking. I would be really mad if I didn't get my ice cream tonight."

Theo took a deep breath. "I'm sorry I got a little upset, love."

"A little upset?" I asked incredulously.

"Just a touch," he responded, finally breaking into a real smile. It transformed his face, making him even more breathtakingly handsome than usual. Theo's smiles were rare, and each one felt like winning a prize.

"Just a tiny murderous rage," I teased.

Theo grunted, pulling up outside the ice cream shop and parking. He turned to me, cupping my face and pulling me in for a kiss. He rested his forehead against mine and breathed deeply, scenting me.

"You're really okay?" he asked.

"I'm really okay."

He took a shuddering breath. "I want to hear more about the class. I promise I'll listen."

"Thank you," I whispered.

"How about we get ice cream to go—there's a spot we can drive to near here with a great view of the city."

"Do I still get extra sprinkles? Even though I didn't help with body disposal?"

"You get as many sprinkles as you want. You get anything you want, my love."

His voice sounded so sincere it made tears come to my eyes. I blinked them away and kissed him again, his lips gentle against mine. Theo kissed my forehead, holding my gaze for a moment before getting out of the car. He quickly opened my door, took my hand, and hugged me tightly.

"Thank you for caring about my safety. And for wanting to listen to me," I murmured into his chest.

"You're the most precious thing to me, Josie. The most important, sweetest part of my life."

I felt like my heart would explode with love and happiness as we went in to get ice cream. Theo glared at the beta teenager preparing my order to make sure they put enough sprinkles on it. I ate my ice cream as Theo drove us to the lookout spot. I may have stolen a few bites from his cone when he was distracted. He growled at me playfully, but the smile on his face told me he didn't mind. The dirt road we turned onto ended abruptly, and I saw we were on top of a hill with trees framing us on either side and the lit-up city below us. We finished up our cones, using copious napkins to clean up the mess we made.

"Will you tell me about the class, love?" Theo asked, gently running his thumb across my bottom lip. I shivered, but not from the cold. I felt myself heating under his gentle touch, wanting more. I nodded, my eyes locked on his warm brown ones.

Chapter Thirty-Five

Theo

I gazed into Josie's beautiful green eyes, capturing her hands with both of mine. I needed her warmth to ground me. My heart pounded at the thought of any alpha using his bark on her, but I had promised to listen. *Fuck.* Now I realized how excited she had been when she got into the car after class, her scent bright and happy without a hint of stress. I had jumped to conclusions without paying attention, but I vowed to pay attention now.

"Luc asked us if we wanted to practice resisting an alpha bark. Because no matter how good we get at self-defense, we're always going to be vulnerable—an alpha could bark at us and that would be it. Even once I'm bonded, another alpha's bark will still influence me. But Luc said if we practiced, we could get better at resisting. We *wanted* to practice. He didn't force us or anything. And by the end of class, I got pretty good at it."

Once I'm bonded. Once I'm bonded. Once I'm bonded.

Her words ran around my head in a giddy spiral until everything else faded away. My grip on her hands tightened, and I had to fight to keep myself from getting out of the car and running victory laps. Josie had been so skittish around us just days ago, and now she was talking about *bonding*. My alpha roared with excitement. I wanted to text the guys and tell them.

"Theo?" Josie's sweet voice jolted me back to reality.

I breathed through my whirlwind of emotion, sobered by the reminder that she *was* vulnerable anytime she was around alphas. I also noticed the pride seeping into her voice when she shared she had gotten good at resisting. It was so rare for her to say anything positive about herself.

"Of course, you were good at it. You're fucking amazing," I said, a hint of a growl in my voice.

Josie preened at my praise, seeming to glow as her incredible, sweet scent grew thicker around us.

"How did he have you practice? He better not have crossed any lines. Did you feel safe?" I asked rapid-fire.

Josie giggled and it was like the brightest sunshine.

"He had us stand across the room from him, and one by one, he barked at us to cross the room. We had to try to stay where we were. It was totally safe. Poppy and Westin did it, too. Clementine was there, but she just cheered us on since she's not susceptible to barks. By the end of class, I only took a few steps towards Luc before stopping myself."

I took in what she was saying, grimacing at how much I had overreacted. None of us fully trusted another alpha around her, but I had to admit that what Luc had done was smart, and he'd helped Josie feel more confident.

"That's so good, angel," I said, smiling as I saw her squirm happily at my praise. I hated that praise had such an impact on my girl because she'd received so little in her life, but I loved that I could make her feel good about herself. "It's not a bad idea to practice, but you should never be in a position where you have to resist a bark. There are laws against alphas using it."

Josie's face fell and she turned towards the window, biting her lip as she took in the view of the city. I gently tugged her lip away, soothing it with my thumb. Her scent had turned to sharp, burnt sugar.

"Has someone used their bark on you?" I asked, my anger rising. I resisted gripping her chin to force her to look at me.

"Yeah," she said softly, glancing at me quickly to gauge my reaction. Suddenly, I had to have my arms around her. I couldn't handle the car console separating us.

"Wait there," I said before getting out of the car. I got a blanket from the back—the only thing in there, despite what I had told Josie earlier—before opening the passenger door.

"Where are we going?" she asked, lips parting as she looked up at me.

"On top of the car," I said as I pulled her out of her seat.

"On top of the car?" she repeated skeptically, looking up at the tall, flat top of my Range Rover.

Before she could say anything, I grabbed her by the waist and hoisted her up. She squeaked out the cutest gasp as she reached out her arms to pull herself up. My hands lingered on her ass as I gave her the final boost she needed to settle herself on the car before swinging myself up next to her.

"Ugh, no fair how sexy you just looked doing that," she said with a disgruntled expression. I laughed and laid the blanket out before sitting on it, pulling her in between my legs with her back resting firmly against my chest. She leaned her head back, turning to look at me.

"Why are we on top of the car, Theo?"

"Because I couldn't wait one more minute to have you in my arms."

"Oh," she said with a smile, and she snuggled closer. The

movement rubbed her ass against my cock, which hardened immediately.

"Oops," she said, a sly smile crossing her face.

"You're much naughtier than you put on, my love," I whispered into her ear before tugging her earlobe gently with my teeth. She shivered in pleasure.

"Now, I want to hear about who used their bark on you," I said, keeping my voice calm. Josie's sweet scent was still burnt vanilla, and I hated how anxious she was. I kept one arm banded around her and moved my other hand to rest gently on her throat, tipping her face towards mine. "I've got you, love. You're safe."

"I know," she whispered. "Will you... I mean, would you mind..."

"What, angel?"

"Could you purr for me?" The request came in the softest whisper, so quiet I barely caught it.

Warmth flooded through my body at her request. An alpha purr was usually only reserved for a bond mate. It was intimate and had an immediate relaxing effect on an omega. I had wanted to purr for her so many times but had held back, so I didn't make her uncomfortable with the implication.

"You don't have to," Josie said quickly, sitting up as if to pull away from me.

"There's nothing I would love more," I responded.

Before she could panic at having asked for something, a rolling vibration started in my chest as I purred for my omega, my love, my *everything*, for the first time. She relaxed against me, her muscles going soft and her scent returning to its earlier sweetness. I rubbed my face against her neck, breathing her in and scent-marking her.

"Thank you," she murmured, trailing her fingers down my arms. Then she took a deep breath. "In my community, any alpha can use their bark against an omega as long as it's justified. Of course, the alpha dictates when the bark is justified. Growing up, it was mainly my pack fathers who used it against me. They would forbid me from talking or force me to stay in my room all day when they grew tired of me."

Her voice hitched and she paused, taking another breath to steel herself. I forced myself to tamp down the rage rushing through me, focusing instead on soothing the deep crescent marks in her palms from her fingernails. I kissed her palms, wishing I could erase all her pain.

"The law says that fathers and bonded alphas can use their bark on their omega, but it also says that certain officials can as well. The alphas at the DA are allowed to use their bark on omegas, and they did it all the time. They forced us to follow their rules and to submit to medical exams. Some alphas did it just because they enjoyed feeling in control. Sometimes I would try to fight it, but when I did, I would get punished more. So I didn't fight it. I just did whatever they said."

Tears fell down her face and I intensified my purr.

"Those fuckers," I growled. "They shouldn't be allowed to get away with that. That never should have happened to you. And none of it was your fault. Of course, you didn't resist. You didn't have a choice." My voice grew louder and I was worried it would stress her more. She surprised me by relaxing against me, her tears slowing.

"No, it shouldn't have happened," she said quietly.

Her hand squeezed the spot on her arm where her scar was. I felt like there was more she wasn't saying, and I almost asked her about it when she turned in my arms to face me.

"Thank you," she said softly.

"What are you thanking me for, beautiful?" I brushed her hair out of her face like she had done for me earlier in the car. That simple gesture had almost killed me.

"Thank you for being angry *for* me."

I didn't know what to say, my fury and sadness mixing with the tenderness of my love for her. I put my hands on her waist and maneuvered her so she faced me fully, her legs straddling my waist.

"Once we moved to North Woods," I said, pulling her in so her face was tucked into my neck, "my pack fathers started using their bark on my mother and sisters. They pressured me to do the same. At first, I refused. I didn't want to be that kind of alpha. We had lived in a progressive community in London, and I had never seen an alpha abuse his bark as they did in North Woods. But they started beating me if I refused, telling me I needed to 'alpha up' and be tough. I did it to avoid being punished, but I should have resisted. I can't believe I did that to other omegas," I confessed, a tear escaping down my cheek.

I was so ashamed of what I had done, the way I had forced omegas to do my bidding. I didn't deserve this perfect omega in my arms. I felt a slight vibration coming from Josie's chest. I stilled as it grew stronger. It was the sweetest, cutest fucking purr I had ever heard. *She was purring for me. My mate was purring for me.*

I don't know how long we held each other, but when Josie's purr petered out, she rubbed her face against my neck and then sat up, her green eyes meeting mine. She brushed my tears away.

"It wasn't your fault, Theo."

I released the breath I didn't realize I'd been holding as the weight of the guilt I'd held onto for years eased. I could see the sincerity in her eyes, feel her warmth against my skin. She wasn't running, wasn't condemning me.

I pulled her in for a kiss, not knowing what else to do with the deep well of emotion I felt for her. Our kisses grew more heated. Josie rocked against me, my cock growing hard again as we built friction between us.

I broke our kiss, my lips quirking at Josie's disgruntled growl. A thrill of fear went through me at the thought of speaking the words burning on my lips, but then Josie caressed my face with tenderness, giving me the courage to speak.

"I love you, angel," I said, tightening my arms around her as if I could keep her from running away. I wanted to make love to her, bond her, make her mine forever.

Josie's face broke into the most stunning smile I had ever seen. Her cheeks flushed and her lips parted in surprise. Her beauty was breathtaking.

"I love you, too," she said, joy radiating from her.

A rush of relief and giddy happiness washed through me. We stayed on top of the car, exchanging drugging kisses, her sexy body rocking against mine until she shivered.

"Let's get you home," I said, pressing one last kiss to her forehead before helping her down.

Chapter Thirty-Six

Cam

"I can't believe Theo gets to have Josie all to himself tonight," Ben complained, angrily pounding on his laptop keys.

"Stop whining and work," I grunted, checking my phone for the hundredth time to see if Josie had texted me back.

"Like you're any better," Ben muttered.

I sighed, turning my swivel chair to face him. I struggled to keep my tone measured.

"I know this fucking sucks, but the sooner we finish this job, the sooner we can return to her."

"Fine, fine," Ben said, lifting his hands in surrender. "Don't mind me, just hacking away at a server I already know is secure because *I* secured it."

I rolled my eyes, shifting back towards the security monitors. I knew Ben was right. He was the best hacker I'd met. If he said the system was secure, it was. But the idiots at Greytex Industries were obsessed with ensuring their systems were impenetrable. A kernel of unease settled in me. They had been vague when they described what they manufactured, describing it simply as "pharmaceutical tech." I wondered again why they were so anxious about security. I shrugged it off. The amount we were billing them was enough to buy three more houses. *I wonder where Josie would want a vacation home...*

My phone vibrated, and I almost fell out of my seat in my rush to grab it.

"Sure, I'm the only one who's jealous," Ben muttered.

I flipped him off and read Josie's text.

BABY GIRL

Finished class and headed back home. Everything's good here! Miss you!

My eyes bored into the screen as if I could teleport my way through it and show up at her side. I had gotten as much of her scent on me as I could, but the haze of vanilla wasn't a substitute for the real thing.

"What did she say?" Ben asked, scooting his chair to read the text over my shoulder. He paused for a moment before asking, "Do you think they're going to have sex tonight?"

I grunted noncommittally. I thought there was a good chance they would. The alpha in me growled in displeasure at the thought of someone else being inside her before me. But it wasn't just someone else. It was Theo.

I took a deep breath.

"Probably," I responded. "We promised each other we wouldn't get jealous. We're all pack, and it will make her feel bad if we do."

"I know," Ben said. "I'm not... I'm not really jealous. I love them both. I just didn't realize how hard it would be to be away from her. It's like a part of me is missing."

"Yeah," I responded. He described how I was feeling perfectly. I hoped it would get easier to be apart once we were bonded, but deep down, I knew I would still want to be by her side as much as possible. Fuck, I loved her so much. I hadn't told her yet. I still didn't think I was good enough for her. She was pure sunshine and perfection. Every step she took towards me, showing her trust, knocked the wind out of me.

We returned to our work. I flipped to the video feeds of the Greytex labs. They had been concerned that their lab cameras had blind spots. After meticulous testing, I found a six-inch area in Lab Room C that wasn't visible from the two cameras in the room. I rolled my eyes at installing a third camera to give six inches of coverage.

I felt a burst of surprise through the bond. Ben muttered, "Well fuck, would you look at that."

He was hunched over his laptop, his eyebrows furrowed in concentration. A few moments passed before he sat up and stretched his arms above his head.

"I don't know if I should be disappointed in myself or impressed. Probably both," he said.

"What happened?"

"I did it. I hacked into the server."

"I thought you said it was impossible."

"It was," he said, running his hand through his hair in a Theo-like gesture. "But I just did it. I really outdid myself here. Figured out a new way to manipulate the code."

"So... what did you find?" I asked, rolling my chair over to his desk.

"A bunch of lab reports."

Ben clicked on a file. It looked like a medical chart.

He read from the top of the page, "Initiation of Pilot Program for Project Excer with Omega Test Subject 001. Completed successful device implantation in 001's upper arm."

"What the fuck is this?" I asked, my unease growing.

"Some product test, I guess," Ben said, shrugging his shoulders.

I skimmed the report, much of which contained data from whatever device they implanted.

"Wait, look at that," I said, pointing out a small handwritten notation at the bottom of the page. "No anesthesia given. Physician noted that 001 appeared to be in severe distress during the procedure but that implantation was still possible as 001 was fully strapped down. Anesthesia recommended in future trials unless otherwise specified."

I felt Ben's growing unease through the bond. He scrolled through a few more pages.

"Efficacy trial one," he read out in a low voice. "Upon device activation, 001 showed 90 percent increased compliance within three minutes. Compliance lasted for approximately twenty-eight minutes before 001 regained awareness. Subject 001 was commanded to engage in pre-specified tasks as outlined in list 21.38 and completed 62 percent of tasks before regaining awareness, at which time 001 was severely distressed and attempted to physically harm a trial attendant. Once the testing team regained control, 001 was questioned about what she remembered during the activation period. 001 demonstrated significantly reduced memory during the twenty-eight-minute period. 001 expressed understanding that an unknown amount of time had passed but could not disclose specifics of what had occurred during that time."

A sick feeling settled in my stomach, and my palms were slick with sweat.

I typed a note on my phone: *Can you copy all the files and cover up the hack?*

Ben gave me a curt nod.

We had already swept the security control room for bugs when we got here, assuming that a company so paranoid about security would also want to spy on us, but we couldn't be too careful.

We quickly wrapped up our work, my heart pounding a mile a minute.

I didn't know what the fuck those files meant, but this was way beyond the scope of a typical pharmaceutical company.

"I'll work on the final report in the car," I said gruffly. "Let's go home to our girl."

Chapter Thirty-Seven

Josie

Theo gripped my hand tightly as he led me inside. The soft light from the entryway lamp cast a glow over the room. I breathed in the scents of all my alphas, pleased with how my sugary vanilla had become intertwined with theirs.

The soft *click* of the lock sliding into place sent a little jolt through me. I turned towards Theo, my hand squeezing his with anticipation. *This is happening*. Every nerve felt raw and alive as his hungry gaze swept down my body.

Theo pulled me in close, his hands skimming down my back.

"I need you," he whispered, lips caressing my ear.

I shivered at the sensation, and a flood of slick drenched my underwear. Theo groaned, pressing his face into my neck, taking deep drags of my scent as his body shook with want.

My breath stuttered, and I struggled to find air as a wave of desire crashed over me.

"Need you," I gasped, feeling brave.

"You're so fucking perfect for me. I can't wait to touch you and taste you," he said, voice shaking.

My arms twined around his neck, pulling him in as close as I could. I needed to feel him against me—his heat, his hardness, his *love*. Theo's hands wandered down my back until they caressed my ass. He gripped me tightly and I whimpered.

The sound seemed to break his restraint, and he suddenly picked me up. I squealed at the sudden movement, wrapping myself around him with a giggle. He kissed me with a growl rolling through his chest. We barely came up for air as Theo carried me towards my room. I threaded one of my hands through his hair, loving the soft feel of his messy strands as I nipped his lower lip. I was lost in our kiss, lost in the feel of him, until we lurched.

"Fuck. No kissing and walking," Theo said, huffing a laugh as he tightened his grip on my thighs.

I giggled and moved my kisses to his face and neck before licking the long column of his throat. He swore and stopped, pressing me against the wall in the stairwell.

"Are you trying to get me to fall down the stairs, little omega?" he growled, pressing his cock against me, sending little lightning bolts of pleasure through my stomach.

"Seems like you're easily distracted," I said, boldly sucking on his neck.

"Fuck," he cursed, picking up his pace.

We tumbled into my room, my feet hitting the ground as he released my legs. His hands were on me, fisting my hair, caressing my breast, and cupping my ass.

"You want this, angel?" he asked, tilting my head back so he could see my face.

"Yes," I gasped.

"Fuck yes," he growled.

He pulled off my sweatshirt and started tugging off my shirt when I froze. The heated arousal coursing through me seconds earlier transformed into icy fear. I curled away from him, tugging my shirt back down so it covered my soft stomach. My friends' voices chorused in my head, telling me that Theo already knew what I looked like and I didn't need to be self-conscious, but an image of him seeing my body and turning away in disgust flashed through my mind. I tried but couldn't hold on to the confidence I had felt earlier in the night. It was as if every one of my fat rolls was shouting *not good enough.* He would see them and find me disgusting.

"Josie?" Theo's voice was tender as he ran a gentle hand down my arm.

"I just... I..." I blinked furiously, trying to stave off the tears threatening to fall. I was messing everything up, ruining this.

"Oh, my love, what's wrong?"

He hesitantly wrapped me up in his arms as if he was scared of hurting me. I leaned into him without hesitation, the heat of his body melting some of my paralyzing anxiety. He was still here. He hadn't run out of the room at my freak out. I took a deep breath, filling my lungs with his comforting scent.

Okay, Josie, get yourself together. You just have to fucking do it.

"Do you want a massage?" I almost shouted, my voice sounding borderline hysterical.

Theo's body stiffened and he tried to catch my eye, but I kept my face pressed to his chest.

"Umm, you want to give me a massage?"

"Yes," I squeaked.

"Will you tell me what I did wrong? What upset you?" he asked, pressing his face into my neck.

"Nothing's wrong. I just want to give you a massage."

I was acting nonsensical, but all I could do was cling to Poppy's suggestion. Giving him a massage didn't require me to get undressed.

"We don't have to do anything you're not ready for," he said, stroking my hair.

"I want to," I said, squeezing my arms around him. He was so solid, so warm. *Safe*. "I'm just nervous."

"I'm nervous, too, angel."

"Really?" I asked, his confession making me brave enough to peek at him. There was no anger or impatience on his face.

"Yes, love. But it's just you and me here. There's no pressure. I want to do whatever you want, whatever feels good for you."

I took a deep breath, exhaling slowly. The tiniest spark of confidence fluttered through me.

"Okay," I said, pulling away from him. "Then I want to give you a massage."

A slow, sexy smile spread across Theo's face. "Alright. Tell me what to do."

Unbidden tears sprang to my eyes as it sunk in: an alpha was giving me control. Theo was giving me control because he loved me, trusted me, and wanted me to feel comfortable.

Alarm flashed across his face at my tears.

"Everything is fine," I said, furiously wiping the tears away. "I'm just emotional! It's all okay!"

My voice was coming out too loud, my movements frantic, and I'm sure my eyes were wild. Theo raised his eyebrows as if trying to make sense of my behavior. We looked at each other for a few silent moments before simultaneously bursting out in laughter. He pulled me into a hug, his chest shaking as he squeezed me tight. Nothing about this had been normal so far. I was an emotional wreck, my desire for Theo warring with my insecurities and trauma. *And yet, he's still looking at you like he wants you. Just keep going.*

"Will you lie down on the bed?" I asked, finally pulling away from his embrace.

"Of course." He kissed me on the nose before lying down on his stomach.

Shoot. I should probably tell him to take off his clothes. Or take off his clothes for him. Seduction, Josie!

"Oh, umm, you should undress?" My voice came out as a squeaky question.

Theo sat up, facing me.

"I might need some help," he said, his eyes twinkling.

I suppressed a smile. "Did you forget how to take your shirt off?"

"Yes," he breathed out, eyes glued on my body as I crawled onto the bed towards him. "Must be because I'm staring at the world's sexiest omega. She's very distracting."

My cheeks flushed with pleasure as I straddled Theo and tugged off his shirt.

"You're so beautiful," I murmured, daring to run my hands down the smooth planes of his chest.

"That's my line," he said, pulling me closer with one hand around my neck and the other on my hip. "So fucking gorgeous."

I leaned in for a kiss and he immediately deepened it, his tongue dancing with mine. More of my anxiety melted away as sensation overwhelmed me: the pleasurable sting of his hand gripping my hair, the luxurious rocking of his cock against my clit, the heat of his bare skin burning through my clothes.

Theo's groans and whispered praise bolstered my confidence.

"Those pants look so uncomfortable," I gasped between kisses, rubbing my core against the ridge of his jeans.

"*Unbearably* uncomfortable," he responded, his lips curving up in a smile against mine.

"I should help you with that," I said, my hands fumbling with the zipper.

Good job, Josie. Excellent work. Very smooth.

And then I let out a very non-sexy shriek.

"You're not wearing underwear!" My hands flew up to cover my eyes, and Theo burst out in laughter.

"A little omega said she wanted her alphas to go commando in a certain questionnaire." He tugged my hands from my eyes, but I still had them squeezed shut.

"It's not going to attack you." His voice was amused but gentle.

I cracked my eyes open, keeping them firmly on his face. His mouth twitched.

"No laughing at me," I said, sticking my lip out in a pout.

"Sorry, angel," he said with a smile. "Fucking cute." He cupped my cheek, the warmth of his hand sinking into my skin.

I rolled my eyes and pursed my lips, trying to stop myself from smiling. "I'm just going to, umm, sit over here and you lie down on your stomach for your massage."

I fixed my eyes on the ceiling as he pulled off his pants and rolled over. When I finally allowed myself to look at him, to *really* see him, heat suffused me.

He looked like a Greek god.

I took in his smooth, pale skin, the muscular expanse of his back, and then finally down to his butt. His sexy, cute butt with a bond mark in the center of the right cheek. My mouth watered. I wanted to lick it, bite it, and place my bond mark on him so he would know he belonged to me.

"You have a nice butt," I blurted out.

"Thank you, angel," Theo said. There was no mocking in his tone.

My body was hot, and I didn't know if it was because of my arousal or embarrassment. I eyed Theo, realizing the best way for me to massage him would be to straddle him. My pussy tingled at the thought of being pressed against his bare skin.

"Is this okay? Am I too heavy?" I asked as I settled myself on the backs of his thighs.

"Never. Feels good."

I ran my hands up and down his back, slowly increasing the pressure. Theo groaned in pleasure, emboldening my movements. I got lost in the feel of him, the softness of his skin, his deepening scent. I noticed after a while that I was having *fun* exploring his body. The DA had always presented sex as something serious, warning us that we needed to ensure we satisfied our alphas at any cost to ourselves. But as I moved my hands over his back, squeezing, kneading, and admiring, I understood this kind of intimacy was supposed to be enjoyable.

Theo shifted his hips, moving me off him. "Fuck, your hands are magic. You can massage me anytime you want. But now it's my turn." His voice was a quiet rasp, laced with want, as he turned over and sat next to me.

I wanted him to touch me.

I was terrified for him to see me.

"You have absolutely nothing to worry about, love," he murmured, nuzzling my cheek. I tried not to but couldn't help sneaking looks at his cock. It bobbed up and down as he shifted on the bed. Theo caught the direction of my gaze, and I quickly looked away, feeling like I had been caught doing something naughty.

"Look all you want," he said with a smile.

I felt like I was in a trance as he pulled off my top and sports bra. His gaze didn't stray from my face as he ran his hands up and down my side, skimming across my ribs and breasts. I fought the urge to hide under the blanket, turn off the lamps, *anything* to stop him from seeing me.

Our breaths synced as we gazed into each other's eyes. My heart rate slowed, and I allowed myself to sink into the moment. Finally, his gaze trailed down to take in my body. I tensed. This was the least flattering position he could see me in.

"I wish you could see yourself like I do right now. You are an angel." His voice was a reverent whisper.

Theo continued his exploration, caressing my nipples and placing hot kisses down my neck. I relaxed into the sensation, closing my eyes. He wasn't insulting me. He was here, touching me because he wanted to. Because he wanted *me*.

Even still, I couldn't stop myself from asking, "Are you sure you're not disappointed?"

His touch paused. "Josie, love, look at me."

My cheeks flamed, and I slowly met his gaze.

"There is no world, realm, or universe in which you or your body could disappoint me. I love every part of you. I've never felt this kind of attraction—"

He paused, then gently guided my hand to his cock. I felt the soft skin covering his rigid member. A bead of moisture got on my hand, and his scent thickened so much I was almost dizzy with it. I could hear the playfulness in his voice as he added, "—and I've never, in my entire life, been this hard."

I bit my lip as I finally looked down to where my hand circled his penis. Even though I had nothing to compare it to, I thought his was particularly nice.

A+ dick.

10/10.

Fuck, I'm such a nerd.

I gave it a small pump with my hand, biting my lip in concern at how much longer and thicker he was than the dildo. My fingers were unable to close around him. And then I noticed something else.

"Umm... is that a piercing?" I asked, my eye catching on two silver metal balls.

"Yeah," Theo responded, looking sheepish, running his hand through his hair.

My Theo, *reserved, serious, wears-a-tie Theo,* had a penis piercing.

"I lost a bet with Ben. It fucking hurt, but once it was in, I decided to keep it. I heard it can feel really good for a partner during sex." He mumbled that last part.

If I hadn't already been in love with him, hearing that he had been walking around with a piercing in his dick because one day it might feel good for his partner would have sealed the deal.

Theo's cock stood straight up, leaving a trail of pre-cum on his abs. My omega was mesmerized by it. He cleared his throat and I realized I had been sitting in silence, staring at his cock with laser focus, my hand wrapped around him. His grip on my thigh was tight as if he was trying to hold himself back.

"I'm nervous I won't be any good at sex," I blurted out, removing my hand from him.

"Not possible," he murmured, leaning in to kiss my nipples. The sensation almost distracted me enough to lose my train of thought.

I pushed him away so I could look him in the eyes, sighing with frustration. "You have to say that, but you don't know." I wasn't sure why I was arguing with him, but it felt important that he go into this with low expectations.

"Angel, I... haven't done this either."

I blinked. "Wait, what? Had sex?"

"Yeah." Theo ran his hand through his hair, making it stick up wildly.

The gesture was so endearing, so *Theo.* I blinked at his revelation. A smile tugged at my lips and warmth filled my chest as I thought about being each other's firsts, when I noticed an anxious edge to his usually warm coffee scent.

"Are you disappointed?" he asked, his hands shaking.

"What?" I grabbed his hands in mine and squeezed tight. "Why would I be?"

"I might not make it as good for you as Ben or Cam would for your first time," he responded, his face a fiery red.

I put my hand on his cheek. "I'm really happy to share this experience with you. It feels special. Even though I don't know how you haven't had sex before since you look like that," I said, gesturing at his magazine-worthy body.

"And you look like that," he said, gesturing at me.

I wrinkled my nose. "Exactly, which is why I don't know why you're attracted..."

Theo let out a fierce growl before tackling me. He pinned me down, still careful to ensure his weight wasn't crushing me. I arched automatically at the feel of his cock against my core.

Theo growled again, the vibration rocking through my body. "I never want to hear you say you're not attractive again. No one insults my girl, not even you. Understand?"

My eyes widened and I nodded. He kissed me before moving down my body, kissing and licking a line down my stomach. I sucked in involuntarily, needing to do something to hide my fat rolls from him.

"One day, you'll see yourself like I do," he murmured, grasping my hip to stop me from shifting away.

"Sorry," I whispered to the ceiling. "I can't get it out of my head that you'll be disgusted. My body's not good enough for you."

"Just means I'll need to get you naked as often as possible so I can convince you of how enraptured I am by you." He tugged the waistband of my leggings. "May I, love?"

I nodded, forcing my body to relax into the bed as he carefully stripped my leggings and underwear off. Theo didn't say anything. Anxiety whirled through me as I propped myself up on my elbows to gauge his reaction.

He was staring at my pussy with something that looked like awe.

"Your pussy is so cute," he said, his pupils wide as he met my eyes. "No more underwear for you. It's a crime to cover this up."

"You can't tell me what to do," I said with a pout.

"Mmm, that's where you're wrong," he said, squeezing my ass tightly. His heated gaze burned a trail down my skin.

"I need to taste you," he said.

Before I could panic, he had already shifted down my body, planting more kisses on my stomach until he reached my mound. I tried to close my legs, but his hands kept my thighs in place as he slowly licked his tongue from my opening to my clit.

Holy.

Shit.

The warm drag of his tongue felt *incredible.* It was more pleasure than I ever could have imagined.

"You taste like heaven," he murmured, his breath hot against me. "Want to spend all my days between your thighs with the taste of your sweet pussy on my lips."

His filthy words rendered me speechless, reducing me to little whimpers and moans. I shifted my hips, chasing more sensation, more of him, but he pinned me down with one arm, keeping his other firmly planted on my thigh. His tongue moved steadily, firmly across my sex, circling my clit.

"Just relax, love. I'm going to make you feel so good."

I released the breath I'd been holding with a *whoosh.* He looped his arm around my leg, bringing his hand around to rest on the top of my mound. I whimpered as he circled my clit with one hand and lapped up my slick with his tongue.

"You want my fingers, angel?"

My vagina clenched in anxious anticipation, but I forced myself to breathe through the anxiety. There was no one else here besides Theo, and I ached to have him inside me, filling me up.

"Yes," I gasped as Theo's rhythmic fingers continued circling my clit.

"My brave omega."

He kissed my inner thighs, scraping his teeth along my sensitive skin. I held myself back from begging for his bite. I wasn't ready to be bonded with him yet, but as he gently slipped his finger inside me, I realized I already thought of myself as *his*.

"Look how wet you are for me. I want to be drenched in your scent so everyone knows you're mine," he growled, pumping his finger in and out as he lowered his mouth to my clit.

My body shook as he drove my arousal higher. My vagina clenched on his fingers, but this time in pure pleasure.

"That's it, angel. Fuck yourself on my fingers."

I moaned at his dirty words as my orgasm drew closer. He slipped another finger inside me. There was a slight sting with the stretch.

"You're okay, love, just relax. You're doing so well. Can't believe how fucking lucky I am."

I breathed deeply, the mix of our scents calming me. I reached down and ran my fingers through his soft hair.

"Love your hands on me," Theo groaned, thrusting his fingers again. He sucked on my clit and curled his fingers inside me, hitting all my omega pleasure spots. I whined and gasped his name as I came, my orgasm moving through me in waves. He kept licking me, his tongue rocking against my extra sensitive clit.

"Too much," I said, trying to close my legs.

"Want you to come again," he said, his hands digging into my thighs. "If you want to," he added, looking up at me.

I giggled, letting my legs relax and fall open in silent permission. His tongue and fingers were gentle as they eased me through a second orgasm. A heavy, pleasurable feeling settled on my limbs. Theo took one final, long lick before working his way up my body with kisses. His lips were glossy with my slick, a self-satisfied smile on his face.

"You look well-pleasured, my love." He moved so he was under me, firmly placing my head on his shoulder and wrapping me up in his arms.

"Oh my god," I mumbled, nuzzling my face into his bare chest. "You've killed me with orgasms."

"I hope not because I have more plans for you." He palmed my butt, squeezing hard. My hips shifted against him, seeking friction. How could I already want more? I was addicted to Theo, floating in a sea of pheromones.

Theo kissed my temple, wrapping my messy hair around his hand.

"Was that okay?" he asked in a vulnerable voice.

I lifted my head, running my hand down the side of his face.

"That was amazing. I've never felt anything like that."

"It wasn't triggering?"

I shook my head, my heart warming at his concern for me. "No, it was perfect. Thanks for being patient with me," I whispered.

"Anything for you. *Anything*." His hand tightened in my hair and we locked eyes. My emotions swirled within me, and I knew this moment would be imprinted on me forever.

"I love you," I said, barely able to speak with the emotion between us.

"I love you so much."

I wanted to make him feel as good as he'd made me feel. I shifted so I was straddling him, my core pressing against his hard cock. I felt the urge to suck in my stomach, to cover myself, but I forced myself to sit bare before him. The heat in his eyes spoke only of pleasure, his hands coming up to cup my breasts.

"My turn," I said.

"Are you going to have your way with me, omega?" he asked, breathless.

"Yes, alpha," I said, licking my lips slowly.

I moved down his body, teasing him the best I could with my mouth—nipping, licking, and kissing down his beautiful chest until I was between his muscular thighs.

"You don't have to do that if you don't want to, angel," Theo said, his cheeks blushing bright red.

His shyness fueled me, giving me the confidence to be bold. "Don't you want me to?" I pouted. "Maybe you don't think I'll be any good." I made sure to widen my eyes as I crawled closer. My breasts gently swayed side to side, almost touching his erect cock.

Theo groaned, his eyes fixated on my breasts. "Believe me, I want you to," he said, sounding pained.

I smiled and leaned down to lick the pre-cum that had beaded on the head of his cock. Oh, Poppy was right. It *did* taste good. I gripped the base of his cock where his knot had already started to inflate and moved my other hand up and down. Theo groaned, his hips jerking up involuntarily. I lowered my face and licked a long, hot stripe, starting at his knot all the way to the tip, before taking him into my mouth and swirling my tongue around the head.

"Fuck, how are you so good at this?"

I moved my mouth off with a *pop*, unable to stop a wide smile from spreading across my face.

"Am I doing good?" I asked, desperately wanting approval.

"So. Fucking. Good. You look so sexy on your knees for me," he groaned, his hand squeezing the back of my neck, adding a comforting pressure without forcing my movements.

The heady feeling of being in control washed over me. I was choosing this, giving my alpha pleasure. I took his cock back in my mouth with renewed enthusiasm and sucked hard, keeping pressure on his knot with one hand. I used my tongue to play with his piercing until he was shouting a continuous stream of curses.

He tugged me off of him and I whined.

"You're way too good at that, angel, and I want to come in that cute little pussy of yours."

Yes, please.

"Okay," I said with a smile. "You can come in my mouth next time."

I let out a squeal as Theo grabbed me and flipped me onto my back, laying his body on top of mine. My slick dripped down onto the sheets and I moaned as he ground his cock against me, drenching it.

"I want you inside me," I said, rocking my hips to match his movements.

He gently gripped my chin so I was looking into his eyes.

"Tell me if you want to stop at any time," he said. He waited for my nod before fitting himself at my entrance and pressing in slowly.

There was a slight sting, the stretch taking my breath away, but mostly what I felt was love. To have my first time with someone as gentle and kind as Theo was an immeasurable gift. My eyes fluttered closed and I whimpered as he pressed in another inch.

"Angel?" His voice sounded distant, as if it was making its way through the fog of arousal surrounding me. The pressure had transformed into pleasure. I wanted *more,* wanted him to *move.*

"Josie, I need you to talk to me." There was an urgency in his tone, and my eyes flew open. He shifted away as if to pull out, and I growled, gripping his hips tightly with my legs.

"Need more," I whined.

Theo released a breath and his head fell down on my chest. He sucked one of my nipples into his mouth, nipping gently with his teeth.

"You have to use your words, love. Almost gave me a heart attack."

"Not my fault your dick rendered me speechless."

Theo choked out a laugh, biting my other nipple in gentle punishment.

"Naughty girl," he said.

And then he eased into me completely, filling me, stretching me, until his knot bumped against my clit. I was beyond words, unable to do anything except whimper as I pulled Theo into a kiss, licking into his mouth.

He thrust into me again.

"*Ohmygod* your piercing," I cried in pleasure.

"Too much?" he asked, caressing my face.

"No, it's perfect."

He gave me a heartbreaking smile and kiss before he continued moving in and out.

For so long, I hadn't allowed myself to imagine that I could have *this.* When I had been trapped in the darkest parts of my abuse, all I wanted was to survive. And once I got away from *them,* I hadn't allowed myself to hope for the future. Feeling Theo inside me, the gentle pressure of his weight against my body, his heady scent... it was so much more than physical pleasure. It felt like coming home to a part of myself I thought I'd lost forever—the part of myself who dreamed, who thrived, who *lived.*

My eyes pricked with emotion and a single tear escaped, trailing down my cheek.

I didn't want to close my eyes, didn't want to forget that I was here, with Theo, choosing this. I breathed through the anxiety scraping at my chest. *Theo Theo Theo.*

"Is this real?" I asked, my eyes wide as he thrust in and out.

Theo furrowed his brow, running his thumb tenderly down my cheek.

"It's real. You're here with me."

He ran his lips down my jaw, his breath hot on my skin. "Can you feel me, love?"

"Yes." I gasped as his hips shifted angles and he hit a new spot inside me. "Fuck," I cried out.

"Love hearing you swear," he said with a smile. "I never expect it."

I couldn't respond, my orgasm stealing away any train of thought I'd had.

"I love you," I whispered, meeting Theo's concerned gaze. "This is *everything.*"

Warmth and understanding filled his face, and he tenderly kissed away my tears, pressing gentle kisses on my eyelids.

"You are my wildest dream made flesh," he said. "I would wait an eternity for you, for this."

Emotion ballooned in my chest and made its way out to my arms and the tips of my toes. It was as if there was too much feeling for my body to hold. The only place I could channel it was into his body, to share myself with him.

I gripped his hips more tightly with my legs and matched his thrusts with my movements. Theo cupped my ass with his hands, lifting me slightly. The change in position meant his knot was grinding against my clit with every thrust, his cock dragging against my pleasure spot. I dug my fingers into his back, running my nails down his skin.

He snarled, his thrusts growing wilder and deeper, his knot teasing my entrance. The pressure was enough to cause an orgasm to break over me. The strength of it stunned me. It was all warm electricity holding my body.

"Fuck, you're perfect. So beautiful when you come," Theo growled, thrusting harder until he came with a roar, my name a chant on his lips.

He slipped out of me and rolled us so I was on top of him. We were both breathing heavily, and I clung to him, reveling in the perfection of this moment.

"That was..." Theo trailed off, sounding awed.

"I know," I said, grinning widely, pressing a kiss to his chest before snuggling in against his body.

Chapter Thirty-Eight

Theo

Holding my beautiful mate in my arms after making love was something I had dreamed of for years. We lay in a dreamy post-sex haze until I realized I needed to tend to her. I reluctantly untangled my limbs from hers. Josie whined, trying to hold on to me.

"I'll be right back, love," I said with a kiss.

I returned from the bathroom with a warm cloth. Josie tried to take it from me, but I insisted on cleaning her up. She blushed so beautifully when she parted her legs, and I grew hard again, both at the sight of her and at the gift of her trust.

"You sore, angel?" I asked, throwing the towel in the hamper in the corner.

"Just a little," she said with a stretch.

She was curled up under the blanket but hadn't said anything about putting her clothes back on. I took that as a victory. It killed me how worried she had been about me seeing her naked. Josie was so gorgeous and soft, determined and strong, and I would make it my mission to show her how much I loved every part of her until she believed it herself.

I slipped back under the blankets, pulling her body flush against mine. I'd thought nothing could compare to the feeling of her wet mouth surrounding me, sucking me off, but I had been wrong. Being inside her, feeling her come on my cock, had been the best experience of my life.

She was pliant against my body, every muscle soft and relaxed, her scent a happy, sugary cupcake vanilla. Flashes of memory flitted through my mind—the feel of her legs gripping me, the softness of her skin, the grip of her tight heat, the sensation of coming inside her, marking her as mine. A primal satisfaction rose in me and my cock twitched, urging me to take her again. I stopped myself from sliding home between her legs, not wanting to add to her soreness.

Josie stroked my chest, the light touch of her fingers a perfect agony, as we lay in comfortable silence.

I was drifting to sleep when Josie asked in a quiet, vulnerable voice, "Did you not want to knot me?"

Fuck. We hadn't talked about knotting ahead of time and I hadn't wanted to bring it up when I was balls-deep inside her.

I shifted us so we were lying side by side.

"I thought it might be too much for the first time," I said. "But I definitely want to," I added hurriedly, remembering from my research that denying an omega a knot could make them feel rejected.

Josie just gave me a soft smile and snuggled closer to me.

"Thanks for not pressuring me. I want to, just so you know."

"Next time," I said, kissing her forehead. I hoped the next time would be soon.

We lay in a sleepy, comfortable silence. One of my hands drifted until it cupped Josie's ass. I couldn't believe what a lucky bastard I was.

"Theo?"

"Yes, love?"

"Why haven't you had sex before?"

I stilled, residual insecurity from my upbringing coming to the fore.

"You don't have to tell me," she said quickly.

"No, I want to tell you. Just trying to figure out where to start."

I pulled her in close as I gathered my thoughts. My hand brushed against the jagged scar on her upper arm, wondering again where she'd gotten it.

"Does this hurt, love?" I asked.

"No, it doesn't hurt," she whispered.

I knew there was more to the story, but I could be patient if she wasn't ready to tell me. She flinched as I ran my fingers down the scar, but her body softened as I continued my movements, steadily caressing my hands down her body.

"My pack fathers had rigid expectations of what it meant to be an alpha, and those beliefs only got more extreme once they moved us to North Woods from London," I said, ripping off the band-aid.

"Why did you move?" she asked.

"We lived in a progressive community in London. My sisters are both omegas and had the freedom to go to school and make friends and all that normal shit. But as we got older, and they had my two younger brothers, my parents got more obsessed with what they called *traditional designation roles.* Things changed quickly at home. They wanted me in the gym all the time and started homeschooling my sisters. Eventually, they fell even deeper into the ideology and moved us so they could be with like-minded families, and we would be forced to fall in line."

"That's terrible." She grabbed my hand, intertwining my fingers and giving mine a squeeze.

"Thanks, angel." I had wanted an omega for our pack for years. My alpha needed someone to dote on, protect, and care for. But I hadn't anticipated what it would be like to *receive* that care. It was more than I could have imagined. I pressed my face into her hair, breathing in her scent, before continuing.

"My fathers sent me to a sex worker on my sixteenth birthday so I could finally become a true alpha, whatever the fuck that means. Most alphas had already had sex by sixteen and my parents felt I was falling behind, not meeting the standards. But I struggled with feeling attracted to anyone. When faced with the beta woman they hired for me, my body felt cold. She was beautiful, and her scent was nice enough, but I didn't feel anything towards her. I... um... couldn't get hard. I didn't want my first time to be with a stranger.

"We ended up just talking for a couple of hours. She told me it was okay to wait until I was ready to have sex and gave me pointers on how to please a partner when I had one. I took notes so I would remember everything she told me."

"They wanted to force you to have sex at sixteen?" Josie exclaimed angrily. She tried to push herself up from my chest, but I wrapped my arms around her more tightly, keeping her body flush against mine.

"I know, love. It's all messed up. When I came home, I pretended that I'd done it. My father slapped me on the back in congratulations. It was one of the rare times he was proud of me, and it was all a lie. I spent the rest of my time in North Woods, pretending to have a slew of partners. It felt like something was broken inside me. I didn't feel sexual attraction like other alphas.

"I went back and saw the same beta woman a few times. She was only a couple years older than me, and I thought she seemed lonely. She liked having someone to talk to, and I took down notes each visit. Even back then, I knew that one day I wanted to find my partner... my mate. And when I did, I wanted to please her.

"I realized I need a strong emotional connection with someone before I feel attraction. I've wanted to have sex, just haven't had someone I wanted to do it with. But, love, I need you to know—I was so attracted to you in that Trader Joe's. I was following you around like a fucking stalker because you're irresistible. I get hard when you walk into the room. I have never wanted someone like I want you, and I can't believe how lucky I am to have you, my mate, my omega."

Josie pulled me in for a fierce kiss, washing away any lingering fears of her judging me. After a few moments, we were both gasping. She pulled away and ran her hands through my hair.

"I'm angry at your parents for putting that on you, for making you feel like your sexuality had to look a certain way. And I'm jealous that you spent time with another woman, even if nothing happened." Her lip jutted out in an adorable pout.

"I love you being possessive of me," I said. "But I've only ever had eyes for you."

Josie smiled and wiggled happily into my embrace. "Have to say, though, the note-taking paid off," she said cheekily.

I barked out a laugh and pulled her close. *Fuck, I'm so gone for her.*

Chapter Thirty-Nine

Theo

A soft hand ran down my bare chest, and the scent of sweet vanilla surrounded me. Gentle lips pressed down my jaw. This was the best dream I'd ever had.

"Theo," the sweetest voice in the world said.

I shifted, pressing my face into Josie's hair. *Not a dream.*

"Need you," she whispered, running her hands down my chest to my cock.

Fuck. Now I'm awake.

I cracked my eyes open and saw Josie's face inches from mine. Once my eyes adjusted to the dark room, I could see her eyes were glassy with need. I ran my hands down her bare back. Her skin was hot. Having sex earlier had probably caused a spike in her hormones, like a mini version of a heat.

"Roll over on your side, love."

She whined.

"Shh, it's okay, angel. I'm going to give you what you need. Do you trust me?"

"Yes, alpha," she said, and fuck if I didn't almost blow my load right then. Her trust was a drug.

Josie rolled onto her side, facing away from me.

"Good girl," I murmured, pulling her body flush with mine. My cock jerked as it pressed against her soft skin. I couldn't help running my hand down her front, tweaking her nipples before dropping my fingers to her core.

"Fuck, love, you're soaking. Is this all for me?"

"Yes," she whimpered, arching into my hand.

"Lift your leg," I said, grasping her delicious thigh and pulling it back over mine. I played with her clit as I entered her from behind in a slow thrust.

We both moaned. Her tight pussy squeezed me, the angle allowing me to push even deeper into her.

Josie reached her arm back until her hand was entwined in my hair. I vowed never to cut my hair short, wanting her hands in it always. I kissed her neck and throat, savoring her taste and the sound of her sweet whimpers.

I returned my hand to her nipples, pinching them harder than before. She gasped, pushing back into me. I smiled into her shoulder, dragging my teeth against her skin. I wanted to bond her more than anything, longed to sink my teeth into her soft, sweet skin and mark her as mine forever.

Josie shouted my name when she came, her pussy pulsing around my cock. I gasped at the sensation, wanting more, always more with her.

"Need your knot," she gasped.

"You sure, angel?" My breathing was labored with the effort of holding back as I gripped her hips. "Need you to be sure."

"Yes, yes," she breathed. "Please, Theo."

I banded my arm around her waist to keep her pressed against me as I thrust my already-inflated knot into her. The sensation was like nothing I had ever felt before. Her hot cunt surrounded me, gripping my knot in an unbelievably tight hold.

Josie whimpered as if in pain as my knot settled behind her pelvic bone. A spark of anxiety ignited in my chest at the thought of hurting her. I needed to keep calm, though. Otherwise, she might tense up more.

"Shh, you're okay, angel. Just relax for me." I teased her clit, murmuring soothing words in her ear until I felt her tensed muscles release with a sigh.

"Good girl, look at how well you take me."

This time she whimpered in pleasure. I had dreamed of this moment, dreamed of being locked inside her, but the reality was so much better than anything my fantasies could conjure. I thrust into her as much as possible, my knot grinding against her omega pleasure spot. She cried out again with another orgasm. After a few more thrusts, pleasure like I'd never known shot through me as I came inside her. The knowledge that she was filled with my cum, would carry my scent, filled me with primal pleasure.

"I love you," she gasped out.

I groaned, pleasure shooting through me again at her words. Suddenly, being locked inside her didn't feel enough. I wanted to be in her skin, to merge my body with hers. The thought of being away from her squeezed my chest. She was my heart, my soul, my everything.

"You're mine," I growled, wrapping both arms around her, shifting so my knee was pressed firmly between her legs. "I'm never leaving this sweet pussy. Need to be in you forever."

Josie whined, grinding against my leg. She came for a third time, shouting my name. My release built as her orgasm pulsed around my cock. I ground my knot against her, my movements languid as relaxed exhaustion covered us both. I came inside her again, my hot cum trapped in her pussy.

"Love you," I murmured against her skin. She snuggled into me, her body relaxing as she fell back asleep. I smiled that she felt safe enough to sleep with my knot in her.

I curled around my omega, and her scent lulled me to sleep.

Chapter Forty

Josie

"We've got cereal and toast," Theo muttered. "Why don't we have more prepared foods in this house?"

I hid my smile behind my hand as he puttered around the kitchen, grumbling about the lack of gourmet breakfast options.

"Cereal is fine," I said soothingly.

Theo turned to me with a scowl. "You deserve better than that. I'll order something."

I couldn't hide my giggle this time. Theo stalked over to my perch on the island stool, wrapping his arms around me, his chest against my back.

"Are you laughing at me?" he asked with a hint of a growl.

God, I wasn't sure there was anything hotter than a growly British accent.

"Not at all," I said, biting my lip to keep from laughing. "Thanks for taking such good care of me." I shifted in the chair so I could kiss him.

Theo returned the kiss, looking pleased when we finally parted. He pulled out his phone and started a takeout order.

"Cam and Ben should be back soon, so we'll get food for them, too," he said.

I did a happy wiggle in my chair, excited to have all my alphas around me again. I loved my alone time with Theo, but I missed Cam and Ben. There was an emptiness in my chest anytime I was separated from them.

"Are you excited to have them back?" Theo asked, kissing my forehead as he continued to add food to the order.

"Yes," I said happily before pausing. "But I was really happy to have alone time with you, too," I added quickly.

"It's okay to miss them, angel," he said thoughtfully, gripping my chin. "But selfishly, I'm bloody thrilled we had this time together." He winked, a smirk tugging at his lips as he slowly ran his eyes down my body.

I wasn't wearing a bra and felt my nipples hardening against my tank top. I shifted in my seat again, a sore twinge in my vagina reminding me I'd had sex twice last night and fallen asleep *with his knot still inside me.* Even with my soreness, I wanted to feel him inside me again. I let out a contented sigh, thinking about how patient and gentle he had been, how good he'd made me feel. I had been so scared to have sex, but now I wanted more. I blushed, wondering what sex with Cam and Ben would be like when icy anxiety seized me.

"Wait, do Ben and Cam know we had sex?" I asked, my chest feeling uncomfortably tight.

Theo looked up from his phone. "I haven't told them," he hedged, gently wrapping his hand in my hair. "But they probably felt it through the bond. Why, love? Do you not want them to know?"

"Are they going to be mad?" I asked, my voice almost a whisper. What was the etiquette around sex in a pack? I needed to ask Poppy.

Theo's brow furrowed. "Of course not, angel. We all want

you to be happy, and that includes making sure you get alone time with each of us. And even if they are jealous, that's not for you to deal with."

I scrunched my nose, confused. "Why wouldn't it be my issue to deal with?"

"Because you're not responsible for how we feel."

I heard Theo's words, but I couldn't make sense of them. "Growing up, it was always my fault if someone was angry at me," I blurted out.

Theo's grip on my hair tightened as he tilted my head so I met his gaze.

"It was never your fault. They just wanted to break you down," he said fiercely.

A gush of slick soaked my underwear at his intensity, and I suppressed a whimper.

"Fuck," he groaned, pulling me into his arms. "You smell so good."

I took a deep breath and snuggled into his embrace. I still felt anxious about Ben and Cam finding out, but if Theo said it wouldn't be a problem, I needed to trust him.

He had me review the food order to see if I wanted to make any changes before submitting it.

"You want to watch something while we wait?" he asked, keeping his arms around me. Theo had been the most hesitant about physical touch, but since last night, he hadn't stopped touching me. I loved it.

"I actually had another idea," I said, twisting my fingers together.

"What is it?" He held me a little tighter as if sensing my nervousness.

"I was wondering if maybe you could help me practice resisting your bark."

I'd gotten the idea last night but knew it was a risky request after Theo told me about his history of using his alpha bark. I had a feeling he needed to redefine his relationship with his bark just as much as I did. I wanted to erase the guilt he felt for what he'd been forced to do. I hoped if he used it on me, it could help him get more comfortable with that part of himself again.

Theo's hand paused its soothing exploration of my back, and his breath hitched. "You would want me to do that?" he asked, his eyes filled with vulnerability. "You would trust me? After what I told you yesterday?"

I looked at Theo with confusion. "Why wouldn't I trust you? What happened when you were younger wasn't your fault. I know you won't use your bark to actually force me into anything I don't want to do."

He said nothing for a long time, his eyes looking into the distance.

"We don't have to. Forget I asked," I said, my skin prickling with anxiety.

Theo's gaze locked back on mine. "Sorry, I was lost in thought. Your trust means everything, my love. I'd like to give it a try."

I smiled, pulling him in for a kiss. "Thank you," I murmured.

"How do we do this?" he asked.

"We could do the same thing I tried in class? We stand across the room from each other and you tell me to walk towards you."

"There's only one problem with that, angel."

"What?"

"I promised myself I wouldn't go a single moment today without touching you. This puts a damper on my plan."

"Well, maybe I'll be terrible at resisting you."

"You saying I'm irresistible?"

"Yes," I breathed.

Theo groaned, running his eyes slowly up and down my body, making me feel like I was slowly catching on fire. I perfumed and he smirked, adjusting his pants where I could see a hard bulge.

"We better do this quickly before I change my mind," he said in a low growl.

I giggled, escaping his embrace and walking over to the other side of the room. I might have tried to add a little extra swing in my hips.

When I turned, I saw Theo adjusting himself again before running his hand through his hair with the sweetest blush on his cheeks.

"Okay," he said. "Let's do this." He went to issue the order and froze. His fists clenched and unclenched as he shifted side to side, and I caught a bitterness in his scent.

"Theo, it's okay. Remember, you're not forcing me," I said softly. Maybe this was a bad idea. I shouldn't have pushed him.

"I know, I'm okay," he said quickly. "I can do this. You ready, love?"

I nodded, still uncomfortable with his distress.

"Come here," Theo barked, his voice low and calm but infused with an undeniable command.

Before I knew it, I was in front of him, throwing myself into his arms. He reached out to catch me, pulling me flush to his body. I jolted with a stunned awareness of where I was, of what I had done. My lip jutted out in a disappointed pout.

"What the hell! I did way better in class." My body heated with embarrassment. Theo was going to think I was such an idiot.

To my surprise, he chuckled at my outrage and pulled me closer.

"Don't laugh at me," I whined. Despite my anger at myself,

I melted into him. "That was terrible. I didn't even realize I had done it until I was already across the room."

Theo pressed his face into my hair as I burrowed into this neck, my omega loving her alpha's soothing comfort.

"Josie, love, did you want to come over here?"

"What do you mean?"

"Before I barked at you, did you want to come over here?"

"Yeah, I wanted to make sure you were okay."

He squeezed me a little tighter. "Thank you, angel. You take such good care of me." He brushed little kisses all over my face, kissing away my pouty lip. "You didn't want to resist my bark, so you didn't. Also, the more connected you are with an alpha, the harder it is to resist their bark. I'm sure you did much better with Luc."

"So what do we do?" I asked.

"I need to tell you to do something you don't want to do. That way, you'll have the motivation to resist."

"That makes sense," I said, reaching up to push Theo's hair out of his face.

"I could tell you to do something truly terrible, like walk away from me," he said teasingly.

"This is building your ego way too much," I grumbled.

"The way you looked at my cock last night already destroyed any chance of you keeping my ego in check," Theo said, a heated look in his eyes as he squeezed my ass cheeks with both hands.

I was seconds away from suggesting we ditch this whole practice in exchange for a pre-breakfast quickie, but I wanted to prove myself.

"Fine, fine, okay. Bark at me again," I said.

Theo smiled and pulled me in for a kiss. I was confused but couldn't help molding my body to his and deepening the kiss. Then he barked.

"Stop kissing me."

I stopped immediately, my face frozen inches from Theo's. I let out a frustrated whine as my omega submitted to the bark. I took a breath as Theo held still in front of me, the warmth in his eyes giving me confidence. Slowly, painfully, I brought my face closer to his until our lips brushed together, breaking the command. I could feel his smile against my lips as he wrapped one hand in my hair, the other firmly cupping my ass.

"You did so good, omega," he said before kissing me until I was breathless.

"Thank you, alpha," I responded.

We continued practicing, my resistance coming faster and easier until Theo barked at me to go to the living room and I responded with an almost immediate "no," standing my ground.

"Good job," he exclaimed, lifting me in his arms and twirling me around. "You're amazing, angel. I've never seen an omega be able to do that."

I felt like I was glowing from his praise. Just then, we heard the front door open.

"We intercepted a delivery person in the driveway. You couldn't manage on your own for one meal?" Ben called out as he walked into the kitchen and set down two brown takeout bags.

"I said I would be fine with cereal," I said, leaping into his arms.

"Psh, no. You deserve better than cereal," Ben said, pulling me in for a kiss.

I giggled and squeezed closer to him. Ben paused and pressed his face into the crook of my neck.

"You smell delicious, precious," he said, a sly hint in his tone.

I stiffened, knowing he scented Theo on me. I waited to see if he was angry.

"Did Theo make it good for you, beautiful?" Ben murmured softly, his lips brushing the shell of my ear.

I nodded, sucking in gulps of his sweet scent.

"He better have," Cam said gruffly. I jumped, not having heard him come in.

I moved out of Ben's arms and threw myself at Cam. He picked me up and I automatically wrapped my arms and legs around him.

"Missed you," Cam murmured.

"Missed you, too," I responded, pressing my face into his neck to see if there was any anger in his scent. When there wasn't, I allowed my body to soften fully, finally letting myself believe they weren't mad at me.

Cam set me down on the counter with a gentle kiss as Ben and Theo started pulling food out of the bags.

"How did it go?" I asked, taking in Cam's exhausted expression.

"Fine," he responded, sharing a look with Ben I couldn't quite interpret.

Before I could ask more, Theo put a plate of food down in front of me and Cam gathered me up in his lap.

"You going to cuddle with me today, sweetheart?" he asked.

I hid my smile at the big alpha asking for cuddles.

"Of course," I said, placing a soft kiss on his lips.

Chapter Forty-One

Josie

I woke with the bed shifting around me, the room still pitch black.

"Sorry, baby girl, go back to sleep." Cam kissed me on the forehead as he slipped out of bed.

"Where you going?" I mumbled, pressing myself further into the warmth of the sheets.

Yesterday, after breakfast, we'd spent the day cuddling and lounging by the pool. Cam had a similar reaction as Theo to hearing about self-defense, but Ben took it in stride and helped me practice resisting his bark. We'd watched a movie before going to bed early, and I'd fallen asleep pressed between all my alphas.

"We're going to work out," Theo said, kissing my cheek.

"Too early," I responded, disgruntled.

"I completely agree," Ben said, pulling me towards him and pressing his body against mine.

"Then stay here with me," I said, nuzzling my face in the crook of his neck and breathing in his rich, spiced scent.

"I wish, precious," he responded, reluctantly rolling out of bed and tucking the covers around me.

The three of them quietly exited the room, the click of the door letting me know I was alone. I whimpered as I curled up in a ball, covering myself with the blankets. I shouldn't react this strongly—they spent most of the day and night wrapped around me. But I hated mornings, and having to spend them in bed alone made me feel abandoned.

I drifted back into a fitful sleep, jerking awake whenever I thought I heard a sound. At the Designation Academy, staff members often barged into our rooms in the mornings unannounced. They would yell at us to get up quickly and head to a surprise assembly, uncaring if we were still asleep or in the middle of getting dressed. It taught me not to let myself sleep too deeply. The exception had been the past few days with my alphas. I'd barely had any nightmares, as if my body knew I was safe with them.

I yelped when my phone rang, jolting me fully awake. I fumbled around in the dark until I found it on the nightstand. As I squinted at the bright screen, I registered two things simultaneously: it was eight o'clock on the dot, and my mother was calling.

I stared at my phone, wondering if I should answer. The call would leave me unhappy and stressed, but I knew my alphas and I had to play nice until we bonded.

My cell stopped ringing before I made up my mind. *Well, that solves it.* I went to lie back down when the phone started ringing again. Who was I kidding? This was my mother—she would keep calling until I answered, and if I didn't, she would just show up. I didn't want her intruding in the space that already felt more like home than anywhere I'd lived. I reluctantly answered, trying to make myself sound as awake as possible.

"Josephine, are you still in bed? It is eight o'clock in the morning. We have talked about this."

"No, mother, I'm not still in bed. I got up bright and early this morning. What can I do for you?" I asked, rolling my eyes.

"I know you're lying. No one likes a lazy omega. You need to be up early and be a productive member of your pack. You need to cook breakfast for those alphas and ensure you please them and run the home properly, just like I taught you."

I tried to hold in a long-suffering sigh, but apparently, she heard me and launched into a tirade. I tried my best to dissociate from her words, but I caught the highlights: I was a disappointment. I must have chosen Pack Ashwood to spite her because I was a terrible daughter. If I didn't watch my figure, my alphas would lose interest and start sleeping around. They only wanted me to join their pack to elevate their status as bonded alphas.

"Josephine, are you even paying attention to me?" she screeched.

"Yes. But I have to go. My alphas are waiting for me to eat breakfast."

"I hope they're following the diet the DC doctor created for you. God knows you need all the help you can get."

I quickly said goodbye and ended the call, cutting off whatever else she was going to say.

A dark mood settled over me. My alphas would probably be done with their workouts soon. I should go downstairs to join them for breakfast, but my mom's poisonous words seeped into my bloodstream. What if she was right? What if Cam, Theo, and Ben got up early because they didn't want to be with me? Or maybe they had wanted me to get up and work out with them. They could easily find more attractive women to sleep with.

My thoughts spiraled and I was helpless to stop them as my

body shook with the fear of rejection. Maybe I could do something to prove that they should keep me.

I threw the covers off. First step was to get my ass out of bed.

A good omega is the first to rise.

A good omega cares for the home without complaint.

My mother's barbs had hit their target as I felt the DA's lessons bubble to the surface. Old wounds I thought had healed now bled out painfully. I threw my hair up in a bun and pulled on sweatpants and a sweatshirt on autopilot.

I would prove to them I was useful.

I heard the showers going when I crept into the hallway. Good. I could get started with cleaning the gym. Luc had always approved of my work, so I didn't think I could mess it up too badly.

I headed downstairs until I found the door to the gym. I flipped the light switch, revealing a massive room that rivaled Luc's gym. State-of-the-art equipment lined the walls. There was a large fridge, a wall of mirrors, padded floors, and multiple TVs. It was absurdly over the top for a home gym.

I found a cabinet with cleaning supplies and started wiping down all the equipment, wishing I had some music playing.

A good omega is a quiet omega.

I wasn't sure how much time had passed, but I was hot and sweaty when I returned the cleaning equipment. I stretched, looking over the gym. I'd disinfected everything, mopped the floors, and started a load of towels. The smell of bleach was so intense my nose stung and I felt a bit lightheaded. I breathed through my mouth as I did a final once-over of the space.

Alright, what next? I bit my lip, wondering if the guys had already eaten breakfast. I should have prepared food for them. I hadn't cooked for them at all since being here. *Shit.* I was frustrated with how quickly I'd let my guard down. I needed to remember my DA lessons on pleasing alphas.

A good omega serves her alphas with a smile.

A good omega defers to her alphas' authority.

I could at least prepare lunch, vacuum the main floor, and do a few loads of laundry. I nodded to myself, feeling better about my plan.

I padded back up the stairs, my limbs shaking slightly from exertion, rattling off a mental list of what I needed to do next. I rounded the corner towards the kitchen and almost ran into Ben.

"Josie!" he exclaimed, shooting his arms out to steady me. He glanced towards the stairs and back at me, brow furrowed. "Theo just went to wake you up. Where have you been?"

I opened my mouth and closed it again, suddenly embarrassed.

"What happened to your hands?" Ben asked, gripping mine gently. "They're all red."

"Oh. I was just cleaning," I said, hearing how mechanical my voice sounded. I tried to tug my hands out of Ben's grasp and forced a smile.

A good omega doesn't complain.

He didn't let go.

"What were you cleaning, precious? We need to get some cream on your skin. This looks painful."

He led me over to the sink and turned the water on, testing the temperature before gently rinsing my hands under cool water. My omega melted at our alpha taking care of me, but I clenched my jaw. This was exactly the problem. I needed to be the one taking care of *them*. Why was I so defective?

"They're fine," I said, pulling my hands out of the water with more force than necessary and drying them off. "I was going to make lunch. Any requests?"

"You haven't eaten breakfast yet." Ben frowned. "And you didn't answer me—what were you cleaning?"

I shifted side to side and avoided his gaze before I realized I was disobeying… *again*.

"The gym," I finally said.

Ben's expression was bewildered, but before he could say anything, Theo shouted from upstairs.

"Josie isn't in bed!"

"She's down here," Ben shouted back, his brow still furrowed as he stared at me.

Theo and Cam thundered down the stairs. Cam was gathering his hair up in a bun as he walked into the room, and, for a moment, I was distracted by my desire to run my hands through it.

"Where were you?" Theo asked, wrapping his arms around me. "And why do you smell like bleach?"

I stiffened. Theo smelled fresh and clean like he had just gotten out of the shower. Part of me wanted to lean into his embrace, but a sick feeling gripped me as he nuzzled into my neck. I didn't deserve his touch and attention. A nasty voice said he was only here with me because I was an omega and his inner alpha compelled him. There was nothing special about me, nothing to make my alphas want me.

"Sweetheart," Cam said softly, brushing his hand under my chin to lift my gaze. "You're shaking."

"Sorry," I whispered, my throat tight as I looked away.

I needed to get away from them before I burst into tears. My mind was all tangled. Everything seemed clear when I was alone in the gym. I didn't know why I expected them to leave me alone to do chores, except that it was what I'd been taught my whole life.

Then Cam's arms were around me. He lifted me onto the kitchen island and caged me in with his body.

"She needs something for her hands," Ben said softly.

A growl rolled through Theo's chest as he took in the raw skin before he stormed off.

I watched him leave with wide eyes.

Ben cupped my face. "He's just worried, precious. We all are."

"What were you doing?" Cam asked, frowning at my hands.

Ben responded when I didn't answer. "She said she was cleaning the gym."

"Why would you do that?" Theo asked, stomping back into the kitchen with a small tub of lotion.

"Just wanted to be helpful," I said, my lower lip trembling.

"We have people who come clean," Theo said, rubbing the cream tenderly onto my hands. They stung a bit but weren't too bad.

"You do?"

"We asked them not to come while you're settling in," Theo responded. "Research shows omegas settle in better to a new place when there aren't strangers coming in and out."

"Oh."

"Is the house not clean enough for you, sweetheart? Because we can clean," Cam said, his hands firmly planted on my thighs.

I shook my head.

Fuck, now they thought I was criticizing their house. I didn't understand how this entire day had backfired so spectacularly. My chest squeezed with anxiety. I wanted to run back to my nest and cover myself with blankets.

Ben wrapped an arm around me. "I don't know what's happened to make you so upset. If you're not ready to tell us, that's okay." He glared at Cam, who looked very much like he disagreed, before continuing. "But we're not going to leave you to be upset alone. You have us now. That means you don't have to suffer alone."

His sweet words broke through the barriers I'd erected, and I released a sob.

All three of them pressed against me immediately, arms wrapping around me in a tangled pile.

"Sweet omega, what happened?" Cam asked as he held my face to his chest.

My sobs intensified, and he kissed my cheeks before grabbing some tissues and gently wiping my face.

"You shouldn't be with me," I whimpered.

"Why not?" Theo asked, eyes darkening.

"Because I'm not good enough for you. You should make me leave."

"What? That's not true. What are you talking about, gorgeous?" Ben asked, gripping my neck.

"You deserve someone better." I tried to move away, needing to create some distance between us. None of them gave me an inch.

"Josie, what happened? I thought you were happy here with us," Theo said.

"I am happy here," I whimpered. *Happier than I've ever been.*

"Good, because we're not letting you go. Now, what happened?" Theo asked again.

"My mom called," I whispered.

"Ahh, charming woman, a real ray of sunshine," Ben said dryly.

I let out a startled laugh.

"I'm guessing she said some nasty things that got you doubting yourself," Theo said.

"Yeah."

"I can say confidently that whatever she said, it's a load of shit," Cam growled.

"I just want to be useful around the house. A good omega keeps a perfect home for her alphas."

All three of my guys raised their brows in a look of pure incredulity that would have been funny in a different circumstance.

"What Stepford Omega bullshit is that?" Theo sputtered.

"That's not what we want. Please don't let her poison your thoughts," Ben said gently.

"But what if she's right? What if you change your mind about me? I need to make sure I'm useful."

Cam gripped my chin, forcing me to meet his gaze. My breath caught when I saw his blazing eyes.

"We will never change our minds about you. Don't fucking say things like that," he growled. His scent was bitter with agitation, and his body was practically vibrating. Ben and Theo looked equally unhappy.

They were upset.

Not because I hadn't been cooking and cleaning but because I doubted my place with them.

Shit.

My mother was profoundly unhappy in her relationships, so why had I let her get in my head? And when had my guys ever indicated they wanted a traditional house omega?

"Oh," I breathed out, slumping against Cam's chest. The solidness of his body soothed me.

He wrapped his arms around me, cradling my body to his.

"Are you back with us?" Theo asked, leaning in to press soft kisses down the side of my face.

"Yeah. Sorry, brain got hijacked there for a bit."

"We want you just how you are," Ben murmured, pulling me in for a sweet kiss. I must have looked hideous, my eyes red and puffy from crying, but Ben didn't seem to care. He placed gentle kisses on my eyelids.

"Did you actually want to make lunch? Because I thought we could order in," he said.

"Umm..." I was a good baker, but cooking was not my strong suit.

Ben grinned. "Take-out it is."

"What about Thai?" Theo suggested, pulling out his phone but keeping one hand in mine. Then he froze. "Wait, do you actually like Thai or was that another joke on the questionnaire?"

I giggled. "No, that one was true. I think you've discovered all the lies by now."

I glanced up at Cam. He was standing between my legs, his hands resting on the island on either side of me.

I bit my lip, worried about how quiet he was being.

"You okay?" I whispered.

He huffed and rested his forehead against my shoulder.

"Fuck, baby girl, still recovering from hearing you say we should *make you leave* when you're the best thing that's happened to us."

"You're too sweet to me," I said, pulling his hair down from its bun and running my fingers through it.

"No such thing," Cam grumbled, leaning into my touch. "You deserve all the sweetness."

A smile tugged at my lips at hearing my gruff alpha say something so sappy.

"Will you cuddle with me?" I asked, repeating his request from yesterday.

"Fuck yes."

Cam lifted me off the island and carried me into the living room. Ben and Theo followed, piling around us as we turned on a movie.

I tried to get my body to relax, but an uncomfortable restlessness still gripped my chest. Guilt wormed its way into my stomach—guilt for messing everything up this morning, for making my alphas worry... and for not being good enough for them. They might disagree, but deep down, I knew it was true.

The Thai food arrived and Ben dished me up a big plate. I was hungry, but my mother's warning about gaining weight haunted me. I ended up picking at my food, something the guys were clearly unhappy about. They kept looking down towards my plate.

"Can you eat any more, love?" Theo asked, tenderly cupping my face.

I shook my head. "I'm not really hungry."

His eyes were tight, but he didn't say anything as he took my plate.

Chapter Forty-Two

Cam

I slammed my laptop shut, frustration coursing through me. Why couldn't I fix whatever was going on with my omega?

The energy had been subdued all day after Josie's upsetting conversation with her mother and the *cleaning*. I scoffed. I couldn't fucking believe our omega thought we wanted her to clean the house. Didn't she know we weren't like the alphas she grew up with?

She'd settled down after we all talked, but things were still off. She'd been too quiet, her smiles too forced.

I fucking hated it.

She'd gone upstairs to shower a few minutes ago, and I had to resist following her up like a stalker. Maybe giving her space right now was the wrong thing to do. My alpha agreed.

I stomped into the kitchen, where Theo was bent over a book.

"What're you doing?" I asked.

He jumped, quickly shutting the book.

I raised my brows and he huffed, showing me the cover: *When Your Loved One is Traumatized*.

"Catchy," I said.

Ben pulled a chocolate cake from the fridge to frost and joined us at the island.

"Anything helpful in there?" he asked, leaning over Theo's shoulder to flip through the book. I felt the weight of his helplessness through the bond. We all hated seeing Josie so dejected.

"Looks like you've already read it," I said to Theo, noting how worn it was.

"I got it years ago," he mumbled. "When we left North Woods."

His words hung in the air, and it took me a moment to realize he must have gotten the book for *me* back in the day. My throat tightened and I pulled him in for a quick hug.

"The three of us have seen some shit," I said, clearing my throat.

"No kidding," Ben said, putting his arm around me. "And I think Josie might have us all beat."

Theo lifted his head from the book. "I feel like she's hiding the worst of it from us because she thinks we'll think less of her." He looked lost in thought for a moment before adding, "We have to figure out how to get her away from her family for good."

Theo's analytic mind shifted from one problem to the next, focusing on strategy and logic in a way I couldn't when it came to our mate. All I knew was that my Josie was hurting, and I felt lost.

My mind went again to the files Ben and I found last night. Something about it tickled at the edges of my memory, but I couldn't quite figure out what.

"So," Ben said, interrupting my thoughts, "what does the book say?"

"A lot of it is about being patient and knowing healing takes time," Theo said with a frown.

"Nope. Don't like that," Ben muttered as he fought the chocolate icing, frustration lacing his tone.

"I just want her to be happy," I said, pulling my hair up in a bun. Josie seemed to like running her hands through it, and I secretly hoped she would pull it back down again.

"Is there any other advice—oh, shit," Ben said. "Did you see this about the senator?" He held out his phone.

Theo and I shook our heads.

"It just came through from Charlie."

Charlie was a hacker Ben worked with through the Alliance.

"Apparently, a senator accused Jericho of stealing his omega in a late-night legislative session."

"What?" I asked, my chest tightening.

"Why isn't this on the news?" Theo asked, now flipping through his phone.

"I'm sure Jericho made plenty of threats to cover it up," I growled.

"What about Jericho?" a sweet voice asked from the doorway.

We whirled to face Josie, whose hair was still damp from the shower.

I held out my arms and was relieved when she came to me, but I hated how stiffly she held herself.

"Jericho?" she prompted.

For a moment, none of us said anything. I hated that she'd overheard. I didn't want to add to her stress or burden.

Ben hesitated. "A video clip just came through from Charlie. She hacked the system and pulled it before it was permanently wiped."

My jaw clenched as frustration flared within me. I threw

Ben a dirty look I knew he didn't deserve, but I didn't want Josie to watch something that would upset her. Ben's jaw clenched, and he averted his eyes.

"You don't have to watch it," I said, caressing Josie's face and wishing I could shield her from everything bad.

"I want to," she responded quietly.

Ben turned his phone around and pressed play on the video. For the first few minutes, it seemed like regular footage of the senate floor until one of the senators stood up. The video was a wide shot of the senate, but the agony on his face was still clear.

"I know you have her, you sick son of a bitch. Give her back to me!" the alpha shouted, pointing an accusing finger at Jericho, whose face didn't betray any emotion. "You took her from us, my omega. Where is she?"

Josie trembled in my arms, blinking quickly to stop her tears. I held her tight to my side.

Something caught Jericho's eye outside the frame, and he snapped his fingers. Immediately, a swarm of guards descended on the alpha and carried him away. Jericho turned back to the assembly and calmly read the next agenda item as if nothing had happened.

Josie pulled away from me, and I fought every instinct screaming to pull her back in, press her close to me and offer whatever comfort I could.

"You think he did it?" she whispered, not making eye contact.

"Possibly," Theo said, trailing his hand down her arm.

Josie's jaw was set, and she gave a little nod.

"I think I'll go to bed," she said.

"Okay," I said, holding out my hand to her to go upstairs.

"Alone," she said so softly I almost didn't catch it.

Fuck. That was like a dagger to the heart.

Was she upset with me? About the news with Jericho? Or something else? I couldn't fucking fix it, and that made me livid.

Theo cleared his throat, raising his eyebrows at me.

Yeah, yeah, time and patience.

"Let me walk you up at least," I said, cupping Josie under the chin.

She said goodnight to the other two and walked ahead of me up the stairs. We paused at her door, the energy awkward between us.

"If you change your mind or need anything, come and get me. No matter what time it is. Understand, baby girl?"

"I will," she said.

I pulled her in for a tight hug, trying to send all my love and warmth into it.

"I'm respecting your space for tonight because you've dealt with a lot today. But soon, you won't be able to hide from me."

She shivered and put her arms around me. For a second, I thought she might ask me to stay. But then she slipped away with a quiet goodnight.

Leaving me alone in the hallway.

Chapter Forty-Three

Ben

I wasn't even trying to sleep. I knew I wouldn't be able to when Josie was in her room, alone and upset. I wanted to do unspeakably horrible things to her mother for whatever she had said to my beautiful mate.

Cam and Theo had finally made their way to their separate rooms, and I was sitting in the library downstairs, a soothing record playing in the background, my hand gripping a large glass of whisky. I didn't know how to make this better. *Should I just go into her room and force her to talk to me?*

The record stopped, and as I got up to turn it over, I heard a sound in the kitchen. My heart lurched—was it her?

I found Josie standing in the dark, illuminated by only the refrigerator light. She was hunched over the counter, quickly eating the chocolate cake I made this afternoon. Based on how much was left, it looked like she had already eaten two or three slices. Her eyes were glazed over, and she didn't notice me standing in the doorway.

"Josie, precious, you okay?" I asked quietly.

She jumped and gave a little scream, throwing her fork at my head. I deflected it before it hit me.

"Damn, you have good aim. Although I think I preferred being hit with the brownie." As I walked closer, I noticed her scent was burnt with fear.

"Gorgeous, why are you shaking?" I lifted my hand to touch her but hesitated when she let out a whimper and flinched away from me.

"Josie," I whispered. "I would never hurt you."

"I'm sorry," she sobbed. "You shouldn't touch me. I'm dirty."

"What are you talking about? Why would you say that?" I almost growled.

Her trembling increased, and I couldn't stop myself from picking her up. I was relieved when she didn't fight me—her arms and legs wrapped around me and I squeezed her tighter. A rumbling started in my chest as I began to purr. Everything about this situation was stressful as fuck, but satisfaction filled me as I purred for my mate for the first time.

I didn't say anything, just held her close and rocked gently back and forth. Her trembling slowly stopped, and she took a deep, shuddering breath. I leaned back against the counter, one arm holding her up beneath her ass and the other cupping the back of her neck so her face was tucked into mine. I pressed my face into her hair, relieved to find her scent was settling down.

"You are my sweet, precious mate. You're such a good girl. You just tell me what's going on when you're ready." I kept up a steady stream of reassurance and praise, holding back my inner alpha pressuring me to push her to tell me everything so I could make it all better. I knew it was important to give her the time she needed.

Finally, she said, "I ate most of your cake." Of all the things she could have said, I was not expecting that.

"What did you think?" I asked.

"What?"

"Did you think it was a good chocolate cake? It's a new recipe."

"Ben! You should be upset with me. I ate most of the cake."

I placed her down on the island so I could see her better. I was missing something, but I wasn't sure what. My legs spread hers wide as I stepped in between them, pushing up the tiny sleep shorts she had on. I placed one hand firmly on her upper thigh, and the other gripped her chin lightly.

"Why the fuck would I be upset? I made the cake because I thought you would like it. You didn't eat nearly enough food today. I'm thrilled you ate some, and there's still plenty left. I'll feed you the rest if you're still hungry."

Josie's eyes filled with tears again.

"Precious, please. I can't handle it when you cry. Please tell me what's going on."

"I binge eat," she whispered, unable to meet my eyes. "I try to control what I eat, but there's something wrong with me. I can't control it and I'm too fat and nothing like an omega should be." Her breaths came faster as she worked her way into a panic.

"Take a breath for me, precious." I pulled her in, resting her head on my chest so she could hear my heartbeat.

"I don't know if there's anything I can say to convince you how beautiful you are, but here," I grabbed one of her hands and guided it down to my hard cock. "I shouldn't be hard right now. You're in distress. But my cock is an asshole and doesn't know that. All it sees are your delicious thighs bracketing mine, your sweet little nipples poking through that tank top. I love your softness and your curves. I wouldn't trade them for anything and certainly don't want you to starve yourself to change your body."

"But I should have more self-control," she said, unable to meet my gaze. My heart was breaking, watching her so lost in pain.

"Says who? I'd be more than happy for you to lose control around me." I brushed my lips down the side of her face and she shivered.

"It's not easy when you three look like Greek gods or something," she said. "Like, *come on*. Makes me feel hideous in comparison."

"You think I look like a Greek god?" I asked in my typical teasing tone. Josie gave me a small, watery smile and looked away. I realized I had messed up. Josie was being vulnerable with me, and I needed to be brave for her.

"No, sorry, that's not what I meant to say." I cupped her cheek and gently urged her to look at me. "I don't know exactly what you're going through. But I know a little bit of what it's like to feel pressure to look a certain way."

Her eyebrows crinkled and her lip jutted out in adorable confusion.

"I'm not saying it's the same thing as what you've gone through. Fuck, it makes me want to cry thinking of how people have treated you. I can't imagine being starved or repeatedly told that something was wrong with my body. It's not the same, but I do feel pressured to be really buff. I was always told alphas had to be the strongest and most muscular. I've been working out daily since I was a kid. And I actually pretty much hate it. I was always told an omega wouldn't be attracted to me if I didn't have a six-pack and wasn't solid muscle."

"What? You don't like working out?"

"No, I would much rather spend the time doing other things like baking or spending sleepy mornings with you. Alpha biology means that I'll probably stay pretty muscular and reasonably strong even without tons of intense workouts, but I wouldn't look like this if I slowed it down," I said, gesturing down my torso.

"But that would be okay," Josie said, her eyes shining earnestly. "You don't have to be super muscular or have a six-pack. You should do what makes you happy."

"Ahh, but you won't be as attracted to me if I gain some fat."

"Says who?" Josie said, crossing her arms in indignation. "I totally would be. You would still be one of the three hottest alphas in the world."

"So fucking cute." I placed a gentle kiss on my mate's rosy lips. "You could just be saying that, though, and not mean it."

"I wouldn't do that. I don't care what you look like, Ben. I love all of you, and I'm always going to be attracted to you."

"Then it shouldn't be hard to believe I feel the same way about you." I raised my eyebrow at her.

She opened her mouth as if to argue and then paused. Her nose scrunched again as if she was trying to figure out a complicated math problem.

"It's going to take me a while to believe that," she finally said.

"That's alright, beautiful. We have time. Until you believe it, I'm going to make sure you eat regularly, okay? And if you want to come down and eat more at night, you don't have to hide it. I'm never going to judge you for it. In fact, I rather like our late-night kitchen tradition."

She leaned against my chest and I purred again, pulling her close. I realized how at ease I was feeling having my mate in my arms and knowing that I was the one who had soothed her.

"It made me sad when you all left this morning," she said, breaking the silence.

"Wait, what?" I asked, confused. "When did we leave?"

"Never mind, forget that I said anything. It's fine. I'm being stupid." She tried to wriggle away from me.

"Wait, none of that. I want to know why you were sad. Please explain, beautiful."

Her eyes shone with tears, and her lips trembled. "When you left the bed this morning. I just... I felt like you didn't want me, like you were rejecting me, which is so stupid because you were just going to work out, and I shouldn't be so needy, and I just need to get over it."

I took a deep breath. Fuck, we messed up.

"Precious, I need you to listen to me. You have three alphas who are completely obsessed with you. You do not have to *get over* anything. You need to tell us when we do something to upset you. Of course, we weren't rejecting you, but we should have realized that you weren't expecting us to all leave before you even woke up. I can imagine that felt jarring. Good thing we've already established that it's literally the last thing I want to do, so we'll make sure it doesn't happen in the future."

"But I'm being unreasonable."

"No, you're not." I gripped her chin firmly, forcing her to make eye contact. "I'm not saying there won't be mornings where we have to get up early or you'll be in bed on your own. But we'll do a better job communicating and ensure you're feeling okay. Before you protest, let me be clear that I *want* to do this. Beautiful, you're my mate. I'm completely taken with you. I love you." Saying the words felt like a huge fucking relief. I needed her to understand how I felt about her.

"You love me?" she asked, eyes wide.

"Yes, precious, I love you. You have my whole heart, and that's not going to change."

"I love you, too," she blurted out, almost like she couldn't get the words out fast enough.

"Don't know how I got so lucky," I murmured, smiling widely.

I ran my hands slowly up and down her bare thigh, getting closer and closer to her sex with each pass. She perfumed and I heard the slight hitch of her breath.

"Are you still hungry?" I asked, placing gentle kisses on her nose and across her cheeks. She shook her head, closing her eyes and leaning into my touch.

"Tired?" I slipped my hands under the bottom of her shorts, my fingers teasing the edge of her panties. She shook her head again and squirmed against me, trying to get my fingers to move where she wanted them.

"Are you feeling needy, precious?"

She let out a soft whine and tugged at my shirt. I quickly helped her pull it off me and groaned in pleasure as she ran her hands up and down my bare chest. I moved to strip her of her tank top. She made an anxious little noise and tried to pull away from me, but I held her firm.

I gripped her chin and nipped at her bottom lip. "Let me see you, gorgeous. I'm so hungry for you. I need to have you sprawled before me, naked, so I can kiss, lick, and bite every inch of your sexy body."

She hesitated before finally nodding. I moved quickly before she changed her mind. I pulled off her tank top before gripping the waistband of her shorts.

"Lift," I commanded gruffly. My cock was straining so hard against my boxers that I thought I was going to explode. I stripped her bare and ran my eyes up and down her delicious body. Josie sat stiffly, her eyes wide and breathing fast. I knew this was hard for her, but I had to show her that there was absolutely nothing about her body to be ashamed of.

"I think we need a new rule in the house," I murmured, pulling her in tightly and resting her head on my bare chest. It was torture holding myself back from touching every inch of her, but I knew she needed some reassurance right now as I rocked her gently in my embrace. "No clothing for you when we're home. It's a crime to cover up this body."

I moved one hand down to her dusky nipples and started teasing and pinching until she softly whined. She tilted her head back, searching for my lips, and I kissed her. Her mouth tasted so sweet, and her little moans and whimpers almost took me over the edge. I shifted her even closer so she rubbed against me, her core right against my hard cock, leaving a wet patch on the front of my underwear. I took a deep breath, needing to get myself under control so I could make this good for her.

"You're going to be a good girl and let me do what I want with your sweet little body, aren't you?"

Her eyes were glazed with lust, her cheeks flushed and mouth parted. "Yes," she breathed out.

"Of course you are. You're my good little mate, my perfect omega. Now, lie back for me."

I helped her lay down on the island, pulling so her ass was right at the edge. I placed kisses down her stomach, causing her to tense up. She tried to cover her stomach, but I gently moved them aside. I continued kissing her soft skin, murmuring praise, and running my hands all over her soft curves. When she finally relaxed, I moved further down. I gripped her calves and kissed up her thigh, teasing her by getting close to her sweet pussy but not touching her there. I wanted her so overcome with need that she couldn't think of anything else.

"Ben, please," she whimpered.

"What, precious? What do you need?"

"Touch me," she whined needily.

"I am touching you," I said as I nipped her inner thighs. I was trying to draw this out, but the sweet scent of her overwhelmed me. She had the prettiest fucking pussy I had ever seen. I blew softly on her pink folds, causing her to jerk her hips.

"Please touch me there."

"Where, beautiful? Use your words."

She growled at me in frustration. "Touch me down there."

I chuckled, amazed at how she could still be so shy when my face was an inch away from her. "You want me to touch your plump little pussy? To lick your slick off your sexy cunt?"

"Yes, please."

"Look at my good girl using her manners. So adorable."

Without warning, I buried my head between her legs, breathing in her scent and licking along her slit. I threw her legs over my shoulder, holding her thigh in a bruising grip as my other hand parted her folds. Her soft whimpers fueled my own enjoyment. I had never felt this overwhelmed with desire. Her taste was exquisite as I circled her clit with my tongue. I plunged a finger into her tight channel, groaning as I imagined my cock sliding into her. I added another finger, stretching her and getting her ready for me. Her breathing grew heavier, and she clenched on my fingers.

"What a perfect omega, so beautiful. Are you going to come on my tongue?"

I curled my fingers to hit the pleasure spot omegas had inside of them and sucked on her clit. She came with a scream and whimpered as I continued to lick her, devouring her slick.

"You're going to come again for me, beautiful," I said, adding a third finger and continuing to pump into her.

"I can't, I can't."

"Yes, you can. Just relax and breathe into it."

I banded my arm across her hips, keeping her in place as I built up her orgasm again. When she came a second time, her scream was louder than the first.

I pulled back and took her in. She lay on the island, looking relaxed and sated, her cheeks rosy. She met my eyes as I brought my fingers up to my mouth and sucked her sweet juices off them.

Chapter Forty-Four

Josie

"Fucking delicious," Ben said with a grin, pulling his fingers out of his mouth.

I lay on the counter in a daze, still trembling with the aftermath of my two orgasms. At least it had distracted me from the shame I had felt at Ben catching me bingeing. I remembered the one and only time my mother caught me eating late at night in the kitchen. She berated me so loudly that half the house had woken up, causing a furious Jericho to storm down the stairs to investigate what was happening. She had called me a fat pig and told me no one would ever love me if I continued eating. The next day, I came down for breakfast and found a lock on the fridge.

"Hey, precious, you here with me?" Ben asked, pulling me into a sitting position. I realized I had zoned out, lost to my memories.

"You really aren't mad at me?" I asked, hating how small and unsure my voice sounded.

Ben took a slow breath and looked me in the eye. "Never,"

he said, and his voice was so sure, so genuine, that a shard of shame I'd been carrying around all this time fell away.

"Thank you," I whispered, wrapping my arms and legs around him. Our chests rose and fell together as our breaths synched, the rest of the world falling away as my alpha held me.

After a few long moments, Ben moved in my grasp, and I realized he was trying to shift his hard-on. A shiver of pleasure washed through me and my core clenched, as if knowing it needed to be filled.

It was stupid to feel nervous about initiating sex with Ben when he had just eaten me out and given me two orgasms on the kitchen island, but old insecurities still welled up. I pressed my face to his neck.

"I want you," I murmured.

"You have me, precious," Ben said.

Okay, direct approach needed. "Umm, no, like I want you," I said, trailing my hand down his front until I cupped his cock.

Ben made a noise that was a mixture of a strangled choking sound and a growl.

"I don't want you to think you have to do anything more tonight."

"I don't feel like that," I said. "I want this. I want to feel you inside me." I finally met his eyes and what I saw there was pure lust.

A beautiful smile spread across his face and his spicy apple scent intensified. I couldn't help breathing in thick gulps of it.

"I've always wanted to fuck in the kitchen. It's my favorite room in the house, you know," he said, a mischievous glint in his eye.

"Who am I to deny your fantasy?"

"Precious, you are my fantasy."

With that, he pulled me off the counter and grasped my

hips, turning me around and bending me over the island. I squeaked as the cold marble pressed on my nipples and Ben's hands squeezed my ass. He ran his hands up and down my back, soothing me for a moment.

"This okay?"

God, it was more than okay. I loved how his body pressed against mine, the feel of his hands on me, and I wanted more.

"Don't stop."

"Fuck, you're goddamn perfect. You're going to give me what I want, right, beautiful? You're going to take my cock like a good girl."

Who knew Ben was such a dirty talker? His cock slid against my slit. I arched my back so he was hitting perfectly against my clit, my slick dripping down my thighs.

"I need you, alpha," I whined.

"Fuck, how can I say no to that?"

He lined himself up and I moaned as he eased his way into me, pleasure lighting up every nerve ending. His thrusts were slow and smooth as he wrapped one hand around my hip and the other on the back of my neck, pinning me to the counter.

"More," I whimpered, my omega taking over with her demands. "Harder."

He swore and leaned his body over mine, his skin hot against my back. "I don't want to hurt you."

"You won't. I need you."

Ben snarled and started thrusting harder, his firm grip the only thing keeping me from sliding forward on the island. His knot ground against me, and I whined with pleasure. Every thrust erased my mother's harsh words and my hatred towards my body. How could I hate my body when it allowed me to feel *this?*

I let out a small cry as he continued to slide in and out. With every thrust, his knot pushed against my entrance, igniting my nerve endings. I arched back to meet him, eager for more as he held me secure. On the next thrust, Ben started pushing the base of his knot in me. The stretch was too much and everything I needed. Except I didn't want to be knotted in the kitchen.

I opened my mouth to tell him to wait, but he had already thrust forward, seating his knot fully inside me. It seemed to inflate even more, the angle making him feel impossibly huge. It was too much, too many sensations. I let out a whimper and tried to shift away, but he curled his body over me and whispered as he placed tender kisses down my spine.

"I've got you. Such a good omega taking my knot."

That was what I needed to transform the overwhelming pressure into pleasure. He rocked against me in small movements, grinding against my clit and slick gland until an intense orgasm rippled through me. I came with a scream as he shouted my name and scraped his teeth against my neck in a promise of the bond mark he wanted to place there.

We both lay pressed over the counter, breathing heavily, until Ben stood up and tried to pull away, putting intense pressure on my core as my sex clenched around his knot.

I squealed. "Stop, stop, stop! What're you doing?"

There was a long pause. "Fucking shit. We're locked together."

I choked out a strangled laugh. "Yes, you knotted me. What did you think would happen?"

I heard the hesitation in his voice. "I didn't think we would be stuck together. I guess I thought when people said they were locked together, they were speaking metaphorically. Like, you know, now we're locked together emotionally."

I looked over my shoulder, taking in his shocked expression and the blush working its way across his cheeks.

"Ben, you have a massive balloon at the base of your cock

inflated in me, and you thought people were speaking *metaphorically*?"

Ben leaned over me and grabbed my hips so we were firmly tucked together.

"Fuck, I'm so sorry, precious. I really didn't think we were going to be literally stuck together. Fuck, fuck, fuck. I wanted our first time to be romantic, but instead, I knotted you over the kitchen counter."

The ridiculousness of the situation took away my residual distress from earlier in the day. I couldn't believe my alpha hadn't understood what knotting meant. I laughed so hard that little contractions rippled through my core. Suddenly, Ben grunted as he came again, which set off my orgasm. I moaned into the counter with pleasure.

"Did you just fucking make both of us come through *laughing*?" he asked incredulously, making me laugh harder. Finally, he joined in, the two of us caught up in giggles, folded over the kitchen island in the middle of the night.

Once our laughter settled down, Ben ran his hands gently down my spine. "I can't believe I did this. Are you in pain? Am I crushing you?"

"I'm fine, definitely not in pain," I said as I pushed back against him, and pleasure lit up my insides. "I hope you know I won't ever let you live this down, though," I teased.

Ben groaned and leaned forward, resting his head on my shoulder. "How long are we going to be stuck like this?"

"It depends," I said, resting my head on my arms with a smile. This position was definitely not the most comfortable for an extended time, but being connected to Ben made me feel giddy and safe.

"Depends on what?" he asked, his hips jerking in another involuntary thrust. "Did Theo knot you?"

"Mmm, yeah, he did. I'm not sure how long we were locked together. I fell asleep. But maybe like thirty minutes?"

"You're kidding me. Why didn't people explain knotting to me more clearly?"

"I mean, I think they did. You're the romantic one who thought they weren't being literal." I wiggled my ass at him, and he moaned. "Okay, here's what we're going to do. Grab my hips and hold me to you. Then slowly lean back and use the wall to help lower yourself down. Then we'll both be sitting, which will be more comfortable."

Ben grumbled, but he did it. His hands wrapped around my hips so hard I knew I would bruise, but I loved it. I wanted his marks all over me.

I groaned and whined in pleasure as he moved me into a seated position in his lap, and his knot tugged and ground against my most sensitive parts. Once I was seated on his lap, he banded his arms around me—one around my waist and the other around my breasts.

He murmured in my ear, "I'm so sorry. I really had no clue it would be like this."

I smiled. "So, I'm guessing you've never knotted anyone."

"Obviously," he groaned out.

"Do you... do you like it?" I asked, suddenly feeling unsure. I was realizing how much praise my omega needed—that *I* needed—to feel secure.

"Do I like it?" he asked incredulously. "This is by far the hottest, sexiest fucking thing I have ever experienced. Your pretty little cunt is gripping my knot so hard I'm on the verge of coming again just sitting here. If we weren't in such an inconvenient location, I would see if we could beat the record for longest time locked together because I never want to leave the heaven of your sweet pussy."

My lips parted in a small gasp as slick gushed around his

knot at how turned on I was at his words. I wriggled in his lap, needing friction.

"If you don't want to be here all night, you need to stop moving, precious. That feels too damn good."

I ignored him and kept rocking against him. "It makes me really happy that I'm the first person you've knotted."

"Me too. Nothing could feel as good as you do right now." He kissed the back of my neck and cupped my breasts.

I experimented with trying to bounce up and down on his knot. "I'm pretty comfortable right now, actually. And you feel so good, alpha."

Ben growled, grabbing my hips and guiding my movements, thrusting as much as he could with the way we were locked together. Pleasure shot through me like little lightning bolts. After a few moments, Ben snaked a hand around to play with my clit, quickly building my orgasm.

"So beautiful, my perfect mate."

His praise pushed me over again, pleasure rushing through me. His hot cum burst in me and I collapsed back into him, my orgasm so intense I felt like I was floating. He ran his hands gently over my skin, massaging my arms, shoulders, and thighs.

"You back with me, beautiful?" he murmured.

"You're trying to kill me with orgasms."

Ben grasped me underneath my knees so I didn't have to hold myself up, and I relaxed further into his hold.

"If we don't come again, your knot should go down in a few minutes," I said, snuggling my face into his bare chest.

"At least our first time will be memorable," he grumbled.

"Ten out of ten for memorability. Two out of ten for location choice," I said cheekily.

"And what about pleasure?"

"Five hundred."

Ben let out a purr.

"What about for you?" I asked.

"Five hundred thousand for sure," he said, stroking a hand through my hair. "Can't believe how lucky I am right now."

"Same," I said quietly.

His spiced apple scent was delicious as it swirled around me. We sat in comfortable silence, Ben's warmth keeping me from getting cold. I felt myself drift off, even though his knot was still in me. *I guess five orgasms will do that.*

I jolted awake slightly as Ben spoke. "Josie, do you want to see someone to help with everything you've gone through? Like a therapist or something?"

I stiffened. My parents were firmly against mental health help and always acted like I was being dramatic. But Ben wasn't saying there was anything wrong with me. He was actually seeing me and wanted to help.

"I don't know," I said, unsure if I could talk to a stranger about what I'd gone through. "But I love you for asking."

He nuzzled the back of my neck, breathing deeply. "Let me know, precious. You know we'll do anything to support you."

I let out a soft sigh, which turned into a whimper as Ben's knot deflated enough for him to lift me off of him. I shifted forward on all fours, my legs still too weak to support myself. A gush of fluid rushed out between us, and I giggled at Ben's exclaimed, "Woah."

"Wait there. I'll get a towel to clean you up."

I flinched as Ben pressed a warm towel to my sex.

"You sore?" he asked as he tenderly cleaned me up.

"Just a bit, but not in a bad way," I mumbled, my eyelids heavy.

"Come on, let's get you to bed."

I curled my arms and legs around him as he carried me upstairs. The scent of my other alphas reached me as we neared the bedroom.

"About fucking time," said a disgruntled Cam. "What took so long? Did you knot her in the fucking kitchen?"

I giggled as Cam pressed against my back.

"You fucking didn't," Theo said, laughter in his voice. He moved to my side and pressed his face into my hair. "How are you doing, love?"

"Good," I said, smiling. "Let's go to bed."

"Fucking finally," Cam growled, stealing me out of Ben's arms and carrying me into my room. The four of us piled onto the bed, and I was pressed firmly between them.

"You better now, baby girl?" Cam murmured in my ear, playing tenderly with my hair.

"All good with my alphas around me."

I breathed them in as I drifted off to sleep.

Chapter Forty-Five

Josie

A ringing jolted me awake.

"Shit, sorry," Theo groaned, rolling over to grab his phone off the nightstand.

Ben's arms tightened around me as I stirred. I was warm and comfortable and automatically hated whoever had called for interrupting our morning. I had no idea what time it was besides *too early o'clock.*

"Go back to sleep," Theo murmured, brushing his hand along my face before getting out of bed to take the call. I whimpered, not wanting any of my alphas to leave. Cam shifted closer, throwing an arm and leg across me, sandwiching me between him and Ben. The warm pressure of their bodies against mine and their spiced apple and cinnamon roll scents settled me.

"How're you feeling, precious?" Ben asked, his voice heavy with sleep.

"Good," I responded, nuzzling into his neck.

"Not too sore?" His arms tightened around me, and I noticed a slightly worried edge to his scent.

"All good," I murmured, pressing a kiss to Ben's bare chest. I was lulled asleep by the soothing sound of his purr.

I woke to low voices. Theo was back, his scent bitter. My eyelids were too heavy to pry open, but I needed to touch him. I reached out my hand, flailing in his general direction until he grasped it and kissed my wrist.

"Good morning, angel," Theo said softly.

"Morning," I mumbled. "What's wrong?"

"Nothing's wrong."

My eyes popped open. "You lying to me?" I asked. Theo's eyes were tight and his smile forced.

He sighed. "Nothing is wrong, but that was Amirah on the phone. She needs us for an Alliance job this evening."

"What's the job?" I asked. Ben still looked half asleep underneath me. Cam was wide awake, soothing his hand up and down my back.

"There's a pharmaceutical development team working with the Alliance," Cam said. "They've developed tablets for omegas that can incapacitate any alphas in close proximity."

"What?" I gasped, trying to sit up.

Ben grunted and pulled me closer to him, pressing his face into my neck. "If we have to have a serious conversation this early, I need you on top of me, precious."

I smiled as Cam and Theo rolled their eyes. Ben might even be more of a monster in the mornings than me.

"They've been in development for a while," Theo said. "They found a way to infuse omega pheromones with a toxin that will render alphas helpless for up to thirty minutes. The omega just has to chew the tab to release it."

My body tensed before I registered Theo's words. Stinging

pain shot through my arm, radiating from my scar. I breathed through it, knowing the pain wasn't real—it was the cost of remembering what had happened to me.

"What's wrong, sweetheart?" Cam asked, his hand settling on the back of my neck in a firm, comforting hold. "Is your arm hurting you?"

Shit. I had reached out to grab my scar without thinking.

"No," I said quickly, dropping my hand. I didn't want to go there, wasn't ready to tell them about my past.

Cam's gaze narrowed, and I thought he would push me to talk. Instead, he took a deep breath and gave me a nod. "Only when you're ready to tell us."

"Thanks," I said, breathing in his cinnamon roll scent, trying to force my muscles to relax again.

Ben's arms tightened around me, and he pressed a kiss to my forehead.

"What happens to the alphas?" I asked, breaking the silence.

"It's described that they go into a sort of trance state where they'll do whatever they're told," Theo said, a slight frown on his face as he looked at me.

"Sounds like what they were doing with omegas," Ben said.

"What do you mean?" I asked, trying to keep my voice steady as the grip on my chest tightened. Were they talking about the device? How would they know about it? A pit in my stomach formed as horror washed over me. Of course, the DA must have used the device on other omegas. How could I have thought that I was the only one? How many more omegas had they experimented on?

"Doesn't matter," Cam muttered, twining his fingers with mine. "We'll keep you safe."

Usually, Cam's protectiveness made me feel warm and cherished, but irritation prickled at his words. *I've already been unsafe, and there's nothing they could have done about it.* I knew I should tell them about the device, about what Glen did to me. But I couldn't bring myself to do it. I didn't want to see the pity in their eyes. Or worse, their judgment. Would they think I was dirty after what happened? Unworthy of being theirs?

"So, what did Amirah want?" I asked, proud of how unaffected my voice sounded. I couldn't fool them with my scent, though.

Theo hesitated before continuing. "The tabs are finally ready to be distributed. We keep Alliance hand-offs discrete, using public events to avoid suspicion. Another alpha pack was supposed to go to a cocktail party at Donovan Turro's home tonight to deliver the tabs to an Alliance member leading the distribution effort, but something happened and they're not able to go anymore."

"Isn't Donovan Turro that male omega artist?" I asked, his name vaguely conjuring images of large, colorful abstract paintings. Male omegas were the rarest of all designations—literally one in a million. I had never met one but had always been curious about what life was like for them.

"Yeah," Theo said. "He and his alphas are part of the Alliance. They occasionally host these art gallery cocktail party events. Mostly, it's an excuse for the wealthy to come together and drink."

"And gawk at Donovan," Ben added sleepily. "It's gross."

"His alphas should shield him from scrutiny," Cam muttered.

His words made me feel defensive. "Unless he doesn't want that. Maybe he wants to be involved."

Cam furrowed his brows. "It's an alpha's job to make sure their omega is safe and cared for."

"Okay, but that doesn't mean we have to be shielded from

everything. Omegas aren't just like, I don't know, fragile little creatures that have to be hidden away."

The energy in the room turned tense at my sharp words. I wasn't sure Ben was even breathing under me, and Theo's eyes were wide.

"I know that," Cam said carefully, caressing my hand. "Omegas are strong and capable. I didn't mean to suggest otherwise."

I knew I was overreacting, knew he hadn't meant anything bad by his words, but I still felt unsettled. I shifted off of Ben, sitting up with my back against the headboard, wrapping my arms around my bent knees.

"So, Amirah wants you to go instead?" I asked, wanting to forget the last few minutes.

"She wants us all to go together, as a pack, and do the hand-off. The tabs will be delivered here in an hour, and we'll get them to the other Alliance member at the party. Amirah also said this could be a good chance to show you're part of our pack. There's likely going to be higher-ups from the Designation Center and government there," Theo responded, running his hand through my hair.

I leaned into his touch, but it didn't ease the prickling of my skin at the thought of having to be around those people again. Growing up, my parents forced me to attend formal events. Even though I was a constant disappointment to them, I was still an omega and, therefore, worth parading around. I could still feel the weight of my parents' judgment and the predatory stares I got from alphas. The only good part of those events was when Sam and I attended together. At the last one we'd gone to, we had snuck into the kitchen and stocked up on champagne and snacks before stealing one of the owner's golf carts and joy-riding around the local golf course. A lump formed in my throat as I thought about how much I missed my best friend.

"It's too dangerous," Cam grunted. "Josie doesn't need to deal with that stress. Two of us can go, and someone can stay here with her."

I bristled. I didn't even *want* to go to this party, but I hated being told what to do, hated how Cam was talking about me like I wasn't even in the room. Before I could say anything, Ben spoke up.

"What do you want to do, precious?" he asked, kissing me on the cheek.

"I think if Amirah thinks it's good for us to go together, we should go." I set my jaw firmly and met Cam's eyes, waiting for him to argue.

"Sounds like a plan to me," Ben said quickly, picking me up and settling me in his lap.

I resisted him for a moment, unsure if I wanted to be soothed right now, but then I breathed in his spicy scent and the fight went out of me. The stress of my mother's call, the shame of being caught binging, the joy of finally having sex with Ben... all the emotions of the past day caught up with me. I slumped in Ben's hold, exhausted by it all.

"We'll have to think of a plan to ensure your safety," Theo said, his hand resting on my leg. "But I agree. I think going as a pack shows our strength."

Cam clenched his jaw, glaring at Ben and Theo. "Fine. But we are leaving at the first sign of any danger. The Alliance mission isn't as important as your safety."

His scent was burnt cinnamon, so strong I could choke on it. My omega whined, wanting to please our alpha, but I refused to back down. I wasn't going to let Cam hide me away for the rest of my life, and I owed Amirah and the Alliance everything.

"I want to be helpful," I said, my throat tight. "If it wasn't for Amirah, I wouldn't be here with you."

The tension in the room broke at my words. Cam met my gaze, his eyes soft, and Ben peppered little kisses down my cheek.

"We need to get you something to wear for the party, love," Theo said, a smile playing on his lips. "Let's get some breakfast and then go to Jewel's."

I nodded, disentangling myself from Ben and heading into the bathroom. I felt shaky as I closed the door behind me. I couldn't believe I had snapped at one of my alphas. Of course, he hadn't lashed out at me—he would never do that, but my fingers trembled as I pulled off my clothes.

I caught a glimpse of my naked body in the full-length mirror. I tried not to fixate on my stomach rolls and flabby arms, but I couldn't help it. The prospect of trying to find a dress that would fit me filled me with dread. The chorus in my head shouted back at me: *ugly, fat, useless omega*. I wiped a tear that escaped my eye before pulling on my clothes and turning away from the mirror. Last night with Ben had been a dream. Now I felt all tangled up inside.

I emerged from the bathroom and was startled to see Cam waiting for me. He opened his arms to me and I automatically stepped into his embrace.

"Have you been crying?" he asked, horrified. He wiped at my face as if he could soothe away invisible tears.

I shook my head, not ready to talk about it, and pressed my face into his chest. I might feel frustrated with him, but I still wanted his comfort.

"Are we okay, sweetheart?" His voice was as unsure as I had ever heard it.

"Yeah. I'm sorry I was so defensive."

"I'm the one who needs to apologize. I never want you to feel like I see you, or any omegas, as less than. You know that, right?" He hugged me closer to him, one hand cupping the back of my head.

"I know... but sometimes I find myself believing the messages I heard at the DA," I confessed. "That omegas are weak, we can't do anything without the guidance of alphas, we're too ruled by our hormones. I know it's not true, but it's like those thoughts have their hooks in me, and it makes me feel like I shouldn't even try to do hard things because I'll just fail, anyway."

"What? Baby girl, no, that's not true at all." The look of sheer horror on Cam's face reassured me even more than his words. "Look at how much you've accomplished. You survived that fucking nightmare of a place, lived on your own, started a self-defense group. I am in constant awe of you."

I melted into his embrace. Cam believed in me. He didn't think I was useless.

"I want you to call me out on my bullshit, sweetheart. Push back if I'm being overbearing or making you feel insecure."

"I like when you get all growly and overprotective and take care of me. But I'm also capable of doing things on my own," I said, trying to convince myself. Where was the girl who used to be so fierce and independent? I wasn't sure where she had gone, but I wanted her back.

"I know, baby girl. I get so fucking scared when I think about you being around those assholes. The thought of anything happening to you kills me." Then, as if he couldn't stand the thought of there being any space between us, he picked me up. I wrapped my arms and legs around him.

"You get scared?" I couldn't remember an alpha ever admitting to feeling afraid.

"Fucking terrified. You mean so much to me."

We stayed like that for a few quiet minutes, Cam's arms wrapped around me. I could feel his heartbeat, the rhythmic sound soothing me.

"Ben and Theo are getting impatient. You need to eat and then we'll get going to Jewel's."

My scent turned bitter, and Cam froze.

"What's wrong?" he demanded. "And don't say it's nothing. I can scent how stressed you are. Do you not want to go to the party?"

"It's stupid. I'm just worried about finding a dress that fits," I mumbled.

Cam pulled away enough to see my face. He looked totally bewildered. "Of course, you'll find something," he said. "And if Jewel doesn't have the right dress, we'll go somewhere else."

"I wish I looked like a normal omega," I said, my voice sounding small.

"Why the fuck would you want to look different when you're the sexiest fucking woman I've ever seen?" Cam's voice was raised, his grip on me tight.

He sounded just as sincere as Ben had last night. My alphas seemed to love my body, something I couldn't understand but was grateful for. I thought about Ben's suggestion to see someone to help me deal with my body image issues and trauma. The idea of telling a stranger my deepest secrets made my skin crawl, but I also didn't want to keep feeling this way.

"Thank you," I said, pressing a kiss to his lips.

Cam deepened the kiss, running his hands down my body and squeezing my butt. I wiggled in his arms, wanting to feel the friction of him against me.

Suddenly, the door opened, causing me to pull away from Cam with a startled squeak.

"Stop trying to keep her from breakfast," a cranky Ben said, striding into the room and taking me from Cam's arms. He carried me out of the room, grumbling about needing to feed me while Cam winked at me as he followed us downstairs.

Chapter Forty-Six

Cam

I tried not to stare too intently at Josie while she ate breakfast, contenting myself to sit pressed up against her, but my mind whirled. I hated myself for hurting her. I had never wanted to suggest she wasn't capable when the reality was, she was braver and stronger than I would ever be. My inner alpha's need to protect her was all-consuming, and I wasn't sure how I would get through this fucking day. Why should she be pulled into the Alliance? She had been through enough.

When I'd held her earlier, I had been so close to saying *I love you* but had been too chicken-shit to do it. She had told Ben and Theo she loved them and had sex with both of them. Insecurity bubbled up in me. What if she didn't love me or want me like the other two?

Josie leaned into me, her bright green eyes meeting mine. "You okay?"

I nodded and pressed my face to her hair, pulling her in tightly. There was nothing more endearing than her messy morning waves. I couldn't get enough of her, needed to touch her at all times. I thought of all the people who would be at the event tonight, and rage washed through me. None of them deserved to breathe the same air as my mate.

Josie placed her hand on mine, and I realized I was shaking.

"We'll be careful. I know you'll keep me safe," Josie murmured in my ear.

I plucked her up from her chair and sat her on my lap. No reason for her to have her own seat if I had anything to say about it. I let her scent soothe me and reminded myself I wasn't alone in protecting her. Ben and Theo would also do anything to keep her safe.

After breakfast, I reluctantly let Josie out of my embrace so she could finish getting ready while we picked up the kitchen.

"She's worried about not finding a dress that will fit," I muttered, turning towards the guys once I heard the quiet click of her bedroom door.

Ben grimaced. "That doesn't surprise me. She was really upset last night when I found her downstairs."

"What happened?" Theo asked, joining our tight huddle by the kitchen island. "Besides the obvious. The whole fucking kitchen smells like sex."

Ben grinned, his hand caressing the island. "Yeah, that part was great. I heard her in the kitchen, and I came in to check on her." His smile fell. "She was standing here, eating some cake. She thought I would be mad at her for it," he said, adjusting his glasses.

"Mad for eating cake?" I asked, my brows furrowing.

"Is it that hard to believe after hearing how her parents talked to her? After seeing the DA meal plan?" Ben spit out, disdain coloring his tone.

"How could she think we're like the DA or her fucking parents?" I growled.

"I don't think she believes that," Theo said. "It takes a long time to heal from those wounds."

I was not feeling patient. I wanted my girl to know how fucking hot and beautiful she was right now.

"I'm going to call Jewel and make sure she has plenty of shit in her size," I said, pulling out my phone.

Chapter Forty-Seven

Josie

I stared at myself in the full-length bathroom mirror, my stomach in knots. How could I go out wearing this? I'd felt so confident in the shop with Jewel, but that confidence quickly fizzled out once I put the dress back on in the privacy of my room.

Jewel had already pulled several outfit options for me by the time I got to her shop. All were more revealing than anything I'd worn before, and I was hesitant to leave the dressing room to show the guys. I should have known I had nothing to worry about—my confidence built every time I emerged from the room and took in their stunned expressions and arousal-filled scents. Jewel had complained about needing to air out the shop.

When I had tried on this dress, a floor-length blue-gray gown with a plunging V-neck and voluminous skirt with layers of gauzy fabric, Jewel told me in no uncertain terms that this was the dress and that I should wait to show my alphas until right before the cocktail party.

"I'm pretty sure I won't ever get those toxic fumes out of my shop if they see you," she said, rolling her eyes. I just smiled and twirled again. I was getting more used to Jewel's prickly exterior, but she couldn't hide her inner sweetness.

But now, uncertainty seeped in. Was the front too revealing? Were my boobs sagging? The tiny straps did nothing to hide my arms, my scar prominently displayed. When I asked Jewel if she had any long-sleeved dresses, she scoffed.

"Wear your scars proudly, omega. They're the proof you survived." I didn't argue with her after that.

I started at the knock on the bathroom door.

"You okay in there, precious? It's almost time to go," Ben said.

Well, if they thought I was hideous in this dress, it was too late to do anything about it. I opened the door, and my brain stuttered as I took in Ben's black tux. The suit fit him perfectly, clinging to his muscular arms and thighs. My eyes slowly raked over his body, stopping at the tightness in his crotch. A burst of slick trickled into my underwear, and I had to reign in the urge to throw myself at him.

Ben cleared his throat and adjusted himself.

"You look... wow. I mean... so hot."

My cheeks pinkened. "You like it?" I asked, my voice soft.

He cleared his throat again, his eyes landing on my cleavage. "Understatement, precious."

"We've got to go," Theo said, looking at his watch as he stalked into the room. He did a double-take when he saw me. Theo's suit was also black, but the jacket was freaking velvet. I wanted to rub myself on it like a kitten before I pushed him down to the floor. Maybe I could lie on top of the jacket while he fucked me. Then he would never be able to get the scent out, and everyone would know he was mine.

Ben's laughter jolted me out of my fantasy, and I realized

Theo and I had been staring at each other in silence for an awkwardly long amount of time.

Theo ran his hand through his hair and choked out a laugh. "Fuck, angel. Just... fuck."

Heavy footsteps sounded on the stairs before Cam stormed into the room.

"What is taking so long?" he growled. His gaze landed on me, hot and heavy, as he raked his eyes down my body.

"What are you wearing?" he gritted out, his eyes fixed on my cleavage. "That's not one you showed us in the shop."

"Jewel said I should keep it a surprise. Don't you like it?" I bit my lip, my earlier insecurity coming back in full force with his almost angry reaction.

"What? No, I hate it. You look too fucking hot in that. Take it off," he said, prowling towards me.

It took my brain a minute to catch up to what he'd said.

"I look... too hot?" I asked.

"Too. Fucking. Hot," he gritted out. "We need to get something that covers you." He looked around as if searching for a parka to materialize.

I closed the small gap between us and ran my hands down Cam's chest. He was dressed the most casually, wearing a black jacket over a white button-down shirt. The first few buttons were open so I could see the beginnings of his chest tattoos.

I leaned forward and licked them.

Cam choked, a purr roaring through his chest.

"Did you just lick me?" he asked, grasping my chin.

"No, I would never," I said, keeping a straight face.

Cam growled, pulling me flush to his body. His hardness pressed against me, and I whimpered as more slick gushed into my underwear.

"Sorry you hate the dress," I murmured as I scent-marked his neck.

"I fucking hate it so much," he whispered back, his breath hot on my ear.

I smiled, extricating myself from his grasp. "I need one more minute, and I'll be ready."

"What do you need, gorgeous?" Ben asked.

"To put on scent-blocking underwear," I responded, cheeks heating.

I may have added an extra swing in my hips as I walked into my closet, enjoying the groans from my alphas.

"Let me hear the plan again," Cam said, his body pressed close to mine in the backseat. His arm was around my shoulders, and his eyes kept flitting to my cleavage.

Ben and I both groaned.

"Are you worried about my short-term memory?" I asked, elbowing Cam's side.

He responded by wrapping both arms around me, pulling me as close as my seatbelt would allow. "Please humor me, baby girl."

His body vibrated with tension. Cam was making an effort and I wanted to do what I could to put him at ease. *It's called compromise, not that I've experienced that before.*

"We'll all go in together," I started to say before the view out the window distracted me. Icy cold tendrils gripped my chest as we drove past Glen Jacoby's home. Many wealthy packs lived in Forestside, where I'd grown up, but I hadn't expected us to pass by his mansion on the way to Pack Turro's.

"Josie?" Cam prompted, running his finger down the side of my face.

I blinked, turning back towards him with a smile I hoped was convincing.

"After we have eyes on the contact, Theo and I will look at the paintings," I continued. "I'm going to pretend to be interested in buying one. The contact will move to either get drinks or food. Cam will go to the food station, and Ben will get drinks. One of you will do the handoff, and then both will return with food and drinks for me."

"You will not—"

"Go anywhere without one of us by your side," Ben and I finished in unison.

Cam growled, pulling me closer. "Brat," he murmured in my ear.

A delicious shiver went through me and goosebumps broke out across my skin.

"Fuck," Theo said as we turned into Pack Turro's long, circular driveway. "Whatever you just said to her, say it again when we're home."

I giggled, realizing I wasn't embarrassed by my arousal. I wanted Cam to know I was aroused because maybe he would finally do something about it. I thought having sex would quiet down my desire, but all it had done was stoke the flames. I felt hot and needy.

My cheeks heated as memories of last night flashed before my eyes—Ben's face between my thighs, the feeling of his knot inside me. Ben turned from the front seat and winked at me as if he could hear my thoughts.

"Baby girl, whatever you're thinking right now, you need to stop. I don't want anyone else to scent how fucking delicious you smell when you're turned on," Cam said with a groan, burying his face in my hair and breathing in deeply.

"I told you I should wear de-scenter," I said.

"No," Theo said firmly. "Hate smelling that shit on you."

I pressed my smile into Cam's shoulder. I loved how much they loved my scent. I was anxious being around other people without de-scenter, but having my guys with me helped. I wouldn't want them to cover up their scents, either.

We pulled up to the front of the house, and Theo handed the keys to the valet. After a graceless exit from the car, my alphas escorted me inside. We were met by a beta butler at the door, an older man with gray hair and a kind smile. He ushered us into the foyer and gently helped me out of my coat, winking at me when Cam growled at his closeness.

I turned around, already in awe of Pack Turro's home. The foyer alone was stunning, with its herringbone floors, tall ceilings, and dark wood wainscoting on the walls. The butler gestured for us to enter the main room, but the second we entered, my breath caught.

"What's the matter?" Cam asked, gripping me so tightly it almost hurt.

"Too many scents," I said. It had been so long since I'd been around other people, let alone a party with alphas in attendance, and all the scents hit me like a truck.

"Shit," Theo said. "I didn't even think about that."

"It's okay," I said, breathing through my mouth. "Just caught me off guard. But I need all your scents on me."

Any worries about being too whiny or demanding vanished at the readiness with which my alphas responded to my request. They pulled me to a quiet corner and boxed me in, each scent marking me in turn. My omega settled once I was covered in their scents, and I could take in the room. We were in what could only be described as a grand hall. Party-goers dressed in finery mingled in the space as servers passed champagne and hors d'oeuvres. I quickly scanned the room, making sure I didn't see any familiar faces.

"Okay, sweetheart. Ben and I have to go. Stick with Theo. We'll be back in just a moment," Cam said, his hands cupping my face.

I bit my lip, suddenly feeling very stressed about my alphas leaving me. But I wanted to prove that I could do this, that I was capable. Theo gathered me to his side, guiding me into one of the quieter rooms. I barely took in my surroundings, my anxiety about Cam and Ben almost dizzying. We stopped in front of one of Donovan's massive paintings so I could pretend to be interested in it.

"Everything is going to be okay, angel. Take a deep breath," Theo murmured. I forced myself to breathe in his scent, allowing it to fill my lungs and ease some of the tension I was feeling. I rested my head on his chest, taking deep, calming breaths.

Theo stiffened. I pulled back, alarmed at what caused his reaction. An older man walked towards us. His black hair was streaked with silver, his skin a deep golden brown. As he got closer, I caught a faint hint of caramel. *Omega.* This must be Donovan Turro. He stopped in front of us, and his gaze softened as he took me in.

"I heard we had a special guest attending tonight and I had to introduce myself. I'm Donovan Turro," he said, holding his hand first to me and then to Theo.

"I'm not a special guest," I said, furrowing my brow.

"Having a bright, beautiful, young omega like yourself in my home is an honor, Josie," Donovan responded. "I'd love to have the honor of showing you around."

I smiled shyly, appreciating that he asked me directly. I turned towards Theo, who nodded.

Donovan led me to the corner of the room and then winked at me before pulling out one of the books on the shelf. I heard a soft *clunk* and Donovan pushed the wall, which swung open, revealing a hidden room.

"Oh my god," I gasped as Donovan gestured for Theo and

me to enter the secret room. "This is the coolest thing I've ever seen."

Donovan chuckled. "Now, that's the kind of reaction I love to see. I thought you might like it here. It's quieter and there are fewer scents."

I was a little awed by how smoothly Donovan had ensured my omega was comfortable without making me feel like a nuisance. I smiled as I twirled to take in the room. Cozy lamps cast a warm glow on rows and rows of built-in bookcases with sliding ladders. A picture light shone down on a large abstract art piece.

"This room is magical," I said. "Feels like something out of *Beauty and the Beast*."

Donovan chuckled. "I certainly know which one I am in that equation."

I threw him an incredulous look. Donovan was the textbook definition of a silver fox.

He laughed good-naturedly at my expression. "You look truly radiant tonight, Josie. How is your new pack treating you?"

"Good," I said, my eyes automatically drawn to where Theo was standing near the secret entrance. I jolted when I saw two surly-looking alphas standing next to him, their gazes fixed on Donovan.

"Are those your alphas?" I asked.

Donovan snorted. "Yep. We also have a beta in our pack, Jackson, but he's out of town. Close to thirty-five years bonded, and they're still as overprotective as ever. Puts them on edge having all these alphas in our home."

I was surprised that Donovan's pack had a beta. These days, bonded pack status was only reserved for alphas and omegas, but things had been different thirty-five years ago. They'd certainly been different since Donovan had been allowed to openly bond with male alphas. Although, I supposed he couldn't have been expected to bond with a pack of female alphas. I felt slightly bitter when I thought of everything Sam had gone through to be with Gerald, but none of that was Donovan's fault. I just wished things had been different. Wished this government had never taken over.

"I guess age doesn't mellow them out," I muttered.

"I hate to break it to you. I wouldn't expect any of your alphas to ever relax when it comes to your safety."

I glanced up at him, taking in his radiant smile.

"But you don't mind?"

"No, I don't. And if it gets to be too much, I just put them in their place," he said with a wink.

I hesitated before asking him the question that had been ping-ponging around my mind the past couple of weeks. "You don't think it makes me weak? To want them to take care of me?"

Donovan's brow furrowed. "Not at all. All of this designation bullshit has fucked everything up. Things were different when I revealed as an omega. Fewer anti-omega laws, no Designation Academy. I can't imagine what it's like to try to grow into yourself and come to terms with your inner omega when everyone is trying to punish you for just being yourself."

My eyes watered and I blinked quickly to prevent tears from spilling over.

"Everyone underestimates omegas. Even our alphas to some extent. Early on, when I first bonded with my pack, there were a few attempts to kidnap me. People were obsessed with getting access to a rare male omega. It took a long time before they let me out of their sight. I knew they wanted to protect me, and I loved them for it, but it also made me feel weak. I wish I had pushed back against them more those first few years."

"But things changed?"

"*I* changed," he responded, his eyes crinkling. "I became more confident in who I was. I started pursuing my art and giving my alphas shit when they drove me out of my mind. You'll find your rhythm with your pack. But don't ever believe that you're weak."

"Thank you," I said softly.

I stared at the art piece before me, taking it in for the first time. Layers of soothing blues and greens surrounded the edge of the canvas. But at the bottom left corner, there was a splash of red and orange, an almost aggressive contrast to the serenity of the rest of the piece. I'd never studied art, couldn't pretend to understand anything about it, but it touched me and made me feel... something.

"This is incredible," I said after a long silence, looking back at Donovan.

"This is actually one of my earlier works. I was trying to process what it meant to be an omega."

My eyes returned to the painting. "I've never met a male omega."

"Few have," he said. "It can be lonely." His jaw clenched and his caramel scent took on a slightly bitter edge.

I jumped as one of Donovan's alphas, a tall Black man who was almost as massive as Cam, seemed to materialize out of thin air. He wrapped his arm around his omega's shoulder and pressed a kiss to the side of his face.

"What's wrong, baby?" he asked, his voice low and soothing.

Donovan looked at me, his lips twitching as he rolled his eyes.

"They never grow out of it," he said, shaking his head as Theo wrapped his arms around me from behind. "Everything's fine, Ter. Just talking to beautiful Josie here."

The alpha kept his firm grip on Donovan but smiled as he looked at Theo and me.

"You okay, angel?" Theo murmured.

I shifted to look at him. I knew Pack Turro was part of the Alliance, but I still didn't want to say anything that could jeopardize our safety.

"Everything went to plan," Theo whispered in my ear.

"They're done?" I asked, feeling dizzy with relief.

"Yes, love. They're getting you something to eat and drink." Theo kissed my forehead.

"Not hungry," I responded. My stomach still felt tangled up in anxiety.

Theo frowned. "You haven't eaten much today."

"I know, I just... Can we go home?"

"Shh, don't stress. Okay, we'll get something at home."

"It was so lovely to meet you, Josie," Donovan said, kissing my hand. "I hope we find each other again soon."

I blushed at his kindness and gave the secret library one final longing glance before pressing myself to Theo as he led me back to the main room.

"I need to use the restroom," I said, looking around.

"I'll wait here for you."

The bathroom was located through a large dressing room with vanities and mirrors. As much as I loved this house, it was definitely too grand for me.

I stared at the toilet and then down at my dress. How was I supposed to pee? I realized I would have to unzip it and sit naked on the toilet before pulling it back up. *Talk about losing your dignity when wearing fancy dresses.*

As I was finally maneuvering the dress back on, I heard voices outside the bathroom. When I opened the door, I saw three beta women touching up their makeup. I gave them a tight smile and tried to walk past them quickly, intimidated by how stunning they looked. They were all tall and thin with perfectly curled blonde hair.

"You're with Pack Ashwood, right?" one of the betas asked, looking me up and down. "I saw you walk in with them." Her lips curled into a sneer, her hand resting on her perfectly tiny waist.

"Cam is here?" another one of the betas asked. "He is so dreamy. We fucked all summer a while back." She giggled, causing her hand to shake and smear the eyeliner she was applying. "Wait," she gasped, finally looking at me. "*You're* their new omega? You're not Cam's type at all."

I knew I should walk away, but I couldn't stop myself. "What does that mean?"

"Oh well, you have this sweet, innocent thing going for you, don't you?" she said with a smirk. "Cam likes a woman who can handle him in the bedroom. He likes it rough, as you know." Then, taking in my blank expression, she continued, "Or maybe you don't," she giggled. "Cam's into BDSM, but I guess he holds that back with you."

"Or maybe this is just some sort of business arrangement," the first beta added. "It's not like Pack Ashwood needs to slum it with fat bitches."

My face burned with anger and shame. I opened my mouth, willing the perfect snarky retort to come out, but nothing did. I was rooted to my spot in the corner, frozen.

"Ben is such a hottie, too," the third beta said as she adjusted her corset top. "He was so sweet when we were dating. He bought me these," she said, gesturing at her diamond earrings as she touched up her already flawless makeup.

"You dated Ben?" I choked out.

The room felt like it was closing in on me, and I finally unfroze my legs and bolted towards the exit before I could hear anything else. I entered the main hall again, breathing heavily. I needed to hide, to nest. I needed my alphas. Except right now, I wasn't sure I wanted them around me.

My cheeks burned with embarrassment, but anger quickly flooded me. How dare those bitches speak to me like that? How dare they touch *my* mates? I looked around the room, trying to spot my alphas. I wasn't sure if I wanted to punch them or kiss them. *I guess I'll just fucking see how I feel when I see them.*

I spotted Theo coming towards me. He was smiling and holding a glass of champagne. I was momentarily distracted by how handsome he looked in his tux. As he got closer, I shook myself out of my lust-filled stupor and scowled. His face filled with concern as he took me in.

"What's wrong, love?"

I reached out and snatched the champagne out of his hand and chugged it. Immediately bubbles went up my nose, which had me sneezing and sputtering. *Champagne, not the best beverage to chug. Duly noted.*

Before Theo could say anything, I snarled, "Do you have any ex-girlfriends here I should know about? Maybe you should just go ahead and introduce us so she can give me pointers on how not to disappoint you in bed."

Shock flashed across Theo's face for a moment before it was replaced with understanding. He glanced around the room and I growled.

"Are you fucking looking for her right now? That's fine, *fine*. You know what, I'm just going to leave. That way, you three selfish, cheating assholes can go off and have your orgy without me being in the way."

I turned on my heels and took a single step before Theo's hard body pressed against my back. One of his arms wrapped tightly around my waist and the other gently grasped my throat.

"You know you're the only one I have ever been with, love,"

he growled in my ear. "I've only ever sunk my cock into your sweet cunt, only heard your breathy moans and whimpers."

He tilted my head to the side and kissed my neck, gently scraping his teeth against my skin. My anger melted away—at least my anger at Theo—as the jealous fog I'd been in started to lift.

"Are you ready to tell me what happened?"

I leaned back into his chest, his scent grounding my wild emotions. I nodded and he rotated me to face him. Suddenly, embarrassment at my outburst washed over me and I felt myself getting teary.

"I'm sorry for what I said," I whispered, tears spilling out.

"Oh, my love, you don't have to apologize."

He crushed me to him, one hand firmly on my ass and the other running soothingly up and down my back.

"Is you holding me by the butt supposed to relax me?" I asked dryly.

"Mmm, no, that's for me. Seeing you all riled up and jealous was fucking hot, except that you were upset. Also, I just like holding your ass. I should do it more."

I grinned. "If you did it anymore, I think you'd have to surgically remove your hand."

"I'll risk it," he said with a smile, pulling away so he could wipe away my tears and give me a kiss.

I nuzzled into Theo's chest, melting into him as he held me. I sensed someone behind me and caught Ben's spiced apple scent. The tension returned to my body as my inner omega bristled at his presence. I pulled out of Theo's arms and whipped around to face Ben, whose smile fell when he saw my expression.

"What happened?" he asked, his gaze flickering between Theo and me.

I felt a pang in my chest, hating that he was unhappy, but

for once, my omega held firm, driven by her rage and insecurity.

"Precious, what's wrong?" Ben asked tenderly.

Tears pricked my eyes as I looked away from him. Having him close, looking so sexy and smelling comforting and arousing at the same time, started to break down my resolve. I loved Ben. I trusted him. I knew he hadn't done anything wrong, but I couldn't silence that voice that said he would be happier with someone else, someone skinnier and more attractive.

Ben made a distressed noise in the back of his throat, and I was horrified to see that he had tears glistening in his eyes. I couldn't stop from launching myself into his embrace. Startled, he quickly wrapped his arms around me.

"I'm mad at you," I said, my voice lacking any conviction as I pressed myself closer to him.

"I'm sorry for whatever I did," he murmured in my ear, his voice achingly sad.

I took deep gulps of his scent and was reminded of how tender he was with me last night, how it had felt to make both of us come just by laughing at the ridiculousness of the situation. Ben was my sunshine.

"Why don't the two of you go out to the courtyard?" Theo suggested, running his hand down my back and kissing my cheek.

Ben wordlessly moved to the back exit, not allowing an inch of space between us as he pulled me into the courtyard.

"I'll make sure no one interrupts," Theo said.

With the quiet click of the door, Ben and I were alone. I was momentarily distracted by the courtyard, which could only be described as magical. Twinkling string lights lit up the space, illuminating the ivy climbing over the brick walls.

"Will you tell me what I did to make you upset, beautiful?" Ben asked, sadness seeping into his scent.

"You didn't do anything," I said, lifting my gaze to his face and running my fingers down the stubble on his chin.

"Obviously, I did," he said.

"I feel like I'm going crazy," I said, tears spilling down my cheeks. "I know you haven't done anything wrong, but my omega is so upset."

"What happened, precious?" he asked, kissing away my tears.

"I went to the bathroom and there was a group of betas in there. It seemed like all of them knew you guys and had had sex with you or Cam. And, of course, they all looked perfect and thin and beautiful, and you'd probably be happier with them," I blurted out. My cheeks heated at my confession. Suddenly, I was overcome with the need to hide, but Ben wouldn't let me pull away.

"God, precious, you have to know we don't want anyone but you. *I* don't want anyone but you. No one could be more perfect or beautiful, no one."

His intensity startled me. I was used to Ben being laid back, but there was nothing relaxed about the determined, heated look in his eyes.

"Do you miss being with betas?" I asked, chewing my bottom lip.

"Precious, I don't miss being with anyone who is not you. It wouldn't matter what designation you were; I would be just as obsessed with you."

His words made me feel like a warm glow was emanating from within me, but the lingering insecurity wouldn't let me drop it just yet.

"Omegas are a lot of work."

Ben furrowed his eyebrows, an incredulous look on his face. "How are you a lot of work?"

"I'm all needy and hormonal," I said, unable to meet his gaze.

"Josie, you're allowed to have needs."

I didn't trust myself to speak, sure that I would burst into tears the second I opened my mouth. When had I been allowed to need anything? Ben's hand cupped the side of my face and I leaned into his touch. He didn't demand I say anything, content to hold me close and gently rock us back and forth.

"Besides," he added, "*Alphas* are a lot of work. Don't know how you put up with us."

A smile tugged at my lips. "That's a good point."

Ben's laughter rang through the space, his bright scent filling the air. "You're trouble," he said, twirling me around. I squealed, gripping him tighter as my feet left the ground.

He set me back down and beamed at me, pressing his face to my hair and breathing in my scent deeply. I'm sure it was much sweeter now than a few minutes ago.

"Sorry I freaked out," I said, kissing him softly.

"I want you to always tell me when you're upset. Anytime you're feeling jealous or angry or sad. And, for what it's worth, I've dreamed of bonding an omega since I was young. You have exceeded every single one of my desires."

My insides went warm and gooey at his words, and slick drenched my underwear. I guess this was a test to see if the scent-proof underwear worked. Ben's flared nose and expanding pupils told me it hadn't.

"Why didn't you want to bring an omega into your pack before now?" I asked. The guys had been a pack before the Designation Government took over. They would have had plenty of time to match with an omega during those years but hadn't.

Ben sighed, and for a moment, his eyes held a haunted, faraway expression that took my breath away.

"I know Cam is planning on telling you what made us leave North Woods, so I'll let him share that part of the story. It took us a long time to recover from the pain of what happened. After a couple of years, I was ready to find an omega. I worked hard to convince them. What they had experienced with their families was worse than anything I ever had, and I think they were scared and maybe feeling unworthy of bonding an omega."

Ben grinned at my outraged expression and kissed my nose before continuing.

"You and I know they're two of the best alphas in the world. But they've always struggled to see themselves that way. Anyway, I finally convinced them to sign us up for omega interviews. I wish we could have met you then. You can't even imagine how different it was. The interviews were meant to be fun, with the omega's wishes front and center. For one of them, we went to a local carnival. With another, we went to a bread-making class. That's when I started baking. But it was never right. We never found the right match for us, and the guys were still too wounded to really consider bonding someone.

"As the years went by, I got lonely and I started dating betas. The relationships never lasted long. I wanted to share a mate with my brothers and they weren't interested in any of the betas. I can guess who you met in the bathroom. We were together briefly last summer. Honestly, she was much more interested in being with Theo than me. It became clear pretty quickly that she was just hoping being with me would give her access to him."

"What a bitch," I snarled. *How dare she treat Ben like that?*

"Ahh, don't judge her too harshly. I hear a British accent is almost impossible to resist," he responded with his usual lighthearted bravado, but I wasn't having it.

"Ben, you deserve someone who is totally obsessed with you and sees you for who you are."

"I know," he said tenderly. "You've taught me that. You see me like no one else has."

He cupped the back of my neck and pulled me in for a kiss, his hands digging into my backside.

"You smell so good, precious. So sweet, so perfect," he said, pulling away. I whined, trying to pull him back to my lips.

"Gorgeous, believe me when I say there's nothing I want more than to peel that dress off you and fuck you right here..."

"Yes, let's do that," I said, trying again to pull him in for a kiss.

Ben snorted. "I've learned my lesson on suitable locations," he said with a wink. "But the main issue is I can feel Cam through the bond and he's about three seconds away from losing his shit and breaking down the door."

His words cut through my fog and I remembered what the betas told me about Cam. My chest tightened again, insecurity coursing through me.

"Whatever you're thinking, I promise you're wrong. But let's get you home so you two can talk."

Chapter Forty-Eight

Cam

The car ride back to the house was fucking torture. Josie sat stiffly next to me—a stark contrast to our closeness on the way to Pack Turro's. She stared out the window, her body angled away from mine. But when I offered her my hand, she took it and held on tightly.

Theo had filled me in on what had made Josie upset, and I felt like the lowest piece of shit. I knew the time had come to tell Josie everything about my past. I trusted her with all of it, but I was terrified it would change how she saw me.

When we got to the house, Josie was out of the car before any of us could get the door for her. Ben clasped me on the shoulder.

"She's feeling jealous and insecure," he said, "But she still loves you."

I took a deep breath, steeling myself before following Josie through the house to the backyard.

She whipped around towards me, and my heart clenched in agony when I saw the tears in her eyes.

"I talked to some of your previous lovers. They had a lot to say about your expectations in bed. Is that why we haven't had sex yet? Because I don't have enough experience, and you don't think it will be good?" Her lip trembled, but her look was defiant.

My chest tightened with panic. I realized how deeply I had fucked up by holding back. That she could believe for even a moment I didn't want her fucking killed me. I had been terrified to do anything to scare her, convinced I would be too much for her, but my caution left her questioning my feelings.

"Baby girl, please listen, that's not..."

She cut me off. "Well, that's fine. I'm sure those women are still there, so you don't have to worry about it anymore. Just go fuck them."

I growled, anger shooting through me. Josie's eyes grew wider as I stalked towards her, unwilling for there to be any space between us. She took a few stumbling steps back until she was pressed against the brick wall. Her eyes were wide, and I was momentarily worried she was afraid of me when I caught her sweet scent deepening with arousal. *Fuck*, this whole time, I'd been holding back because I thought I would frighten or trigger her, but maybe I had gotten it all wrong.

"You want me to fuck another woman?" I growled, crowding her against the wall. "You'd be okay if I went back and fucked a beta in the bathroom? You would be fine with me putting my hands on someone else? Because baby girl, let me be crystal clear—if you ever touch someone outside of our pack, I'll fucking kill them. You. Are. Mine."

She was breathing rapidly now, her pupils dilating.

"That's barbaric. And possessive."

"Fuck yes, it is." I ran my hands up her body before capturing her hands and pinning them to the wall over her head. "And you like it."

She scowled and shook her head no, but her little whimper as I pressed my body firmly against hers gave her away.

"I've never in my life wanted someone like I want you. My thoughts are filled with you every single waking moment. I'm fucking obsessed with you, baby girl. I want to do anything I can to make you happy, to keep you safe. And to give you more pleasure than you've ever experienced."

Her hips rolled against mine.

"You didn't answer my question," I said as I pinned her harder, my lips hovering an inch from hers. "Do you want me to leave to fuck someone else?"

Fire blazed in Josie's eyes. "Never," she said fiercely.

"Mmm, you sure about that?"

"You're mine," she said in an omega growl so adorable I had to bite my cheek to keep from smiling.

"Damn right I am," I said, closing the gap between us and kissing her.

I cupped her ass with one hand, squeezing it until she whimpered, pressing her firmly against me. My other hand had a possessive hold on her neck as I deepened the kiss, thrusting my tongue into her mouth. She threw her arms around me, one hand curling into my hair and pulling my face tightly to hers. I ground against her core, wishing I could rip her dress off of her right now.

I forced myself to pull away. We were both breathing heavily, and Josie's pupils were dilated. She whined at the distance I created, trying to pull me back. I was tempted to throw her over my shoulder and take her to bed.

"Hold on, sweetheart, we need to talk."

She made a frustrated sound as I led her to a chair and sat down, pulling her so she was straddling my lap. Her cheeks were flushed, and her hard nipples peeked through her dress. It was almost enough to make me abandon my plan of having a rational conversation, but I remembered her tears and knew we needed this.

"What happened back there?" I asked, playing with a strand of her hair. Her head tipped towards my hand, greedy for my touch. I forced myself to keep my touch light when all I wanted was to twist her hair around my fist as leverage to guide her where I wanted her.

"There were some betas in the bathroom, and one of them said that you used to sleep with them and that you like BDSM, and that I'm not your type and wouldn't satisfy you in bed."

My blood pressure and self-loathing rose in equal measure. I had a feeling I knew exactly who had cornered Josie in the bathroom, and I fucking hated them for it, but ultimately it was *my* choices that had made my mate feel crushed and rejected.

"I'm so sorry they said that to you, but you have to know they don't know what they're fucking talking about."

"So, you're not into... dominating me?"

I opened my mouth and then closed it again. That was not the question I expected her to ask. I needed to be honest, but I was scared shitless that I would make her afraid of me.

"Well, I mean, I am. But I would never push you to do something you didn't want or do anything to hurt you. I promise I will never abuse you. I don't need to have that kind of sex and don't want you to feel..."

Josie placed her hand over my mouth, cutting me off. My chest tightened, sure that this was when she would leave me when I noticed a small smile playing across her face.

"You're panicking without letting me respond," she said.

I immediately went to say something, but her hand still covered my mouth. She arched an eyebrow. Josie was here with me. She wasn't running away or yelling, even though I wouldn't blame her if she did both. I gazed into her deep green eyes and nodded slowly. Then, because I couldn't resist, I licked her hand. She let out a startled laugh and scrunched up her nose before wiping her hand on my shirt. Her laughter loosened the tension I was carrying in my chest, and I couldn't resist pulling her in for a quick kiss.

"I'm listening, sweetheart," I murmured in her ear, allowing her vanilla cupcake perfume to soak into my clothes and calm me further. The burnt edge to her scent had dissipated, and she was relaxed and pliant in my arms.

"Cam, I know you would never hurt or abuse me. Since we met, you've been caring for me and protecting me. I trust you."

I pulled her in closer until her head rested on my chest. She wrapped her arms tightly around me and squeezed.

The words I'd never spoken to anyone outside Ben and Theo started tumbling out.

"You know we all grew up in North Woods. My father was, and still is, one of the leaders. He and my pack fathers put a lot of pressure on my brothers and me to be the most aggressive, dominant alphas. They thought that any kindness or sensitivity was a weakness. My fathers tested me by forcing me to fight them all at once. I was a kid, so I could never overpower them. If I cried or backed down, they would tell me I was weak and often punished me by locking me out of the house for days without food. No one in the community did anything to help me because they knew they would have to face my fathers if they did."

Josie jolted upright from where she was curled against my chest. Her eyes blazed with anger. "You were a kid and no one helped you? No one put a stop to it?" She was shaking with rage, her hands clenching my arms.

"They didn't have much of a choice. I used to be angry with my mom because she just stood by and watched it happen. But she was abused, too. She couldn't risk herself."

"That's crap," Josie said, putting her hands on either side of my face. "Others should have stepped in. You didn't deserve any of that."

Warmth spread through my body at my mate's indignation at what I had gone through.

"People should have stepped in and stopped what was happening to you as well, sweetheart," I said, gently cupping her face with my hand and running my thumb across her cheek.

She leaned into my touch. "Yeah, well..." She took a deep breath. "Will you keep going?"

"Things got better once Theo moved next door. At the time, I was aggressive, getting into fights at school. Theo somehow saw through that, and we quickly decided to become a pack. It was the first time I felt like I had someone on my side, especially since my two younger brothers are fucking clones of our pack fathers. People didn't mess with us once we formed our pack, including my fathers. Soon after, we noticed this younger alpha who was friendly and sensitive, all the shit alphas shouldn't be. Oh, and he liked to talk all the fucking time."

Josie smiled at my description of Ben.

"I saw him for the first time at school. He was a couple grades below us and was just a fucking nice person. He wanted to make friends with everyone, which put a target on his back.

"We decided quickly that we wanted to protect Ben. It was crazy shit to see this alpha be so happy and easygoing. He was getting bullied at school and we stepped in to protect him. He annoyed the shit out of me at first with his positivity, but we quickly realized he was pack, too. The three of us stuck together. Theo and I served the year of military service our community required. Theo stopped after the first year, but I kept going with it, not because I liked it but because I didn't have anything else I was good at."

"Did Ben do the year of military training?"

"We left before he had to," I said.

Josie looked at me with such sweetness and curiosity. None of us had told her why we left, and I dreaded saying it out loud.

"We talked about leaving for years but knew it meant we wouldn't have contact with our families anymore. We all had omega sisters we wanted to look out for."

"You have a sister?" Josie asked, confused.

"No, not anymore," I said. I looked away from my mate, trying to get my emotions under control. I never talked about my sister. It was still too painful, even over a decade later.

"Oh, Cam," Josie said, pulling me in for a hug and placing gentle kisses on my face. "You don't have to tell me what happened if you don't want to."

I took a shuddering breath. "No, I want to. It's just hard for me to talk about."

My voice was tight and I felt tears building behind my eyes. I wasn't sure how I would get this next part out when I felt a slight vibration run through Josie's chest. The vibration strengthened, and I realized my mate was purring for me. I held her close, allowing her purr to work through my body. I had never dreamed of being gifted an omega purr, and a tear spilled onto my cheek.

"Thank you," I said gruffly. Josie pressed her face into my neck and intensified her purr.

"My sister's name was Ellie. She was four years younger than me and the best fucking person in the world. She was an omega but was always really mischievous and a risk-taker. I would catch her sneaking out of the house to go to the movies or pull pranks, and she would just give me this haughty look and ask if I was coming with her. She became close with Ben's sister, Lilah, and they were total fucking terrors. They had this asshole teacher they hated, so one night, we went to the teacher's house and stole his car."

"Wait, what? What did you do with it?" Josie asked, her eyes lighting with laughter.

I chuckled. Ellie had been fourteen at the time and very focused on righting injustices.

"We stole the car and drove it to the school so the teacher wouldn't be able to get to school in the morning, but the staff would think he was there. Then we broke into his classroom, and the omegas rigged a glitter bomb so when the teacher eventually arrived at school and sat in his chair, glitter would rain down on the whole classroom."

"Oh my god, that's so ridiculous. Did it work?"

"Fuck yeah, it did. We recruited Ben and Theo to erase all the security footage and help us break into the school, but hot-wiring the car and rigging up the glitter bomb was all Ellie and Lilah. You would have loved them." My heart clenched with the reminder that Josie and Ellie would never get to meet.

"When she was seventeen, our parents sat her down and told her they had arranged for her to join a pack. The alphas were all in their forties and had previously been bonded with an omega who had mysteriously died. Ellie was terrified and tried to contact me, but I was on a training mission. Now I know my fathers arranged it so I would be gone when they told Ellie. They made her move into the pack house the next day, and her alphas bonded her immediately. By the time Theo and Ben were able to make contact with me, it was too late.

"Her alphas wouldn't allow me to see her and kept her locked in the house. We tried to break in one night when we thought they were gone, but it had been a trap, and I was arrested. I didn't know what to fucking do and my mother was absolutely useless, just telling me to let it go. Within a month, Ellie was dead."

Josie gasped, her hands tightening their hold on me.

I knew if I stopped, I wouldn't be able to finish the story, so I pressed ahead.

"Her alphas said she tried to leave the house through her window and had fallen and died instantly. Everyone knew Ellie had a habit of leaving my parents' house growing up, so no one questioned it. But her room was only on the second floor. There's just no way that fall would have killed her. They didn't even bring her into the hospital, and they refused an autopsy. They murdered my little sister and I couldn't do anything to stop it."

My voice broke and I couldn't keep going. The memory of my mother calling me to tell me the news, her voice numb and detached as she shared that her only daughter had died, flooded me. I had immediately gone to my parents' house and demanded an investigation. When my father walked in, I'd jumped him, punching him in the face until my pack fathers pulled me off. Then they all set on me. I had been convinced they would kill me, and they probably would have if Ben and Theo hadn't barged into the house and gotten me away.

Josie held me tightly, running her hands soothingly over my body and pressing little kisses to my neck and chest as she continued purring. I tried to hide the tears rolling down my face, but she cupped my cheeks with both hands.

"It's okay to cry. Not a single bit of what happened was your fault," she said softly, wiping away the tears as they fell.

"I should have done more to protect her," I choked out between sobs.

"You did everything you could. It sounds like you were Ellie's everything, the best big brother she could ever hope for. I can't imagine she would want you to blame yourself for what those horrible alphas did."

"I wanted to kill my parents and those alphas. They don't deserve to live after what they did to her."

"What stopped you?" she asked without judgment.

"Theo and Ben convinced me that if I went after them, I would end up dead or in prison for the rest of my life. They said the best thing I could do for Ellie was to live my life and help fight for other omegas. That's why we joined the Alliance." After a pause, I added wryly, "They also kept me locked in a hotel room for days while I healed from the beating my fathers gave me and refused to let me leave until I promised I wouldn't go after them."

"That sounds about right," she said with a small smile.

"We left the community, and they officially banned us from coming back. Theo and Ben aren't allowed to talk to their sisters since they're bonded to packs in the community. I was in a really dark place and didn't think I deserved to have an omega since I couldn't protect my sister." The final part of my sentence came out in a whisper, and the fear that Josie would agree with me swept over me again. My hands were in fists and I tensed my whole body, waiting for her response.

"Cam, I need you to hear me on this. I've spent my life around terrible alphas. Alphas that wanted me to be scared and under their control, that didn't listen to me, that violated me. I know what cruel alphas are like. Do you think I would be here if you were anything like that? I love you."

I exhaled, tentative hope seizing my chest. "You love me?"

"Of course, I do," Josie said with a smile.

"I love you, sweetheart, so fucking much."

More tears spilled down my face, but I knew Josie wouldn't judge me for it. We both went in for a kiss and came together fiercely. I cupped the back of her neck with my hand, keeping her glued to me as I deepened the kiss. A thought occurred to me, and I pulled away.

"I haven't been with anyone in the past year," I blurted out.

"Oh?" Josie said, looking dazed from our kiss and the sudden change in topic.

"I haven't wanted to be with anyone in the past year until I met you. The way I want you is something I've never experienced before. I only chose betas to sleep with who I wouldn't form an emotional attachment with, but baby girl, I am so attached to you."

"Good," she said, doing her happy little wiggle from her perch on my lap. A pensive look crossed her face, and she looked like she was going to ask me something before she stopped herself.

"What is it?"

"*WillyoutellmeabouttheBDSM?*" she asked, her words coming out so fast I almost didn't catch what she had said.

"What do you know about BDSM, baby girl?" I asked.

"I read books," she mumbled, her cheeks flushing.

"I think I need to know what books you're reading. They sound very naughty," I whispered in her ear, relishing the shiver that ran up her spine.

"Answer my question," she said with a pout, her cheeks flushing a darker red.

I chuckled. "I met this guy, Liam, through a job. We were helping him do a security eval for his company. Anyway, he's a cool guy and we started hanging out some. He was in the scene and went to clubs. He told me about it and convinced me to give it a try." I watched Josie for any signs of disgust, but she just looked curious.

"What do you like about it?" she asked.

"Liam showed me that being an alpha and wanting dominance wasn't inherently bad. My fathers always used violence to get their way, but that's not what BDSM is about. It gives me an outlet to be myself, but everyone involved consents and wants to be part of the scene. It helped me accept being an alpha."

"That makes sense," Josie said slowly. "What kinds of things do you like?"

"Liam used to tease me about how vanilla I am. I'm not into anything extreme. I like some bondage, spanking my partner, controlling her pleasure and orgasms." Josie perfumed with arousal and my cock grew hard under her. "I also like the more nurturing aspects of BDSM. It's not something I've explored at clubs or with any partners, but you bring out that side of me. I want to make sure you're safe, make sure you follow the rules and care for yourself, punish you if you put yourself in danger or disobey," I said. Her breaths were coming faster now and her cheeks were flushed.

"You like that idea, baby girl?"

"I felt like there was something wrong with me when I read things like that in romance books and wanted it."

"There's nothing wrong with you," I said firmly. "What did you like about it when you were reading?"

"I liked the idea of letting go of control but knowing that my partner was safe and looking out for me. And, I don't know, it was just hot to read about."

"Would you ever want to try it?"

"Yes," she said, her pupils dilating.

"It's really important that you know you are ultimately always in control. You would have a safe word and I would always, always listen to it."

"I know. I trust you," she said.

"That's the greatest gift you could give me, sweetheart," I responded, pulling her in for a kiss.

Chapter Forty-Nine

Josie

My emotions swirled as I leaned into the kiss.

I felt devastating sadness for Ellie, my chest tightening with the reminder that hers could have easily been my fate if not for my alphas. I breathed through my sadness, letting Cam's scent soothe the pain.

Cam's vulnerability, his trust, filled me with gratitude. I knew the time was coming to tell my alphas everything that had happened to me, but right now, I had other things on my mind.

I circled my arms around Cam's neck, falling deeper into the kiss as his chest rumbled and he planted a hand on my ass.

I needed an outlet for my emotions, the chance to let go and just *feel*.

Cam broke our kiss and my lip jutted out in an automatic pout. He chuckled, running his finger along my lip.

"Do you want to find the guys and get some food?" he murmured, his voice deep and gravelly.

Wait, what? Confusion and a flash of insecurity ran through me. I was definitely *not* thinking about food right now. I thought we were gearing up for something different than *let's go eat something*. Unless that something was me. *Ugh, my dirty talk is terrible.*

I paused before responding, sorting through my emotions. My insecurity was still there, the fear that, deep down, he didn't actually want me. Except, that argument no longer felt convincing. I *knew* he wanted me.

The confidence of that thought pulled me up short. When had I become so sure of my desirability? Happiness bloomed in my chest as I realized how much my time with my alphas had grown my confidence. Cam was holding back because he was afraid of scaring me, not because he didn't find me attractive. I knew he would never do anything to harm me, but he didn't trust himself. I had to do something that would help him drop his inhibitions. And then a mischievous idea took root.

"No," I responded. "I want to spend time with just you." I trailed my hands down his chest and lower until I cupped his cock through his pants.

His eyes heated, and a low growl rumbled through his chest. His hand wrapped around my wrist but didn't pull me away. "Careful, baby girl, I'm on edge right now. It's been an eventful day. You should go rest."

"Don't you want me?" I asked, making sure my eyes looked wide and innocent, slightly poking out my lip in a pout.

"Fuck, more than I can say, but I'm not fully in control right now. I would be... too much for you. Go with Ben and Theo for a bit."

My lips twitched, almost breaking into a smile. My sweet cinnamon roll alpha.

"Mmm, no, I don't think so," I said, squeezing his cock tightly. His responding growl caused another gush of slick, and I knew he could scent me. "I think you need to catch me."

Before he realized what I was doing, I threw myself off his lap and took off. I headed for the patio doors and pulled them open. Ben poked his head out of the kitchen and looked surprised and a little concerned when I rushed in, my cheeks flushed and hair wild. I winked at him, causing him to laugh before I continued my sprint through the house.

Cam's roar followed me as I ran up the stairs, slick dripping down my legs. I looked over my shoulder to see him standing at the base of the steps, his eyes dark and his hair falling out of his previously neat bun. Excitement bubbled in my stomach as I realized he was toying with me.

I picked up my pace, knowing he could catch me in a heartbeat, especially as I tried to avoid tripping over my skirt. I turned the corner and sprinted into my room. My chest heaved as I turned to shut the door behind me, but before I could, firm arms gripped me around my waist and pushed me against the wall. I let out a little scream. Cam's cock pressed against my back, his cinnamon roll scent thick around me.

"That was very naughty. You should know better than to run away from a predator."

My body trembled with anticipation and I pressed my legs together, trying to create some friction.

"What are you going to do about it?" I asked, trying to sound as unaffected as possible, but the breathiness in my voice betrayed me.

"I think my baby girl needs to be punished," he said, his hips thrusting against me.

Fuck, yes. I really, really did.

He ran his hands down my sides before grasping my wrists and pinning them to the wall above my head.

Cam breathed in deeply, scenting me. "That excites you. You know you need to be punished, don't you, baby girl? You need me to strip this dress off you, take you over my knee, and redden that sexy little ass of yours."

"No, you can't do that." *Oh, please do that.* I squirmed

against him, unsure if I was trying to get away or press myself closer.

"No avoiding it now, baby girl. You need to learn not to disobey your alpha."

He ran one hand down my body and cupped my ass hard. I groaned as his fingers dug in. Suddenly, he spun me around and picked me up. I wrapped my arms and legs tightly around him, trying to subtly rub my core against him.

"You want this?" he asked softly. "I don't want to remind you of other alphas."

"You could never," I said. There was such vulnerability in his eyes I couldn't help but lean in for a kiss.

"I love you," he said, running his nose down my face.

"I love you, too."

The words felt too insignificant for what I felt. My chest was going to burst with happiness and wholeness.

"I don't want to scare you, sweetheart. You need to tell me your limits."

I'd read enough BDSM romance books to know that communication was essential. I needed to be brave, honestly share my desires, and trust my caring, loving alpha to honor my boundaries.

"I'm not entirely sure," I said. "But I don't want to be, um, humiliated."

Cam hugged me tighter. "Of course not. Don't think I could, even if you wanted me to. You're my precious omega." He placed gentle kisses on my forehead and cheek. "What else?"

"Um, no blood or, like, water sports," I squeaked out.

Cam burst out laughing. "Fuck, sweetheart. What books have you been reading?"

I blushed and hid my face in his neck. He tugged on my hair, the move sending a shiver through me.

"No hiding. Need your eyes."

I pulled back and saw a heartbreaking smile on his face, his eyes crinkling with happiness.

"Good girl, you're doing so well."

I whimpered, another gush of slick drenching my underwear.

"How do you feel about spanking? Bondage?"

"Two thumbs up," I said before blushing again. "Ugh, pretend that sounded sexy and not super dorky."

"Everything you say sounds sexy," Cam responded with a chuckle. "If you get overwhelmed and need a pause, say yellow. If you need to stop everything, say red. I promise I won't get upset if you use your safe words, but I will be very upset if you need to use them and don't. Understand, baby girl?"

I nodded.

"Use your words," he growled.

I whimpered. "Yes, alpha."

"Good girl. Now, time for your punishment."

I gasped as he lowered me to the ground and quickly unzipped my dress, pushing it off my body before I realized what was happening. I was standing before him, wearing only the useless scent-blocking underwear I had put on earlier. I froze, trying not to cringe and cover my body. Cam pulled me close and rubbed his face in my hair.

"No feeling self-conscious when you're standing there looking like a fucking goddess. You are so beautiful. I dream about these curves every night, have fantasized about this from the moment I saw you."

He cupped my ass tightly and pulled me in for a kiss, his tongue sweeping into my mouth. My skin felt hot and electric, his touch washing away my anxieties about my body. He pulled away, leaving me gasping for air.

"But you definitely do need to be punished."

With lightning speed, Cam tugged me over to the bed, pulled me over his lap, and pushed my panties down to my knees. I tried to pull myself off his lap, but he pinned my arms firmly behind me.

"The more you struggle, the longer your punishment will be, little omega."

A thrill rushed through me like little sparks in my stomach. To my embarrassment, more slick gushed out of my sex. I kicked my legs, trying to dislodge his grip, but my underwear limited my movement. I knew we both wanted this and were both getting off on the fight.

I flinched as Cam's hand rubbed my ass.

"Shh, just relax and take it. I know you want to be my good girl."

Before I had the chance to respond, his hand came down hard.

Crack.

I let out a whimper at the sting, gasping when his hand smacked my other ass cheek. Cam squeezed both cheeks hard.

"Love that pretty pink color," he said, making me moan as he massaged my warm skin.

Crack.

I cried out again, the sting radiating through me. Cam continued to pepper my ass, creating an even rhythm. I lost count of how many he had given me. My skin throbbed and grew hot under his touch. He stopped and rubbed in the heat.

"Good girl for taking that warm-up so well."

I squeaked. That was the warm-up? My ass felt like it was on fire.

"No, I don't want anymore," I whined, trying to get away again, all the while hoping he would continue pinning me to his lap.

Cam's hand came down heavy, harder than any of the previous spanks, and I squealed at the pain.

"No lying, baby girl. I know you want this. I can smell your pussy, the sweetness of your arousal."

I shook my head, struggling against the vise grip on my wrists.

"No, you don't want this? Your cunt isn't drenched right now?"

I shook my head again.

"Well, there's one way to check which one of us is right."

I groaned in pleasure, instinctually widening my legs and arching my back as Cam's finger stroked down my slit, circling my clit. He pressed his finger to my entrance but paused before entering.

"Is this okay, sweetheart?"

I loved him for checking, for always taking care of me.

"Yes, don't stop," I gasped.

Cam's thick finger entered me, curling so it rubbed against my slick gland. I arched against him, needing just a tiny bit more to push me over the edge.

"Oh, you don't get to come that easily," he said with a chuckle, removing his finger and slapping my ass again *hard*.

I moaned as he continued to build heat in my ass and the tops of my thighs, my body relaxing and letting go as the pain morphed into pleasure.

"Next time, are you going to be a good little omega and listen to your alpha?" he asked between slaps.

No, definitely not if it leads to this. "Yes, alpha, I'll be good."

He stopped and rubbed my heated skin again, his touch stinging and soothing at the same time.

"I'm not sure I believe you," he said teasingly. "But you've been such a good girl taking your punishment so well for me. Your little red ass is so pretty under my hand."

He slipped his finger into me again, shortly adding a second one. The sensation was too much and not enough at the same time. I whined incoherently, needing him to anchor me.

"Shh, sweetheart, I've got you. Just relax. I'll give you what you need."

He worked his fingers around my clit, building heat and tension. I rocked against his hand, needing the friction, needing anything he could give me as my core tightened.

"Fuck, you're squeezing me so tightly. That's right, I want to feel you come on my fingers."

My orgasm broke over me and I screamed. I felt like I was floating underwater, deep in a sea of pleasure. My body felt alive and electrified.

My core was still contracting as Cam slipped his fingers from me. He released my wrists and massaged my arms before lying down on the bed, arranging me so I was lying on top of him. He threw a blanket over us and ran his hands slowly up and down my body, murmuring soothing words. I was overwhelmed by how cherished he made me feel.

"How are you doing?" he asked softly.

"So, so good," I said with a smile.

I trailed my hands down his chest and scrunched my nose as I realized he was still fully clothed.

Cam ran his finger down my nose, cupping my cheek with a chuckle. "Why do you look so disgruntled?"

"Get undressed," I whined. "How are we supposed to fuck when you're clothed?"

Cam swiftly flipped us so he was on top of me, pressing his hard cock against my core.

"Did you forget who's in charge, little omega?"

I arched my back, rubbing my pussy against the seam of his pants. "No, alpha," I said sweetly. "Feel free to order me to fuck you any time that works for you."

Cam's laughter boomed out around us. He captured my lips in a kiss, twining his hand in my hair and creating delicious tension. "Well then, omega, present for your alpha."

A shiver went through my body as Cam stood and stripped off his shirt. The dark lines of his tattoo stood out against his tan skin and my mouth practically watered at each hard ridge of muscle. I sat up and ran my fingers down his bare chest. He groaned in pleasure.

"Get going unless you want another punishment," he said with a wink.

I quickly shifted to face the headboard on my hands and knees. I presented to my alpha, my ass high in the air, head on the bed, and arms stretched out in front of me. I whimpered as I felt him behind me, his now-bare legs pressing firmly against mine, the coarseness of his leg hair a contrast against my smooth skin. I couldn't stop myself from looking back at him, taking in his naked form for the first time. His fist was wrapped around his cock, which was thick, slightly curved, and leaking precum. I licked my lips, eyes wide.

He grinned at my perusal, grabbing my ass and squeezing hard.

"You're so perfect, baby girl. Can't wait to slide into that sweet, tight cunt of yours, feel your heat around me."

I wiggled my ass teasingly. "Why are you being so slow, then?"

"Brat," he gritted out, slapping my ass.

There was laughter in his voice, and warmth bloomed in my chest that I brought out his playful side.

Cam's fingers dug into my hips as the head of his cock brushed against my entrance. I pressed my face against the bed, taking a slow, shuddering breath as he slid slowly inside me. I moaned as his cock rubbed against my pleasure spots, sending bright bursts of lightning through my stomach.

"You feel like fucking heaven," he groaned. "I'm never going to get enough of this, enough of your sweet cunt. Can't wait to tie you up, spread out on the bed." He pushed in deeper and cupped his hands around my breasts, squeezing my nipples. "Going to decorate these beautiful tits with nipple clamps as I paddle your ass."

I whimpered, positive I could come from listening to him talk alone. His legs were pressed on either side of mine, adding to the stretch and feeling of fullness. The slight curve of his cock rubbed deliciously against my slick gland.

"Yes, that feels so good," I moaned, pressing back against his thrusts.

His hand moved to my neck, keeping me pinned to the bed, and I cried out at the possessiveness of his touch. I craved being dominated by him, held in place by his hands, legs, cock. I trusted him to do whatever he wanted with my body because he would always put my needs first.

"My good little omega," Cam said, thrusting deeper and faster now. "Look at you, taking my cock so well."

My noises turned into sobs as pleasure overwhelmed me. Cam's swollen knot ground against my clit, and my hands clenched the blanket as my next orgasm shuddered through me. *How many was that now?*

Cam swore as he finally thrust his knot into me, breathing hard as he came, warmth filling my insides. I screamed at the stretch, a hint of pain accompanying the incredible pleasure as he lodged himself firmly inside me.

I sighed as a wave of peace washed over me. Being connected like this made me feel complete, a reassurance that we belonged together. I'd always thought knotting would be scary, but just like with Theo and Ben, Cam's knot felt like a physical reminder of our love and connection.

"I've never felt anything like this," he said, breathing heavily. "This is my new addiction, feeling your hot pussy squeezing me."

He released my neck and started gently massaging my back. I relaxed into his touch, exhaling a shuddering breath.

"You okay, baby girl?"

I moaned and nodded my head. He had killed me with pleasure. My body felt like it was still vibrating, like a single touch could throw me over again.

"Use your words," he commanded sternly.

"I'm sooo good, alpha."

"Damn right," he said, the smugness in his voice unmistakable.

I moaned as he started moving.

"Shh, just going to change positions so I can tend to you better."

Cam arranged us so we were both lying on our sides. He pressed one of his legs between mine, pinning me even more firmly to him. I reached back behind me and pulled his hair loose from its bun. He purred as I ran my hand through it. The vibration set me off again and I pressed my ass back, shifting his knot deeper inside me.

"You're going to come again for me," he said in my ear, running his hand down the soft rolls of my stomach and cupping my mound.

"I can't," I whined.

"You can," Cam growled. "Because I demand it. You'll do it because you're a good girl, and your alpha wants to feel you come on his cock again."

Well, when he said it like that.

He placed gentle bites down my neck, not breaking the skin but lighting me up with desire all the same. I groaned as I realized I *wanted* his bite, wanted him to bond me.

He twisted my nipples, the pain going straight to my clit, as he rocked his knot deeper inside me. I cried as I came, tears streaming down my face as the rightness and safety I felt with him in this moment, that I felt with all my guys, overwhelmed me.

Cam's arms tightened and he brushed my tears away.

"Baby girl, why are you crying? Did I hurt you?" he asked, a hint of panic edging into his voice.

"Good tears," I managed to choke out. "This feels so good and safe."

Cam exhaled with relief, tenderly brushing the hair away from my face. "I love you, sweetheart. I can't believe how lucky we are to have found you," he murmured, never stopping his gentle stroking up and down my skin. "Are you sure you're okay?"

"Better than okay, alpha."

"So... I take it you would give this experience two thumbs up?"

I groaned and hid my face in my hands. "Why am I such a dork?"

"You're my dork, baby. And I love it."

"Definitely two thumbs up."

Cam chuckled and wrapped me up in his arms. His knot was still pulsing inside me as I drifted off.

I wasn't sure how much time had passed, but I woke as Cam slipped his cock out of me. One of his hands massaged my still tender ass, the other wrapped firmly in my hair. My sex clenched with emptiness. I was too sore for anything else right away, but my body hadn't quite realized that.

"I still haven't had enough of you," I sighed without thinking, still drunk off the many orgasms.

"Thank fuck for that because I'm not done with you, little omega."

His cock was hard underneath me, pressing against my thigh. I popped my head up so I could look at his face.

"How can you be hard again? It's been like three seconds," I exclaimed with a laugh.

"I get hard when you walk into a room. The question is, how am I ever *not* hard around you?"

My cheeks heated and I automatically ground my pussy against his thigh. Maybe I wasn't too sore to go again.

"Easy, sweetheart. I'm going to get you in the bath first to help with any soreness."

"Too tired to get up," I whined, pressing my head back against his chest.

"You just stay relaxed. I'll take care of everything."

My eyes were closed as he carried me to the bathroom and sat me on the counter while he ran the hot water. The cool counter felt good on my heated butt cheeks. Even though the skin was tender, I loved the reminder of his hands on me.

Cam returned, pressing my legs apart so he could stand between them, hugging me to his body.

"Thank you," I murmured.

"For what?" he asked as he gently massaged my neck.

"For taking such good care of me. And for being yourself, for giving me all of you."

Cam lifted my face so we were looking at each other. He was all warmth, from his brown eyes to the soft caress of his hands.

"Thank you for giving me you. The sweetest gift I could ever be trusted with," he said, voice tight. He pulled me in for the gentlest kiss before picking me up and moving us into the bath.

Chapter Fifty

Cam

I took a minute to observe my mate from the office doorway. Josie was in the study, her back to me as she peered at Theo's book collection. Fuck, she was gorgeous. She was running a finger lightly over the book spines, and I almost groaned at the memory of her fingers trailing down my bare skin last night.

The light streamed through the window, making her brown hair shine like gold. She was wearing one of my sweatshirts with nothing underneath. It came down to her thighs, but my cock hardened at the reminder that if I slipped my hand underneath the fabric, I would feel her bare ass and pussy.

Josie turned towards me, her nostrils flaring as she scented my arousal. I stalked towards her, my excitement rising as she backed away from me until her back hit the wall. I kept going until I was inches from her. Before she realized what I was doing, I grabbed her wrists and pinned them above her head with one hand, placing my other possessively on her hip. She let out a disgruntled noise. My little omega had been irritable all morning. My guess was it was due to a combination of her hormones trying to stabilize after her heat was cut short, along with everything else that had happened the past couple of weeks. I almost purred, realizing that next heat, she would have us to care for her and satisfy her. My cock strained against my sweatpants, and my hips gave a small involuntary thrust.

"My sweet mate, you've been in a bad mood all day."

"Is this how you charm the ladies? Because if that's the case, I'm not surprised it's taken you this long to find an omega," she bit out.

My insides danced in delight at her fiery snark. "Mmm, you saying you don't find me charming?"

Josie scowled and tried to pull her hands from my grip. Her struggle barely registered.

"I know there have been so many changes lately. It's a lot to cope with," I murmured in her ear, running my nose down the side of her neck so I could breathe in her heady scent. "What do you need, sweetheart?"

I heard a little sniffle and pulled back to see a few tears fall down her face.

"I don't know," she whimpered. "I felt so good waking up with you this morning, but now I just feel all messed up."

"Oh, baby girl, you should have told me. You know you little omegas need the guidance of us big, strong alphas," I teased, but a twinge of insecurity rolled through me. Maybe I had been too much last night, too alpha.

She choked out a surprised laugh. "I hate you," she said, but her lips twitched into an almost smile.

Relief rushed through me at the sound of her laugh. "I don't think you do. In fact, I heard a rumor that you love me." I kissed her forehead and then each cheek. "You know what else I think?"

Josie made a noncommittal noise, but her breathing sped up.

"I think you need a good fuck." I pressed my cock firmly against her. "Your hormones are still unregulated after your heat."

Josie snorted. "Your idea of dirty talk is terrible. Yeah, let me stick this big cock in you to regulate your hormones," she said in a terrible impression of my voice.

I snorted. "Is that what you think I sound like? No wonder I'm not scoring."

"You scored three times last night and twice this morning, so I think you're fine," she said primly, her cheeks flushing that delicious pink I couldn't get enough of.

Fuck, how was it possible she was even cuter when grumpy?

I hid my smile in her hair. "Maybe you didn't come enough last night? I thought a dozen orgasms was enough, but apparently not." Yeah, I'd kept count.

Josie's hip rolled against mine, and she whimpered as she strained against my grasp. I'd forgotten I still had her hands pinned above her head and quickly released them, gently rubbing her arms. She melted against me and her eyes fluttered shut. My heart clenched as I realized my omega was fucking exhausted.

My brothers had left earlier for a company meeting we couldn't get out of. I knew they were jealous that I stayed home with Josie, but after our intense play session, I needed to stay close to her. She'd been clingier than usual, growing distressed if I left her side. I wasn't sure if it made me a bastard to admit I loved it. I was thrilled to give her lots of reassurance and aftercare, wanted any excuse to touch her at all times. This kind of connection is what I'd been missing when I went to clubs. There, I'd scene with a sub and spend a few minutes on aftercare, making sure they were alright before sending them away. I didn't realize how much I craved being needed and how strongly I wanted to nurture my partner.

"You hungry, baby girl?" I asked as I moved my attention to massaging the back of her neck. As much as I wanted to fuck her, making sure she was taken care of was my number one priority.

She shook her head and leaned more of her weight on me. I grabbed her by her thighs and picked her up, reveling in the feel of her soft legs wrapped around my waist.

"Theo and Ben will be home soon. How about we wait for them in the nest? Then you can be surrounded by all your alphas."

Skin-to-skin should help regulate her hormones and reduce the restlessness she was feeling.

"You're not going to leave, right?" she asked, her voice cracking.

"Course not, baby girl. You can't get rid of me even if you want to. Ben and Theo only left because they had to, and they're coming back as fast as they can."

Most of the time, Josie was practically stoic for an omega. I'd seen little glimpses of her inner omega during her heat, when she nested, and in her lightning-quick jealousy at the cocktail party. But most of the time, she seemed uncomfortable with her designation. I hoped this vulnerability meant she was getting more comfortable showing us her omega.

"You just let it out, baby girl," I said as she sniffled again. "I'm right here. You can fall apart if you need to, because I'll never let you go."

She didn't say anything but tightened her hold around me, her lips pressing against my neck in a soft kiss.

Chapter Fifty-One

Josie

I bounced happily on the couch, feeling much more settled than earlier. I'd rolled my eyes at Cam's comment about getting my hormones regulated, but he was right. I still felt messed up after my heat. Or maybe this was just what being an omega felt like—needy, emotional, and vulnerable. A small smile tugged at my lips when I realized the thought didn't immediately fill me with hatred for my omega. We were learning how to get along.

Theo sat down beside me with a little huff. He threw an arm around my shoulder, pulling me into his side. He was wearing a soft black t-shirt instead of his usual button-down, and it made me want to rub myself against him like a kitten.

"Are you sure we need to watch this?" he asked, eyes crinkling with a smile.

My heart skipped a beat. I wasn't sure there was anything more beautiful than Theo when he smiled.

"Yes," I said, leaning into his side. "*Twilight* is essential education."

Cam walked into the den, setting down the Chinese

takeout containers on the coffee table. He sat down on my other side and laced his fingers with mine.

"How're you feeling, baby girl?" he murmured.

"Good," I said, kissing the side of his neck. "Thanks for taking such good care of me."

Cam had been so attentive and patient with me, and I loved it, but I was a little worried I was being too needy. I bit my lip. Maybe he would decide that sex with me was too high maintenance.

"It's my pleasure to take care of you," he said with a hint of a growl. "It fulfills a need inside me, so whatever you're thinking, stop."

His words loosened the tension in my chest. "Yes, alpha," I responded, running my nose down his stubbly jaw.

"Alright, are we all prepared for some complete and utter garbage?" Ben said with a gleam in his eye, bringing in the rest of our food.

"Hey!" I responded. "Complete and utter *entertaining* garbage."

"Next time, we're going to watch something good," Cam grumbled as he dished up large portions of everything we'd ordered.

"Oh yeah? Like what?" I asked, looking around for a plate.

"Like *The Godfather*," he said as he handed me the food he'd plated.

I locked eyes with Ben, who pursed his lips to hold in his laughter.

"*The Godfather*, really?" I asked. "How old are you?"

Ben guffawed, and Cam narrowed his eyes.

"Young enough to spank your ass," he muttered.

My body heated, my butt tingling from the spanking I'd received the night before. I broke eye contact with Cam before I spontaneously combusted and looked down at my plate.

"This is for me?" I asked incredulously, staring at the heaping portions.

"Yes, and you're going to eat it," Cam said sternly.

"What he means is, eat as much as you want," Theo said, kissing me on the cheek.

"No, that's not what I fucking mean," Cam responded. "She's barely eaten all day."

I should bristle at him for telling me what to do, but I was too busy reveling in the warm feeling of someone *wanting* me to eat.

I picked up the fork and took a bite of lo mein. "I'm not sure why you're assuming this movie is going to be bad," I said. "Maybe it will be your new favorite."

Cam simply shifted closer to me on the couch until our bodies were pressed together.

"Good girl for eating," he murmured, playing with my hair. "But I'm still going to punish you for calling me old," he said with a wink.

I bit my lip to stop myself from whimpering. Now all I could think of was getting a repeat of last night—for him to throw me over his lap and spank me for being naughty and then fuck me for being his good girl. But what about Theo and Ben? Would they watch? Join in? My body was on fire and I took another bite of food to distract myself.

Ben's nostrils flared and he cleared his throat. "Are we going to watch this movie or have an orgy?"

I almost choked on my bite of chicken.

"Movie," Cam said, his voice deep and heated. "Our omega needs to eat to keep up her strength."

The thought of being with all three of my alphas at once sent a thrill of nervousness and lust through me. Luckily, the movie started before I had time to overthink it. Soon I was laughing and quoting the movie, loving Cam and Theo's outraged commentary. Ben settled between my legs on the floor, and I played with his hair. Cam kept scowling at Ben, and I wondered if he was jealous. I was itching to play with Cam's long hair. It was currently up in his signature bun, and I wanted to pull it down and run my hands through it, preferably while he was on top of me...

As the credits started playing, Cam said, "I thought there were werewolves in this movie."

"Oh, just wait for the later movies," I responded.

"Wait, how many are in the series?" Cam asked, his eyes wide.

"Umm, five."

I giggled at Cam's groan, snuggling up to him.

"Admit it," I said, my lips skimming his ear. "You liked it."

"Did not," he snorted.

"You liked it, right Theo?" I asked, leaning to give him a kiss.

Theo cleared his throat. "It was an experience." He grabbed the remote. "I want to check the news."

Theo switched the TV input. Chills skittered down my spine as I heard Glen Jacoby's sneering, condescending voice. My stomach churned with nausea as I turned towards the TV. Glen stood at a podium, flanked by Jericho on one side and Marshall Whiteburn on the other.

"I want to thank Director Marshall Whiteburn for doing such an exceptional job with the Designation Academy and our legislators for passing a generous funding package to expand DA services. It brings us closer to our vision of every pack finding the perfect omega. The funding will quickly be deployed to create the Pack Cohesion program, an innovative alpha/omega matching service..."

"Shut up," Ben muttered, grabbing the takeout containers.

"What an asshole," Theo said, muting the TV.

My guys bustled around me, cleaning up the takeout containers, but I barely caught anything they said. Dizziness overtook me, and my stomach churned. I realized I was going to throw up. I managed to keep myself upright as I stumbled to the bathroom, getting there just in time. Tears streaked down my face as I threw up everything I'd had for dinner. My throat burned, my scar screamed in pain, and I wanted to disappear.

I curled up on the bathroom floor, grabbing one of the towels under the sink to throw over myself. I was shaking from the cold and shock. I'd been so careful this past year to never turn on the news, to try to forget that Glen Jacoby existed. Now I felt like he had infiltrated my safe space with my alphas.

"Josie, are you in there?" Ben asked, knocking lightly on the door a few minutes later.

I couldn't let them know how messed up I was. I had to hide it. The cruel voice in my head kicked up again. *Once they know how defective you are, they won't want you anymore.*

"I'll just be a minute," I called out, relieved at how steady my voice sounded.

I picked myself up off the floor, my muscles screaming, and washed my face with cold water. I cleaned up the bathroom and rinsed my mouth with mouthwash before opening the door. Ben looked me over with concern.

"What's wrong, precious?" he asked, tenderly pulling me in for a hug.

"Nothing," I said, the lie feeling like ash in my mouth. "I think I ate too much."

"You don't feel good?" he asked.

I shook my head, soaking up his body heat.

"I'm so sorry. Let's get you to bed."

Ben led me upstairs and stripped off all my clothes before tucking me in under a pile of blankets. I raised my eyebrow at him questioningly when he took off his shirt.

"Not for sexy time," he said with a little smirk. "Just skin to skin."

He got me medicine from the bathroom, tenderly holding me upright as I drank some water. I shuddered in relief when he slipped in next to me, his skin soothing against mine.

Chapter Fifty-Two

Josie

"That's right, baby girl. Take all of me."

Cam pushed his cock into me in a single thrust, the sting of pain taking my breath away. I wriggled, trying to create some space between us. It was too much. I was stretched tight around him, each thrust causing a burning friction in my channel. I tried to breathe in his scent, but there was... nothing.

"Ah ah, no getting away from us," Theo whispered in my ear, his hand coming up and gripping my throat. "We're going to do whatever we want. This is our body."

A gush of slick rushed out of me as Ben pinned my hands above my head, but it felt wrong. Nausea swirled in my stomach. I didn't like this. Darkness surrounded me, and I realized someone had slipped a blindfold over my eyes. I tried to relax into Cam's thrusts, tried to tell myself it felt good, but the panic in my chest grew and grew.

"Look at that little whore, taking cock like the omega slut she is," Cam growled. Theo's hand squeezed tighter and tighter. I tried to tell them to stop, scream, whine, anything, but no sound

came out. A hint of a scent tickled my nose, but I couldn't place it.

"Omega sluts, all the same." I heard Ben's words, but they didn't make sense. My alphas wouldn't talk to me like this.

Cam came with a grunt before ripping his cock out of me and grabbing my ankles, holding them to the bed.

No, not the bed. A metal table.

It had all been a lie. Everything they had said and done leading up to this moment. Betrayal turned my skin hot and cold at the same time.

Steel bands wrapped around my waist, tightening until I knew they would leave deep bruises. Shackles clicked around my hands and legs, keeping me spread-eagled on the examination table. Theo's hand lifted from my neck, and I took a ragged breath before a cold, metal collar wrapped tightly around my neck, holding it in place.

"Why are you doing this?" I croaked out. "I thought you loved me."

Tears leaked from behind the blindfold, wetting my face and hair.

"Who could ever love a fat, ugly, defective slut of an omega like you?"

It was him.

I choked and gagged on Glen Jacoby's rotten fruit scent—initially sweet and then stomach curdling.

"Activate the device," he commanded with a laugh.

"No!" My scream echoed in my ears, my throat feeling like it was bleeding from the force of it.

"Josie, baby girl, wake up now." The voice hovered on the edge of the fog surrounding me, but I couldn't bring the words into focus.

My alphas. They hurt me. Betrayed me.

"Why won't she wake up? Precious, please come back to us."

"Fuck, she's going to hurt herself. Sweetheart, open your eyes now."

"Josie, wake up!" Theo's bark ripped me out of the nightmare.

My eyes flew open at the command. I was on my back on the bedroom floor. Cam, Ben, and Theo were around me. Looming over me. Trapping me.

"No!" I shrieked. "Stay away!"

I curled into a ball and then remembered the device. They would use it against me. My hand flew up to where I knew it was implanted and I dug my nails in, trying to dig it out.

"Angel, please stop. You're bleeding." Theo pleaded, his coffee scent acidic.

His scent.

Every muscle in my body froze. I took a deep, shaky breath. Bursts of coffee, cinnamon roll, and spiced apple hit me.

My mates.

I whimpered, relief coursing through me like a deluge before a sob tore out of my chest. It had been a dream. My mates were here.

I breathed in again, needing to convince myself this was real. Each inhale convinced me a little bit more.

"I'm going to turn a light on," Theo murmured.

The glow of the table lamp illuminated the mess around me. The bedding was in a twisted pile on the floor. I realized I was naked, something that had felt fine when I went to bed but now made me want to vomit. I whimpered as I tried to cover myself, curling into a tight ball.

Ben dug through the bedding pile until he found my favorite soft blanket. He slowly moved towards me and laid it over me. I realized he was crying. They all were. I had made my alphas cry. Another sob burst from my chest.

"Can I touch you, baby girl?" Cam asked, his voice hoarse.

I shook my head. I couldn't handle any hands on me, my skin still crawling from the nightmare.

Theo got up and I whined. "Don't leave me."

I knew it was irrational to want them to be near me but not touching me, but the thought of him going anywhere constricted my chest. He crouched down in front of me.

"I'm just going to get the first aid kit from the bathroom," he said carefully. "I promise I'll be right back. Is that alright, angel?"

I nodded, tightening the blanket around me. My upper arm felt like it was on fire, and wet drops of blood dripped down my skin. Shakily, I pushed myself into a seated position, using the wall at my back for support. Ben and Cam sat close in front of me. Not touching, not saying anything, just lending me whatever support they could with their presence. There was such sadness in their eyes and their scents were sharp with distress. I wanted to reach out and comfort them, erase the devastation from their faces, but fear kept me frozen.

Theo returned with the first aid box.

"Can I look at your arm, love?" he asked, sitting down at my side. He moved hesitantly as if I was a wounded animal about to bolt. Which, I guess I was. My face heated. God, I was such an inconvenience. Other alphas got fun, perky omegas who slept without waking up screaming and were... *normal.* My mates were stuck with me.

Defective. Glen's voice snarled through my mind, making me whimper.

"Baby girl, we're right here. Nothing's going to happen to you." Cam's voice grounded me enough to peek out from where I'd pressed my face to the blanket.

I took a deep breath, trying to focus on Cam's words. I realized Theo was waiting for me to give him an answer. "Okay," I whispered, untangling my wounded arm from the blanket.

I kept my eyes on his face, not wanting to see what I'd done to my arm. Tension filled his gaze as he frowned at the cuts. He caught me looking at him and threw me an apologetic smile.

"Sorry, love. It doesn't look like it needs stitches. I'd like to clean it up and bandage it if that's okay with you. I won't touch you more than I have to."

Part of me wanted to throw myself at my alphas and demand that they wrap themselves around me. But I wasn't quite ready yet. I gave Theo a non-verbal assent and continued taking deep breaths, allowing the scents of my mates to pull me further and further away from the dream.

Ben sat close to my other side, his shoulders shaking with silent tears. I wanted to ease his pain, but I didn't know how. I pushed my left hand out of the blanket and threaded my pinky with his. His teary gaze met mine as he squeezed my little finger.

"I love you," he mouthed at me.

"Love you," I mouthed back.

Theo's hands were achingly gentle as he cleaned my arm—the place where the *scar* was, not the device. I took a shuddering breath. It wasn't in me anymore. The adrenaline of the dream drained from me, leaving me boneless. I rested my head on Ben's shoulder, unable to remain upright. He shifted slightly so my face rested close to his neck, as if he knew I needed his scent right now.

"All set," Theo said, causing me to jump a little. I still wasn't ready to look at my arm, the evidence of what I had done to myself.

"Do you want to go back to bed, sweetheart?" Cam asked, his voice hesitant.

I lifted my head, meeting his devastated gaze. Last night he looked at me with heat in his eyes as he made love to me repeatedly. That seemed like a distant memory.

"I... I don't think I'm ready to go back to bed," I whispered. "Can I sit in the den for a bit?"

"Of course, precious," Ben said, giving my pinky a little squeeze.

"I don't want to keep you up," I said, shame curling in my stomach.

"We want to be with you," Theo said firmly. "Unless... unless you want to be alone?" His voice sounded strained.

"No!" I said, panic filling me at the thought.

"Not leaving you," Cam said with an air of possession.

Memories of nightmare-Cam tried to encroach. I needed to replace them with something good. I released Ben's finger and shakily held out my arms to Cam.

"Will you carry me?" My heart was pounding, and my scent was bitter with stress.

"Always," Cam grunted out.

With tremendous tenderness, he scooped me up. I wrapped my arms and legs around him and breathed in big gulps of his scent. This was Cam, *my* Cam, who was so worried about hurting me I had to goad him into having sex. My Cam, who had been so tender while he dominated me. I rubbed my face against his neck, scent-marking him. I needed their scents covering me, grounding me. I tightened my hold and he responded in kind, exhaling a deep breath.

"I love you, baby girl."

"Love you so much."

I wanted to apologize to all of them for my reaction, for waking them, and upsetting them, but I knew they would just growl at me and tell me I had nothing to be sorry about. The ghost of a smile tugged at the corner of my mouth.

Cam settled down on the sectional with me still wrapped around him. I reached my arms out on either side of me, needing to feel Ben and Theo. They were there immediately, pressing their bodies against mine. Theo's hand threaded in my hair, and Ben held me around my waist. For a moment, it was too much. Reminders of being held down in the nightmare flooded me. The guys stiffened, noting my distress. I forced myself to take a deep breath, inhaling their scents. *You're safe, you're safe.*

"It's okay," I said, my muscles unclenching.

I knew the guys were dying to ask me what had happened, but they refrained, simply caressing me and planting tender kisses on my skin. I needed to tell them everything. If I didn't do it now, I would chicken out.

"Glen Jacoby has been a friend of my parents for a long time." I kept my face pressed into Cam's neck, eyes closed, focusing on their scents to keep me grounded. I felt Cam's breathing hitch before he relaxed again.

"When I was younger, he was at the house a lot. I realize now he was working with my parents to plan the Designation Government takeover. I hated being at home anyway, so I tried to stay out of the house or in my room. But sometimes, my parents would force me to come down and sit through these long, formal dinners. Glen would almost always be there, along with a group of their friends. Director Whiteburn was there once, and several other people who now have government positions. But I remember Glen the most. He was the loudest, always saying anti-omega things.

"After I revealed, the insults became more pointed. He mocked my body, talked about how much I was eating, and gave my parents suggestions on how to control me better. He acted like he hated me. But sometimes, I would catch him staring and it felt... I don't know. It felt like he was a predator and I was his prey. His eyes tracked me all the time."

Cam vibrated underneath me, and I heard Ben's sharp intake of breath. I glanced over at Theo, who was sitting stiffly, a blank mask on his face.

"When the Designation Government came into power and founded the Academy, I was in the first class mandated to attend. At first, it was like a strict boarding school. But then things got worse."

My throat felt like it was closing up. I'd never shared the full story of what happened to anyone besides Sam, and I had been drunk when I had told him. Cam pressed a gentle kiss to my temple.

"They implemented a whole system of punishments. If you didn't follow their rules, they would take away your weekend privileges, meaning you could never leave campus. They would also strip your room of anything comfortable, like blankets and pillows. You already know about the meal plan they put me on."

My three alphas growled.

"We got word that they were going to start doing... medical exams on us. Specifically, pelvic exams to make sure we were virgins."

"Fuckers," Cam snarled.

I squeezed my eyes shut and clenched my hands tightly, pushing ahead.

"I made a few friends while there—Poppy and... Genevieve." God, even saying her name was painful.

"Our rooms were next to each other, and we had classes together. Poppy was only there for two months before she bonded with her alphas. She left before things got bad. When Genevieve and I found out the medical exams were scheduled to start, we decided to escape. We couldn't make it another year and a half, and we'd been punished so much that we hadn't been allowed to do any pack interviews. We were trapped. So we planned out the whole thing, but the night before we planned to go, the guards came to my room. They said Genevieve told them about our plans to escape. She betrayed me." I choked on those last words, the pain as fresh as it had been years ago. Cam's chest vibrated with a steady growl, and I wasn't sure any of them were breathing.

"So they took me to this room. Glen was there with Dr. Bishop, my fathers, and other DA board members. Glen announced to all of them I was a defective omega and could never bond with a pack the way I was. But they had just created a new training program to transform omegas like me to fit the expected designation standards."

My tears fell heavily. Cam wrapped the blanket around me tighter.

"Take a breath, baby girl."

I forced the air into my lungs and then continued, trying to get the words out as fast as possible.

"They forced me onto a metal table and strapped me down. Everyone stood around me, watching me as I screamed. Glen said they had a new device they could implant into an omega's arm that would force compliance and deliver punishment, all to train the omega to obey alphas at all times. So, then they cut open my arm and put the device in."

"Shit," Ben said, looking wide-eyed at Cam, whose jaw clenched. Cam shook his head almost imperceptibly, and I wanted to ask about their reactions, but I was shaking too hard to get words out.

"Shh, you're going to make yourself sick," Theo said, running his hand up and down my back, his pace too rapid to be soothing. "I'm going to get you some water." He kissed me on the cheek before getting up. The silence in the room was stifling, broken only by my sobs and Cam's growl. I reached out blindly for Ben's hand, unable to stomach looking any of them in the eye. He immediately captured my hand, squeezing it tightly and kissing my wrist.

I heard shattering glass from the kitchen and flinched.

"Theo?" I asked.

"Don't worry," Cam said. "He's just trying to process it all."

I curled into myself. "I'm making you upset."

"We're upset because we love you more than anything. You're being so brave, so strong to tell us."

Theo returned with a glass and tissues. I met his gaze for a split second, and the rage and love I found there took my breath away. I managed a few sips of water before exchanging the glass for tissues, cleaning up my face and blowing my nose. I could feel my mates' eyes on me intently as I grabbed more tissues to blow my nose again. For some reason, the idea of them staring so seriously at my snot caused a hysterical giggle to burst out of me.

"Never thought I'd have an audience for blowing my nose," I quipped. None of them said anything, the tension still crackling in the room.

"Okay, Josie, not the time for joking," I muttered.

"I think you're very funny," Ben said gravely.

I snorted, casting him a grateful smile. He winked and that gesture, more than anything, helped me continue.

"After they put the device in me and sewed up the cut, Glen activated it. I lost consciousness. When I came to, all I knew was some amount of time had passed. Everyone in the room, my fathers included, were clapping and congratulating Glen for his work. I realized I was naked." I dug my fingernails into my palms more deeply, trying to keep myself from returning to that room. Theo's hands captured mine, soothing the marks on my skin.

"Squeeze my hand as hard as you want to," he said. "Use your fingernails on me."

I whimpered. I could never cause him pain. But I gave his hand a squeeze in gratitude.

"I was terrified of what had happened and lashed out at the doctor and assistant. Then Glen activated the device again, but this time it gave me an electric shock. I didn't know if the pain would ever end. After that, I didn't fight them."

"During the rest of my time at the DA, Glen visited frequently. We had monthly medical exams, and he would be there for them. He would activate the device so I would be unconscious for the exam. It feels almost worst that I wasn't awake for it. I don't know what they did to me," I sobbed. "I'm dirty."

"No," the three of them growled at the same time.

"You are so strong, precious. Such a survivor," Ben said, kissing away my tears. "I'm so in awe of you and how you've kept going, kept resisting, kept *living*."

"But I stopped fighting," I confessed. "Anytime I did anything they didn't like, they would take more things away. I lost track of time. I think I spent more time in solitary than out of it. And Glen would visit and use the device—shocking me if I didn't obey him and then putting me unconscious whenever he wanted. When it was finally time to leave the DA, my parents came to collect me and bring me back to their house. I hadn't been outside for almost two years. Those first few weeks, I stayed in my room. I wanted to die," I whispered.

"That's how Sam found me. I hadn't gotten to speak to him for two years. He was about to move to Sol. He told me he wrote to me the whole time I was at the DA but had been told that I didn't want to talk to him—I was too busy having fun at boarding school. He panicked when he saw me. He was going to give up moving to be with Ger..." I stopped, aware that I was about to betray his secret.

"We are forever in debt to Sam," Cam said, sensing my hesitation. "He's part of your family, which makes him a part of ours. We would never do anything to hurt him."

I nuzzled my face into Cam's neck. "He was going to give up moving to be with his boyfriend just to make sure I was okay. But I told him... I told him I would kill myself if he gave up his happiness for me."

Ben made a distressed noise.

"Our compromise was that he would keep paying for his apartment so I could move in. At that point, political opposition to the Designation Government was ramping up, and they weren't paying me a lot of attention. Sam moved me out without telling my parents. Once they found out, they tried to threaten me to get me to return. I told them I would make everything that happened to me at the DA public if they tried to force me back home. That scared them enough to back off."

"Did the DA remove the device before they sent you home?" Theo asked, running a gentle finger over my bandages.

"No. I got really drunk with Sam before he left and told him everything. I forced him to cut it out."

"Fuck!" Cam shouted. A snarling growl tore through his chest, and I could tell he was torn between punching something and keeping me on his lap. In the end, he tightened his grip on me.

"What was the nightmare about, precious?" Ben asked, cupping my face with his hand.

"I think seeing Glen on the news last night triggered it." I paused, unsure how much to tell them. In the end, I decided they didn't need to know the details. It would only make them hesitant to touch me or have sex with me, and I didn't want that.

"I dreamed of being on that table with Glen. I was scared the device was still in me."

We lapsed into silence. I felt drained, but not in a bad way... I felt lighter, grateful we didn't have this secret between us. I rested my head on Cam's chest, holding Ben's hand tightly. After a while, I realized Theo wasn't touching me. I cracked my eyes open and saw him staring off into the distance.

"Theo?" I asked hesitantly. "Are you okay?"

His eyes snapped to mine, and he forced a smile that didn't reach his eyes.

"No, angel, I'm not okay. I just heard that my mate, the most important person to me in the world, was tortured for *years*. And we didn't do anything about it."

I scrunched my nose in confusion. "What would you have done? You didn't know I existed."

Theo ran his hand through his hair in agitation. The usually styled strands were sticking up erratically. I reached out and fixed a few pieces, and he leaned his face into my hand. I nudged Cam's arms, and he released me with a reluctant sigh. I crawled over to Theo's lap, snuggling up to him.

"It's not your fault," I whispered, running my fingers down his face.

He took a slow, shuddering breath before wrapping his arms around me and burying his face in my hair.

"We're going to take those fuckers down," he said.

A thrill of fear and excitement ran through me. I'd spent the past few years just trying to survive, not thinking about the future, unsure if I would have one. But the thought of taking Glen down, the DA, the entire Designation Government...

"You think we can?" I asked, sitting up.

"Fuck yes," Cam growled.

Ben smiled. "You haven't seen these two in action,

precious. They're fierce when someone hurts someone they love."

A little warm glow settled in my chest. It felt like hope.

"It's going to take me a while to come to terms with this," Theo said. "But I'm so grateful you told us. That you trust us."

"Thanks for being safe," I said, my voice hitching.

"Sweetheart, what do you need from us? I don't want to trigger you," Cam asked, concern etched onto his face. Now that my panic had settled, I realized my mates were all naked. I just had my blanket wrapped around me.

"Umm, maybe just no bondage with metal. And no blindfolds." Cam nodded seriously. "But, please don't... don't be all careful around me. I still want you to see me as desirable. Not like a victim." I looked them each in the face.

Finally, the tiniest hint of a smile touched Cam's lips.

"You have nothing to be concerned about there, sweetheart. You are the sexiest," he gave me a kiss on the forehead, "hottest," a kiss on my nose, "most desirable woman in the universe." A kiss on the lips. I exhaled, my shoulders relaxing. I had been worried sharing my past would ruin everything between us.

Theo's arms tightened around me.

"Why don't we go back to bed?" he suggested. "We can sleep in my room."

I sighed in relief. I loved my room but didn't want to return to my bed tonight. I kissed Theo on the cheek as he stood and carried me to bed.

Chapter Fifty-Three

Cam

"Stop hovering," Ben hissed, bumping me as he headed to the kitchen to make yet another thing Josie would refuse to eat.

"I'm not," I responded, my jaw clenched. Ben just shot me a look.

I was totally fucking hovering.

I stared into the study from my spot in the hall, my eyes drawn to where Josie was curled up in a leather chair with a book and untouched hot chocolate. Theo was in the chair next to her, pretending to read. Every few minutes, his eyes flickered towards her, tension lining his body. I could feel his and Ben's agony through the bond, joining my own. We had known Josie suffered at the Academy, but nothing could have prepared me for the horror of it. Seeing Josie experience such terror, for her to be so lost in her dream, she flinched away from me... it had completely broken my heart. Her cries from last night echoed in my head, serving as a reminder of how I'd failed to protect her, just as I'd failed Ellie.

She'd been subdued when she woke, slipping out of bed to

take a long shower alone. Since then, she hadn't spoken much. Whenever I caught her eye, she looked away quickly, biting her lip as if embarrassed, her scent taking on a bitterness I couldn't quite place. I wanted to punch something, needed to work out the helplessness blanketing my body. But I didn't want to leave Josie. Being by her side was a compulsion.

I strode into the study and knelt by her chair. She was looking out the window, her eyes distant.

"Baby girl?"

She jumped with a whimper, and I quickly snagged the hot chocolate from her hands before it spilled.

"Cam," she said, glancing around the room. "Sorry, I didn't notice you."

A wave of her bitter vanilla scent washed over me, and I finally realized what I was scenting: it was shame. A loud growl snarled from my chest before I realized what I was doing, causing Josie to shrink deeper into the leather chair with a whine.

"What the fuck, Cam," Theo bit out, his voice cold.

"Sorry, sweetheart. I'm so sorry," I said, stopping my growl and kissing the tops of her thighs.

Josie ran a cold, shaky hand through my hair. I had forgotten to put it up in a bun this morning and now, feeling her fingers running through it, I was fucking grateful. I purred, hoping the sound would relax her, and rested my head in her lap.

"You have nothing to be ashamed about," I murmured.

Her fingers paused their movements, and I wanted to beg for her to continue. Her touch was the only thing anchoring me, the only thing stopping me from hunting down Glen Jacoby and fucking ending him.

I glanced up and saw silent tears running down Josie's face. I moved instinctually, picking her up and walking towards the den where we would have more fucking space to cuddle. I jerked my head at Theo, signaling that he should follow. He looked even more out of it than Josie right now.

I settled Josie on my lap on our large sectional. Ben walked into the room holding a tray of sandwiches, immediately setting them down on the coffee table and joining us on the couch. We wrapped our arms around our omega, touching her as much as we possibly could, and purred. It wasn't long before Josie's tears subsided and she fell asleep.

We must have all fallen asleep because hours later, I was woken by Josie stretching on my lap like a kitten. Theo and Ben were sprawled on the sectional, their limbs entwined in mine. I sleepily pulled Josie onto me, kissing her on the forehead.

"Hi," she said, smiling up at me.

"Hi, baby girl. How're you feeling?"

"Better," she responded, rubbing her face against my chest and reaching out to hold Theo's arm. "Sorry about this morning. I just... last night was a lot to process."

I didn't like how small her voice sounded.

"You have nothing to be sorry about. And certainly nothing to feel ashamed about." I gripped her chin gently, forcing her to meet my gaze. She exhaled slowly and nodded.

"Damn, that was a good nap," Ben said, his eyes still closed. He stretched out his arm, reaching it across Josie and settling it on her breast.

"Ben, you're grabbing my boob," Josie said, her nose scrunching. But she didn't shift away or tell him to stop, so I didn't interfere.

"Am I?" he responded innocently.

"Yes," she said, an edge of laughter in her voice.

"Any complaints?" Ben asked, cracking his eyes open.

"No," she said, blushing beautifully.

"Will you eat a sandwich, precious?" Ben asked, giving her breast a squeeze.

She hesitated for a moment and I held my breath. She'd barely eaten dinner and hadn't had anything today.

"Actually, is there any chance I could have some mac and cheese? Like just from the box is fine," she added hurriedly.

"My beautiful, precious, sunshine omega darling, I would love to make you mac and cheese," Ben said, leaping up from the couch. "And it's not going to be from a fucking box," he threw over his shoulder before skipping to the kitchen.

I snorted at Ben's antics, and Josie giggled, her body soft and relaxed against mine. Damn, if I didn't grow hard at the sound of her laugh.

"Thank you," I said, caressing her face.

"For what?" she asked.

"For giving him something to do. For making him so happy." I couldn't resist brushing a kiss against her forehead. I needed to keep touching her, to feel that she was *here* and safe.

She snuggled against me, snaking one hand under my shirt and stroking my bare skin. I groaned, shifting my hand to her ass and cupping it. I wasn't going to start anything sexual, especially after last night, but I couldn't help if everything Josie did oozed sex.

Josie made a contented noise, continuing to trace one hand across my skin and keeping her other on Theo. I could feel through the bond that Theo was awake, but he was pretending to sleep. He didn't "wake up" until lunch was served. He sat next to Josie, always touching her in some way but barely speaking a word. Josie kept casting him worried looks and I wanted to reassure her, but I didn't know what to say. Theo's anxiety could suck him down a deep hole, and it was almost impossible to drag him back out.

We all cuddled back on the sectional after lunch, and Josie turned on some British TV show I'd never heard of. I grabbed my knitting and went to sit next to her when she nudged me.

"Will you sit in front of me?" she asked. "I want to play with your hair."

My insides danced with joy. This was everything I wanted. I kept my cool, simply sliding to the floor with my knitting, but I knew my scent was giving away my excitement. She sat with her legs on either side of my shoulders and started working her fingers through my hair.

Fuck. Me.

It was like her fingers were stroking up and down my cock. The pleasure was so good, her touch so tender, it almost brought tears to my eyes. After a while, I gave up the pretense of knitting, sinking more deeply into my spot on the floor and grasping her calves, which were still slung over my shoulders. Josie moved down to my neck, teasing out all the tension.

I groaned. "Feels so good, sweetheart."

"Can I give you a braid?" she asked.

"You can do whatever the fuck you want."

I felt the gentle tugs on my hair as she braided it and then used the hair tie on her wrist to secure the end.

"All set." She leaned over, wrapping her arms around my chest and kissing me on the cheek.

"Thanks, baby girl," I said, caressing her arms.

"Sounds like you got a text, precious," Ben said, reaching over to snag Josie's phone from the side table.

I didn't want to let her untangle herself from me, but I reluctantly let go of her arms as she took the phone from Ben. I tensed. If it was anyone from her fucking family...

"Oh my gosh," Josie exclaimed. "Sam and Gerald have a last-minute work assignment in the city tomorrow."

Josie's eyes were bright and she smiled widely. The relief it brought me to see her smile was instantaneous, my chest loosening even further as her scent sweetened to its usual cupcake vanilla.

"They're asking if they can stay here. Is that okay?" she asked, looking between the three of us hopefully.

A zing of uncertainty and possessiveness rocked through the bond. I couldn't refuse Josie anything that made her this happy, but the thought of having other alphas in the house right now set me on edge. Alphas had hurt our omega, and we needed to protect her.

I shifted to face the couch, still keeping my hands on Josie's calves. I met Ben's gaze and he nodded, signaling his agreement. Theo would be the greater challenge.

"Are we sure it's safe to have them here?" Theo asked, speaking for the first time in hours.

The fact that he hadn't immediately said no, that *I* hadn't immediately refused, proved how far gone we were for our mate.

Josie's smile fell slightly, and I felt Theo's regret through the bond.

"Why wouldn't it be?" she asked in a small voice.

"It might look suspicious for us to host two alphas from Sol," Theo mumbled, running his hand through Josie's hair in a silent apology.

"But Sam's my childhood friend. I don't think that's weird." Josie's lower lip trembled and she looked away.

"Sweetheart, don't cry. We'll figure this out," I said, giving her leg a squeeze.

"Am I putting you in danger?" she asked, her voice hitching on a silent sob.

"What?" Theo asked. "Of course not. Why would you say that?"

"Glen hates me," she whimpered, tears rolling down her face in earnest. "Having me as part of your pack puts a target on your back."

"You're not just *part of our pack*," I growled. "You're our mate, our omega. If anyone has a problem with that, they can go fuck themselves. You're ours, understand? And if you want to see your friend, we'll make it happen."

"Are you sure?" she asked, looking worriedly at Theo.

He took a deep breath before forcing a smile. "Yes, angel. Why don't you let them know?"

She hesitated for a moment before picking up her phone and sending a text.

"Thank you so much," she said smiling, but she was still a bit subdued. I wanted her bouncing excitement back.

"When will they get here?" I asked.

"Tomorrow afternoon, and then they have to leave the following morning," she responded. Then she said almost shyly, "I'm excited for you to meet them. I haven't even gotten to meet Gerald in person."

"We'll have a great time," Ben said, wrapping his arm around her. "I'm excited to meet them."

This time Josie's smile seemed more genuine.

"Okay, I'm going to go get dressed," she said, kissing each of us before heading up the stairs. We all watched her walk away.

"Why are we letting them come?" Theo asked, keeping his voice low as he turned towards us.

"Why wouldn't we?" Ben asked. "He's Josie's friend."

"And he protected her," I added, clenching my fists. I wished I could have been the one to protect her, to save her from Glen fucking Jacoby.

Theo looked away, running his hand over his face.

"Theo," Ben said, worry in his voice. He moved to the other side of the couch, pulling Theo in for a hug. "It's going to be okay."

Theo returned the hug briefly before pushing himself off the couch.

"I'll go see what we need for the guest room," he said, stalking out of the den.

"I think he just needs time," I said to Ben, who was biting his lip and staring after Theo.

"Yeah," Ben said with a sigh. He turned back towards me. "Nice hair, by the way," he teased, his lips quirking into a wide smile.

I pulled out my phone to look at myself in the camera. I huffed out a laugh. Josie had done a French braid down the top of my scalp and tied it off at the back of my head. I would have gotten beaten up for wearing my hair like this growing up. I found myself not caring. My omega, my mate, had done this for me. I ran my fingers down the neat braid, the look growing on me. And now her scent was woven into my hair, into my very soul.

Chapter Fifty-Four

Cam

A massive alpha, almost as broad as me, stepped out of the car with a scowl. Josie let out a happy squeal and threw open the front door to run out and meet him. Sam Larsson was a tall, Black alpha with a short afro and mistrusting eyes. His face broke into a massive grin as Josie threw herself at him, and he spun her around with a laugh before setting her back down. His eyes locked with mine over Josie's head, the scowl returning. I instinctually flexed my arms and then felt ridiculous. This was Josie's friend. We owed him a shit-ton for protecting her.

"So... Josie didn't mention her best friend looks like a fucking military leader and is built like a tank," Theo muttered.

The passenger side door opened and another alpha stepped out. Gerald couldn't have been more of a contrast to Sam if he tried. He was a ginger with a slight build, nerdy glasses, and a friendly gaze. He gave the three of us a cheerful wave before pulling Josie into his arms.

"Come on," Ben said, a smile tugging on his lips. "Let's go say hi."

Josie made all the introductions, practically bouncing with happiness. Her eyes kept returning to Sam as if afraid he was going to disappear. The possessive part of me didn't want her to pay attention to anyone else, especially not another alpha, but the joy she exuded helped me settle down. I couldn't stop myself from snagging her hand as we walked back into the house. She grasped it with both of hers and beamed at me.

"Thanks for letting them come stay," she said softly, pressing her body against mine.

I melted, amazed at how easy it was to please our omega. If seeing Sam made her this happy, I could put my possessiveness aside for a day.

Jealousy surged through me as I shifted, trying to get comfortable on the lounge chair that was too small and way too empty of my omega. I looked over again to the couch where Josie was giggling with Gerald at the movie they'd put on. Apparently, this was the second movie in the series we started the other night, not that I was paying attention to anything happening on the screen. Sam was on Gerald's other side, and Theo was pressed up against Josie, his face expressionless.

Theo had continued to spiral since Josie's nightmare. Yesterday, I could sense his anxious chaos through the bond, but now he was shielding his emotions, pulling away from us and barely speaking. He also hadn't left Josie's side. I knew it was hurting her, how far he had retreated within himself. I wanted to help him come out of this mood, but right now, I was just pissed that I wasn't the one sitting next to Josie. I didn't know how it was possible to miss someone who was sitting a few feet away, but the absence of her skin on mine felt like a piercing wound. *Maybe you're not as okay as you're pretending to be.* I scoffed. Of course, I wasn't fucking okay.

Josie had another nightmare last night. It wasn't as intense as the first one, and we helped her come out of it quickly, but it still left me off-kilter. I struggled to reconcile the vibrant, smiling woman in front of me with the one curled up on the floor, fear saturating her scent as tears trickled down her cheeks. I had been so convinced I could protect her from anyone who dared try to cause her harm I'd forgotten one crucial thing: I couldn't protect her from the scars left on her mind any more than I could prevent my own nightmares from visiting me each night. *Not each night,* I reminded myself. *Not since Josie started sleeping next to you.*

Helplessness surged through me, gripping my heart like a vise. As if she could sense the direction of my thoughts, Josie looked over at me.

"You okay?"

I nodded and did my best to smile. She didn't look convinced by my effort. I saw her nose scrunch up and realized she *could* sense my feelings through my scent. Fuck, how could I have forgotten that? And once we were bonded, she would have a direct line to my emotions. The fear of burdening her with my feelings warred with my primal alpha desire to see my bite on her.

"I need more snacks," Sam said, giving Gerald a kiss on the cheek. "You want anything?"

Josie and Gerald both shook their heads.

"You sure? Because I know how you both get about snacks. I'm going to come back and you'll want something."

"Shh, you're talking over the good part," Gerald said, gesturing wildly at Sam.

Sam rolled his eyes, but his lips twitched. As he got up, he shot me a meaningful look. Knowing this might be the only chance to talk with him without Josie, I got up and followed him to the kitchen. Theo and Ben followed, making excuses for why they needed to go to the kitchen.

Sam turned to face me behind the island, expression severe and body defensive.

I cleared my throat. "We wanted to get a chance to talk with you alone. But before that, I wanted to thank you."

A brief look of shock flitted across Sam's features.

"Josie told us two nights ago... about the DA and the device. And how much you helped her. We're forever in your debt for what you did for her," I continued.

"I didn't do it for you," Sam said. "There's never a debt when it comes to her. I would do anything for her, always."

I nodded and crossed my arms. "Still, we are in your debt. Josie sees you as family. And..." Fuck. Why was this so hard? My entire upbringing and my inner alpha fought against me. *You should always treat outside alphas as threats. Never let your guard down.* I forced myself to unclench my fists. "We hope you'll consider us part of your family."

This time, the surprise was clear on Sam's face. He chuckled and rubbed the back of his neck. "Well, fuck, I wasn't expecting that."

"Great, have we got the alpha posturing out of the way?" Ben asked cheerfully. "Because our mate definitely needs more snacks." He pulled out a large serving plate and started putting together a cheese board.

Sam smiled. "It's fun to see them together," he said, nodding to where Josie and Gerald were sitting in the other room.

"We do have some questions for you," I said. Theo was standing next to me, his arms crossed. I tried to sense his feelings through the bond, but he was still shutting me out.

I turned my attention back to Sam. "Our company has a

security contract with Greytex Industries." I watched Sam for a reaction, but his face remained blank.

"Last week, Ben and I were called out to their facility for an additional security evaluation. They were worried about someone being able to hack into their servers."

"Paranoid is more like it," Ben muttered, scooping pimento cheese onto the board. Good, that was Josie's favorite.

"We found medical charts for a pilot program they're running," I said.

Sam's gaze snapped to mine. "What was the name of the pilot program?"

"Project Excer," I said.

"Fuck." Sam's gaze went back out to where Josie was sitting. He lowered his voice. "I'm assuming you know what the project is?"

"We didn't when we read the files, but then after Josie told us..." I said, trailing off.

"Do you have the charts?"

"All copied over," Ben said. "And I covered my tracks," he added when Sam opened his mouth.

"We're meeting with Charlie tomorrow and are giving her the files," I said.

"Who's Charlie?" Sam asked.

"She's a hacker with the Alliance. We work together quite a bit," Ben said.

"I'm assuming you've shown Josie what you found?"

I clenched my jaw, guilt swirling in my stomach. "No."

Sam raised his eyebrows. "Why not?"

"We just realized the other night there was a connection."

Sam looked at the three of us, his expression turning to one of disdain. "You're not planning to give them to her?"

"We're trying to protect her," Theo snarled, finally breaking his silence.

The temperature in the room dropped. Fuck, I'd underestimated what Theo was feeling right now.

"You think I'm not looking out for her?" Sam asked, his voice low. He took a few steps towards Theo.

"We don't know you," Theo hissed out.

I grasped Theo's shoulder. "Tone it down." Ben was looking between Theo and Sam, wide-eyed.

"I guess we're not done with the alpha posturing," he muttered, pulling crackers out of the pantry.

"Can you tell us about the device?" I asked. "Josie said you were the one who removed it."

Sam crossed his arms, leaning back on the counter in what some might have interpreted as a relaxed stance, but I knew he was on the defensive.

"Yeah, I removed it," he said. "What do you want to know?"

"How did you get it out?" Ben asked.

The question broke Sam's stoic expression and he shuddered. "It was the night before I moved to Sol. I'd just moved her into my apartment, and I forced her to tell me everything that happened. She told me the device was still in her and she needed it out. I told her we would find a doctor to do it or at least find a way to give her some fucking anesthesia. But she kept crying and screaming that I had to do it now. She said it had to hurt, that the pain was the only way she could be sure it was really out. I didn't know what to do."

My knuckles were white from squeezing the countertop. The haunted look in Sam's eyes was the only reason I didn't punch him. He had cut her open, dug out that device with nothing to block the pain. Flashes of Ben and Theo's distress and anger radiated through the bond, but we all kept silent, needing to hear the rest of Sam's story.

"I kept saying no. Finally, she got a knife and said she would do it if I didn't." Sam took a shaky breath, running his hand over his face. "The device was only about a centimeter wide, but I had to cut quite a bit to have room to get it out. As I stitched her up, she just held the device, staring at it without blinking. It was like she needed to memorize the feeling of it being out of her."

"What did you do with it?" Ben asked. I could tell his mind was spinning with the need to analyze the implant.

"I gave it to my Alliance contact. Amirah told me the other day that analyzing it helped their team develop the new alpha tabs."

"Does Josie know that?" Ben asked.

Sam shook his head. "I haven't had time to tell her, but I was planning to while I was here. It'll make her feel good to know. Just like you need to let her read those files. That fucker, Glen Jacoby, and those doctors did shit to her body without permission. You can't give those files to the Alliance without letting her see them first. She's already been a huge asset to the Alliance without knowing it, and she could do more to take down the government if she wanted."

"She went through all of that, and you want to put her in harm's way to work for the Alliance," Theo growled, his rage dangerously close to the surface. Everyone assumed I was the most aggressive of the three. But I had seen Theo fight when we were younger. He could be a scary fucker when he wanted to be.

Anger flashed in Sam's eyes. "It's because she went through all that she needs to do it. They made her feel powerless, helpless, like her life wasn't worth shit. Fighting back, taking them down, will remind her she's powerful as fuck. You didn't know her before the DA. I've never known someone as vibrant as Josie. She took risks all the time, fighting back in all these small ways. She forced me to teach her to drive, wore all these outfits that pissed her mom off, and argued with her pack fathers even though she knew they would punish her for it. She was so fucking fearless. Honestly, it scared the shit out of me. But nothing has ever scared me as much as seeing her so broken after what they did to her."

My inner alpha didn't want to hear what Sam was saying. He wanted to keep our mate protected and locked away. But part of me recognized the truth in his words. Joining the Alliance and trying to take down the Designation Government had given me a purpose after Ellie's murder. Were we depriving Josie of the same by sheltering her?

"This is as close as I've seen her to the Josie I knew growing up," Sam added begrudgingly. "You three are good for her, but only if you support her in reclaiming these parts of herself. If you hold her back, you're doing her a disservice to satisfy your own selfishness."

Theo growled at Sam, the tension escalating in the room. I caught a faint whiff of burnt vanilla. Someone was eavesdropping. I stepped away from the argument, and sure enough, my little omega was pressed against the wall just around the corner. Her eyes widened when she saw me, and then they narrowed and she set her jaw.

"What are the files you're hiding from me?"

I closed my eyes for a moment, gathering myself.

"Ben and I found some files from that job we went to. We didn't know what they were when we first saw them. But we think it's your medical chart from when they implanted the device."

"You weren't going to tell me?" she asked, her voice high-pitched and betrayal clear on her face.

"Fuck. We would have, eventually. I wouldn't have been able to keep it from you. But I wanted to protect you. Didn't want you to be in any more pain."

"That's not your decision to make," Josie said fiercely.

I would have been tempted to smile if this wasn't such a serious conversation. Seeing the fire behind her eyes, even when directed at me, filled me with joy and hope. Hope that she was healing. She was so fucking strong.

"I know. It was wrong," I said.

"You promise you would have shown me?"

"Yes. I'm sorry we didn't tell you yesterday."

She gazed into my eyes for a long moment, and it was as if time stood still.

"Okay," she said slowly. "But no more hiding things from me."

I nodded my agreement and opened my arms to her. She threw herself into them, and I easily picked her up, her arms and legs wrapping around me. Relief flooded me at her forgiveness.

Josie snuggled into my chest, pressing her face into my neck.

"Did having my device really help the Alliance?"

"Sounds like it, sweetheart," I said, my heart clenching with the vulnerability I heard in her voice.

"Maybe that makes it worth it," she whispered.

I growled, unable to stop myself. "Nothing is fucking worth what you went through. Nothing." I balanced her weight on one arm so I could cup her face. "But it made a difference."

Josie's eyes shone with unshed tears, and her bottom lip trembled.

"Oh, baby girl," I sighed into her hair as she burst into tears.

"I just... feel relieved it wasn't all for nothing," she shuddered.

"I know, sweetheart."

I crushed her to me, holding her through her waves of grief. I felt Theo and Ben's presence as we all gathered into one big group hug. After what felt like way too short a time, Josie lifted her head from my chest.

"Did Amirah really say that?" she asked Sam, who I realized was standing behind me.

"Yeah, she did. Some Alliance scientists used the technology in your device to make the new alpha tabs. And those tabs will help us take down this fucking government."

Josie shivered. "Good," she said, fierceness lighting up her eyes.

I shifted so I could see Sam. His hard gaze met mine and I saw the truth there. Josie needed to be a part of this fight, and it was our job to support her, not shield her.

Chapter Fifty-Five

Theo

I pressed myself to Josie's side, holding myself back from ripping her out of Cam's arms. Ever since her nightmare, I'd been excessively possessive. I'd slept curled around her last night and had been unwilling to have her out of my sight all day. I knew Sam was Josie's friend and had helped her. I knew Gerald wasn't a threat. But my inner alpha wanted my omega locked away, safe.

"Do you want to read your chart?" Cam asked Josie.

Fuck.

I didn't want her to see it. I'd felt sick when Ben and Cam showed it to me, and I hadn't even known it was hers.

She bit her lip. After a few long moments of silence, she said in a small voice, "I'm not sure if I'm ready yet."

Relief was evident through the bond.

"You know what we need?" Sam said with a clap. "We need to do something fun. Josie, have you shown these guys your driving skills?"

Josie squealed in excitement and pushed herself out of Cam's grasp.

"Oh my gosh, it's been forever since I drove. Can we go?" She looked at each of us, her face lighting up with hopefulness.

"Yeah!" Ben exclaimed, picking her up and spinning her around.

"What?" Cam growled, glaring at Ben.

Great. Now it was up to Cam and me to be the bad guys.

"Please," Josie pleaded, staring at Cam with wide eyes and a little pout.

Cam's lip twitched almost imperceptibly. "Only if we can find a safe spot for it, where no cops are going to see," he relented.

I shot him a look of betrayal. Now it was just up to me to stop this plan. Why did no one seem to understand that our mate needed to be kept safe?

Suddenly, she was in front of me. I steeled myself against her persuasive charms.

"Are you okay, Theo?" she asked gently, taking me off guard. I looked down to meet her gaze and saw her eyes were filled with concern... for me?

"It's illegal for you to drive. Too dangerous," I said, avoiding eye contact. If I looked into her bright green eyes, I would be hypnotized, convinced to do whatever possible to make her happy.

"Can we talk privately for a sec?" she asked softly, pulling me by the hand before I responded.

The door to the formal dining room, which we rarely used, closed behind us. I fought to keep myself under control, to shield her from the fear and rage running through me. I didn't realize she had pushed me into one of the dining room chairs until I felt the leather seat underneath me.

"Theo," she murmured, cupping my face. "Talk to me."

"About what?" I asked, trying to sound as nonchalant as usual.

"You're upset," she said softly. "I know I upset you."

"What? No, you didn't."

To my horror, Josie's eyes grew glassy with tears. "I know I did. You've been quiet ever since the other night. You won't look at me. You won't talk to me."

Fuck. I had been so absorbed in my dark, swirling abyss of emotions. I hadn't been caring properly for my mate.

"Angel, I'm not upset with you. I could never be upset with you."

Josie shook her head, not believing me.

"I shouldn't have told you what happened," she said, her voice tight. "You see me differently now."

"No," I growled fiercely, lifting her chin to ensure her eyes were on me. "I don't see you differently, except I know even more deeply what a survivor you are. I just... fuck, you don't need to hear about my problems."

"But I do, Theo. I want to know what you're feeling. Please don't shut me out. I love you." Several tears spilled over, trailing down her soft, round cheeks. I ran my thumb across them, soothing the tears away.

Shit, I needed to be honest.

"I can't handle it when I feel out of control," I confessed. "I know logically that I can't control everything, but it doesn't stop the anxiety from overtaking me. It started when my family moved to North Woods. It was like my whole life was stolen from me. The freedoms I'd enjoyed in London, that my sisters had enjoyed, everything was taken away. It felt like my parents had been abducted by fucking aliens, and not the nice ones in the books you read about."

Josie blushed and I couldn't resist pulling her in for a soft kiss.

"You still need to read them," she mumbled.

A smile tugged at the corner of my lips. This girl. I couldn't believe how happy she made me.

"I will, promise. Things got better once Cam, Ben, and I became pack, but I still get anxiety attacks and shut down when I can't control what's happening around me. Having you in our lives makes me the fucking happiest I've ever been, but it also scares the shit out of me. Hearing how you've already been hurt, been *tortured*, I just... I don't know what to do with that. I'm angry at myself for not protecting you. I'm fucking terrified I won't be able to keep you safe going forward. I don't know if you understand how much I love you, how it would kill me if anything ever happened to you."

Josie crushed her body to mine and purred the softest omega purr. A lump formed in my throat. I wrapped my arms around her waist and reveled in her softness and the vibration of her purr, finally easing the weight of anxiety I'd been carrying.

"I love that you want to protect me," Josie said. "I've never had a lot of people who cared about me and wanted me safe. And now I have you three, and I'm so grateful. But I can't just hide away for the rest of my life."

"Don't see why not," I grumbled, threading my fingers through her wavy hair.

"Now you sound like Cam," she said, a smile on her lips.

"Yeah, well, the bastard has a point every once in a while."

I traced my fingers down her jaw and pulled her in for a kiss. I needed to taste her, feel her, and reassure myself she was okay. She relaxed into my touch, nipping at my lip and sucking lightly on my tongue. I cupped her ass tightly, causing her to gasp into the kiss. I thrust my hard cock against her core, cursing the clothing getting in my way. All I wanted was her.

"Need you," I gasped as I stood up, keeping her pressed against me. Josie's scent was rich and sweet with arousal.

"Yes," she moaned.

Her gasps turned into little whimpers as she unzipped my pants and pulled out my cock. I almost came as she ran her hands down my hard length. I pushed her hand away before pulling down her leggings. I growled when I found she was wearing underwear.

"I thought I told you no underwear at home," I murmured into her ear, walking her back until we were against a wall. "That was very naughty."

I ripped the lace off her, putting the scraps in my pocket. Josie's eyes were glazed over with lust, her breaths coming quicker. I ran my finger through her slit. She was dripping.

"You think Cam's the only one who can spank your ass?" I kept my words soft, aware of how close we were to the others, unsure how much Josie was comfortable with them overhearing. I couldn't hold back from fucking her, though. I was going to make my omega scream.

She whimpered as she arched her back, trying to create friction against my hand.

"It would be no hardship to redden this amazing ass. Then I would take you from behind, spanking you as I thrust into that tight pussy of yours. Bringing you so close to coming over and over again and then leaving you dripping and wanting."

"No, you can't do that," Josie whined, the sound pulling at my alpha instincts. Fuck, she had me wrapped around her finger.

"Well then, angel. You best follow the rules."

I thrust two fingers into her warm pussy, grinding the palm of my hand against her clit.

"You better be a good girl and stay quiet unless you want them all to know what we're doing," I whispered. Her hands gripped my arms tightly.

"Theo," she whined. "I need you. Please."

My cock jerked, a spot of pre-cum dripping on my shirt.

I groaned. "There's nothing sweeter than hearing you beg for me."

I lifted her, my hands firmly under her ass, and thrust into her, seating myself fully. Josie's head fell back with a moan of pleasure, her back pressed against the wall with each rough thrust. I was lost in the feel of her hot cunt wrapped around me, the sensation of *her*. She wrapped her hand in my hair and kissed me with a fierceness that shocked me. My balls tightened and I was already close to coming, but fuck if I was going to come without her. I shifted our angle until I was hitting her sensitive omega spot, grinding my knot against her clit in the process. Josie's cries got louder and a primal satisfaction washed through me that everyone knew I was giving my mate pleasure.

She came with a little squeak that was adorable as fuck. I thrust a few more times, resisting the urge to press my inflated knot inside her before coming with a shout. We held each other tightly, her arms and legs wrapped around me, as we caught our breath.

"You make me feel so good, Theo. And so safe. You have to trust me to make my own decisions, too. And take some risks."

I nodded. "I know, love. I'll try."

"Thank you," she said sweetly. "Now we've got to get ready to go."

My orgasm-induced brain fog made me slow on the uptake as Josie wriggled out of my grasp.

"Go where?"

"For a drive," she said as she pulled on her leggings—sans underwear—and sauntered out of the room.

A bark of laughter burst out of me as I had the distinct feeling that my little omega had played me.

Chapter Fifty-Six

Theo

It was a risk to let Josie drive, and even my post-orgasmic bliss couldn't entirely fend off my anxiety as I walked towards the garage. *The likelihood of us getting pulled over in the mountains is essentially non-existent. This will make Josie happy. I want my mate to be happy, so she'll let me fuck her against the wall again.*

Sam jogged over to me as I unlocked the car.

"How much do you care about your car?" he asked in a low voice.

I raised my eyebrows. A massive grin spread across his face as he glanced over his shoulder to where Josie and Gerald were laughing.

"Because Josie is a terrible driver."

"Er..." I said, my heart clenching. "How bad are we talking here?"

"Oh, truly horrendous," Sam responded cheerfully. "I'm not saying omegas shouldn't be allowed to drive, but Josie definitely shouldn't be able to."

"But you're the one who taught her!" I sputtered. "And suggested this!"

Sam's smile broadened. "I know, but... well, you'll see. She's quite confident in her skills. I'm just saying, if you have a least favorite car, I would go with that one." He winked at me before jogging back over to the group. He kissed Gerald on the cheek and laughed at something Josie said.

"It's just a car," I muttered to myself, eyeing the flawless black and chrome finish on my Range Rover. Beyond the safety of my car, Sam's comments made me worried about Josie's safety. He must be exaggerating—I couldn't imagine my sweet, reserved omega being an unsafe driver.

I pulled out of the garage so everyone could get in more easily.

"Wait, there's not enough room for all of us," Josie said, her lip jutting out in a pout.

"I need to stay behind and get some work done," Gerald said, wrapping his arm around Josie's shoulders. She was so much more comfortable with physical touch now, something that filled me with warmth and satisfaction. Ben and Cam both looked at her with tenderness.

"Drive carefully, please," Gerald said with a wink.

"I'm a great driver," Josie responded, flouncing her hair.

"Uh huh," Gerald said, "I've heard the stories."

Josie pushed his arm off her playfully. "Sam is a very unreliable source," she said as she strode towards the car.

I opened the passenger's side door for her.

"Should I be concerned?" I asked, raising my eyebrows.

Josie rolled her eyes. "Sam likes to exaggerate. I'm a great driver."

She leaned in for a kiss, and my anxieties melted as her soft curves pressed against mine. I reluctantly pulled away and lifted her into the car. Everyone else piled in and we got on the road. I would drive until we were in a secluded spot in the mountains where our mate could drive without the fear of being caught.

"We are going to die," Cam muttered from the backseat.

I would have teased him for his reaction—this was an alpha who had undertaken dangerous missions and seen death and mayhem in his years of military service—but I was too busy gripping my seat, hanging on for dear life as every muscle in my body vibrated with tension.

"Wow, look how pretty the sunset is," Josie exclaimed as we flew over the crest of a hill, revealing the picturesque mountain view at the exact moment our stomachs bottomed out. The car swerved as Josie turned her head to take in the pink and orange sky.

I leaned over to grab the steering wheel and straighten us out so we didn't go *careening off a fucking cliff.*

"Angel, why don't we switch off now? That way, you can take in the views more easily," I suggested in a strained voice.

"Nice try," Sam coughed from the backseat.

I glared back at him. He had a shit-eating grin on his face. Why the fuck hadn't he taught her how to drive more safely? *Yeah, like you're saying anything to correct her.* I rolled my eyes at myself. While I was reasonably confident we would all die in a fiery crash after rolling off a cliff, I didn't want to tamp down Josie's joy. She was beaming, her bright cupcake scent saturating the car.

"I don't think I've ever been this turned on while fearing for my life," Ben muttered, shifting in his seat. His brow furrowed slightly, possibly from the last nausea-inducing switchback, before he added, "Oh my god. Is this my new kink?"

"No, no, it's not," Cam grunted. "No kinks that put our mate at risk." He raised his voice and added, "Baby girl, could we maybe slow down just a touch?"

I smirked at Cam's gentle tone, so in contrast with the commands he used to bark out as a military officer.

"But it's so much more fun to go fast," Josie said, bouncing up and down in her seat.

"Josie-girl, you're scaring the fuck out of your alphas," Sam called out.

"What?" Josie asked, her face falling.

The three of us all turned towards Sam with furious expressions. *If our mate wanted to kill us all in a car crash, she could do that, damn it, and no one was going to make her feel bad about it.*

Sam chuckled at our expressions, completely unphased.

Josie turned to look at us, causing the car to swerve dangerously close to the edge of the mountain. I let out a strangled noise as I grabbed the wheel again.

"You're doing a great job, love. These roads can just be treacherous," I said, trying to keep my voice calm. Josie's face brightened a bit.

"That's true. I could see it being hard for some people to drive on these roads, especially if they're scared of heights," she responded.

We flew over the next hill with so much speed we were practically airborne for a moment. Cam swore loudly.

"Oh, Cam, are you afraid of heights?" Josie asked sweetly, clearly concerned.

"Newly developed fear," he grunted.

"Why don't you take this right turn here so we can trade-off? We'll want to get back before it gets too late," I said.

"Yes, that's a great idea, Theo," Ben said loudly. "I'm sure everyone will be ready to eat dinner soon."

"Oh, okay," Josie said, slight disappointment coloring her voice.

I sighed. *Maybe we should let her drive for a few more minutes?*

She took the right turn I had pointed out so aggressively that the back wheels slid out from under us, kicking up a cloud of dust. She pulled over onto the side of the road with a stop so abrupt we were all thrown against our seat belts. *Then again, maybe not.*

"That was so much fun," Josie squealed. "I was worried I would be a little rusty since it's been so long, but I've still got it."

"Oh, yes," Sam said dryly. "Your driving skills haven't changed a bit."

"I'll sit in the back so one of you can have more space up front," she offered, hopping out of the car and closing the door behind her.

"I swear to god I'm all for removing the Designation Laws restricting omegas except for this one," Cam said.

Sam snorted. "I dare you to say that in front of her."

The three of us were fucking cowards because there was no way we would tell Josie she was the worst driver I had ever seen. I wouldn't trust her to drive a car in a video game.

Josie opened the back door. "Who's moving up front?"

"I will," Sam said, getting out of the car and giving Josie a hug. "Glad we're all still alive after that," he said with a wink.

Josie scowled at him before hopping up into the backseat.

"I'll sit in the middle," she said, crawling over Ben, who squeezed her ass.

Cam wrapped his arms around her and pulled her in close, breathing in her scent.

"You smell a little stressed," she said, pressing her face into Cam's neck. He just grunted in response.

I slipped into the driver's seat and exhaled. I wasn't sure how we would convince Josie she should never drive again, but we would have to think of something.

"I'm a good driver, right? Sam always used to tell me I was awful and that there was a reason omegas were banned from driving. Isn't that terrible?"

"Yes, terrible thing to say, Sam," Ben choked out, covering his face so Josie couldn't see his smile.

"You think I'm a good driver, right Theo?"

I hesitated, unsure of what to say.

Josie gasped and I saw her face transform into the cutest fucking pout in the rearview mirror.

"You think I'm a bad driver!" she shouted, crossing her arms as she looked at the three of us.

"Your skills might be better suited for a racecar track," Cam said, stroking her hair.

"Or a car chase in a movie," Ben said with a chuckle. "We still love you, even though you did just try to murder us all."

Josie huffed, but I could tell by her scent she wasn't too upset. Sam looked positively gleeful as he turned back to Josie.

"I'm vindicated," he said.

"The only thing this has proven is that alphas are total wimps. I bet Clementine, Westin, and Poppy would appreciate my driving."

"I'm sure they would," Cam said, tilting Josie's face so she was looking at him. "But let's not test out the theory, okay?" He pulled her in for a kiss before she had a chance to protest.

I smiled and pulled back out onto the road and headed home.

Chapter Fifty-Seven

Josie

I tried to shimmy my way out of my pile of alphas without waking them. Ben had both arms wrapped around my waist in a vise grip. I allowed myself a small huff as I continued my extraction effort. I tried rolling my way out of his grasp, only succeeding in somehow being pressed more tightly to his chest. A gentle rumbling met my ears, and I realized the chest below me was shaking.

"I'm sorry to tell you, being a secret spy is not in the cards for you, precious," Ben said in a whisper, his voice trembling with restrained laughter. "That was such a weak escape attempt."

I huffed. I should have known there was a reason his grip had only grown tighter.

"Why are you getting out of bed?" he whispered, his breath running down the shell of my ear and making me shiver with pleasure. "Is something wrong? You need food?"

"Everything's fine," I said, stretching so I could plant a kiss on his lips. "I'm just going to meet Sam."

"Mmm, what will you give me to release you from my clutches?"

I smiled in the dark, nuzzling my face against his neck.

I felt happier and lighter than I could remember between Sam's visit, getting to drive, and forcing the guys to watch my favorite movies. Theo and Cam had finally relaxed this evening; even Ben had been more lighthearted than usual.

I decided I wanted to be playful.

"I'll give you a blow job tomorrow."

"Fuck. Fuck!" Ben hissed out, his hips involuntarily thrusting against my core. A shock of pleasure radiated through me. I smiled into Ben's chest, loving that I made him lose control enough to swear.

"So, I take it we have a deal?"

"Only if I get to eat you out. It's been way too long since I got to lick your delicious, plump pussy."

A burst of slick wet my underwear and I perfumed. I glanced over to where the sliver of moonlight through the curtains illuminated Cam and Theo's sleeping forms.

"You drive a hard bargain," I said dryly. "But you've got a deal. Now let me up."

I wriggled out of Ben's grasp and headed towards the balcony. I'd managed to carefully open the balcony door when hands landed on my hips.

"Where do you think you're going?" Ben asked, his whisper sending shivers down my spine and causing me to arch my hips against him.

"I'm meeting Sam outside," I said, forcing myself to pull away from Ben and step out onto the balcony. He followed me out, shutting the door behind him.

He raised his brows at me.

"Sam and I have late-night talks on the roof. It's our thing.

Don't worry about it. Just go back to bed." I made a shooing motion with my hands.

Ben stood back, arms crossed, looking between me and the roofline.

"What's the plan?"

I huffed. "I said don't worry about it."

I dragged the balcony table closer to the roof overhang. I had checked it out earlier and was pretty confident standing on the table would give me enough leverage to pull myself over the roof's edge. While I was not generally physically agile, I'd had enough roof-climbing experience in my childhood that I felt like it was in my wheelhouse.

The moment I got up on the table, Ben's hands returned to my hips. I turned to look down at him from my elevated perch.

"You can't possibly think I'm going to let you climb onto the roof, precious," he said, humor in his voice.

I let out an exasperated breath. "You have to let me. Remember what I promised you." I ran my hand through his hair and he groaned, wrapping his arms around me and pressing his face into my stomach.

"That was for letting you get out of bed. Now you want to get on the roof. I should at least get to plug your ass as a reward for letting you do this. That is, if I survive. Because if Cam wakes up and you're on the roof, he's going to murder me."

A thrill ran through me at the thought of Ben plugging me, of him touching me *there.*

"Okay, deal. If we both survive the night, you can do that."

"What?" Ben sputtered out, his shock making him forget to keep his voice low.

I gestured wildly and covered his mouth. He shot me an apologetic look and mimed zipping his lips.

"While I'm loving hearing this touching conversation about how you're going to defile my best friend, let's get this show on the road," Sam's voice hissed out from above, causing me to let out a small shriek and almost fall off the table. Ben's arms tightened around me, keeping me steady.

"What the hell, Sam," I whisper-shouted.

I could see the outline of his face pop out from the roof overhang, his bright eyes and smile clear.

"I could say the same thing," he whispered back. "First, I have to hear you fuck the grumpy one in the dining room, and now this?"

"Wait, Theo's the grumpy one?" Ben asked, glee in his voice. "I have to tell Cam he's been dethroned as pack grump."

I couldn't resist smiling.

"Help me up," I said to Sam, lifting my arms above my head. He pulled me up with ease, although I was sure I looked a bit like a beached whale with all my flailing.

"Just as graceful as always," Sam said. I elbowed him in the side as hard as I could, causing him to let out a quiet grunt.

Ben popped his head over the edge of the roof.

"You good, precious?"

I shimmied on my stomach over to the edge and gave him a kiss. "All good."

"Please be careful coming down. My ass is on the line here. Or should I say, yours is." He winked before getting off the table. My cheeks must have been flaming red with how hot they felt.

Sam groaned as he hefted me further onto the roof. "I'm scarred for life."

"You'll survive," I said. "Remember that time you butt dialed me while you and Gerald were doing that role play..." I squeaked as Sam lunged at me, covering my mouth with his hand.

"I thought we promised *never to speak of it again*," he growled.

"Anything you say, *professor*."

We both burst out laughing, lying back on the roof side by side. I reached out and grabbed his hand, reminded of all the times we had done this growing up.

Sam squeezed my hand. "You seem happy, Josie."

"I think I am."

"Are they treating you right? Because I'll find a way to smuggle you back with us if not."

"They treat me perfectly," I said, smiling.

"I'm still not sure they're good enough for you."

His voice was grumpy, but he had talked and laughed with the guys at dinner. I had been on the verge of happy tears, so grateful to have the people I loved most at the table. Even if I had had to endure lots of jokes about us eating in the room Theo and I had defiled.

"I want you to like them. You're my family, they're my pack. I want us to all be friends together," I said.

"Cam said something similar, actually."

"He did?"

"I thought you would have heard when you were eavesdropping."

There was no condemnation in his voice. We promised as kids not to keep secrets from each other. Besides, we perfected our eavesdropping skills at all the dinner parties we attended.

"I didn't hear all of what you said. And I wasn't eavesdropping. I was going to the kitchen for more snacks, and then I heard you all talking about me."

"I'm sorry, Josie-girl. I wasn't trying to hide anything from you."

"I know."

Because I did. I had been frustrated with the guys for not telling me about the files they found right away, but it had been a hard couple of days. I understood why they held back.

Sam and I lay for a while in companionable silence, the cool air washing over my skin and causing little goosebumps to spread across my arms.

"You really think I should help the Alliance?" I asked, breaking the silence.

"I think you should do whatever you want, Josie. You've earned it. I would never blame you if you wanted to sit out of this fight. But I know you, and I think eventually you might regret not taking an active role. I know you don't think you can be helpful to the Alliance. But you're wrong."

"I don't even know what I would do to help them. I can't hack stuff like Ben or do security like Theo and Cam."

"You're brilliant and brave."

Warmth curled in my stomach at his compliment, quickly followed by doubt. "I'm not brave."

"Fuck yes, you are. I've never met someone braver than you. The life you've lived, Josie? You're brave to keep waking up every day, to keep fighting, to keep living."

"But I'm afraid all the time."

"And you keep doing it, keep moving forward, keep living with the fear. It's the bravest thing you could ever do. The Designation Government is crumbling, Josie. Support is waning. Glen barely shows his face anymore. They're getting desperate and making mistakes. Now that we have the alpha tabs, we have another advantage in this fight. The Alliance is confident we can end them soon."

I wanted to believe what he was saying, but I was scared to get my hopes up. It hit me that I'd resigned myself to living under the Designation Government. My two years at the DA had taken the fight out of me.

"No one will blame you if you don't want to take part. Giving them the device has already given us a leg-up no one expected us to have. You've done enough for the Alliance. The question is, have you done enough for yourself?"

"What do you mean?"

"You've spent the last few years being their victim."

I breathed in sharply, ripping my hand from Sam's. Hurt bloomed in me.

"You think I've just sat around being their victim? Like that was a choice?" I asked, my voice getting louder.

"Fuck. No, that's not what I meant."

Sam moved closer towards me and I scooted away.

"Josie-girl, please listen," Sam said quickly, desperation in his voice. "I don't mean that any of it's your fault. You fought as hard as you could. You fought every day to stay alive. I've never seen you as a victim, have never thought you didn't do enough. What I'm concerned about is that *you* see yourself as a victim and not as a survivor. You see yourself as weak. I just thought that taking a more active role in the Alliance could show you how fucking strong you are. But I'll back off if it's too much. You never have to do anything to prove something to me. I already know how incredible you are. I never need convincing."

I lay back down, breathing hard. Sam tentatively reached out to grasp my hand again, and I let him.

"Sorry," he said softly.

I took a deep breath, forcing my jaw to unclench.

"It's okay. I'm just feeling sensitive about it all. I had a bad nightmare the other night and it just brought it all back."

Sam didn't say anything; he just squeezed my hand.

"I've really missed you," I choked out, tears falling down my face.

"I've missed you, too," Sam said, his voice tight.

He pulled me closer to him and put his arms around me.

"You know I would do anything for you, right?"

"I know. I wouldn't be here without you," I sniffled.

Sam held me for what could have been minutes or hours. I breathed in his floral scent, so steadying after all these years without it.

"So..." he said once we pulled apart, a slyness in his voice. "When are you and those hunks in there going to bond?"

"Hunks?" I asked with a smile. "You've spent this whole time threatening them."

"Yeah, well, had to make sure they were a bit intimidated," he said with a stretch. "But I have eyes."

"They're so hot, right?"

"You're avoiding my question."

I huffed in irritation. "We haven't known each other that long," I hedged. "Is it... weird that they haven't talked to me about it?"

I knew it was probably because they didn't want to pressure me, but I couldn't shake the nagging insecurity that they didn't actually want to bond me.

As if reading the direction of my thoughts, Sam said, "Josie, if you woke them up right now and asked them to bond you, I guarantee they would all bite you on the spot. I might not be convinced I like them yet, but I can say with unquestioning certainty that they're fucking obsessed with you."

I squirmed a little, blushing at the thought of my alphas biting me, marking me as theirs.

"It's a big step," I said. "I just want to make sure I'm ready."

"You will be," he said.

The wind picked up and I shivered.

"We should head back in," Sam said.

I sat up and started scooting to the roof edge.

"I wish you didn't have to go in the morning."

"I know. But hopefully, we can take down these assholes soon and then travel between provinces will be easier."

I smiled at the thought of visiting Sam and Gerald's home.

"Travel will be easier. And driving," I said with a giggle. I knew my driving was reckless, but it was one of the few outlets I had for taking risks.

Sam groaned. "Here's to hoping your alphas can keep you in line."

I snorted, jabbing my elbow into his stomach again.

Sam lowered me down to the patio table.

"See you in the morning," I whispered before slipping back into the warm bedroom.

I stared at my three alphas in bed, wondering how to get under the covers without waking them. I crawled up from the foot of the bed until I reached a spot between Ben and Cam. As I was trying to shimmy under the covers, Cam's arms encircled me, pressing me to his hard body.

"Someone's been very naughty," he growled in my ear.

"I was just in the bathroom," I whispered, my heart racing.

"Lying to your alpha. That's just going to add to your punishment." His hand squeezed my ass hard in a promise of what was to come. "But for now, you need to rest, little omega."

A wave of exhaustion hit me, and I snuggled closer to his chest. Ben's body pressed behind me.

"Traitor," I hissed at him.

All I got in response was a chuckle as he leaned over and kissed my cheek.

"Go to sleep, precious. Tomorrow's going to be busy for you," Ben said. I shivered in delight, looking forward to everything my alphas had planned.

Chapter Fifty-Eight

Josie

Ben closed the door and I watched Sam and Gerald pull out of the circular driveway, keeping my eye on them until their car was out of sight. A lump formed in my throat at having to say goodbye, but I also felt a hopefulness that I would see them soon... and maybe the world would be a different place then.

I turned away from the window and saw Ben leaning against the wall, his heated gaze on me. I raised my eyebrows and a smile spread across his face. He pushed off the wall and stalked towards me, a gleam in his eye.

"We have some unfinished business to attend to, gorgeous."

A thrill shot through me as I realized Cam and Theo were also closing in on me.

Oh my god, is group sex about to happen?

I tried to keep my expression and tone nonchalant.

"Oh? I'm not sure we do," I said, shifting away from the window.

"I guess we need to jog your memory," Ben said.

Before he moved into arm's reach, I took off running.

Laughter burst through me as my alphas followed after me. I knew they could catch me in a second if they wanted to, but they were toying with me, and I was ready to be their prey.

They kept almost catching me, their hands brushing up against my body, leaving me breathless with arousal. They corralled me from room to room until they closed in, cornering me in the dining room. My skin was heated, my hair damp with sweat, and slick dripped down the inside of my thighs.

Cam lunged for me and I squealed. I turned to run away but ended up caught in Ben's arms.

"It's cute you thought you could get away," Ben said, his voice low and sultry.

He held me tightly from behind, pinning my arms to my sides. I pressed my legs together. At this point, I just needed to throw out my underwear and skirt. I wasn't sure they could ever recover from the amount of slick gushing down my legs.

"Good work catching her," Cam said, his eyes heated and nostrils flaring as he scented my arousal. "We have a naughty omega to punish."

Yes, please. I craved their hands on me, trusted them with whatever they wanted to do, but I wasn't going to let on quite yet.

"Punish?" I asked indignantly, fighting against Ben's hold.

"Mmm, yes," Ben said, nipping at my ear. "I seem to recall a certain bargain you made last night."

My butt tingled and excitement bubbled in my chest.

"And she needs punishment for making us listen while she and Theo fucked right here," Cam said, staring pointedly at the corner where Theo had taken me against the wall.

I bit my lip to suppress a smile and locked eyes with Theo. His cheeks were pink as he winked at me.

Cam closed the distance between us, gripping my neck and kissing me deeply. All I could do was surrender—to Ben's tight hold, to Cam's tongue dancing with mine as he devoured me. Cam's hands moved under my skirt and he groaned.

"Fuck, she's drenched. Fuck!" He gripped my thighs hard, holding my legs apart. "Are you wearing this skirt to tempt us?"

"Is it working?" I responded coyly.

Cam and Ben locked eyes over my shoulder, and then, as if by silent agreement, they moved at once. Ben pushed down my skirt and Cam threw me over his shoulder.

By the time I registered what had happened, Cam was already striding to the stairs.

"Let me down!" I yelled, flailing as I tried to steady myself. Cam simply banded his arms tightly across my legs and smacked my ass before running his nose along my bare thigh.

"You smell so fucking good. I need to taste you, be drenched in you," he groaned.

I grew wetter at his filthy words. *Goodbye underwear, it was nice knowing you.*

I looked down at Cam's butt, covered only by a loose pair of gray sweatpants, and an idea sparked in my head.

I locked eyes with Ben and Theo, who were following behind us. They both grinned and gestured for me to do what I was already thinking. I reached down and squeezed Cam's butt cheeks as hard as I could. *Holy wow, talk about buns of steel.* I squeezed them again. *How do you even get a butt this muscular?*

Theo and Ben choked with laughter, and I realized I had said that part out loud. Cam groaned as he muttered, "Fucking hell."

I couldn't help but burst out in giggles, Ben and Theo joining in.

"That's going to add to your punishment," Cam growled, opening the door to my bedroom.

"Not fair! Ben and Theo told me to do it!" I cried as he flipped me onto the bed.

"Likely story," Ben responded.

I glared at him. He simply tapped me on the nose, unbothered.

"I think Theo should have to stay back and just listen to us pleasure our omega," Cam said to Ben, moving onto the bed next to me.

"That's mean," I said, my lip jutting out in a pout. *To me and Theo.* I was feeling greedy and wanted all their hands on me.

Cam chuckled. "Never said I was nice, baby girl."

"Too bad. You are," I responded. "So sweet, just a gooey cinnamon roll of sweetness."

Cam growled, flipping me onto my stomach and landing a few heavy smacks on my ass.

"Sweet, am I?" he asked.

"The sweetest, like a marshmallow explosion of sweetness. Like cotton candy martini levels of sweetness," I squealed between my peals of laughter as Cam kept spanking my ass. Finally, he stopped, his chest shaking with laughter.

"Fuck, I love you," he said, gripping my hair so he could turn my head and kiss me. "Love your sass, your brattiness. That doesn't mean you're getting out of your punishment."

"Speaking of which," Ben said, "Thanks for getting her into the right position for me."

Ben held a bright pink object in one hand and a bottle of lube in the other. My butt cheeks clenched in anticipation. I wasn't sure I would like anything *up there*, but the idea got me so hot I knew I wanted to try.

I faced the other way and saw Theo sitting in the chair in the corner, his eyes hungry and his hand cupping his cock through his pants.

I turned back to Cam, chewing on my lip. "Are you actually mad at Theo?" I whispered.

Cam's eyes softened. "So fucking sweet." He ran his hand down my hair in a comforting gesture. "Of course not, baby girl. We'll let him play. Just want to torture him first."

"Don't worry, love. It's no hardship to watch," Theo said with a reassuring grin.

My cheeks heated, but I felt more settled. I wanted to make sure everyone was happy and taken care of.

"What do you say if anything gets to be too much?" Cam asked, his tone serious.

"Yellow to slow down, red to stop."

"Good girl. You use them if you need to, for any reason."

"Yes, alpha."

Cam leaned down and kissed me tenderly on my cheek.

"You know what I think?" Ben asked.

"What's that?" Cam responded.

"Our little omega is wearing far too much clothing."

I squeaked as they stripped me, my heart racing at the thought of all three of them seeing me naked at the same time.

"Look at this body—how sexy, how utterly tempting," Cam said, digging his fingers into my hips.

"Perfection," Ben said, his heated gaze raking down my body.

I propped myself up on my elbows and tugged at his shirt. "Too much clothing," I whined.

"It's cute she still thinks she can make demands," Cam said, landing more quick spanks on my butt.

Every stinging slap built my arousal until I was practically writhing on the bed with need.

"Please," I cried out.

"Does our omega need to come?" Ben asked innocently. To my delight, he quickly stripped off all his clothing.

I nodded furiously.

"Too bad we have something else to attend to first," he said, mock sadness in his tone.

I growled, moving my hand towards my clit. My body was on fire and I needed an orgasm *now*.

"None of that," Cam growled, capturing my wrists. "You get pleasure when we say you do and not a moment before."

Cam placed a pillow under my hips, lifting my ass in the air, and moved his hands firmly up and down my back.

Ben parted my butt cheeks and I flinched as he touched my hole. "Just relax, precious. Tell me if anything hurts or doesn't feel good," he murmured.

Cam shifted so he was lying next to me, stroking my hair. I relaxed into the bed as Ben gently rubbed lube at my entrance before slipping in his finger. I clenched automatically and he stopped, but after a few moments, I relaxed and he eased the rest of his finger in.

"Good girl," he murmured.

The sensation was weird but not painful. I pressed back against him, wanting more friction, more *something*.

"Fuck, that's so hot. You're doing so well, baby girl," Cam said, his voice a low growl.

"I'm going to insert the plug now, beautiful. Take a deep breath for me," Ben said.

I felt the pressure of the plug against my hole. It stung a bit as it went in, but once it settled between my cheeks, I moaned in pleasure.

Every nerve ending was on fire.

"You took that so well for me," Ben said. "Feel okay?"

Okay was not how I would have described it, but I nodded.

"Good," he said. "Can't wait to take you there someday soon. Now, you want my fingers or my tongue?"

"What?" I squeaked out, looking over my shoulder to see Ben's carefree smile, his eyebrows raised seductively.

Cam pressed himself against my side. "Are you going to let Ben lick your beautiful little pussy, baby girl? You want him to lick up all that slick you're making for us and play with that cute little clit of yours?"

Oh. My. God. They were going to kill me.

Ben leaned in close to my ear. "Just so you know, I haven't stopped dreaming about the delicious taste of your pussy on my tongue. I've been craving more."

I inhaled their scents, sinking into the feel of them around me, allowing my body to relax fully. My inner omega took over when I nodded my agreement.

"I want your tongue," I said.

"Fuck yes," he responded, wasting no time flipping me onto my back and spreading my legs wide for him.

Cam grasped my wrists again and pinned them above my head. I struggled against his hold, but I loved it. The lack of control, the surrender to what my alphas were doing, reminded me how much I trusted them.

I sighed as Theo lay down beside me, sliding his hand over my waist, gripping tightly before leaning forward to suck on my nipples. Tension I didn't realize I was holding released now that I had all three alphas touching me.

"Did you like watching?" I asked Theo, nuzzling my face against his.

"I like everything to do with you. Every little sound you make, your expression when you come. Everything about you enchants me," he said, kissing tenderly down my cheek.

"Damn, Theo. Maybe I need to read more romance books. That was smooth," Ben said.

Theo flipped him off and rolled his eyes before returning to my nipples.

Ben teased me, his stubble rubbing against my skin as he kissed, licked, and bit my thighs until I was begging him to lick my clit. He finally gave me what I asked for, licking firmly up my slit and circling my clit with his tongue. His grip on my thighs was bruising as he devoured me. Cam captured my cries with his lips, licking into my mouth with consuming kisses. As Ben spurred me higher, I clenched around the plug. The sensation tipped me over the edge, and I cried out as my orgasm washed over me.

"So delicious, so sweet for us," Ben said, his lips glossy with my slick. He sat up, firmly running his hands up my body until he cupped my breasts. "Now, I was promised a blow job, but I want your pussy instead," he said with a wink.

My cheeks flushed and my sex clenched, wanting desperately to be filled. My alphas flipped me over again, pulling me onto my hands and knees. Ben positioned himself behind me and slid in, my copious slick meaning he met no resistance, even with the plug still in. I arched back with a cry, needing more.

"That's right, such a good girl taking my cock," Ben said. "Nothing hotter than seeing your tight little pussy stretch around me."

Ben's dirty talk took my breath away with its filthiness. And then his hand was on my clit, and my noises became increasingly incomprehensible.

Cam gathered up my hair. His firm hold made me whimper, my eyes fluttering. He fed his cock into my mouth, guiding my head in a steady rhythm since I had lost any ability to move, to think. Then Cam pulled out, but before I could complain, Theo's hands were on me as he fed his cock into my mouth. I moaned at the sensation of being controlled by them. All I could do was *feel* as each of them thrust into me in an alternating rhythm.

"That's so hot," Ben groaned. "Look at you taking all of us." He shifted one hand from my hip and rubbed my back reassuringly, as if he knew I needed something to keep me grounded.

Theo shifted me back around Cam, and I moaned around his hard cock as another orgasm washed over me. I wasn't sure how many that was, but I was so sensitized I felt like I would come again if they just breathed on me the right way. I was overwhelmed with pleasure, with the exquisiteness of their love and care. I never wanted this moment to end.

Tears streamed down my face. Cam pulled out of my mouth, causing me to whine with indignation.

"Where you at, baby girl?" he asked, wiping my tears.

"Green," I whispered.

Theo kissed my cheeks. "You are absolute perfection," he said, his voice hoarse.

The next moments passed in a blur. Each of Ben's thrusts pushed me deeper onto Cam and Theo's cocks. My jaw ached and my breaths became labored, but I resisted each time Theo or Cam pulled me off them. I needed their taste in my mouth, was desperate for more. I hollowed out my cheeks, sucking hard, reveling in their low groans and swears, in Cam's stinging hold on my hair and Ben's grip on my hips.

"I'm going to come, baby girl. You going to swallow me down?" Cam asked, a low growl at the edge of his voice.

Instead of answering, I sucked harder, trying to take him deep down my throat. My eyes watered and I gagged but kept going. I was rewarded by Cam cursing as he came, his cum shooting down my throat. It tasted like fucking frosting.

I licked him, cleaning up every last drop of cum. Cam caressed my face, his touch tender.

"Thank you, sweetheart. That was incredible," he said roughly. He ran his hands through my hair as I caught my breath.

I eyed Theo's cock, hungry for more.

"You don't need to if you're feeling tired," Theo said, lifting my chin so I met his gaze.

I scrunched my nose in indignation. My omega was creeping in, taking over, and she didn't like her alpha depriving her of cum. I made a displeased noise before opening my mouth and taking Theo's cock to the back of my throat in one swift movement.

"Holy shit," Theo gasped, wrapping my hair around his hand.

Ben's knot rubbed against my clit and I whined with the intensity of the pleasure.

"Fuck, angel, I'm going to come," Theo groaned.

I wiggled happily as his cum filled my mouth. I swallowed as much as I could, but some dripped out.

"You are fucking incredible," Theo said, cupping my face with both hands and wiping away the cum on my chin. I opened my mouth and sucked it off his thumb. He chuckled.

"Love you, angel," he murmured.

I sighed happily, lowering my arms and resting my cheek against the bed. I felt exhausted and energized at the same time as Ben continued to thrust into me. I cried out as he played with the butt plug, pulling it out slightly and then pressing it back in.

Theo and Cam stayed close, running their hands over me as Ben continued to move. He grasped my hips tightly, shifting our angle so he was hitting my pleasure spots. I never could have imagined having a pack of three alphas who loved me so well, who I trusted enough to let go like this. My heart felt like it was going to burst with love.

"That feels so good, Ben," I moaned, arching back to meet each movement. I felt overstimulated but still craved more.

"God, precious, you feel like heaven. How did we get so

lucky?" I could hear the emotion in his voice, and it made me crave *feeling* his emotions through a bond.

Ben's knot pressed up against my entrance.

"Can I knot you, gorgeous?" Ben asked, his voice strained as he dug his fingers into the curve of my hip.

"Please," I cried out, needing to feel the stretch.

Ben swore as his knot slipped in, feeling even larger than I remembered. I screamed with my orgasm, panting quickly. The pressure of his knot combined with the butt plug was more than anything I'd ever felt. It was tight and squeezing and *wonderful*. Euphoria overtook me like I was floating out of my body.

I was beyond words. I had never felt this good before. It was a free-fall of sensation, my awareness only registering my alphas' gentle touch and deepening scents. I was out of control but didn't panic, knowing my alphas wouldn't leave me. They were here, protecting me, comforting me, loving me.

When I returned to my body, I was in our massive bathtub. Ben's knot had subsided, and I was cradled in his arms. His face was pressed to my hair, which they had gathered up in a bun at the top of my head to keep it from getting wet.

"Back with us, precious?" Ben asked, kissing me on the forehead.

I nodded, running my nose down his throat and breathing in his scent.

"You're a responsive little thing," Cam said, his hand firmly on my neck. "How're you feeling?"

"Really good," I mumbled.

"Just rest, love; we have you," Theo said. I closed my eyes, knowing it was true.

"Are you asleep, angel?" Theo asked once we were back in bed. He skimmed his nose down the back of my neck.

"Still awake," I mumbled, shivering at his touch. We were a tangle of limbs, and I had achieved that level of cozy where I was the perfect temperature and every muscle in my body was perfectly relaxed.

"We had something we wanted to talk to you about," Theo said hesitantly.

Well, there goes my relaxation. I popped my head up in time to see the three of them exchange a nervous look. I bit my lip, scared of what they were about to say. Even now, sandwiched between them after the world's greatest group sexy time, I was still worried they would say they were done with me.

"Okay," I said, trying to keep my voice steady as my heart rate picked up.

Ben caressed the side of my face. "We haven't been together long, but the three of us can't imagine our lives without you."

"We knew the moment we saw you that you belonged with us. We wanted to make sure you knew that whenever you're ready, we want to make it official," Cam said, his arm tight around my waist.

My breath caught, and tears pricked at my eyes.

"You want to bond me?" I asked, sniffling.

"Of course, we do, angel," Theo said with a frown. "Why are you crying?"

"I'm crying because I'm happy," I sobbed.

My alphas wore expressions of bewilderment and relief as they gathered me up in their arms, kissing me and murmuring sweet words.

"I love you all so much. You make me happy," I choked out.

"Does this mean you want to bond us?" Theo asked, vulnerability in his gaze.

"Yes," I said, trying to wipe away my tears. "I just... I'm not sure I'm ready quite yet. Is that okay?"

Part of me wanted to just bond them now. I loved them and trusted them. But bonding was *forever*, and while the past couple of weeks had been better than anything I ever could have imagined, there was a part of me that was afraid it was all too good to be true.

"Of course, love. There's no rush," Cam said with a gentle kiss.

I snuggled into them, running my hands down their bare skin.

"It's like I'm getting everything forbidden to me—love, pleasure, the freedom to choose the life I want. I'm scared it's all going to be taken away," I confessed softly.

All three of them tightened their hold on me, but it was Theo who spoke up.

"You're not alone now, love," he said, gripping the back of my neck and bringing his forehead to mine. "We're going to do whatever we can to make sure you have the life you deserve, filled with happiness and love."

I shuddered, soaking up his words as I leaned into his touch. I wanted his words to be true, but I still carried with me the fear that the government or my fathers would do something to separate us.

Cam reached over, grabbed a tissue box off the nightstand, and started wiping my tears, his expression serious.

"You alright?" I asked, running my thumb over his lips.

"Don't like seeing you cry," he said.

"They're happy tears," I reassured him.

"Still don't like it," he grumbled.

Ben and I made eye contact and had to keep from laughing. Our sensitive alpha.

I pulled Cam in close and kissed him on the cheek.

"You make me happy," I whispered in his ear, planting more kisses up and down his jaw until he broke into a smile.

"We're going to make it special for you," Cam said. "Whenever you're ready."

Theo's hand moved down to cup my ass. I pushed back into his touch. If he kept doing that, I would be ready to go again soon.

"I've already decided where I want my mark. Right here," Ben said, pointing to a spot high up his neck. "That way, everyone will know I belong to you."

I snuggled closer to him, leaning over and sucking on the spot he'd indicated. He groaned, pressing his erection against my leg.

"You're so sweet," I said. "That line was almost enough for me to tell you your scent." I licked a long stripe up his neck.

"You vicious little omega," Ben said with a grin.

"That's my girl," Cam said as Theo laughed.

Chapter Fifty-Nine

Josie

"Let's just get an assortment of desserts for the table," Poppy said, putting down the menu and signaling the waiter.

"Poppy, that's too much food," Westin said with a laugh. I eyed her carefully. She looked pale today and was quieter than usual, but she brushed off my concern when I asked if she was alright.

"Nonsense, we have to sample it all," Poppy said.

A young beta waiter with messy brown hair appeared, his eyes wide as he took us all in.

"Hi, cutie. We would love one of everything, please," Poppy said, giving him a thousand-watt smile. He nodded and fumbled as he gathered up the menus, throwing awed glances at Poppy over his shoulder as he walked away.

"You're shameless," I said, smiling as I took in the baby blue and gold decor of the French bakery Poppy had suggested. The design felt a little stuffy, and the chairs were uncomfortable. If Ben and I opened a place together, I would make sure we had cozy chairs and flowers on every table...

"Now he might throw in some free desserts," she responded, a twinkle in her eye.

"Don't let your alphas catch you flirting," Westin said.

Poppy just grinned. "Maybe I want them to catch me. I love when they get all possessive." She leaned to the right, trying to see out the window. "I bet anything they're standing by the entrance with your alphas, Josie. Such stalkers."

"Probably," I said, a smile tugging at my lips. "Ben was all grumpy when I told him where I was going. He said he didn't want me to eat anyone else's baked goods."

Cam and Theo had lectured me about safety during the drive, while Ben worried I would prefer the café's pastries to his.

"Oh, I bet he doesn't want you tasting anyone else's goods," Poppy said with a sly smile.

Clementine choked on her coffee.

"You're the worst," I said with a laugh.

My smile quickly faded when I saw three alpha police officers emerge from the back of the bakery. I quickly averted my eyes, not wanting to draw their attention, but they were already headed our way. My heart pounded, and my stomach churned with nausea.

"Shit," Westin said when she spotted them.

"Good afternoon," the largest officer said as he came to a stop right next to our table. He stood between Clementine and Poppy's chairs, looming over us. Their uniforms were almost identical to the ones the DA guards wore. I crushed my fingernails into my palms, trying to stay in the present and not let dark memories drag me under.

Poppy cleared her throat and then smiled up at the alpha. "Good afternoon. What can we help you with, officers?"

Her tone was clear and pleasant, and relief washed through me that she was here. I almost jumped out of my skin when I felt Westin's hand brush against mine under the table. Without a word, I took it, clenching her hand tightly.

"I'm Officer Kennedy. This is Officer Lee and Officer Tucker. We're just visiting the neighborhood to ensure everything is in order. We noticed your table and were concerned to see four omegas, alone and unprotected."

Clementine met my gaze. They hadn't noticed she wasn't an omega. I didn't know if that was good or not. Probably a good thing since the Designation Government liked to keep omegas segregated from society.

"Oh, don't worry," Poppy said, a little giggle slipping out. "Our alphas are waiting for us just outside. We needed a little girl time to ourselves. You know how it is."

She batted her eyes in the best fucking acting performance I'd ever seen.

Officer Lee stepped forward. His eyes were focused on Westin, his expression hungry.

Fuck. Westin couldn't help but stand out with her silvery white hair and supermodel looks. I rubbed the back of her hand with my thumb in a way I hoped was soothing.

"So, you're all bonded?" he asked, still staring at her.

Poppy hesitated for a moment. "The two of us have packs," she said, gesturing to me.

"And you?" the officer asked Westin, openly leering.

"I'm ineligible," she said, lifting her chin slightly.

"Doesn't mean you're ineligible for a good time," he said, licking his lips.

Officer Tucker, who had been standing back, cleared his throat. He looked almost embarrassed by the other officer's behavior. "We just need to see your identification."

We all reached in our bags and got our IDs. I clenched my jaw when I realized I hadn't gotten a new one since joining

Pack Ashwood. Of course, I wouldn't be able to update my ID until we were officially bonded.

We handed them over to Officer Kennedy. He held them up, inspecting them one by one before fixing his eyes on me. "Your ID doesn't say you're bonded."

"My alphas are outside. I just haven't updated it yet," I said, hating how timid I sounded.

"That's a citable offense," he said.

"Oh, that's not necessary, right?" Poppy asked.

She had pulled her phone out of her bag with her ID, and I knew she was ready to text her alphas if needed.

Officer Kennedy pursed his lips, turning towards Clementine.

"What's a beta doing with omegas?" he asked.

"I work at the Designation Center," she said, her tone cool and unbothered. "I help facilitate pack interviews for omegas, so that's where I met them."

Officer Kennedy was about to say something when his radio went off, a request for backup coming through the static.

"We need to go," he said, jerking his head at the other two cops. He turned towards me. "Next time, it's a citation. Fix your ID, omega. You would all do your best to remember the dangers of being out without supervision."

And with that threat lingering in the air, they left out the back, Officer Lee giving Westin one more hungry look before turning away.

I let out a shuddering breath. My body trembled and everyone in the café was staring at us.

"For fuck's sake," Poppy said. "They're going to have to get used to omegas existing out in the world soon."

"Poppy," I hissed, terrified someone would overhear her words as support for the Alliance.

"Sorry," she mouthed, glancing around.

I'd been in such a good mood since Sam's visit and so hopeful about life and the world. Now, I felt thrown back into my life before I met my alphas. A life where I was afraid to move around, terrified of being picked up by the police.

"Are you okay?" Westin asked, putting her arm around me.

I glanced up from where my eyes had been fixed on the table.

"Do you want me to get your alphas?" Poppy asked, her voice gentle.

I did want my alphas. I wanted them to cuddle me and tell me everything was okay. But I knew if my guys saw me like this, they would insist on bringing me home, and I didn't want to let the officers ruin this.

"No," I said finally. "We need to see if this place is any good."

Before I could figure out how to lighten the mood, my phone vibrated and I pulled it out of my bag.

CAM

Police officers just left out of the back.
U ok?

JOSIE

They talked with us for a few minutes, but all good now.

"They must have seen the cops leave," Poppy said. "Mine are texting me, too."

"How many seconds until they're in here?" Clementine asked with a small smile.

"Less than thirty sec... oh wait, here they are," Westin said with a chuckle.

Cam stormed into the bakery, a furious expression on his face. He was followed by Maximo, one of Poppy's alphas, who looked equally angry.

Cam came to my side, crouching down so we were closer to eye level. "What happened?" he asked, taking my hands in his.

"They just asked us some questions," I said, my voice barely above a whisper. "But then they were called away."

"How fucking dare they harass you? It's not illegal for you to eat out," Maximo said, jaw clenched as he leaned over Poppy.

Cam's nostrils flared as he took in my scent, and his eyes immediately softened.

"You're scared," he said, cupping my cheek.

I leaned into his touch, letting his scent wash away those of the cops. His thumb ran across my hand and he frowned, looking down at the indentions on my palm.

"Josie," he said disapprovingly.

"I know," I said. "I'm okay now."

"Do you want to go home?" he asked.

I bit my lip. "I'd like to stay."

Cam didn't say anything, and I knew he was stuck between needing to keep me safe and wanting to make me happy.

"Okay. I'm just going to stand right there by the wall. You won't even notice I'm there."

I snorted, laughter bubbling up in my chest. I looked over at my friends, who were grinning.

"I won't even notice you?"

"What?" Cam asked, looking around.

The table next to ours was filled with teenage beta girls who were openly gawking at Cam and Maximo.

"Cam, you're an enormous, hot alpha. I'm pretty sure people will notice if you're standing against the wall, glaring at everyone," I said, smiling. "Why don't you go back with the others? We should be fine now."

"Yes, no boys allowed," Poppy announced, giving Maximo a little shove. He looked about as amused as Cam.

Cam growled and gripped my chin. "You will call immediately if something happens."

"I promise." I ran my hand through his hair, which he'd kept down today, and his face softened again.

He huffed out a quiet sigh. "Fine."

But before he left, he pulled me in for a kiss. I thought it would be a light peck, but he deepened it, gripping my face in his hands. I surrendered to it, forgetting where we were until Poppy cleared her throat.

I broke away from Cam, my cheeks burning.

He smirked. "Now everyone here knows you're mine."

He trailed his hand through my hair before leaving with Maximo.

"Whew," Poppy said, fanning her face.

"I was going to ask how things are going with your alphas, but I think that's all I need to know," Westin said, her eyes dancing with humor.

"Fuck that," Poppy said. "I want to know *everything*." She raised her brows suggestively.

"Everything's going really great," I said primly, taking a sip of my chai latte.

"Come on, Josie," Clementine said. "I'm living vicariously through you. Give us more details than that."

I bit my lip. I had been looking forward to meeting my friends today because I needed their advice.

"Well, yesterday they told me they wanted to bond me," I said slowly, my voice drowned out by excited squeals.

"I'm so happy for you," Clementine said.

"They said they'll wait until I'm ready, but it's what they want." My face heated as flashes of last night flitted through my mind.

"Girl, I see that blush. Now I want to know what you were doing when they asked you," Poppy said.

I shot her a dirty look and she just laughed. Damn her for being so perceptive.

"Just as I thought," she said. "While I always say the more alphas the better, three really is a great number. No one is left out—you have one for every..."

"I swear to god, Poppy, if you finish that sentence, I'm going to dump this water on you," Westin said quickly.

Poppy just smiled and winked. My face was seconds away from going up in flames.

But also... she wasn't wrong.

"Ignore her," Westin said. "I'm so happy for you. You deserve this, Josie."

"Thanks." I bit my lip and fidgeted with the napkin in my lap. "I just... how do I know if I'm ready?"

"Why wouldn't you be ready?" Clementine asked. "You love them, right?"

"Of course," I responded. "But I haven't known them that long and bonding is a forever decision."

My unspoken fears danced through my head: What if they changed their minds? Realized they'd made a mistake? Met a better omega and cast me aside? I felt so secure in our relationship when I was with my alphas, but doubt pricked at me the moment we were apart.

"Josie, those alphas are obsessed with you. That won't change," Clementine said, reaching over to squeeze my hand. "Poppy, how did you decide it was time to bond your alphas?"

Poppy looked thoughtful. "My process was a little different because my alphas courted me for a month while I was at the DA. I felt a connection with them right away because we're mates. But honestly, when they asked me to move in, all I could think about was getting out of the fucking Academy," she said with a grimace.

The briefest bolt of jealousy went through me that she had

only spent two months at the DA, but I quickly shoved it aside. I didn't want anyone to suffer like I had, least of all Poppy, who I loved.

"Once I moved in, we still had a couple weeks until my heat. We ended up bonding during my heat, which was, like, the hottest experience of my life. But yeah, we had known each other longer than you've known your alphas, Josie. You've also gone through a lot more than I have." Poppy's voice was unusually soft and sincere as she reached over and squeezed my other hand. "I'm so confident you'll love being bonded to them, but you get to take all the time you need."

"Thanks," I said, touched by her support.

"I didn't realize your alphas are your mates, Poppy," Clementine said. "I guess it really is more common than the government says." She whispered that last part, glancing around the small café to make sure no one overheard.

"I wish I could feel it," I said, scooting closer to the table and keeping my voice low. "My alphas said they knew right away that I was their mate, but I can't feel it yet."

"Do you think they're lying?" Westin asked, her voice sharp.

"No, I don't," I admitted. "But it would be helpful if I could actually feel it myself. And besides, fated mates just means we're biologically a perfect match, right? It doesn't necessarily mean anything about actual compatibility."

"I'm not sure," Westin said. "I think fated mates go deeper than that. I don't know of any fated mate packs that aren't also emotionally compatible, you know?"

"I agree with that," Poppy added. "What I have with my alphas goes much deeper than physical compatibility."

We all stared at her with amused smiles. Poppy had already told us one graphic sex anecdote before we even sat down at the table, and I was sure she would have told us more if she wasn't trying to ply me for information.

Poppy waved her hand dismissively. "I mean, the sex is really good. But they're my soulmates in every way."

"Okay, think of it this way," Westin said, turning towards me. "Imagine your alphas bonding with another omega..."

I let out a growl before she even finished her sentence. The idea of them bonding with another omega, touching another omega, filled me with unspeakable rage.

"I think we got our answer on that one," she said with a smile. "Now imagine yourself bonding with another pack."

My chest tightened and my stomach churned with disgust at the thought of being with any other alphas.

Westin, Poppy, and Clementine all grinned.

"That doesn't mean I'm ready to bond them," I said, scowling at my friends.

"I didn't realize you were having such big doubts," Poppy said, twirling her hair.

"I don't have doubts about them," I snarled.

"Oh, so you *are* sure of them," Clementine said with a smirk.

I covered my face with my hands. "You all are impossible."

Clementine put her arm around me. "We're just teasing," she said soothingly. "I know it's a lot of change at once. You're doing great."

Just then, the waiter came with a massive tray. He blushed as he arranged the desserts in front of us.

"Is there anything else you need?" he asked Poppy.

"Oh no, cutie, that's all," she said with a wink. The waiter turned tomato red before scurrying back to the kitchen.

"You think he's back there hyperventilating?" Westin asked dryly.

Poppy just tossed her hair as she picked up her fork.

"Enough serious talk. Josie, what I *really* want to know is which one of your alphas has the biggest dick. Because I think it might be Theo. It's always the quiet ones."

I averted my eyes, taking a bite out of a berry tart.

"I knew it!" Poppy squealed.

I cleared my throat. "I can neither confirm nor deny. But... there might be a piercing situation."

"*Ohmygod,*" Poppy gasped. "I can't believe you've been holding out on me. Is it good? Is there a piercing shop near here? Which one of my alphas can I convince to get one?"

Poppy pulled out her phone and started typing away. My face felt hot, and I hoped Theo wouldn't be upset that I'd mentioned his piercing. Suddenly other parts of me felt hot as I thought about how his piercing had felt inside me...

I cleared my throat, needing a distraction before I abandoned the pastries and jumped my alphas.

"Has anything happened between you and Dave?" I asked Clementine, taking a bite of a slice of cheesecake.

"No," Clementine said, biting her lip. "He's flirted with me and looked out for me since I started my job, but he's never made a move. Lately, I've been working from home, and he isn't responding to my texts. The last time I was in the office, he dropped me off at my house after work, and I totally embarrassed myself."

"What happened?" I asked, furrowing my brows.

"I ended up just asking him why we weren't together and if he wanted an omega instead of me. He was kind of evasive, but then he finally said an alpha's health declines if they can't knot their partner, so unless I can practice stretching to take a knot, it would be impossible for us to be together."

Dave had been so kind to me when I was going through the interview process, but now a red-hot rage stirred in my chest. How dare he say that to Clementine?

"That's not true," Westin bit out fiercely.

"She's right," Poppy said, scowling. "That's total propaganda. Alphas enjoy knotting, but it's not a requirement for their health. What bullshit."

"None of my alphas had knotted anyone before me," I said. "And I don't like that he's making it seem like you're not good enough for him."

Clementine sniffled. "But alphas are happier with omegas, right? Betas don't fit into packs."

"Why not? You're so incredible and kind and beautiful. If he can't see that, it's his loss," I said. Now it was my turn to grasp Clementine's hand.

We sat in silence for a few moments, and it struck me how hard life was for women of all designations.

Eventually, Poppy saved us with light-hearted small talk as we tried and ranked all the pastries.

"None of them live up to Ben's baking," I said. "Maybe once things settle down, we could have you all over." My throat tightened and I suddenly felt vulnerable. What if they rejected my invitation? I had so little experience with female friends.

"That's so sweet," Clementine said. "I would love that."

I looked up to see my three friends smiling at me, and the lump in my throat vanished with the realization that maybe we all needed each other.

We finished up our food and Poppy insisted on paying for us. The guys had given me my own credit card tied to their account, but I wasn't sure how I felt about spending their money.

I pulled Clementine aside as we made our way out of the café.

"Hey, I was wondering if you got the go-ahead to do the pack inspection." I was antsy to have it over with.

Clementine looked unsure. "I've been meaning to talk with

you about that. Things have been pretty scary at the DC. They keep changing rules and procedures. We tried to schedule your home visit, but they keep blocking it for some reason. Amirah doesn't want me in the office anymore for my safety, but I'm more worried about *her* safety."

"How worried should I be?" I asked, my chest tightening.

"I don't want you to worry yet, which is why I didn't say anything. I mean, there's a chance they'll just forget about it and approve your pack."

I raised my brows skeptically. That seemed too good to be true for the life I'd lived.

"I mean, slim chance, but it's a possibility," she said. "The government is starting to fall apart. It can't happen soon enough."

The fear I'd often felt that the DC's downfall wouldn't be fast enough for me returned. What if we bonded, and then the government took me away from them? I hadn't heard of them separating a bonded pack, but I wouldn't put it past them.

I took a deep breath. "You'll keep me in the loop?"

Clementine gripped my hand. "We're going to figure this out. It's one tiny hurdle before you're official."

I forced myself to take a deep breath, willing my scent to be relaxed. I didn't want to stress any of my alphas, especially since I didn't know if there was anything to be panicked about.

"I'm sorry I don't have better news for you."

"It's okay. Like you said, just another hurdle."

I forced a smile as I pushed open the front doors.

My heart leapt as I saw my alphas standing next to Poppy's pack. Poppy threw herself at one of her alphas with long hair. He picked her up and his eyes widened as she whispered something in his ear. I turned away to hide my laughter, pretty sure what she had asked him.

"Did everything else go okay?" Cam asked, pulling me into a tight embrace.

"Yeah," I said, giving him a soft kiss.

"Did you have fun?" Theo asked, kissing my cheek.

"It was great," I said, leaning into him.

"How were the desserts?" Ben asked, scowling at the café.

"You know, it was rather disappointing," Clementine said loudly.

"I agree," Westin said, catching on. "Just average."

Poppy joined in. "Josie was telling us how everything you've made is *so* much better, Ben."

Ben puffed out his chest, a huge smile spreading across his face. "Is that right, precious?"

"Of course," I said, giggling as he twirled me around.

"Fuck, I love you," he murmured against my ear. "I'm feeling hungry for that sweet pussy of yours." I shivered in pleasure. His heated gaze met mine as he stopped spinning and I slid slowly down his body, feeling his hardness.

"We'll have to have you all over soon," Ben said, turning to the group.

Poppy's alphas did a bro chin-lift in acknowledgment. I caught Westin's gaze, and we both rolled our eyes. Alpha posturing was so ridiculous.

As I looked at Westin, I realized she looked unsteady. "Westin, can we give you a ride?" I asked.

"Oh no, I'm fine. My aunt's place is just around the corner." She smiled, but it didn't reach her eyes and her scent was stressed.

Part of me wanted to push her to tell me what was going on, but I also knew what it was like to feel vulnerable and need to protect yourself. "If you ever need anything, I'm here for you." I pulled her into a hug, surprised at myself for initiating physical contact. Westin's smile looked genuine when we pulled away.

"Thanks," she said. "See you soon?"

"Absolutely."

My alphas ushered me to the car and I slipped into the back with Ben.

"Do you actually think my desserts are better or were you just saying that?" Ben asked the second the car door was closed.

"Yours are definitely better," I said, snuggling into him.

"Of course they are," he said, kissing me on the forehead as Theo pulled out of the parking spot and headed home.

Chapter Sixty

Ben

I flipped through my recipe list while waiting for Josie to get out of the bath. She kept weaving the idea of me opening up my own bakery into conversation, and now I couldn't stop thinking about it. Her confidence in my abilities bolstered my own, and I felt genuine excitement about the future for the first time in years. I knew I should catch up on my programming work, but more and more, it felt like drudgery.

Suddenly, a jolt of anxiety and anger rang through the bond so strongly I almost doubled over. I took off towards Theo's office. Cam came up the stairs from the gym just as I was rounding the corner, eyes wide as he scanned the hallway for threats. We shook our heads, unsure of what was going on, as we barreled our way into the office.

Theo looked up from his chair as we barged in, his face drawn. Cam closed the door behind us.

"What's going on?" he barked. "Where's Josie?"

"Upstairs in the bath," I responded.

Theo ran his hand through his hair. "That was Amirah on the phone."

A chill ran down my spine.

"Remember Glen's press conference that we caught on TV the other night?" he continued.

"How could we forget," Cam muttered.

"Yeah, well, he was talking about this new Designation Center department called the Center for Pack Cohesion. Basically, they're going to be interfering with packs even more than before."

"They can't take Josie away from us," I blurted out.

"Course they're fucking not," Cam said, his eyes flashing with anger. "What does this mean for us?"

"It means we have to go into the DC tomorrow and do an in-person interview," Theo said with a grimace.

"Why can't Clementine come here for the interview like we originally planned?" I asked, my heart racing.

"It's not procedure anymore," Theo spit out. "Amirah didn't know what the interview would involve but said we need to practice our answers and make sure we say we're doing everything by their instructions. After the interview, they should approve us as a pack, and we'll be done with them."

"Are they going to split us up for the interview?" I asked. My chest felt tight like I could barely get air. Cam reached over and clasped my shoulder, the heavy weight of his hand grounding me.

"No, the protocol is for us to be kept together," Theo said. He took a deep breath before sitting up straighter in his chair. "We need to stay calm when we tell Josie the news to reassure her that nothing bad will happen tomorrow."

"Nothing bad will happen," Cam snarled. "We'll protect her."

"Of course," Theo responded. "But that place holds bad memories for her."

"So, we just pretend we're fine with this?" I asked, a sick

feeling growing in my stomach. The thought of returning to the DC made me anxious enough with their constant surveillance. I couldn't imagine how hard it would be for our mate.

"We don't have to act happy about it," Theo said with a frown. "But we can't fall apart."

Cam grunted. "I agree. We have to be steady for her."

I looked between them. "I guess so." I wasn't sure we would be able to hide our emotions from Josie, anyway. I felt like she understood me better than I did myself.

"Why are they doing this now?" Cam asked, sitting down heavily in the seat across from Theo.

Theo tapped his pen on his desk and looked out the window. "Everything is falling apart for the Designation Government. Protests are increasing and the Alliance is making significant progress against them. They've created this new Pack Cohesion program to regain control."

His voice was calm, almost clinical, but I could feel his riot of emotions under the bond. I shifted my weight, frustrated. It felt like we were back in our teenage years when the two of them thought I couldn't handle their honest thoughts and feelings.

"I think Glen's taking out his fucking anger on Josie," Cam said. "He obviously has it out for her."

Memories of Josie's nightmare haunted me. I would be in the middle of doing something and remember a new detail and have to find her and hug her close. I didn't know how to deal with the fear of being unable to protect her.

"I don't understand how all these legislators still support Glen," I said.

"He must have something on them," Theo responded. "At least that's what Amirah believes, and I agree. Some of those alphas are good guys, or at least I thought they were. And now they're all in bed with Glen."

"Fuck, I don't want to tell her about tomorrow," Cam groaned, gripping the chair's armrest. "She's been so happy."

"We'll tell her as soon as she comes downstairs, yeah?" Theo said.

"Let me shower real quick," Cam said, standing up with a stretch.

"Wait," I blurted out. "Wouldn't it... I don't know. Wouldn't it be safer for us to leave the province?"

Cam's jaw clenched and he ran his hand through his hair. "Not sure we could get out, even if we tried."

Theo tapped his pen more quickly on the desk, the tension in his body telling me he'd already thought about this.

"They've increased the number of guards at the border. They obviously won't approve a visa for Josie to leave, and I don't think there's a safe way to smuggle her out," he said.

Tension hung in the air.

"Well... then wouldn't it be better if we bonded her before tomorrow? That way, they can't take her away from us." The moment the words were out, they felt wrong. I was anxious to be forever tied to my girl, but I didn't want to bond out of fear.

"We can't pressure her," Cam said. "Bonding should be special."

"I agree," Theo said. "We shouldn't rush it just because of the DC. I can't imagine them actually trying to separate us. Alphas would revolt against them if they started taking omegas away from their packs."

"Yeah, you're right. Sorry," I said, rubbing the back of my neck.

"It's going to happen, just at the right time," Cam said confidently, grasping my shoulder before heading out of the room.

———

I kept stealing glances at Josie. She was curled up in the corner of the sectional under a heavy blanket, even though it was an unseasonably warm day outside. She had accepted the news of the DC interview calmly... too calmly. She seemed almost resigned when Theo told her, as if she expected something like this to happen. Anxiety clawed at my insides, and I wanted to scream in frustration. But instead, I sat quietly, following Theo and Cam's lead. They were both laser-focused on prepping for the interview and didn't seem to notice our mate's silent, vacant gaze.

Theo had decided we all needed to review the DC's omega manual. He'd made copies for all of us and occasionally read passages out loud as if he were leading a college study group. Josie hadn't touched her copy. It sat on the side table next to her as she stared out the window.

"We're not supposed to let you have any nesting materials outside your heat? What the fuck," Theo muttered. He read from the manual, "Omegas frequently test their alphas. It is their nature to be manipulative and try to gain control of the pack. Therefore, it is essential to utilize punishments to keep the omega on track. Examples of punishments include sleeping apart from the pack, sleeping on the floor, removal of all blankets and pillows, removal of physical touch and affection, and corporal punishment. These punishments should persist as long as necessary for the omega to learn her lesson and earn back the privileges."

Theo put down the manual, his eyes wide.

"Fucking barbaric," Cam growled. It was a testament to how worried he was about the interview that he wasn't engaging in his favorite pastime—staring at Josie. Instead, he thumbed through the manual, a scowl on his face.

I couldn't stand any distance between Josie and me any

longer, so I moved from my chair to the spot next to her, our bodies pressed together. The blanket shifted and I realized her skin was cold and small trembles racked her body.

"Josie?" She didn't turn to acknowledge me. "Precious, can you hear me?" I gently shook her arm, causing her to jolt out of her haze and turn towards me.

"Sorry, did you say something?" she asked softly. Even though she was looking at me, her eyes had a glazed quality that made me feel like she wasn't really seeing me.

"Where'd you go, beautiful? You were lost in thought there," I said, trying to keep my voice low and soothing.

She shrugged, but her lower lip trembled ever so slightly.

Cam and Theo finally noticed what was happening, their heads snapping up.

"Sweetheart, what's wrong?" Cam asked. "You don't have to worry about tomorrow. Nothing bad is going to happen."

Josie stiffened next to me. "You're probably right," she said. "I just... I already know this stuff. I might go upstairs to rest for a bit."

Theo looked unsure. "Did I upset you by reading it out loud? I'm sorry, love. I shouldn't have done that."

Josie just shrugged again. "It's fine. It's nothing I haven't lived." She stood up, keeping the blanket wrapped around her like a protective cape. "I'm just going to lie down."

I desperately wanted to follow her as she disappeared up the stairs, but first, I needed to talk to my brothers. I turned towards them, a spark of anger moving through me. "Your decision to be all stoic about this is making it so she can't show her feelings," I hissed.

"You want us to be all dramatic and fall apart? How is that going to help her?" Theo bit out.

"I want you to act like a fucking human being," I snarled.

"I'm trying to hold this all together and get us ready for

tomorrow because, if you hadn't noticed, Ben, a lot is riding on us doing well in this interview," Theo said. We were both standing now, glaring at each other.

"If you haven't noticed, Theo, Josie needs us right now," I sniped back, hands clenched. Part of me knew it wasn't really Theo I was angry at. He was doing what he always did—leading us through any challenge—but I couldn't stop the avalanche of my emotions.

Cam stepped in between us. "We're all on the same side here," he growled. "Let's just fucking calm down."

I huffed. "Yeah, I'll just do that. Our pack is being threatened, but I'll just keep calm."

"Ben," Cam said, frowning, his brows furrowing with concern.

I looked away. I never rocked the boat and couldn't remember ever being this angry with my brothers. I forced myself to take a deep breath.

"I'm going to go check on her," I said, leaving the room before they could respond.

I walked into Josie's bedroom without knocking, my body trembling with anger. The moment I saw her, my rage melted away. She was sitting on the side of the bed, staring at the wall. Seeing her like that made me want to cry.

"What do you need, precious?" I murmured, sitting down next to her.

She didn't move, didn't say anything. I wondered if she needed me to back off or to take control like I had during her heat. The idea of leaving her alone like this was unthinkable, so instead, I went to her dresser and got out a pair of sweatpants and one of my sweatshirts she had pilfered. I moved back towards her carefully.

"I'm going to get you changed, precious, so we can lie down and be more comfortable."

She kept staring at the wall, but at least this time, she gave me the tiniest nod of acknowledgment. I quickly changed her clothes and tugged her onto the bed so she was curled up against my side.

"We'll all be together tomorrow," I murmured, holding her tightly. "We won't leave. We're not going to let anything happen to you."

Her breath hitched and tears streamed down her face.

"I'm scared," she whispered.

"Me too, precious. But you're not going in there alone this time."

She entwined her legs with mine and we held each other close, as if by clinging to each other, we could prevent anything bad from touching us.

The door clicked and Cam and Theo walked in, both looking anxious and uncertain.

"I'm sorry," Theo said, sitting down on the edge of the bed, running his hand down Josie's hair as he met my gaze. "To both of you. I panicked and went straight into solution mode. I don't know how to deal with this."

"I'm sorry, too," I said.

"It's okay," Josie said, reaching out to hold Theo's hand.

"What do you need, baby girl?" Cam asked, brushing the hair out of Josie's face.

"Will you lie down with us?" she asked hesitantly. "Unless there's other stuff you need to do," she added quickly.

"Nothing I would rather do than be here," Theo said. They lay down on either side of us, wrapping us in their embrace.

Chapter Sixty-One

Josie

"Josie, sweetheart, you're so tense you're going to hurt yourself," Cam said, scooting his chair closer to mine so he could rub my neck. I leaned into his touch, trying to focus on the feel of him, but nothing could soothe me while sitting in the Designation Center lobby.

"I just have a really bad feeling about this," I whispered, fidgeting in my seat.

Ben squeezed my hand from the seat beside mine, his leg bouncing as he looked around the hall.

"We'll go in there, answer their questions, and be out of here before you know it," Theo said. "Where do you want to go for lunch?"

I shrugged. My stomach was so twisted up I wasn't sure I could eat anything.

"I just want to go home," I whispered.

"We'll be back home so soon, baby girl," Cam said, squeezing my thigh. "Just hold on."

I nodded and forced myself to take a steadying breath.

A door opened down the hall, and laughter filtered into the

lobby. I gripped Cam and Ben's hands as tightly as I could as heavy footsteps sounded on the marble floor.

An alpha I'd never seen before strode towards us with a mild smile plastered on his face. His blond hair was perfectly coiffed and his dark navy suit was tight across his chest, as if it were a size too small. The very lines of his body felt sinister, and it took everything in me to stay in my chair when he raked his eyes over me, licking his lips. Cam and Ben tensed, and Theo subtly angled his chair to partially block me from the alpha's view.

Then, heavy footsteps echoed in the lobby as a group of security officers filed in and lined up against the wall.

No, no, no.

There was a ringing in my ears, and I didn't understand how I was sitting silently when everything inside me was screaming.

"What the fuck?" Cam muttered, putting his arm around me.

I couldn't feel his skin against mine. I couldn't feel anything.

"Welcome, Pack Ashwood and Ms. Porter. It's always an exciting day to have a newly formed pack visit us."

His voice raised the hairs on my skin, and I had to suppress a whimper. Ben moved closer to me on my other side, running his hand up and down my arm as if he knew my scar was aching.

"Who are you?" Theo asked.

The alpha's smile didn't falter, even at Theo's curt tone.

"My name is Todd Cross. I am the newly appointed Director of Pack Cohesion here at the Designation Center. My department was created specifically to help alphas find the perfect omega for their packs and to ensure a seamless transition to pack life." His voice was robotic, as if each word was carefully rehearsed. "Now, we're ready to begin the interviews. To ensure the highest quality of care, you will each be interviewed separately. This is to ensure everyone feels free to express themselves fully."

I felt myself falling into a haze. Theo and Cam stood up, and I saw Theo's lips move, but I didn't hear what he said. The sound around me grew muffled and I noticed, as if I were observing myself from a distance, that I was on the verge of a panic attack.

"That is not what we were told," Cam bit out, his raised voice startling me back to reality.

"New procedure," Director Cross said smugly.

Ben gripped my arm tighter. My eyes flitted to the guards.

"No," I whimpered.

Director Cross fixed me with an ice-cold stare. "Omegas do not contradict alphas," he snarled, his tone no longer mellow. "It's not a good sign when alphas can't keep their omega in line."

"We want to do the interview together," Theo said. "That's what we were told would happen."

"Like I said, the policy has changed to better serve the needs of our pack alphas. If you refuse to follow procedure, we will be forced to determine you are unfit to have an omega."

"You can't fucking do this," Cam snarled, taking a step towards Director Cross.

Immediately, two guards stepped up on either side of the director, their hands on their weapons. Acting on sheer instinct, I lunged out of my chair at Cam, wrapping my arms around his waist. I pressed my face against his back and held on as tightly as I could. His entire body vibrated, his hands clenched into fists.

"Cam," I said, my voice coming out in a hoarse whisper.

No response.

"Alpha, please," I whimpered.

I didn't know what I was asking for, except that it was clear the DC had planned all of this with precision. They would delight in denying our pack status. Before meeting my alphas, all I wanted was to spend the rest of my life alone. Now I wouldn't survive being separated from them.

Something must have broken through to Cam because he placed his hand over mine on his stomach. He gently broke my grip enough to turn around to look at me.

I bit my lip to keep it from trembling. If I lost it right now, so would my alphas. It would be my fault if anything happened to them.

"We have to do what they say," I whispered, hating that we had an audience.

"Omegas are always so dramatic," Director Cross said with condescension. "Such emotional manipulators. You'll all be led back to your individual interview rooms in a moment. The interviews will be brief, nothing to get worked up about."

My gaze was still locked with Cam's, and I silently begged him to go along with it. He was breathing heavily, his eyes unfocused. I wanted to reassure him, to tell him this wasn't like when he lost his sister, but the words wouldn't come out. How could I tell him everything would be okay when I felt like I was being marched to hell?

Another alpha entered the hall.

"Ahh, Dave. Perfect timing. You will take Ms. Porter back for her interview," Director Cross said, looking down at his watch impatiently.

I peered around Cam to see Dave standing there next to the director, a blank expression on his face. He gave me a curt nod and the tightness in my chest eased enough for me to take a deep, shuddering breath. If Dave was here, Amirah must have had a hand in this.

Theo, so used to being in control, looked stricken. "I'm so sorry, love." He kissed my cheek before whispering, "I texted Amirah for backup. I'm going to make sure everything's okay."

Ben simply pressed up against my side, holding me as tightly as he could.

Cam shook his head, his eyes becoming more focused. He turned to look at Dave, his expression hard.

"We are not leaving here without you," Cam said in a low growl, gripping my chin. "We are all walking out of here together as a pack. You belong with us, sweetheart."

I nodded, desperately wanting to believe his words. Cam tucked me into his chest, briefly purring for me before letting me go.

I forced myself to take steady steps away from my alphas. *I'm doing this for them. I have to protect them.* I walked past the guards, their menacing stares quickening my footsteps.

Panic overtook me as I followed Dave down a long corridor off the main lobby. I looked back, my alphas' desperate gazes meeting mine. Every muscle in my body screamed at me to run back to them, to escape this place once and for all. But Director Cross's threat hung in the air. I needed to show them I could be a good omega. So I forced myself to turn away from them, to follow Dave deeper into the bowels of the Designation Center.

We left the brightly lit and luxuriously decorated lobby, the halls turning bleak and gray the further we walked. I wished Dave would talk to me, comfort me like he had when he escorted me for my interviews. But today, he walked in stony silence, setting a quick pace that forced me to almost jog to keep up as he led me through the twisted maze of hallways. My harried footsteps and pounding heart were the only noises breaking the eerie silence.

Dave stopped abruptly at the end of a small hallway tucked away at the back of the building. My wide eyes met his as he pulled open the metal door. I wanted to ask him what was going on, to scream, anything, but my throat was closed up.

"They're expecting you," Dave said in a gravelly voice, gesturing for me to enter the room.

I forced myself to put one foot in front of the other, feeling like I was dragging my limbs through concrete. As I walked past Dave, I caught a whiff of his scent—*his deeply distressed and acidic scent.* Alarm gripped me, my omega whining at the intensity, my body on full alert. I whipped back to the door, ready to bolt down the hallway back to my alphas. I no longer cared about following the procedures. I needed to get out.

Just as I lunged towards the exit, Dave shut the door.

Locking me inside.

Alone.

Panic consumed me as I clawed at the door, the solid metal expanse refusing to give way. I tried to scream, but no sound escaped. I clawed at my throat, trying to breathe. Blackness encroached on my vision and the room started to spin. I leaned against the door, the coolness of the metal a contrast to my heated skin. I dug my nails into my palms, wishing it was Theo's soothing hands I was feeling instead, but the pain was enough to bring me out of my panic spiral. *You can get out of this, just fucking pull yourself together.*

I pushed myself off the door and turned to face the room. In the haze of my panic, I registered a vaguely familiar scent I couldn't quite place underneath the medical antiseptic smell. A warning tickled in the back of my brain, something alerting me to danger, but I didn't know what. I scanned the room to see if there was any other way out and saw two things I hadn't noticed before.

The first was an exam table with wide leather straps.

The second was a metal door just to the left of the table.

My mind went blank and I crumpled to my knees.

I was trapped.

Keep going, keep fighting, don't give up.

My arms shook and tears I didn't realize I was crying hit the floor.

Keep going, keep fighting, don't give up.

The mantra played on repeat in my head. And it was my alphas' voices. And Luc's, and Sam's, and all of my friends.

I pressed my nose to my sweater, the combination of cinnamon roll, apple spice, and coffee clearing my mind.

I started crawling towards the metal door, silent tears streaming down my face, my shaky arms barely able to drag me to what I hoped beyond hope that it was an exit.

I cowered as I reached the medical table, momentarily frozen by flashbacks, the scar on my arm burning with memory. I lifted my head, forcing myself to focus on my destination—the door in front of me.

And then it opened.

Out stepped an alpha in a perfectly pressed black suit.

The smell of rotten fruit assaulted me.

Glen Jacoby met my gaze with a sinister smile. "Hello, Josephine."

To be continued in book two.

The Story Continues...

I know, you hate me right now for that cliffhanger. Don't be worried, though. Read what happens next in ***Forbidden: Part Two.***

And if you enjoyed this book, it would mean the world if you left a review. Reviews are so important for indie authors!

Acknowledgments

I read the Acknowledgements section of every single book I finish. Writing can be a solitary, sometimes lonely act, but books aren't written alone. There's something magical about peeking behind the curtain and seeing the team that helped bring a book into the world.

First and foremost, this book would not exist without TikTok. At the start of the pandemic, I (along with seemingly every millennial) found myself trying to figure out this new social media app. I found my way onto Booktok where I discovered the world of reverse harem and omegaverse, joined reader groups on Facebook, and connected with new friends over our love of reading romance. The pandemic was a profoundly isolating experience, and feeling connected to all these incredible readers helped me in more ways than I can say.

Darcy, this book wouldn't be where it is now without you. In fact, I probably never would have finished it. You have been the absolute best critique partner I could ever hope for. I'm so grateful you took a chance and messaged me on Instagram all those months ago. Your encouragement and critique has made me a better writer, and this story is all the better for it.

Alex, I would have stopped writing this book many times if not for you. You were the first person I told about this book, the one I constantly texted throughout my writing process. I am so grateful for your encouragement, feedback, and editing support. Thanks for being the best book friend and never judging me for my smutty reading or writing.

Lindsay, even though you've never read a reverse harem or omegaverse book (or even a sex scene!), you have been the greatest friend and encourager through this process. Thanks for being convinced that this book would be a success without ever having read a word.

To my Tenacious Writer's critique group: Patricia, Jenny, and Robyn. Your excitement about this book made a world of difference! It's hard to overcome my inner critic, and hearing you all speak positively about my writing was a gift. And to Rachel and Emily, thank you for creating such an incredible coaching program. The community you created is one I will cherish forever.

Olivia, it's absolutely unhinged the way you love this book. Thanks for being my number-one fan.

Celina, thanks for answering all of my "give me a list of names for four unlikeable guys" texts. Oh, and you also came up with the title! You get the number one award for naming things.

To my friends, co-workers, that random middle-aged guy on the plane, and everyone who fully believed in this book when they had absolutely no good reason to: sorry not sorry for explaining omegaverse to you.

And finally, thank you, lovely readers, for taking a chance on a debut author. Writing this series has been an absolute dream come true.

About the Author

Emilia Emerson loves to embroider, take naps with her dog, read filthy smut, and do projects around the house. She works in mental health and loves that writing romance allows her to explore worlds with guaranteed happily ever afters, cozy characters who love each other, and found families who overcome challenges together.

Stay up to date on new announcements:

Facebook Group: Emilia Emerson's Reader Group
Newsletter Signup: www.emiliaemerson.com
Instagram & TikTok: @emiliaemersonauthor

Printed in Great Britain
by Amazon

37682081R00320